THE AWAKENING
AND OTHER WRITINGS

broadview editions
series editor: L.W. Conolly

Kate Chopin, 1899. Courtesy Stone and Kimball Collection,
The Newberry Library, Chicago, Illinois.

THE AWAKENING AND OTHER WRITINGS

Kate Chopin

edited by
Suzanne L. Disheroon
Barbara C. Ewell
Pamela Glenn Menke
Susie Scifres

broadview editions

Library and Archives Canada Cataloguing in Publication

Chopin, Kate, 1851-1904
    The awakening and other writings / Kate Chopin ; edited by Suzanne L. Disheroon ... [et al.].

(Broadview editions)
Includes bibliographical references.
ISBN 978-1-55111-349-4

    I. Green, Suzanne Disheroon, 1963- II. Title. III. Series: Broadview editions

PS1294.C65A64 2011   813'.4   C2011-901318-5

Broadview Editions
The Broadview Editions series represents the ever-changing canon of literature in English by bringing together texts long regarded as classics with valuable lesser-known works.

Advisory editor for this volume: Martin Boyne

Broadview Press is an independent, international publishing house, incorporated in 1985.

We welcome comments and suggestions regarding any aspect of our publications—please feel free to contact us at the addresses below or at broadview@broadviewpress.com.

North America
Post Office Box 1243, Peterborough, Ontario, Canada K9J 7H5
2215 Kenmore Avenue, Buffalo, NY, USA 14207
Tel: (705) 743-8990; Fax: (705) 743-8353
email: customerservice@broadviewpress.com

UK, Europe, Central Asia, Middle East, Africa, India, and Southeast Asia
Eurospan Group, 3 Henrietta St., London WC2E 8LU, United Kingdom
Tel: 44 (0) 1767 604972; Fax: 44 (0) 1767 601640
email: eurospan@turpin-distribution.com

Australia and New Zealand
NewSouth Books
c/o TL Distribution, 15-23 Helles Ave., Moorebank, NSW, Australia 2170
Tel: (02) 8778 9999; Fax: (02) 8778 9944
email: orders@tldistribution.com.au

www.broadviewpress.com

The interior of this book is printed on 100% recycled paper.

Typesetting and assembly: True to Type Inc., Claremont, Canada.

PRINTED IN CANADA

Contents

Acknowledgements

As with any project of this magnitude, we owe a debt of gratitude to a host of people without whom this project would literally not have been possible. Our long-suffering families, especially, have been endlessly patient with the lost weekends, piles of manuscript pages stacked around our respective houses, and frenetic spurts of activity. Kathryn Green, J. Alex Green, and Jason Kuilan, especially, were very understanding of their moms taking on "another damn commitment" when time always seems to be at a premium. And Sheila Geha and Jerry Speir were, as always, partners *par excellence*. Our long-time friend and colleague Kathryn Nance worked tirelessly with us over several weekends simply out of the goodness of her heart. She offered invaluable advice on the organization of the introduction to this volume and helped in the revision process.

The research for this project was greatly expedited and enhanced by Mary Linn Wernet, head archivist at the Cammie G. Henry Research Center at Northwestern State University, and Gail Kwak, government documents librarian at the Northwestern State University Library. We are also grateful to Lauren Leeman, reference specialist at the State Historical Society of Missouri, for locating sources for us and sending them out very quickly.

Elizabeth Rubino, professor of French at Northwestern State, generously assisted us with the translation of the many French phrases and terms that Chopin uses in her novel. Kristina McBride typed the reviews and the *At Fault* excerpt for us in her capacity as a graduate assistant at Northwestern State.

Finally, without the seemingly endless patience of Marjorie Mather at Broadview Press, this volume would never have been completed. This project had a long and convoluted journey, and we are indebted to her for her grace and flexibility. Similarly, Broadview Editions series editor Leonard Conolly and volume editor Martin Boyne have been great sources of assistance and support, and we are grateful for their efforts to make this the best volume possible.

Introduction

During her lifetime, Kate Chopin was best known as a writer of local color fiction set in the mysterious bayous of Louisiana. Local color, or regionalism as it is now more commonly called, presented readers with a slice of life from distinctive parts of the nation that seemed exotic or romantic, precisely because of such differences. Louisiana, with its alien French, Spanish, and African roots, coupled with its lush landscapes, unfamiliar social customs, and soft Creole *patois*, provided effective backdrops for the stories that flowed from Chopin's pen.

Kate Chopin did not begin writing until later in life, after she had married, borne six children, and buried her husband. She herself grew up in St. Louis, the gateway to the new frontier as well as a thriving commercial and social center in its own right. The world of Chopin's youth was one characterized by dichotomies: the ongoing tension between the city's older French traditions, typified by the French language that she learned at home, and the newer American culture, reflected in the English that was used for instruction at the Sacred Heart Academy; the clash between Northern anti-slavery sentiments and the Southern insistence on states' rights and the ongoing struggle to forestall the collapse of its labor-intensive economy; and the divergent expectations of the roles women were culturally conditioned to fulfill and the reality of life in her matriarchal family, headed by her grandmother and her mother, who had been widowed young upon the death of Kate's father, Thomas O'Flaherty, in a train accident. By the time Chopin returned to St. Louis, herself a widow with six young children, these dichotomies were further complicated by her experiences in south Louisiana and the more urban sensibilities of New Orleans. The result is the extraordinary body of fiction that Chopin produced over the short course of her career, stories that, despite their distinctive settings and popular motifs, incorporated a range of issues important to women: conventional roles, sexuality, marriage, friendship with other women, and the effects of variables such as race, class, and region on the ways in which women conducted their daily affairs.

The Awakening: Contemporary Critical Reception

Certainly Chopin's best-known and most critically acclaimed work is *The Awakening*, a novel that ignited a firestorm of controversy when it debuted in 1899. Reviewers criticized the book for its tacit endorsement of adultery, its frank depiction of a woman's sexual frustration, and its overt rejection of conventional expectations for women's roles and behavior. (See Appendix A for a selection of contemporary reviews.) Edna Pontellier's abandonment of her marriage and children was deemed tasteless, at best, especially since Chopin neglected to inscribe any clear rebuke of her heroine's irregular behavior. Her hometown paper, the *St. Louis Post-Dispatch*, described the novel as being "too strong drink for moral babes, and should be labeled 'poison'" (21 May 1899; see Appendix A4). The fact that Chopin examined depression, the capricious nature of love in its many forms, sexuality, and all of the assorted implications of these topics from a woman's point of view contributed to the general recoil against the "morbid ... sex fiction" (Toth, *Kate Chopin* 21) that she had produced. Contrary to the myth that arose suggesting that Chopin was so wounded by the reviews of *The Awakening* that she never wrote again, her biographer Emily Toth has demonstrated that Chopin was rarely one to take reviews—or their writers—too seriously. She once quipped that book reviewers with "a worthy critical faculty might be counted on the fingers of one hand" (Toth, *Kate Chopin* 20), and later observed that "in answering questions [about herself and her work] ... the victim cannot take herself too seriously" (Seyersted 723). *The Awakening*'s numerous negative reviews, however, begged for some response, and Chopin complied with an ironic retort that confirms her continuing confidence in her work. A few weeks after *The Awakening* appeared, this wry comment appeared in a national periodical, *Book News*:

Having a group of people at my disposal, I thought it might be entertaining (to myself) to throw them together and see what would happen. I never dreamed of Mrs. Pontellier making such a mess of things and working out her own damnation as she did. If I had had the slightest intimation of such a thing I would have excluded her from the company. But when I found out what she was up to, the play was half over and it was then too late. (28 May 1899)

But the reviews were not all negative. In fact, a week earlier, in the *St. Louis Post-Dispatch*, C.L. Deyo had praised the novel, describing it finally as sad and mad and bad, but it is all consummate art. The theme is difficult, but it is handled with a cunning craft. The work is more than unusual. It is unique. The integrity of its art is that of well-knit individuality at one with itself, with nothing super-fluous to weaken the impression of a perfect whole. (20 May 1899)

Most early critics acknowledged Chopin's literary artistry: her subtle prose, her skillful evocations of southern life—precisely the qualities that readers had come to expect from her short fiction. The problem was that she had applied those talents to themes that many Americans still considered unsuitable.

In the years following its publication, another misconception developed: that *The Awakening* had been banned in Chopin's native St. Louis soon after its publication. This erroneous but exasperatingly persistent belief is rooted in three sources: comments made by Chopin's son, Felix, in which he accused the St. Louis Mercantile Library of taking *The Awakening* out of circula-tion (Toth, *Kate Chopin* 367); the complicity of Chopin's first biographer, Daniel Rankin, who so wished to portray Chopin as a good Catholic who wrote quaint local-color stories that he sup-pressed some contradictory evidence, secreting many of Chopin's papers and manuscripts in a bus-station locker; and, finally, an account by a librarian at the St. Louis Mercantile, Clarence E. Miller, that was taken out of context. Miller described a scene to Chopin's second biographer, Per Seyersted, in which Chopin came with a friend to the library to ask for the novel, but when she was told it had been removed from circulation, she simply walked away (Toth, *Kate Chopin* 367). In reality, copies of *The Awakening* were removed from the library's collection when the books were too worn for further use. The St. Louis Public Library had purchased three copies of the novel upon its publi-cation. One was lost in 1901 but was later replaced, and the other two were marked "condemned," which was the standard notation applied to a book removed from circulation after being de-acces-sioned due to excessive wear or damage (Toth, *Kate Chopin* 368). Furthermore, neither Bill Reedy nor Orrick Johns, two well-regarded critics of Chopin's day who argued vehemently against censorship in any form, ever mentioned Chopin's book being banned (Toth, *Kate Chopin* 369), despite the fact that Reedy and Chopin remained good friends to the end of her life. Toth points out that "Billy Reedy—who loved to fulminate about censorship—would have gone into a volcanic rage if such a thing had happened to his friend Kate Chopin" (Toth, *Unveiling* 227). Scandalous though the novel became, no evidence exists to prove that *The Awakening* was ever banned in its author's home town.

Despite these lingering reports that Chopin was somehow defeated by the reception of her novel, perhaps the only real consequence of the unfavorable reviews of *The Awakening* was the cancellation of her contract to publish a new collection of short stories, *A Vocation and a Voice*, with Herbert S. Stone, the original publisher of her novel. The publishers insisted that they were simply trimming their list, but *The Awakening*'s slow sales and poor reviews may well have been a factor in their decision. Chopin's third and final collection remained unpublished until the late twentieth century.

In fact, the fuss over Chopin's novel was short-lived. Not really scandalous enough to generate increased sales or lasting controversy, *The Awakening* fell into obscurity soon after Chopin's death in 1904. For more than 60 years, the novel, along with most of Chopin's other work, went out of print and was generally unavailable to readers. A few short stories remained accessible, such as "Désirée's Baby" (1893), which often appeared in anthologies of American literature. Only in the last half of the twentieth century—largely due to the efforts of scholars such as Per Seyersted and Emily Toth—has Chopin's body of work again become available to readers in its entirety.[1] Since Seyersted's *Complete Works* appeared in 1969, *The Awakening* has become an integral part of the American literary canon, to the point that scholars have argued that it has even surpassed Melville's *Moby Dick* in terms of popularity and significance. In her second biography, *Unveiling Kate Chopin* (1999), Emily Toth wittily asserts that *The Awakening* is "far more of a grabber than *Moby-Dick*, which in the 1970s was being taught as the required great American novel.

---

1 The bulk of Chopin's works is available in Per Seyersted's *The Complete Works of Kate Chopin* (1969), as well as in various collections. Editions of each of Chopin's three collections of short stories—*Bayou Folk, A Night in Acadie*, and *A Vocation and a Voice*—have been published as she originally arranged them; Chopin's first novel, *At Fault* (1890), is also available (U of Tennessee P, 2001). Uncollected works can be found in various sources, including *Kate Chopin's Private Papers*, edited by Emily Toth (1998), and *A Kate Chopin Miscellany* (Northwestern State UP, 1979). The editors are unaware of any extant Chopin works that are not generally available.

Chopin's main character—a thoughtful, sensual woman—was much more interesting than an angry white whale" (Toth, *Unveiling* xx).

The Awakening continues to be a classroom favorite not only because it provides insight into late nineteenth-century life, but also because it explores issues that remain relevant, even pressing, for readers today. Chopin explored many of these issues in her short fiction—the lingering nature of unrequited love as shown in "The Storm" or the unasked-for temptations of adultery, as in "A Respectable Woman"—examining the social, intellectual, and emotional consequences for women who defy the expectations of their culture, family, or religion, as well as the lengths to which women will go to escape such limits when the stakes are high enough. Chopin's short fiction plainly prepared her to write the novel that created so much controversy. Indeed, not only do the ruminations on moral conflict, isolation, sensuality, solitude, and despair occur in Chopin's earlier fiction, but so too do some of the minor characters of *The Awakening*, such as Gouvernail and Tonie, make their first appearance in Chopin's short stories. The awakening itself, which many readers assume is primarily sexual, has, in fact, a much broader reference. Though sexuality plays a critical role in Edna's development in *The Awakening*, the visceral represents only one element of a series of awakenings that Edna experiences. Her growth into the "solitary soul" that is at least one measure of human maturity—recognizing one's relationship to the world within and without—also involves Edna's efforts to find a place for herself as an artist, as a woman, as a wife, and as a lover, all matters that would appear to have been best left unexamined by a late nineteenth-century Southern woman, whether she be character or writer.

Exploring Gender

For many years prior to the Civil War and the abolition of slavery, progressive thinkers and activists were urging the reconsideration of the legal and social position both of women and of African Americans. By the final decades of the nineteenth century, profound economic and social changes were making that reconsideration unavoidable. In 1878, the first women's suffrage amendment was introduced in Congress, although forty years were to elapse before the Nineteenth Amendment, which finally granted women the Constitutional right to vote, was passed by the US Congress. England had passed its Qualification of Women Act two years earlier in 1918, granting the vote to women who were over the age of 30, who were property owners or wives of property owners, or who were university graduates. Occupying a prominent place in public discussions throughout the 1890s, "the Woman Question" was rooted in the liberalism of the Enlightenment, which promoted equality and individual freedom as essential human rights. The rights of married women to own property, to initiate divorce, to retain custody of their children, or to enter the professions of law and medicine, as well as to vote, became potent political issues in Western Europe as well as in the United States. In the course of the struggle for women's suffrage, American culture underwent dramatic changes, being transformed from an agricultural to a manufacturing economy, from the isolation and homogeneity of rural villages and farms to the challenges of an increasingly diversified urban life, from an emerging nation pressing its own frontiers to an imperial power with impressive ambitions.

Within these dramatic cultural shifts, women's roles were necessarily changing as well. New options for education and employment emerged, and women eagerly—from both need and ambition—sought entry into the professions and public life; they took up work in mills and factories and offices, mastering new technologies such as the telephone and typewriter. Earlier models of womanhood became increasingly unmatched to contemporary experience: the figure of the modern woman did not fully embody "true womanhood"—i.e., the domestic saint and mother who ruled the private sphere, protected, supported, and spoken for by her husband, with no self of her own. As men and women struggled to adjust to these difficult changes, the implications of gender were widely and passionately debated in the periodicals, scholarship, and fiction of the time. What *was* the proper role of women? What part should nature—childbearing, for example—play in determining the options for women or in defining their characters? Questions about these new roles became a fixture of commentary in the 1890s, and "The New Woman" became a byword and magnet for the varied hopes and anxieties surrounding the transformation of gender roles that the culture was witnessing.

Two prominent contemporaries of Kate Chopin who worked actively to transform women's roles were Elizabeth Cady Stanton (1815-1902) and Charlotte Perkins Gilman (1860-1935). Stanton's tireless lecturing and activism on behalf of women's rights shaped the contours of what the "New Woman" personified. Having argued for women's suffrage for decades, Stanton finally addressed the Judiciary Committees of Congress in January 1892, articulating her clearest statement on the liberation of women. Entitled "The Solitude of Self," Stanton's important speech echoes many of the notions implicit in Chopin's novel: that women are individuals, who, like Edna, must learn "to realize her position in the universe as a human being" (52), one who cannot sacrifice her essential self, even though she might willingly sacrifice her life. Interestingly, Chopin's working title for *The Awakening*, "A Solitary Soul," echoes the published title of Stanton's landmark speech, "Solitude of Self" (1892), reminding readers of how profoundly radical the notion of female autonomy still was in the 1890s.

Gilman was even more directly identified with the "New Woman," and her concerns about women's lot in contemporary society mirrored those that Chopin addressed in her fiction. In 1898, Gilman published her most famous work, *Women and Economics*, a witty and satiric critique of women's subordinate role in history and in contemporary society. The book was an international success, and Gilman's 1899 lecture tour included two stops in St. Louis, one in January when Chopin was eagerly awaiting the publication of her new novel, and another in November when its disappointing reception had clarified the risks Chopin had taken with Edna. Although it is unclear whether Chopin ever heard Gilman speak, *Women and Economics* articulates many of the arguments that defined the "New Woman" and that implicitly shape Chopin's critique of marriage and motherhood in *The Awakening*. Additionally, Gilman's most famous fiction, "The Yellow Wallpaper" (1892), anticipates Edna's ambivalence about her children and both authors' opinion that motherhood is neither instinctive nor appropriate for every woman.

Though Chopin allows Edna to experiment with the elements of new womanhood, she also acknowledges the power of the conventional notions of womanhood, creating in Adèle Ratignolle both a foil to Edna and a confirmation of the enduring appeal of these more familiar roles. Opposite in appearance and temperament, Adèle and Edna become fast friends, and, in fact, Adèle is the last person that Edna sees prior to going back to Grand Isle at the novel's end. Adèle is the model of the "mother-woman" (46) as Chopin describes it: the perfect mother and doting wife whose life's goal is to create a beautiful and comforting environment for her family. Her role is rewarded by the fulfillment that she finds in her marriage to a man who apparently appreciates her and her efforts. Though Chopin represents Adèle's contentment with her role and the admiration that that role typically exacts from others, she also (less typically) portrays Adèle as a lushly sensual woman, even in pregnancy. Rather than closeting herself during pregnancy, as was conventional during this era, Adèle revels in her condition, referring to her state constantly and even regaling male guests at the Grand Isle *pension* with tales of the more harrowing aspects of her *accouchements*, i.e., childbirth. Though Adèle is the consummate wife and mother, whose husband adores her and whose children worship the ground she walks on, Chopin reminds us of the sensual ground of that familiar role, even though Adèle herself seems oblivious to its sources.

Edna, on the other hand, is Adèle's antitype. She is pale and slim, and arguably more self-absorbed than a wife and mother should be, one who loves her children intensely but fitfully, one moment wanting to hug them tightly, the next nearly forgetting their existence. Her well-meaning husband is consistently befuddled by her choices, and he does make an effort to accommodate what he views as her capriciousness, as long as she helps him in what he considers to be her most critical role—keeping up appearances so that his business remains unaffected. While Adèle personifies the traditional wife and mother, Edna departs radically from that model. But in a break with much other fiction that preceded *The Awakening*, Chopin does not punish Edna for her unconventional behavior. She is not shunned by polite society, even when she allows the notorious womanizer Alcée Arobin to visit her late at night and alone; and, at the end of the novel, when Edna abandons her marriage and then her children, Chopin imposes no clear judgment on Edna's otherwise unconventional—even abhorrent—actions. Edna's continuing relationship with Adèle—the constancy of both women toward one another—remains a mark of the potential acceptability of Edna's radical choices, choices that echo those of Chopin herself.

Though Edna embodies significant attributes of the "New Woman," she in fact spends much of the novel drifting from diversion to diversion and, indeed, from man to man, searching for some activity, some relationship, some connection that will relieve the *ennui* that stalks her with increasing intensity. Today, we might diagnose her as suffering from depression, or perhaps even a bipolar disorder. Her periods of enthusiasm and energy are followed by dark, bleak periods when nothing satisfies her, and during one of these darker moods, Edna ultimately takes her final swim in the Gulf. While Chopin's ending leaves indeterminate the extent to which that final swim is an intentional suicide or an accidental drowning, the incident itself foregrounds Edna's ongoing emotional distress, much as Gilman does in her famous story, "The Yellow Wallpaper." For both writers, women trapped in marriages whose contours did not fit their own needs or abilities for mothering experienced inexplicable emotions and bleak choices. More than half a century later, women writers such as Betty Friedan[1] struggled to identify "the problem that has no name" and, like Chopin and Gilman, understood how deeply—and with what dire consequences—social convention can bury female experience.

Indeed, the significance of *The Awakening* lies, in part, in its unprecedented willingness to examine issues that were rarely mentioned, much less understood, in the late nineteenth century, but that were—and remain—central to many women's experiences. Unlike the mother-women who populate Edna's social strata, Edna cannot bring herself to sacrifice her inner needs for her children. Ultimately, she "eludes" them altogether (163), leaving them in the hands of their grandmother, a more traditional woman who is ostensibly better equipped to manage them and plainly able to love and care for them. In fact, Chopin herself often eluded social expectations, especially after the death of her husband and as her own children grew up—smoking cigarettes, walking in public unaccompanied, and pursuing her art rather than engaging solely in such domestic objectives as "struggl[ing] with the intricacies of a pattern" for a new dress or "try[ing] a new furniture polish on an old table leg"—tasks she ironically describes in an 1899 essay (Seyersted 721), just a few months after the publication of *The Awakening*.

Exploring Sexuality

Critical to Edna's journey from conforming wife and mother to solitary soul is her sensual awakening, a theme that often recurs in Chopin's short fiction. Early in the novel, we learn that although Edna has been married for a good number of years, she has not experienced physical passion. She tells Adèle of the infat-

---

1 Betty Friedan, author of *The Feminine Mystique* (1963), was a leader in the Second Wave of Feminism in the US, during which she co-founded the National Organization of Women and fought for the repeal of anti-abortion laws.

uations of her childhood—a beau of her elder sister's, a tragic actor whose picture she used to cover with kisses—but none of these romantic ideals ever came to fruition; they remained ideals, untouched by the real, visceral world. She married her husband in part because it aggravated her father and sister and because, like other inexperienced youth, she "fancied there was a sympathy of thought and taste between them, in which fancy she was mistaken" (58). As her relationship with Léonce settles into a daily routine, as marriages usually do, she realizes that, in fact, while she appreciates her husband's generosity (at least until the point that she finds it excessive), she does not love him and is not even especially attracted to him. It is not until the summer at Grand Isle, when she meets and falls in love with Robert Lebrun, that Edna experiences the kind of emotional connection associated with romantic love and sexual passion.

Yet Edna's sexuality is not tapped by Robert, for whom she recognizes the "first-felt throbbings of desire" (58), significantly on the heels of connecting with her own physical strength. After weeks of apprehension in the water and failing to learn to swim, Edna suddenly, effortlessly, lifts her body and glides through the waters of the Gulf, which Chopin consistently describes in sensual terms: "the touch of the sea is sensuous, enfolding the body in its soft, close embrace" (53). Despite Edna's at first subtle and then overt urgings to express their love physically—as when she tells Robert that "[n]ow you are here we shall love each other, my Robert" (156)—he cannot bring himself to dishonor either Edna or his Creole moral code in an affair. As Edna kisses him passionately, he wishes aloud that her husband would set her free, but he is then completely bewildered when Edna scoffs at the idea, saying that she gives herself when and where she pleases and that even if her husband consented to release her from their marriage, she would "laugh at [them] both" (156). Instead of fulfilling their mutual desire, Robert flees it at every opportunity, leaving their passion unrequited. It is not Robert but the rogue Alcée Arobin who first causes Edna to become "supple to his gentle, seductive entreaties" (140). When Edna tries to share with Robert her awakened sexuality, "that cup of life" that "had inflamed her" (130), to express physically her emotional passion for him, he demurs. Facing that "monster made up of beauty and brutality" (130), Edna remains unable to combine romance and sexuality, to create a space where she can make love to a man with whom she is in love. Neither Alcée nor Robert can adequately respond to the sexually awakened, new woman Edna has become.

Chopin had explored the nature of women's sexuality in other stories as well, but never more explicitly than in "The Storm" (see Other Fiction, 190), which she wrote in the months after completing *The Awakening* and which she evidently never even tried to publish. "The Storm" continues the relationships established in the 1896 story "At the 'Cadian Ball," by celebrating an adulterous affair as the necessary and unavoidable outcome of an unrequited passion. In contrast to the ambiguities of the ending of *The Awakening*, the conclusion of "The Storm" insists that after the adulterers are reunited with their marital partners, "the storm passed, and every one was happy" (196). Explicitly metaphoric in its description of sexual pleasure, "The Storm" honors the clandestine encounter as a source of relief and rejuvenation for all parties—not just for the adulterers themselves, but for their spouses as well. There is no repudiation of the event or evidence that the transgressors will suffer for their choices. Although "The Storm" is unique in Chopin's oeuvre, she often explores marriage and the temptation of adultery in stories such as "A Respectable Woman" (see Other Fiction, 183) or "Athènaïse," both of which include the character Gouvernail, who appears as a guest at Edna's birthday dinner. Other stories examine the strength of marriage bonds, such as "In Sabine," where domestic abuse entitles a young wife to a clandestine, ultimately comic, escape, or in "Madame Célestin's Divorce" (see Other Fiction, 180), in which another, much neglected, married woman toys with the idea of a divorce. Encouraged by the town's bachelor attorney, whose motives are decidedly mixed, Madame Célestin decides to reconcile with her husband when he returns home and promises to "turn ova a new leaf" (183). Neither the reader nor the lawyer shares Madame's faith in Célestin, but the story, like others in Chopin's canon, reflects the writer's continual—and unconventional—scrutiny of marital relationships and the ways in which they often fall short of the public ideal.

Exploring Race

While sexuality and its role in female development are clearly foregrounded in *The Awakening*, the novel, like the short stories that preceded it, remains deeply embedded in place, specifically the post-bellum South, where race continued to be as critical to identity as gender. Indeed, Edna's story exemplifies many of the unique aspects of race in Louisiana, including late nineteenth-century struggles to redefine the meaning of Creole. Unlike most of the South, which divided race simply into categories of white and non-white, slave and free, Louisianians had historically constructed race differently, albeit with equal rigidity. Partly as a consequence of greater flexibility about racial mixing in the French and Spanish colonial era, a three-caste system had emerged: the descendants of Europeans remained at the top of the social ladder, while those of African heritage languished in the lowest social strata, but between them was a group whose heritage was less determinate. Mingling European and African ancestry, many of these people came to be designated Creoles, a term that originally referred to any person born in the region, but that after the Civil War became a deeply contested identifier. Alice Dunbar-Nelson, writing in 1916, articulates some of the attendant ambiguities (see Appendix D4). To some, she explains, Creole means a

> white man, whose ancestors contain some French or Spanish blood in their veins. But he would be disputed by others, who will gravely tell you that Creoles are to be found only in the lower Delta lands of the state, that there are no Creoles north of New Orleans.... Sifting down the mass of conflicting definitions, it appears that to a Caucasian, a Creole is a native of the lower parishes of Louisiana, in whose veins some traces of Spanish, West Indian or French blood runs. The Caucasian will shudder with horror at the idea of including a person of color in the definition, and the person of color will retort with his definition that a Creole is a native of Louisiana, in whose blood runs mixed strains of everything un-American, with the African strain slightly apparent. The true Creole is like the famous gumbo of the state, a little bit of everything, making a whole, delightfully flavored, quite distinctive, and wholly unique. (Dunbar-Nelson 366-67)

In antebellum Louisiana, Creole specifically included the free people of color—*gens de couleur libres*—who were not fully white or fully black and who populated that unique middle caste. They enjoyed social and economic benefits not available to their darker counterparts who occupied the lowest social strata, but their place was no less closely circumscribed. In fact, this caste system designated race by descriptors that indicated a specific quantity of a person's African ancestry: "To the whites, all Africans who were not of pure blood were *gens de couleur*. Among themselves, however, there were jealous and fiercely-guarded distinctions"

(Dunbar-Nelson 361). These distinctions included terms such as "griffes, briqués, mulattoes, quadroons, octoroons, each term meaning one degree's further transfiguration toward the Caucasian standard of physical perfection" (King 333). These designations were as much a part of identity within African-American culture as outside it, with degrees of darkness paralleling and even guaranteeing social status and economic options. Thus, when Edna's children's nurse is called a "quadroon" (46), Chopin is specifically indicating an individual who is one-fourth black and three-quarters white. In the larger South, that designation would simply mean black, but in Louisiana culture, a quadroon might well be considered a Creole, implying an intermediate degree of autonomy and status.

Being Creole, as opposed to African American, held significant advantages even in post-bellum Louisiana. But earlier in the nineteenth century, Creoles of color represented a distinctive caste, with legal and social ramifications. Creoles of color could, for example, readily do business with their white counterparts and might even have limited social contact. The presumption concerning their legal status was that they were free unless there was proof to the contrary, whereas for an African American, the presumption was the reverse. Creoles could own property and marry at will and, in general, enjoyed similar if not equal rights of citizenship to those maintained by their white counterparts. Although Creoles did not have the full measure of legal advantages and protections as whites in Louisiana, they fared far better than slaves or former slaves of African descent: "under the title of *gens de couleur libres*, free part-white Creoles were accorded special privileges, opportunities, and citizenship not granted to part-Negroes in other states." The preservation of this third caste, however, was "contingent upon strict adherence to the caste system by its members" (Mills xiv). That adherence became particularly pronounced after the Civil War, when racial definitions gradually hardened to the national standard of black or white. At that point, many Louisianians who had once crossed the color line more or less freely were constrained to choose a single race, one of which would be distinctly disadvantageous. On the one hand, Creole, the definition of which had once been racially fluid, became jealously guarded by whites to signify narrowly a French or Spanish ancestry, while, on the other hand, people of color determinedly claimed the label as designating their own uniquely Afro-European heritage.

Common to Creoles on both sides of the color line, however, was their sense of distinctiveness. In the decades after the

Louisiana Purchase, French-speaking natives of all colors shared a common disdain for the English-speaking newcomers, *les Américains*. Self-consciously, they clung to colonial traditions, including the maintenance of a rigid and complicated caste system based on color. Even after the postwar imposition of binary racial classifications separated blacks and whites, Creole culture generally retained its insularity and resistance to outsiders: Euro-Americans to protect themselves from accusations of a tainted Creole/African identity, and African Americans to maintain their privileged difference from darker blacks, who did not share their complex Euro-African Creole history and heritage.

Chopin, who had herself entered Louisiana's European Creole community on her marriage, explicitly informs her readers at the beginning of *The Awakening* that the entire Grand Isle *pension* is populated by Creoles, and their customs and language give the novel its distinctive flavor. But despite such patent and exotic differences from most Americans, Chopin, as Bonnie James Shaker argues, makes clear that these Louisiana Creoles (as well as the Cajuns in her other stories) are racially white. Static characters, such as Edna's children's "quadroon nurse," or Catiche, the *mulatresse*, who makes such good coffee in the suburbs of the city (153), are carefully designated by their skin color, using the remnants of Louisiana's color caste. Other characters, such as the flirtatious Mariequita or Madame Antoine on Chênière Caminada, hint at racial ambiguity, with Spanish names or servant status. But Chopin implies that the lines of color are already drawn, and even outsiders—Americans such as Edna and most of Chopin's readers—need not be confused by the intricacies of Creole culture, at least not in that most important matter of racial identity.

Nonetheless, Chopin also capitalizes on the ambiguities and differences that Creole culture represents, highlighting the conflicts between being an insider—a member of a knowing community—and an outsider—one who does not belong or fully fit in or understand its arcane conventions, whether racial or sexual. Mlle. Reisz, for example, is one such outcast. The pianist to whose music Edna responds so emotionally, Mademoiselle in fact celebrates her alienation from polite society as the just price of an artistic temperament that the Creole insiders simply find unpleasant. Though she lacks Mlle. Reisz's intentionality, it is Edna who is most clearly the outsider among the Creoles of Grand Isle and New Orleans. Hailing from Kentucky, Edna maintains a reserved exterior that makes her seem odd to those who have grown up with the emotional openness and greater fluidity of Creole society. At the same time, Edna cannot quite penetrate the curious candor of her companions. She is embarrassed at being observed reading a racy French novel, while the Creoles do not just read the Goncourt novel publicly, but discuss it freely in mixed company at the dinner table. Unlike her Creole counterparts, who can describe their *accouchements* and the sexual content of books without embarrassment, Edna merely becomes accustomed to such "shocks, but she could not keep the mounting color back from her cheeks" (49). She gradually accepts the Creoles' "freedom of expression [that] was at first incomprehensible to her" and does not question the paradoxical assumption of a "lofty chastity which in the Creole woman seems to be inborn and unmistakable" (48). Assuming her inclusion in the culture, she merely accedes to its customs. However, when she acts upon her erotic impulses in ways that might seem consistent with such candor about sexuality, she ultimately violates the cultural codes of the community, committing transgressive acts that would no more occur to her Creole friends than mistaking a pale octoroon for a social equal. Being admitted to a community of insiders does not ensure comprehension, and Edna, like other transgressors of contemporary racial and sexual codes, must pay a heavy price for her mistake.

Exploring Class

While race remained one of the most visible issues of the period, no less critical to the cultural shifts of the turn of the century was the role of class in structuring human affairs. A major economic text published the same year as *The Awakening* was Thorstein Veblen's *Theory of the Leisure Class*. A major premise of Veblen's revolutionary work was his analysis of the relationship between wealth and women's dependence (see Appendix B9). He exposed many of the disturbing roots of the ostentatious affluence of the Gilded Age, explaining how waste and leisure, as indicators of wealth and social status, rested on the hierarchies of class and gender. Veblen famously coined the phrase "conspicuous consumption" to denote this marker of wealth and argued that women served as its primary sign and instrument.

Léonce Pontellier is a prototype of the "conspicuous consumption" to which Veblen refers. Much admired around Grand Isle for his generosity, Léonce spends money with abandon, handing a wad of cash over to Edna after a successful night of gambling at Klein's hotel, in spite of (and perhaps to atone for) their argument the evening before. When he sends his family enormous boxes of expensive treats after returning to work in the city, the ladies at the *pension* declare him "the best husband in the world," a pronouncement Edna finds no reason to refute (46). Later, when she chastises him for being too "extravagant" and points out that he does not "ever think of saving or putting by" (96), Léonce simply responds that she does not understand how things work and patronizingly suggests that she should take better care of herself.

In awakening to her self, Edna recognizes that the trappings of "conspicuous consumption" are part of what contain and limit her identity. Gradually, she rejects the signs of her husband's possession, which Chopin marks on the opening pages of the novel, when Léonce observes her sunburned face as "a valuable piece of personal property which has suffered some damage" (41)—and then returns her wedding rings, which she has left in his keeping. Later, aggravated by Léonce's criticism of her failure to play her part as a social support to his business, she flings her wedding ring across the room and "striv[es] to crush it" (125). Eventually, these futile gestures become more substantive, as Edna leaves behind the material comfort that her husband provides as a part of their marriage contract and chooses to live on income that she earns herself. By renouncing the conspicuous consumption of her husband, Edna literally creates new spaces for herself that are no longer defined by societal conventions or her husband's expectations, but rather by standards she sets for herself.

As Edna begins to recognize her separate identity, she marks that recognition by a gradual withdrawal from the material privileges that have defined her as a wife and mother. At first simply refusing to maintain her reception day or supervise the household servants, she withholds sex from her husband and finally moves out of the Esplanade Avenue mansion of which he is so proud. She retires to a small cottage, which she can pay for with her gambling money, remarking to Mlle. Reisz that her new dwelling will give her a "feeling of freedom and independence" (125). Edna's behavior and Léonce's reactions indicate how clearly both understand their meaning as markers of female dependence, on the one hand, and economic status, on the other. Her earlier infractions, for example, lead Léonce to remonstrate that "people don't do such things; we've got to keep up with the procession" (94), while her move to a smaller house immediately generates his concern for appearances and "his financial integrity" (140). He promptly orders an expensive remodeling of their house (140). Not interested in correcting the perception he creates with his neighbors and business associates, Edna simply goes about her business, pursuing the peace and contentment that she needs while allowing her husband to create whatever excuses he deems necessary to maintain the image that results from his "conspicuous consumption."

Exploring Place

Although the early designations of Chopin's work as local color served to limit public perceptions of its scope, regional identity undeniably plays a significant role in *The Awakening*, much as it does in her full body of work. In fact, much of the symbolism in the novel derives from the region in which the story is set. The sonorous murmuring of the Gulf of Mexico carries' throughout the narrative. Grand Isle and the smaller, outlying islands such as Barataria Bay and Chênière Caminada provide a unique backdrop for some of the major events that occur prior to Edna's return to New Orleans, such as her trip to Our Lady of Lourdes with Robert and his hasty exit to Mexico under cover of night. The pirogues and sailboats help to construct the uniqueness of this specific place. Even the climate functions to define the spaces and events of the novel: the thick coastal humidity that draws the Pontelliers from their cabin no less than their quarrel; the stiff breezes that blow Edna's and Adèle's clothing when they journey down to the beach one afternoon, freeing their conversation; the lapping waves that draw Edna's attention as Mlle. Reisz provides an evening's entertainment and that echo the power of her music; the daily "bath" in the sea to combat the oppressive heat, which encourages Edna to learn to swim. These and other elements anchor the narrative firmly on Grand Isle, in south Louisiana, even as Chopin carefully uses such details to deepen the significance of her story.

Chopin also constructs the materiality of her characters and their lives through the implicit backstories created in the whole of her fiction and then exploited in her novel. Before William Faulkner created Yoknapatawpha County, or Fred Chappell spun tales of the North Carolina Kirkmans, or Ellen Gilchrist regaled readers with Rhoda's effusive and self-destructive exploits,[1] Kate Chopin populated a fictional community of Louisiana Creoles. Her characters share not only geographic proximity to rural Cane River and urban New Orleans, but also relationships with families and friends and love affairs and gossip. The Grand Isle *pension* becomes synonymous with the Gulf of Mexico, for example, while various neighborhoods of New Orleans are evoked in the novel, with street names and locations that can still be identified: Esplanade Avenue, Carondelet Street, the St. Charles Hotel.

Further, Chopin builds a sense of a thriving community by introducing characters in one story that she later develops in another. The three Santien brothers, sons of the former slave-owner Lucien, appear in several stories, including Chopin's first novel, *At Fault* (see Other Fiction, 165), where Grégoire, the youngest, comes to an untimely end as a consequence of being rejected by his love. The Laballières, Ratignolles, and Pontelliers frequently cross paths in Chopin's stories, socializing with the likes of Gouvernail the bachelor and Mademoiselle Claire Duvigné, the love of Tonie Bocaze's solitary life as well as one of Robert Lebrun's attachments. We learn in "At Chênière Caminada" (see Other Fiction, 169) that Claire dies during the winter in New Orleans, but her demise is also briefly mentioned in *The Awakening*, when Adèle Ratignolle describes Robert as having "posed as an inconsolable" upon learning of Claire's untimely demise (49). Tonie, whom we meet when Edna and Robert sail out to the Chênière Caminada, is also the fisherman who owned the "boat with the red lateen sail" (81) that later carries Robert away from Grand Isle when he leaves for Mexico. This interrelated and recurring cast of characters—who appear as cursory to one narrative only to reappear as the central focus of another—provides solidity to Chopin's fictional conjurations of Louisiana no less than her accurate descriptions of the places and customs that those characters inhabit.

---

1   The majority of William Faulkner's fiction is set in the imaginary Yokna-
    patawpha County, including the two novels that many readers consider
    his masterpieces: *The Sound and the Fury* (1929) and *Absolom! Absolom!*
    (1936). Similarly, Fred Chappell's Kirkman trilogy, *I Am One of You
    Forever* (1985), *Brighten the Corner Where You Are* (1989), and *Farewell,
    I'm Bound to Leave You* (1996), and Ellen Gilchrist's Rhoda stories,
    found in collections such as *Rhoda: A Life in Stories* (1995) and *I, Rhoda
    Manning, Go Hunting with My Daddy, And Other Stories* (2002), create
    communities of families and friends sharing their lives in small, and typ-
    ically rural, southern towns.

Chopin further deepens the materiality and allusiveness of her novel by engaging with its history and legends, particularly that of the pirates and privateers who once commanded these coastal islands. Madame Antoine is the first to tell pirate stories, but Robert and later Edna transform them into images of their own escapes to the criminalized margins of society. Many of these tales had their origins in the Barataria Bay area of the Gulf, which Grace King, a contemporary writer whom Chopin admired, describes in detail:

> The name [Barataria] includes all the Gulf coast of Louisiana between the mouth of the Mississippi and the mouth of the Bayou LaFourche, a considerable stream and the waterway of a rich and populous territory. A thin strip of an island, Grand Terre, six miles long and three wide, screens from the Gulf the Great Bay of Barataria, whose entrance is a pass with a constant, sure depth of water. Innumerable filaments of stealthy bayous running between the bay and the two great streams, the Mississippi and the LaFourche, furnished an incomparable system of secret intercommunication and concealment. (191-92)

For generations, pirate legends haunted the outlying islands, and these are the stories that Madame Antoine tells to Robert and Edna after she awakens from her nap at Chênière Caminada. Clearly, the influence of the Baratarian legend and history on *The Awakening* is more extensive than it might first appear.

Exploring Nature

The Great Hurricane of 1893

While the history of the barrier islands of Louisiana is associated with the pirates who once controlled them, by the late nineteenth century Grand Isle was simply a popular resort and vacation area for wealthy families of New Orleans, who sought temporary escape from the oppressive heat and diseases of the summer. Chopin knew the area well, having herself spent several seasons there with her children. By the time she began *The Awakening* in the summer of 1897, however, the lively resorts on Grand Isle and Chênière Caminada were merely memories. Just four years earlier, in 1893, a powerful hurricane had totally changed the landscape. Striking late in hurricane season, the Great October Storm is still remembered as one of the largest natural disasters in United States history, with a death toll of over 2,000 in the immediate area (see Appendix E). Its ten-foot storm surge decimated Chênière Caminada and left few structures on Grand Isle standing. The Great Storm was national news, and many cities, including St. Louis, offered aid to the stricken coastal communities. Kate Chopin, who had continued to write and visit her deceased husband Oscar's family regularly in Louisiana, could not have helped being shocked by the reports. Those familiar summer places were now just rubble: the *Joe Webre* steamer, the Krantz Hotel, even the little church of Our Lady of Lourdes, whose bell had tolled all night until the steeple collapsed. Evidently stirred by these events, later that month Chopin began writing "At Chênière Caminada" (see below, 169), setting her tale on Grande Isle and populating it with characters and the themes of loss that would recur in *The Awakening*.

Though Chopin never mentions the 1893 hurricane directly in her fiction or in her surviving papers, the knowledge of the recent destruction of these coastal communities clearly shapes her choice of Grande Isle as a setting and its implications for Edna's self-possession (see Ewell and Menke). Indeed, the novel itself makes clear that Chopin intends Edna's struggle to unfold in the very year before the Great Hurricane wiped away every trace of that magical place where her awakening had begun— deepening the poignancy and intensity of all that Edna loses by the novel's end. In fact, Chopin's temporal details are fairly exact: the novel begins in midsummer, with Edna learning to swim, as Robert notes, on the night of the "twenty-eighth of August" (70). Adèle is in the early stages of pregnancy that summer and gives birth early the next spring. As Edna returns with Dr. Mandelet from Adèle's that evening, she notes that Léonce will be return-ing "[q]uite soon. Some time in March" (159). The next day, Edna returns to Grande Isle for the last time. But another detail of the novel fixes the precise year as well as the early spring season of these events: at one point, Mrs. Highcamp casually mentions a meeting of the New Orleans Folk Lore Society, an actual organization founded on 8 February 1892 (Jordan and de Caro 33), thus fixing the period of Edna's awakening between the summer of 1892 and the arrival—just over a year later—of the Great October Storm, which swept everything away.

When Edna steps into the chilly late-February waves, the Gulf was already beginning to warm, stirring up the literal hurricane whose destructive powers would prove no less threatening to the traditional community on its shores than Edna's revolutionary desire to possess her own soul were to American society at the turn of the century. By setting Edna's story on Grande Isle in the very year before the Great October Storm, Chopin not only couples Edna's awakening with the forces of nature—its sensuality along with its power—but also signals the vulnerability of individuals like Edna who would challenge powerful social conventions without possessing, as Mlle. Reisz explains, the "strong wings" of those who would "soar above the level plain of tradition and prejudice" (129).

The Sea

The sea, stirred by powerful winds of hurricanes, that would eventually destroy Grand Isle along with Edna's dreams of selfhood, gives thematic shape to the novel in other ways as well. Both literally and symbolically, the sea becomes the source of many of Edna's moments of self-reflection and insight. Swimming in the sea, whether for the first or for the last time, Edna feels reborn, transformed into a different person from the one controlled by convention. Her emotional response to Mlle. Reisz's music, which directly connects to her artistic aspirations and her internal growth, occurs as she sits on a retaining wall looking out at the whispering, night-time Gulf. The night she learns to swim, she resists her husband's demands for the first time in their marriage, and as the novel draws to a close, she is again drawn into the sea, relishing both the absence of her confining clothing and the "soft, close embrace" (164) of the sea as she immerses herself in its soothing waves until her strength is gone. But while Edna experiences rebirth in the enfolding waters, the consequence of that immersion is death. Chopin does not resolve the ambiguity of that final encounter with the sea, except perhaps to eliminate some of the key phrases of temporality when she repeats the description of Edna's response to the "voice of the sea": it is "seductive; never ceasing, whispering, clamoring, murmuring, inviting the soul to wander *for a spell* in abysses of solitude; *to lose itself in mazes of inward contemplation*" (53; emphasis added). The time for "inward contemplation" has now passed; the "spell" is concluded. Edna is on her own. Is her fatal swim merely an accident, a result of her typical capriciousness and inability to predict the consequences of her actions? Or is her death intentional, the last rebellious act of a woman who systematically rejected the expectations of husband, children, friends, and society, choosing to live and die on her own terms rather than submit to the will of someone other than herself? Partly by her characterization of the sea in this final chapter—"The water of the Gulf stretched out before her, gleaming with the million lights of the sun.... The foamy wavelets ... coiled like serpents about her ankles" (164)—Chopin masterfully leaves these questions open-ended, allowing, indeed forcing, each reader to interpret Edna's final act as a measure of her success or failure.

Birds

Another important and often noted pattern of the novel's natural imagery is that of birds. The novel opens with a bird in a cage that calls out in a loud voice, only to be ignored and then banished from human company. The caged bird is later replaced in Edna's imagination—stimulated by Mlle. Reisz's music—by a wild bird flying away free, as a naked man stands on the beach passively observing its flight, powerless to stop it. That image becomes more literal as Edna prepares for her final swim and sees a bird with a broken wing "reeling, fluttering, circling disabled down, down to the water" (163). The birds echo Edna's efforts to conceptualize what would satisfy her, to understand what would relieve her intermittent but increasingly troubling *ennui*, give her emotional and intellectual fulfillment, or allow her to feel connected to another human being who would not eventually "melt out of her existence, leaving her alone" (163). Like Edna, the birds begin as imprisoned, albeit in a gilded cage; they evolve, encouraged by music, to become the freedom-seeking, natural creatures they are. But, once again beside the sea, their fragile wings broken by the heavy load of convention and social consequences, they sink, like Edna, into the glittering waters of the Gulf.

Conclusion

Biographer Emily Toth has often asked, "How did Kate Chopin know all of that in 1899?" Even in 1899, a reviewer noted that

> Mrs. Chopin appeals to the finer taste, sacrificing all else, even pecuniary profit, to her artistic conscience ... [she] has been called a southern writer, but she appeals to the universal sense in a way not excelled by any other American author. She is not sectional or provincial, nor even national, which is to say that

she is an artist who is not bound by the idiosyncrasies of place, race, or creed. ("A St. Louis Writer Who Has Won Fame," n.p.)

Both Toth and the anonymous reviewer isolate elements of this novel's enduring appeal. On the one hand, Chopin raises questions in this novel that were not resolved in 1899 and that are still problematic over a century later. Though women (and authors) certainly now have greater freedom to express sexuality, the underlying conflict between personal desire and social obligation, particularly the obligations often entailed as a consequence of that desire (i.e., children), remains today. Women continue to struggle with the competing demands of career and family, with the implicit stigma of rejecting motherhood even as they fully claim their femininity, and with the subtle constrictions of female identity and the continuing challenge of personal integrity. Likewise, the moral choices that shape Edna's life remain relevant: the realities and temptations of adultery to which Edna succumbs but which Robert resists; the high moral ground of that resistance and the compelling natural force of love and desire, which Edna embodies and which Chopin leaves unsatisfied, foregoing the happy ending that would unite the lovers in a romantic haze; Léonce's well-meaning but uncomprehending efforts to accommodate both his wife's caprice and the economic and social need to keep up appearances; and whether Edna was right to choose death over life, self over children. Readers continue to recognize the situations that Chopin presents so vividly: spouses who do not understand their mates; confusion over what direction one's life should take; the sexual frustration and the self-loathing that such confusion can engender; the meaning of love and passion and how they are related; the contradictory emotions generated by motherhood and children; depression and despair, and the toll that they take on one's mental and physical well-being; intentional suicide and accidental death. How did she know all of these things? Probably because, as a woman and as writer, she had the courage, as her readings and translations of French fiction writer Guy de Maupassant had taught her, simply to tell us what she saw.

Works Cited

"*The Awakening* by Kate Chopin." *Book News* July 1899: 612.
Deyo, C.L. "The Newest Books." *St. Louis Post-Dispatch*. 20 May 1899: 3.

Dunbar-Nelson, Alice. "People of Color in Louisiana: Part I." *The Journal of Negro History* 1 (1916): 361-76.

Ewell, Barbara C., and Pamela Glenn Menke. "*The Awakening* and the Great October Storm of 1893." *The Southern Literary Journal* 42.2 (2010): 1-11.

Gilman, Charlotte Perkins. *Women and Economics: A Study of the Economic Relation Between Men and Women as a Factor in Social Evolution.* Boston: Small Maynard, 1898.

———. *The Yellow Wallpaper.* Boston: Small Maynard, 1899.

Jordan, Rosan Augusta, and Frank de Caro. "'In This Folk-Lore Land': Race, Class, Identity, and Folklore Studies in Louisiana." *Journal of American Folklife* 109 (1996): 31-59.

Kate Chopin: A Re-Awakening. Screenplay by Anna Reid-Jhirad. Dir. Tika Laudun. Narrated by Kelly McGillis. Louisiana Educational Television Authority. 1998.

King, Grace. *New Orleans: The Place and the People During the Ancien Régime.* New York: Macmillan, 1895.

Mills, Gary B. *The Forgotten People: Cane River's Creoles of Color.* Baton Rouge: Louisiana State UP, 1977.

Nelson, Carolyn Christensen, ed. *A New Woman Reader: Fiction, Articles, and Drama of the 1890s.* Peterborough, ON: Broadview Press, 2001.

"A St. Louis Writer Who Has Won Fame in Literature, Part Four." *St. Louis Post-Dispatch* 26 November 1899: n.p.

Seyersted, Per, ed. *The Complete Works of Kate Chopin.* Baton Rouge: Louisiana State UP, 1969.

Shaker, Bonnie James. *Coloring Locals: Racial Formation in Kate Chopin's Youth's Companion Stories.* Iowa City: U of Iowa P, 2003.

Stanton, Elizabeth Cady. "The Solitude of Self: Address Delivered before the Committee of the Judiciary of the United States Congress." 18 January 1892.

Toth, Emily. *Kate Chopin: A Life of the Author of The Awakening.* New York: William Morrow, 1990.

———, and Per Seyersted. *Kate Chopin's Private Papers.* Bloomington: Indiana UP, 1998.

———. *Unveiling Kate Chopin.* Jackson: UP of Mississippi, 1999.

Veblen, Thorstein. *Theory of the Leisure Class.* New ed. New York: Macmillan, 1912.

Kate Chopin: A Brief Chronology

1850   Born 8 February in St. Louis, Missouri.

1855   Father, Thomas O'Flaherty, dies on 1 November in train accident.

1868   Graduates from Academy of the Sacred Heart on 29 June.

1870   Marries Oscar Chopin on 9 June and settles in New Orleans following a honeymoon in Europe.

1882   Husband, Oscar Chopin, dies on 10 December.

1884   Returns to St. Louis.

1885   Mother, Eliza O'Flaherty, dies on 28 June.

1889   First literary publication, the poem "If It Might Be," appears on 10 January in *America* magazine.

1890   *At Fault* published in September.

1894   Short-story collection *Bayou Folk* published.

1897   Short-story collection *A Night in Acadie* published.

1899   *The Awakening* published.

1900   Contract for short-story collection *A Vocation and a Voice* canceled.

1904   Dies on 22 August, two days after suffering a cerebral hemorrhage.

1991   *A Vocation and a Voice* published posthumously.

A Note on the Text

The Awakening was first published by Herbert S. Stone on 22 April 1899. Kate Chopin originally called the manuscript "A Solitary Soul," but the title was changed to *The Awakening* upon publication. We have used the first-edition text of the novel as the copy text and have made no editorial changes to it. A minor spacing issue has been corrected throughout the manuscript, but otherwise the text presented here is as close a representation of the first edition as possible.

At Fault was privately published in 1890 by Nixon-Jones Printing Company in St. Louis, Missouri. The present text comes from *At Fault by Kate Chopin*, edited by Suzanne Disheroon-Green and David J. Caudle (Knoxville: U of Tennessee P, 2001). The 2001 edition used the first-edition text as its source.

The short stories presented here are all in some way linked to *The Awakening*, either through a recurring character or by a thematic element. The text of each story not specifically mentioned here comes from its first serial publication during Chopin's lifetime. "The Storm" was first published in Per Seyersted's *The Complete Works of Kate Chopin* in 1969, and the text that appears here comes from Chopin's original hand-written manuscript. "Madame Célestin's Divorce" was first published in *Bayou Folk* (1894).

The transcripts of the poetry and journal entries come from Chopin's manuscripts, which are primarily housed in the archives of the Missouri Historical Society in St. Louis. Most of these works have been published elsewhere since Chopin's death.

The original cover of the first edition, published by the Chicago firm of
Herbert S. Stone & Company. Courtesy Special Collections, Howard
Tilton Library, Tulane University, New Orleans, Louisiana.

Surf Bathing, Grand Isle (1885) by the French artist and New Orleans resident, John Genin (1830-1895). Courtesy New Orleans Museum of Art: Gift of Sam Friedberg. 52.42.

THE AWAKENING

I

A green and yellow parrot, which hung in a cage outside the door, kept repeating over and over: "*Allez vous-en! Allez vous-en! Sapristi!*[1] That's all right!"

He could speak a little Spanish, and also a language which nobody understood, unless it was the mocking-bird that hung on the other side of the door, whistling his fluty notes out upon the breeze with maddening persistence.

Mr. Pontellier, unable to read his newspaper with any degree of comfort, arose with an expression and an exclamation of disgust. He walked down the gallery and across the narrow "bridges" which connected the Lebrun cottages one with the other. He had been seated before the door of the main house. The parrot and the mocking-bird were the property of Madame Lebrun, and they had the right to make all the noise they wished. Mr. Pontellier had the privilege of quitting their society when they ceased to be entertaining.

He stopped before the door of his own cottage, which was the fourth one from the main building and next to the last. Seating himself in a wicker rocker which was there, he once more applied himself to the task of reading the newspaper. The day was Sunday; the paper was a day old. The Sunday papers had not yet reached Grand Isle.[2] He was already acquainted with the market reports, and he glanced restlessly over the editorials and bits of news which he had not had time to read before quitting New Orleans the day before.

Mr. Pontellier wore eye-glasses. He was a man of forty, of medium height and rather slender build; he stooped a little. His hair was brown and straight, parted on one side. His beard was neatly and closely trimmed.

Once in a while he withdrew his glance from the newspaper and looked about him. There was more noise than ever over at the house. The main building was called "the house," to distinguish it from the cottages. The chattering and whistling birds

---

1 Go away! Go away! For heaven's sake!
2 A small community in Jefferson Parish, Louisiana, at the southern tip of the state located on the Gulf of Mexico. This resort area was a popular escape for affluent families from New Orleans during the hot, humid summers.

were still at it. Two young girls, the Farival twins, were playing a duet from "Zampa"[1] upon the piano. Madame Lebrun was bustling in and out, giving orders in a high key to a yard-boy whenever she got inside the house, and directions in an equally high voice to a dining-room servant whenever she got outside. She was a fresh, pretty woman, clad always in white with elbow sleeves. Her starched skirts crinkled as she came and went. Farther down, before one of the cottages, a lady in black was walking demurely up and down, telling her beads.[2] A good many persons of the *pension*[3] had gone over to the *Chênière Caminada*[4] in Beaudelet's lugger[5] to hear mass. Some young people were out under the water-oaks playing croquet. Mr. Pontellier's two children were there—sturdy little fellows of four and five. A quadroon[6] nurse followed them about with a far-away, meditative air.

Mr. Pontellier finally lit a cigar and began to smoke, letting the paper drag idly from his hand. He fixed his gaze upon a white sunshade that was advancing at snail's pace from the beach. He could see it plainly between the gaunt trunks of the water-oaks and across the stretch of yellow camomile. The gulf looked far away, melting hazily into the blue of the horizon. The sunshade continued to approach slowly. Beneath its pink-lined shelter were his wife, Mrs. Pontellier, and young Robert Lebrun. When they reached the cottage, the two seated themselves with some appearance of fatigue upon the upper step of the porch, facing each other, each leaning against a supporting post.

"What folly! to bathe at such an hour in such heat!" exclaimed Mr. Pontellier. He himself had taken a plunge at daylight. That was why the morning seemed long to him.

---

1 Comic opera about a pirate, written in 1831 by Ferdinand Hérold (1791-1833).
2 Catholic ritual of praying the rosary.
3 Boarding house or small hotel.
4 Small island community near Grand Isle.
5 A small boat used for fishing or sailing that has two or three masts, each with a sail.
6 A racial designation codified under Louisiana Law more explicitly than in the rest of the South. Rather than labeling individuals as either black or white, Louisiana indicated the percentage of non-white blood an individual possessed. A quadroon was one-quarter Negro and three-quarters white. See Gary Mills, *The Forgotten People* (Baton Rouge: Louisiana State UP, 1977).

sets tone for novel

"You are burnt beyond recognition," he added, looking at his wife as one looks at a valuable piece of personal property which has suffered some damage. She held up her hands, strong, shapely hands, and surveyed them critically, drawing up her lawn sleeves[1] above the wrists. Looking at them reminded her of her rings, which she had given to her husband before leaving for the beach. She silently reached out to him, and he, understanding, took the rings from his vest pocket and dropped them into her open palm. She slipped them upon her fingers; then clasping her knees, she looked across at Robert and began to laugh. The rings sparkled upon her fingers. He sent back an answering smile.

"What is it?" asked Pontellier, looking lazily and amused from one to the other. It was some utter nonsense; some adventure out there in the water, and they both tried to relate it at once. It did not seem half so amusing when told. They realized this, and so did Mr. Pontellier. He yawned and stretched himself. Then he got up, saying he had half a mind to go over to Klein's hotel[2] and play a game of billiards.

"Come go along, Lebrun," he proposed to Robert. But Robert admitted quite frankly that he preferred to stay where he was and talk to Mrs. Pontellier.

"Well, send him about his business when he bores you, Edna," instructed her husband as he prepared to leave.

"Here, take the umbrella," she exclaimed, holding it out to him. He accepted the sunshade, and lifting it over his head descended the steps and walked away.

"Coming back to dinner?" his wife called after him. He halted a moment and shrugged his shoulders. He felt in his vest pocket; there was a ten-dollar bill there. He did not know; perhaps he would return for the early dinner and perhaps he would not. It all depended upon the company which he found over at Klein's and the size of "the game."[3] He did not say this, but she understood it, and laughed, nodding good-by to him.

Both children wanted to follow their father when they saw him starting out. He kissed them and promised to bring them back bonbons and peanuts.

---

1 A sheer linen or cotton material.
2 A local hotel and men's watering hole, probably modeled after Krantz's Hotel, a popular destination on Grand Isle prior to the Great Hurricane of 1893 that wiped out the island.
3 While many people would assume this refers to poker or possibly billiards, the game of bourrée, which is similar to poker, is a popular game played for money in Louisiana.

II

Mrs. Pontellier's eyes were quick and bright; they were a yellow-ish brown, about the color of her hair. She had a way of turning them swiftly upon an object and holding them there as if lost in some inward maze of contemplation or thought.

Her eyebrows were a shade darker than her hair. They were thick and almost horizontal, emphasizing the depth of her eyes. She was rather handsome than beautiful. Her face was captivating by reason of a certain frankness of expression and a contradictory subtle play of features. Her manner was engaging.

Robert rolled a cigarette. He smoked cigarettes because he could not afford cigars, he said. He had a cigar in his pocket which Mr. Pontellier had presented him with, and he was saving it for his after-dinner smoke.

This seemed quite proper and natural on his part. In coloring he was not unlike his companion. A clean-shaved face made the resemblance more pronounced than it would otherwise have been. There rested no shadow of care upon his open countenance. His eyes gathered in and reflected the light and languor of the summer day.

Mrs. Pontellier reached over for a palm-leaf fan that lay on the porch and began to fan herself, while Robert sent between his lips light puffs from his cigarette. They chatted incessantly: about the things around them; their amusing adventure out in the water—it had again assumed its entertaining aspect; about the wind, the trees, the people who had gone to the *Chênière*; about the children playing croquet under the oaks, and the Farival twins, who were now performing the overture to "The Poet and the Peasant."[1]

Robert talked a good deal about himself. He was very young, and did not know any better. Mrs. Pontellier talked a little about herself for the same reason. Each was interested in what the other said. Robert spoke of his intention to go to Mexico in the autumn, where fortune awaited him. He was always intending to go to Mexico, but some way never got there. Meanwhile he held on to his modest position in a mercantile house in New Orleans, where an equal familiarity with English, French and Spanish gave him no small value as a clerk and correspondent.

---

1 A vaudeville operetta by Austrian conductor and composer Franz von Suppé (1819-95).

He was spending his summer vacation, as he always did, with his mother at Grand Isle. In former times, before Robert could remember, "the house" had been a summer luxury of the Lebruns. Now, flanked by its dozen or more cottages, which were always filled with exclusive visitors from the "*Quartier Français*,"[1] it enabled Madame Lebrun to maintain the easy and comfortable existence which appeared to be her birthright.

Mrs. Pontellier talked about her father's Mississippi plantation and her girlhood home in the old Kentucky blue-grass country. She was an American woman, with a small infusion of French which seemed to have been lost in dilution. She read a letter from her sister, who was away in the East, and who had engaged herself to be married. Robert was interested, and wanted to know what manner of girls the sisters were, what the father was like, and how long the mother had been dead.

When Mrs. Pontellier folded the letter it was time for her to dress for the early dinner.

"I see Léonce isn't coming back," she said, with a glance in the direction whence her husband had disappeared. Robert supposed he was not, as there were a good many New Orleans club men over at Klein's.

When Mrs. Pontellier left him to enter her room, the young man descended the steps and strolled over toward the croquet players, where, during the half-hour before dinner, he amused himself with the little Pontellier children, who were very fond of him.

III

It was eleven o'clock that night when Mr. Pontellier returned from Klein's hotel. He was in an excellent humor, in high spirits, and very talkative. His entrance awoke his wife, who was in bed and fast asleep when he came in. He talked to her while he undressed, telling her anecdotes and bits of news and gossip that he had gathered during the day. From his trousers pockets he took a fistful of crumpled bank notes and a good deal of silver coin, which he piled on the bureau indiscriminately with keys, knife, handkerchief, and whatever else happened to be in his pockets. She was overcome with sleep, and answered him with little half utterances.

---

1 French Quarter of New Orleans.

He thought it very discouraging that his wife, who was the sole object of his existence, evinced so little interest in things which concerned him, and valued so little his conversation.

Mr. Pontellier had forgotten the bonbons and peanuts for the boys. Notwithstanding he loved them very much, and went into the adjoining room where they slept to take a look at them and make sure that they were resting comfortably. The result of his investigation was far from satisfactory. He turned and shifted the youngsters about in bed. One of them began to kick and talk about a basket full of crabs.

Mr. Pontellier returned to his wife with the information that Raoul had a high fever and needed looking after. Then he lit a cigar and went and sat near the open door to smoke it.

Mrs. Pontellier was quite sure Raoul had no fever. He had gone to bed perfectly well, she said, and nothing had ailed him all day. Mr. Pontellier was too well acquainted with fever symptoms to be mistaken. He assured her the child was consuming at that moment in the next room.

He reproached his wife with her inattention, her habitual neglect of the children. If it was not a mother's place to look after children, whose on earth was it? He himself had his hands full with his brokerage business. He could not be in two places at once; making a living for his family on the street, and staying at home to see that no harm befell them. He talked in a monotonous, insistent way.

Mrs. Pontellier sprang out of bed and went into the next room. She soon came back and sat on the edge of the bed, leaning her head down on the pillow. She said nothing, and refused to answer her husband when he questioned her. When his cigar was smoked out he went to bed, and in half a minute he was fast asleep.

Mrs. Pontellier was by that time thoroughly awake. She began to cry a little, and wiped her eyes on the sleeve of her *peignoir*.[1] Blowing out the candle, which her husband had left burning, she slipped her bare feet into a pair of satin *mules*[2] at the foot of the bed and went out on the porch, where she sat down in the wicker chair and began to rock gently to and fro.

It was then past midnight. The cottages were all dark. A single faint light gleamed out from the hallway of the house. There was no sound abroad except the hooting of an old owl in the top of a water-oak, and the everlasting voice of the sea, that was not

---

1   A woman's loosely fitting dressing gown.
2   Slip-on shoes.

uplifted at that soft hour. It broke like a mournful lullaby upon the night.

The tears came so fast to Mrs. Pontellier's eyes that the damp sleeve of her *peignoir* no longer served to dry them. She was holding the back of her chair with one hand; her loose sleeve had slipped almost to the shoulder of her uplifted arm. Turning, she thrust her face, steaming and wet, into the bend of her arm, and she went on crying there, not caring any longer to dry her face, her eyes, her arms. She could not have told why she was crying. Such experiences as the foregoing were not uncommon in her married life. They seemed never before to have weighed much against the abundance of her husband's kindness and a uniform devotion which had come to be tacit and self-understood.

An indescribable oppression, which seemed to generate in some unfamiliar part of her consciousness, filled her whole being with a vague anguish. It was like a shadow, like a mist passing across her soul's summer day. It was strange and unfamiliar; it was a mood. She did not sit there inwardly upbraiding her husband, lamenting at Fate,[1] which had directed her footsteps to the path which they had taken. She was just having a good cry all to herself. The mosquitoes made merry over her, biting her firm, round arms and nipping at her bare insteps.

The little stinging, buzzing imps succeeded in dispelling a mood which might have held her there in the darkness half a night longer.

The following morning Mr. Pontellier was up in good time to take the rockaway[2] which was to convey him to the steamer at the wharf. He was returning to the city to his business, and they would not see him again at the Island till the coming Saturday. He had regained his composure, which seemed to have been somewhat impaired the night before. He was eager to be gone, as he looked forward to a lively week in Carondelet Street.

Mr. Pontellier gave his wife half of the money which he had brought away from Klein's hotel the evening before. She liked money as well as most women, and accepted it with no little satisfaction.

"It will buy a handsome wedding present for Sister Janet!" she exclaimed, smoothing out the bills as she counted them one by one.

---

1 Usually depicted as a woman on a wheel that turns at random to determine the events of someone's life.
2 Four-wheeled carriage with two or three seats and a cover.

"Oh! we'll treat Sister Janet better than that, my dear," he laughed, as he prepared to kiss her good-by.

The boys were tumbling about, clinging to his legs, imploring that numerous things be brought back to them. Mr. Pontellier was a great favorite, and ladies, men, children, even nurses, were always on hand to say good-by to him. His wife stood smiling and waving, the boys shouting, as he disappeared in the old rockaway down the sandy road.

A few days later a box arrived for Mrs. Pontellier from New Orleans. It was from her husband. It was filled with *friandises*,[1] with luscious and toothsome bits—the finest of fruits, *patés*,[2] a rare bottle or two, delicious syrups, and bonbons in abundance.

Mrs. Pontellier was always very generous with the contents of such a box; she was quite used to receiving them when away from home. The *patés* and fruit were brought to the dining-room; the bonbons were passed around. And the ladies, selecting with dainty and discriminating fingers and a little greedily, all declared that Mr. Pontellier was the best husband in the world. Mrs. Pontellier was forced to admit that she knew of none better.

IV

It would have been a difficult matter for Mr. Pontellier to define to his own satisfaction or any one else's wherein his wife failed in her duty toward their children. It was something which he felt rather than perceived, and he never voiced the feeling without subsequent regret and ample atonement.

If one of the little Pontellier boys took a tumble whilst at play, he was not apt to rush crying to his mother's arms for comfort; he would more likely pick himself up, wipe the water out of his eyes and the sand out of his mouth, and go on playing. Tots as they were, they pulled together and stood their ground in childish battles with doubled fists and uplifted voices, which usually prevailed against the other mother-tots. The quadroon nurse was looked upon as a huge encumbrance, only good to button up waists and panties and to brush and part hair; since it seemed to be a law of society that hair must be parted and brushed.

In short, Mrs. Pontellier was not a mother-woman. The mother-women seemed to prevail that summer at Grand Isle. It

---

1   Small sweets; preserved fruits served as petit fours or small desserts.
2   French delicacy baked with a crust, as in a pie or loaf, or a spread of finely chopped seasoned meat.

was easy to know them, fluttering about with extended, protecting wings when any harm, real or imaginary, threatened their precious brood. They were women who idolized their children, worshiped their husbands, and esteemed it a holy privilege to efface themselves as individuals and grow wings as ministering angels.

Many of them were delicious in the rôle; one of them was the embodiment of every womanly grace and charm. If her husband did not adore her, he was a brute, deserving of death by slow torture. Her name was Adèle Ratignolle. There are no words to describe her save the old ones that have served so often to picture the bygone heroine of romance and the fair lady of our dreams. There was nothing subtle or hidden about her charms; her beauty was all there, flaming and apparent: the spun-gold hair that comb nor confining pin could restrain; the blue eyes that were like nothing but sapphires; two lips that pouted, that were so red one could only think of cherries or some other delicious crimson fruit in looking at them. She was growing a little stout, but it did not seem to detract an iota from the grace of every step, pose, gesture. One would not have wanted her white neck a mite less full or her beautiful arms more slender. Never were hands more exquisite than hers, and it was a joy to look at them when she threaded her needle or adjusted her gold thimble to her taper middle finger as she sewed away on the little night-drawers or fashioned a bodice or a bib.

Madame Ratignolle was very fond of Mrs. Pontellier, and often she took her sewing and went over to sit with her in the afternoons. She was sitting there the afternoon of the day the box arrived from New Orleans. She had possession of the rocker, and she was busily engaged in sewing upon a diminutive pair of night-drawers.

She had brought the pattern of the drawers for Mrs. Pontellier to cut out—a marvel of construction, fashioned to enclose a baby's body so effectually that only two small eyes might look out from the garment, like an Eskimo's. They were designed for winter wear, when treacherous drafts came down chimneys and insidious currents of deadly cold found their way through keyholes.

Mrs. Pontellier's mind was quite at rest concerning the present material needs of her children, and she could not see the use of anticipating and making winter night garments the subject of her summer meditations. But she did not want to appear unamiable and uninterested, so she had brought forth newspapers, which she spread upon the floor of the gallery, and under Madame

Ratignolle's directions she had cut a pattern of the impervious garment.

Robert was there, seated as he had been the Sunday before, and Mrs. Pontellier also occupied her former position on the upper step, leaning listlessly against the post. Beside her was a box of bonbons, which she held out at intervals to Madame Ratignolle.

That lady seemed at a loss to make a selection, but finally settled upon a stick of nougat, wondering if it were not too rich; whether it could possibly hurt her. Madame Ratignolle had been married seven years. About every two years she had a baby. At that time she had three babies, and was beginning to think of a fourth one. She was always talking about her "condition."[1] Her "condition" was in no way apparent, and no one would have known a thing about it but for her persistence in making it the subject of conversation.

Robert started to reassure her, asserting that he had known a lady who had subsisted upon nougat during the entire—but seeing the color mount into Mrs. Pontellier's face he checked himself and changed the subject.

Mrs. Pontellier, though she had married a Creole, was not thoroughly at home in the society of Creoles; never before had she been thrown so intimately among them. There were only Creoles that summer at Lebrun's. They all knew each other, and felt like one large family, among whom existed the most amicable relations. A characteristic which distinguished them and which impressed Mrs. Pontellier most forcibly was their entire absence of prudery. Their freedom of expression was at first incomprehensible to her, though she had no difficulty in reconciling it with a lofty chastity which in the Creole[2] woman seems to be inborn and unmistakable.

Never would Edna Pontellier forget the shock with which she heard Madame Ratignolle relating to old Monsieur Farival the harrowing story of one of her *accouchements*,[3] withholding no inti-

---

1 Pregnancy.
2 A term that is defined in several ways, depending on the area of Louisiana to which it refers. In New Orleans, Creole generally refers to a white person of French-European descent. In central Louisiana, it more frequently refers to free people of color. Sub-categories of racial designation were codified in Louisiana law, based on how much African-American blood an individual was perceived to possess. For a more complete explanation, see Dunbar-Nelson, Appendix D4.
3 Childbirth.

mate detail. She was growing accustomed to like shocks, but she could not keep the mounting color back from her cheeks. Oftener than once her coming had interrupted the droll story with which Robert was entertaining some amused group of married women.

A book had gone the rounds of the *pension*. When it came her turn to read it, she did so with profound astonishment. She felt moved to read the book in secret and solitude, though none of the others had done so—to hide it from view at the sound of approaching footsteps. It was openly criticised and freely discussed at table. Mrs. Pontellier gave over being astonished, and concluded that wonders would never cease.

V

They formed a congenial group sitting there that summer afternoon—Madame Ratignolle sewing away, often stopping to relate a story or incident with much expressive gesture of her perfect hands; Robert and Mrs. Pontellier sitting idle, exchanging occasional words, glances or smiles which indicated a certain advanced stage of intimacy and *camaraderie*.

He had lived in her shadow during the past month. No one thought anything of it. Many had predicted that Robert would devote himself to Mrs. Pontellier when he arrived. Since the age of fifteen, which was eleven years before, Robert each summer at Grand Isle had constituted himself the devoted attendant of some fair dame or damsel. Sometimes it was a young girl, again a widow; but as often as not it was some interesting married woman.

For two consecutive seasons he lived in the sunlight of Mademoiselle Duvigné's[1] presence. But she died between summers; then Robert posed as an inconsolable, prostrating himself at the feet of Madame Ratignolle for whatever crumbs of sympathy and comfort she might be pleased to vouchsafe.

Mrs. Pontellier liked to sit and gaze at her fair companion as she might look upon a faultless Madonna.[2]

"Could any one fathom the cruelty beneath that fair exterior?" murmured Robert. "She knew that I adored her once, and she let me adore her. It was 'Robert, come; go; stand up; sit down; do this; do that; see if the baby sleeps; my thimble, please,

---

1 A character more fully developed in Chopin's "At Chênière Caminada" (1893) (see below, 169).
2 The Virgin Mary; an important religious figure in Catholicism.

that I left God knows where. Come and read Daudet[1] to me while I sew.'"

"*Par exemple!*[2] I never had to ask. You were always there under my feet, like a troublesome cat."

"You mean like an adoring dog. And just as soon as Ratignolle appeared on the scene, then it *was* like a dog. '*Passez! Adieu! Allez vous-en!*"[3]

"Perhaps I feared to make Alphonse jealous," she interjoined, with excessive naïveté. That made them all laugh. The right hand jealous of the left! The heart jealous of the soul! But for that matter, the Creole husband is never jealous; with him the gangrene passion is one which has become dwarfed by disuse.

Meanwhile Robert, addressing Mrs. Pontellier, continued to tell of his one time hopeless passion for Madame Ratignolle; of sleepless nights, of consuming flames till the very sea sizzled when he took his daily plunge. While the lady at the needle kept up a little running, contemptuous comment:

"*Blagueur—Farceur—gros bête, va!*"[4]

He never assumed this serio-comic tone when alone with Mrs. Pontellier. She never knew precisely what to make of it; at that moment it was impossible for her to guess how much of it was jest and what proportion was earnest. It was understood that he had often spoken words of love to Madame Ratignolle, without any thought of being taken seriously. Mrs. Pontellier was glad he had not assumed a similar rôle toward herself. It would have been unacceptable and annoying.

Mrs. Pontellier had brought her sketching materials, which she sometimes dabbled with in an unprofessional way. She liked the dabbling. She felt in it satisfaction of a kind which no other employment afforded her.

She had long wished to try herself on Madame Ratignolle. Never had that lady seemed a more tempting subject than at that moment, seated there like some sensuous Madonna, with the gleam of the fading day enriching her splendid color.

---

1   Alphonse Daudet (1840-97), French short-story writer and novelist in the naturalist tradition; he was called the French Dickens and influenced by the Goncourt brothers (Edmond and Jules) and Emile Zola.
2   Literally "for example," but used as an all-purpose exclamation similar to "my word."
3   Pass! Goodbye! Go away!
4   Joker, Fool, Dummy, go!

Robert crossed over and seated himself upon the step below Mrs. Pontellier, that he might watch her work. She handled her brushes with a certain ease and freedom which came, not from long and close acquaintance with them, but from a natural aptitude. Robert followed her work with close attention, giving forth little ejaculatory expressions of appreciation in French, which he addressed to Madame Ratignolle.

"Mais ce n'est pas mal! Elle s'y connait, elle a de la force, oui."[1]

During his oblivious attention he once quietly rested his head against Mrs. Pontellier's arm. As gently she repulsed him. Once again he repeated the offense. She could not but believe it to be thoughtlessness on his part; yet that was no reason she should submit to it. She did not remonstrate, except again to repulse him quietly but firmly. He offered no apology.

The picture completed bore no resemblance to Madame Ratignolle. She was greatly disappointed to find that it did not look like her. But it was a fair enough piece of work, and in many respects satisfying.

Mrs. Pontellier evidently did not think so. After surveying the sketch critically she drew a broad smudge of paint across its surface, and crumpled the paper between her hands.

The youngsters came tumbling up the steps, the quadroon following at the respectful distance which they required her to observe. Mrs. Pontellier made them carry her paints and things into the house. She sought to detain them for a little talk and some pleasantry. But they were greatly in earnest. They had only come to investigate the contents of the bonbon box. They accepted without murmuring what she chose to give them, each holding out two chubby hands scoop-like, in the vain hope that they might be filled; and then away they went.

The sun was low in the west, and the breeze soft and languorous that came up from the south, charged with the seductive odor of the sea. Children, freshly befurbelowed,[2] were gathering for their games under the oaks. Their voices were high and penetrating.

Madame Ratignolle folded her sewing, placing thimble, scissors and thread all neatly together in the roll, which she pinned securely. She complained of faintness. Mrs. Pontellier flew for the cologne water and a fan. She bathed Madame Ratignolle's

1 But that's not bad at all! She knows what she's doing; she has a talent, yes.
2 Dressed in finery and ruffles.

face with cologne, while Robert plied the fan with unnecessary vigor.

The spell was soon over, and Mrs. Pontellier could not help wondering if there were not a little imagination responsible for its origin, for the rose tint had never faded from her friend's face.

She stood watching the fair woman walk down the long line of galleries with the grace and majesty which queens are sometimes supposed to possess. Her little ones ran to meet her. Two of them clung about her white skirts, the third she took from its nurse and with a thousand endearments bore it along in her own fond, encircling arms. Though, as everybody well knew, the doctor had forbidden her to lift so much as a pin!

"Are you going bathing?" asked Robert of Mrs. Pontellier. It was not so much a question as a reminder.

"Oh, no," she answered, with a tone of indecision. "I'm tired; I think not." Her glance wandered from his face away toward the Gulf, whose sonorous murmur reached her like a loving but imperative entreaty.

"Oh, come!" he insisted. "You mustn't miss your bath. Come on. The water must be delicious; it will not hurt you. Come."

He reached up for her big, rough straw hat that hung on a peg outside the door, and put it on her head. They descended the steps, and walked away together toward the beach. The sun was low in the west and the breeze was soft and warm.

VI

Edna Pontellier could not have told why, wishing to go to the beach with Robert, she should in the first place have declined, and in the second place have followed in obedience to one of the two contradictory impulses which impelled her.

A certain light was beginning to dawn dimly within her,—the light which, showing the way, forbids it.

At that early period it served but to bewilder her. It moved her to dreams, to thoughtfulness, to the shadowy anguish which had overcome her the midnight when she had abandoned herself to tears.

In short, Mrs. Pontellier was beginning to realize her position in the universe as a human being, and to recognize her relations as an individual to the world within and about her. This may seem like a ponderous weight of wisdom to descend upon the soul of a young woman of twenty-eight—perhaps more wisdom than the Holy Ghost is usually pleased to vouchsafe to any woman.

But the beginning of things, of a world especially, is necessarily vague, tangled, chaotic, and exceedingly disturbing. How few of us ever emerge from such beginning! How many souls perish in its tumult!

The voice of the sea is seductive; never ceasing, whispering, clamoring, murmuring, inviting the soul to wander for a spell in abysses of solitude; to lose itself in mazes of inward contemplation.

The voice of the sea speaks to the soul. The touch of the sea is sensuous, enfolding the body in its soft, close embrace.

VII

Mrs. Pontellier was not a woman given to confidences, a characteristic hitherto contrary to her nature. Even as a child she had lived her own small life all within herself. At a very early period she had apprehended instinctively the dual life—that outward existence which conforms, the inward life which questions.

That summer at Grand Isle she began to loosen a little the mantle of reserve that had always enveloped her. There may have been—there must have been—influences, both subtle and apparent, working in their several ways to induce her to do this; but the most obvious was the influence of Adèle Ratignolle. The excessive physical charm of the Creole had first attracted her, for Edna had a sensuous susceptibility to beauty. Then the candor of the woman's whole existence, which every one might read, and which formed so striking a contrast to her own habitual reserve—this might have furnished a link. Who can tell what metals the gods use in forging the subtle bond which we call sympathy, which we might as well call love.

The two women went away one morning to the beach together, arm in arm, under the huge white sunshade. Edna had prevailed upon Madame Ratignolle to leave the children behind, though she could not induce her to relinquish a diminutive roll of needlework, which Adèle begged to be allowed to slip into the depths of her pocket. In some unaccountable way they had escaped from Robert.

The walk to the beach was no inconsiderable one, consisting as it did of a long, sandy path, upon which a sporadic and tangled growth that bordered it on either side made frequent and unexpected inroads. There were acres of yellow camomile reaching out on either hand. Further away still, vegetable gardens abounded, with frequent small plantations of orange or lemon trees intervening. The dark green clusters glistened from afar in the sun.

The women were both of goodly height, Madame Ratignolle possessing the more feminine and matronly figure. The charm of Edna Pontellier's physique stole insensibly upon you. The lines of her body were long, clean and symmetrical; it was a body which occasionally fell into splendid poses; there was no suggestion of the trim, stereotyped fashion-plate about it. A casual and indiscriminating observer, in passing, might not cast a second glance upon the figure. But with more feeling and discernment he would have recognized the noble beauty of its modeling, and the graceful severity of poise and movement, which made Edna Pontellier different from the crowd.

She wore a cool muslin[1] that morning—white, with a waving vertical line of brown running through it; also a white linen collar and the big straw hat which she had taken from the peg outside the door. The hat rested any way on her yellow-brown hair, that waved a little, was heavy, and clung close to her head.

Madame Ratignolle, more careful of her complexion, had twined a gauze veil about her head. She wore dogskin gloves, with gauntlets that protected her wrists. She was dressed in pure white, with a fluffiness of ruffles that became her. The draperies and fluttering things which she wore suited her rich, luxuriant beauty as a greater severity of line could not have done.

There were a number of bath-houses along the beach, of rough but solid construction, built with small, protecting galleries facing the water. Each house consisted of two compartments, and each family at Lebrun's possessed a compartment for itself, fitted out with all the essential paraphernalia of the bath and whatever other conveniences the owners might desire. The two women had no intention of bathing; they had just strolled down to the beach for a walk and to be alone and near the water. The Pontellier and Ratignolle compartments adjoined one another under the same roof.

Mrs. Pontellier had brought down her key through force of habit. Unlocking the door of her bath-room she went inside, and soon emerged, bringing a rug, which she spread upon the floor of the gallery, and two huge hair pillows covered with crash,[2] which she placed against the front of the building.

---

1 A plain, woven cotton fabric.
2 Inexpensive pillows covered with a rough material.

The two seated themselves there in the shade of the porch, side by side, with their backs against the pillows and their feet extended. Madame Ratignolle removed her veil, wiped her face with a rather delicate handkerchief, and fanned herself with the fan which she always carried suspended somewhere about her person by a long, narrow ribbon. Edna removed her collar and opened her dress at the throat. She took the fan from Madame Ratignolle and began to fan both herself and her companion. It was very warm, and for a while they did nothing but exchange remarks about the heat, the sun, the glare. But there was a breeze blowing, a choppy, stiff wind that whipped the water into froth. It fluttered the skirts of the two women and kept them for a while engaged in adjusting, readjusting, tucking in, securing hair-pins and hat-pins. A few persons were sporting some distance away in the water. The beach was very still of human sound at that hour. The lady in black was reading her morning devotions on the porch of a neighboring bath-house. Two young lovers were exchanging their hearts' yearnings beneath the children's tent, which they had found unoccupied.

Edna Pontellier, casting her eyes about, had finally kept them at rest upon the sea. The day was clear and carried the gaze out as far as the blue sky went; there were a few white clouds suspended idly over the horizon. A lateen sail[1] was visible in the direction of Cat Island,[2] and others to the south seemed almost motionless in the far distance.

"Of whom—of what are you thinking?" asked Adèle of her companion, whose countenance she had been watching with a little amused attention, arrested by the absorbed expression which seemed to have seized and fixed every feature into a statuesque repose.

"Nothing," returned Mrs. Pontellier, with a start, adding at once: "How stupid! But it seems to me it is the reply we make instinctively to such a question. Let me see," she went on, throwing back her head and narrowing her fine eyes till they shone like two vivid points of light. "Let me see. I was really not conscious of thinking of anything; but perhaps I can retrace my thoughts."

"Oh! never mind!" laughed Madame Ratignolle. "I am not quite so exacting. I will let you off this time. It is really too hot to think, especially to think about thinking."

---

1 A triangular sail.
2 A small island west of Grand Isle.

"But for the fun of it," persisted Edna. "First of all, the sight of the water stretching so far away, those motionless sails against the blue sky, made a delicious picture that I just wanted to sit and look at. The hot wind beating in my face made me think—without any connection that I can trace—of a summer day in Kentucky, of a meadow that seemed as big as the ocean to the very little girl walking through the grass, which was higher than her waist. She threw out her arms as if swimming when she walked, beating the tall grass as one strikes out in the water. Oh, I see the connection now!"

"Where were you going that day in Kentucky, walking through the grass?"

"I don't remember now. I was just walking diagonally across a big field. My sun-bonnet obstructed the view. I could see only the stretch of green before me, and I felt as if I must walk on forever, without coming to the end of it. I don't remember whether I was frightened or pleased. I must have been entertained.

"Likely as not it was Sunday," she laughed; "and I was running away from prayers, from the Presbyterian service, read in a spirit of gloom by my father that chills me yet to think of."

"And have you been running away from prayers ever since, *ma chère*?"[1] asked Madame Ratignolle, amused.

"No! oh, no!" Edna hastened to say. "I was a little unthinking child in those days, just following a misleading impulse without question. On the contrary, during one period of my life religion took a firm hold upon me; after I was twelve and until—until—why, I suppose until now, though I never thought much about it—just driven along by habit. But do you know," she broke off, turning her quick eyes upon Madame Ratignolle and leaning forward a little so as to bring her face quite close to that of her companion, "sometimes I feel this summer as if I were walking through the green meadow again; idly, aimlessly, unthinking and unguided."

Madame Ratignolle laid her hand over that of Mrs. Pontellier, which was near her. Seeing that the hand was not withdrawn, she clasped it firmly and warmly. She even stroked it a little, fondly, with the other hand, murmuring in an undertone, "*Pauvre chérie.*"[2]

The action was at first a little confusing to Edna, but she soon lent herself readily to the Creole's gentle caress. She was not accustomed to an outward and spoken expression of affection,

---

1 My dear.
2 Poor darling.

either in herself or in others. She and her younger sister, Janet, had quarreled a good deal through force of unfortunate habit. Her older sister, Margaret, was matronly and dignified, probably from having assumed matronly and housewifely responsibilities too early in life, their mother having died when they were quite young. Margaret was not effusive; she was practical. Edna had had an occasional girl friend, but whether accidentally or not, they seemed to have been all of one type—the self-contained. She never realized that the reserve of her own character had much, perhaps everything, to do with this. Her most intimate friend at school had been one of rather exceptional intellectual gifts, who wrote fine-sounding essays, which Edna admired and strove to imitate; and with her she talked and glowed over the English classics, and sometimes held religious and political controversies.

Edna often wondered at one propensity which sometimes had inwardly disturbed her without causing any outward show or manifestation on her part. At a very early age—perhaps it was when she traversed the ocean of waving grass—she remembered that she had been passionately enamored of a dignified and sad-eyed cavalry officer who visited her father in Kentucky. She could not leave his presence when he was there, nor remove her eyes from his face, which was something like Napoleon's, with a lock of black hair falling across the forehead. But the cavalry officer melted imperceptibly out of her existence.

At another time her affections were deeply engaged by a young gentleman who visited a lady on a neighboring plantation. It was after they went to Mississippi to live. The young man was engaged to be married to the young lady, and they sometimes called upon Margaret, driving over of afternoons in a buggy. Edna was a little miss, just merging into her teens; and the realization that she herself was nothing, nothing, nothing to the engaged young man was a bitter affliction to her. But he, too, went the way of dreams.

She was a grown young woman when she was overtaken by what she supposed to be the climax of her fate. It was when the face and figure of a great tragedian[1] began to haunt her imagination and stir her senses. The persistence of the infatuation lent it

---

1 According to Margo Culley, Edwin Booth was most likely the great tragedian because Chopin "was a fan of the actor and in 1894 published a review of his letters entitled 'The Real Edwin Booth.'" See *The Awakening by Kate Chopin*, ed. Margo Culley, 2nd ed. (New York: Norton Critical, 1976).

an aspect of genuineness. The hopelessness of it colored it with the lofty tones of a great passion.

The picture of the tragedian stood enframed upon her desk. Any one may possess the portrait of a tragedian without exciting suspicion or comment. (This was a sinister reflection which she cherished.) In the presence of others she expressed admiration for his exalted gifts, as she handed the photograph around and dwelt upon the fidelity of the likeness. When alone she sometimes picked it up and kissed the cold glass passionately.

Her marriage to Léonce Pontellier was purely an accident, in this respect resembling many other marriages which masquerade as the decrees of Fate. It was in the midst of her secret great passion that she met him. He fell in love, as men are in the habit of doing, and pressed his suit with an earnestness and an ardor which left nothing to be desired. He pleased her; his absolute devotion flattered her. She fancied there was a sympathy of thought and taste between them, in which fancy she was mistaken. Add to this the violent opposition of her father and her sister Margaret to her marriage with a Catholic,[1] and we need seek no further for the motives which led her to accept Monsieur Pontellier for her husband.

The acme of bliss, which would have been a marriage with the tragedian, was not for her in this world. As the devoted wife of a man who worshiped her, she felt she would take her place with a certain dignity in the world of reality, closing the portals forever behind her upon the realm of romance and dreams.

But it was not long before the tragedian had gone to join the cavalry officer and the engaged young man and a few others; and Edna found herself face to face with the realities. She grew fond of her husband, realizing with some unaccountable satisfaction that no trace of passion or excessive and fictitious warmth colored her affection, thereby threatening its dissolution.

She was fond of her children in an uneven, impulsive way. She would sometimes gather them passionately to her heart; she would sometimes forget them. The year before they had spent part of the summer with their grandmother Pontellier in Iberville.[2] Feeling secure regarding their happiness and welfare,

---

1   Edna was from Kentucky and her family was Protestant. They would have opposed a marriage to a Catholic because it would have required her to convert.

2   Iberville Parish or county is a sugar-farming area south of Baton Rouge named after the founder of Louisiana.

she did not miss them except with an occasional intense longing. Their absence was a sort of relief, though she did not admit this, even to herself. It seemed to free her of a responsibility which she had blindly assumed and for which Fate had not fitted her.

Edna did not reveal so much as all this to Madame Ratignolle that summer day when they sat with faces turned to the sea. But a good part of it escaped her. She had put her head down on Madame Ratignolle's shoulder. She was flushed and felt intoxicated with the sound of her own voice and the unaccustomed taste of candor. It muddled her like wine, or like a first breath of freedom.

There was the sound of approaching voices. It was Robert, surrounded by a troop of children, searching for them. The two little Pontelliers were with him, and he carried Madame Ratignolle's little girl in his arms. There were other children beside, and two nurse-maids followed, looking disagreeable and resigned.

The women at once rose and began to shake out their draperies and relax their muscles. Mrs. Pontellier threw the cushions and rug into the bath-house. The children all scampered off to the awning, and they stood there in a line, gazing upon the intruding lovers, still exchanging their vows and sighs. The lovers got up, with only a silent protest, and walked slowly away somewhere else.

The children possessed themselves of the tent, and Mrs. Pontellier went over to join them.

Madame Ratignolle begged Robert to accompany her to the house; she complained of cramp in her limbs and stiffness of the joints. She leaned draggingly upon his arm as they walked.

VIII

"Do me a favor, Robert," spoke the pretty woman at his side, almost as soon as she and Robert had started on their slow, homeward way. She looked up in his face, leaning on his arm beneath the encircling shadow of the umbrella which he had lifted.

"Granted; as many as you like," he returned, glancing down into her eyes that were full of thoughtfulness and some speculation.

"I only ask for one; let Mrs. Pontellier alone."

"*Tiens!*" he exclaimed, with a sudden, boyish laugh. "*Voilà que Madame Ratignolle est jalouse!*"[1]

---

1 Finally! It appears that Madame Ratignolle is jealous!

"Nonsense! I'm in earnest; I mean what I say. Let Mrs. Pontellier alone."

"Why?" he asked; himself growing serious at his companion's solicitation.

"She is not one of us; she is not like us. She might make the unfortunate blunder of taking you seriously."

His face flushed with annoyance, and taking off his soft hat he began to beat it impatiently against his leg as he walked. "Why shouldn't she take me seriously?" he demanded sharply. "Am I a comedian, a clown, a jack-in-the-box? Why shouldn't she? You Creoles! I have no patience with you! Am I always to be regarded as a feature of an amusing programme? I hope Mrs. Pontellier does take me seriously. I hope she has discernment enough to find in me something besides the *blagueur*.[1] If I thought there was any doubt—"

"Oh, enough, Robert!" she broke into his heated outburst. "You are not thinking of what you are saying. You speak with about as little reflection as we might expect from one of those children down there playing in the sand. If your attentions to any married women here were ever offered with any intention of being convincing, you would not be the gentleman we all know you to be, and you would be unfit to associate with the wives and daughters of the people who trust you."

Madame Ratignolle had spoken what she believed to be the law and the gospel. The young man shrugged his shoulders impatiently.

"Oh! well! That isn't it," slamming his hat down vehemently upon his head. "You ought to feel that such things are not flattering to say to a fellow."

"Should our whole intercourse consist of an exchange of compliments? *Ma foi!*"[2]

"It isn't pleasant to have a woman tell you—" he went on, unheedingly, but breaking off suddenly: "Now if I were like Arobin—you remember Alcée Arobin and that story of the consul's wife at Biloxi?"[3] And he related the story of Alcée Arobin and the consul's wife; and another about the tenor of the French Opera,[4] who received letters which should never have been

---

1 Joker, fool.
2 My faith! Indeed!
3 A resort town in Mississippi on the Gulf Coast, about 85 miles from New Orleans.
4 The French Opera House was built in 1859 to house one of the oldest opera companies in the US.

written; and still other stories, grave and gay, till Mrs. Pontellier and her possible propensity for taking young men seriously was apparently forgotten.

Madame Ratignolle, when they had regained her cottage, went in to take the hour's rest which she considered helpful. Before leaving her, Robert begged her pardon for the impatience—he called it rudeness—with which he had received her well-meant caution.

"You made one mistake, Adèle," he said, with a light smile; "there is no earthly possibility of Mrs. Pontellier ever taking me seriously. You should have me taking myself seriously. Your advice might then have carried some weight and given me subject for some reflection. *Au revoir.*[1] But you look tired," he added, solicitously. "Would you like a cup of bouillon? Shall I stir you a toddy?[2] Let me mix you a toddy with a drop of Angostura."[3]

She acceded to the suggestion of bouillon, which was grateful and acceptable. He went himself to the kitchen, which was a building apart from the cottages and lying to the rear of the house. And he himself brought her the golden-brown bouillon, in a dainty Sèvres[4] cup, with a flaky cracker or two on the saucer.

She thrust a bare, white arm from the curtain which shielded her open door, and received the cup from his hands. She told him he was a *bon garçon*[5] and she meant it. Robert thanked her and turned away toward "the house."

The lovers were just entering the grounds of the *pension*. They were leaning toward each other as the water-oaks bent from the sea. There was not a particle of earth beneath their feet. Their heads might have been turned upside-down, so absolutely did they tread upon blue ether. The lady in black, creeping behind them, looked a trifle paler and more jaded than usual. There was no sign of Mrs. Pontellier and the children. Robert scanned the distance for any such apparition. They would doubtless remain away till the dinner hour. The young man ascended to his mother's room. It was situated at the top of the house, made up of odd angles and a queer, sloping ceiling. Two broad dormer windows looked out toward the Gulf, and as far across it as a

---

1 Goodbye.
2 Hot alcoholic drink perceived to have medicinal qualities.
3 A type of bitters; originally developed as a tonic, it is now primarily used to flavor food and alcoholic drinks.
4 Fine china from France.
5 Good boy.

man's eye might reach. The furnishings of the room were light, cool, and practical.

Madame Lebrun was busily engaged at the sewing-machine. A little black girl sat on the floor, and with her hands worked the treadle of the machine. The Creole woman does not take any chances which may be avoided of imperiling her health.

Robert went over and seated himself on the broad sill of one of the dormer windows. He took a book from his pocket and began energetically to read it, judging by the precision and frequency with which he turned the leaves. The sewing-machine made a resounding clatter in the room; it was of a ponderous, bygone make. In the lulls, Robert and his mother exchanged bits of desultory conversation.

"Where is Mrs. Pontellier?"

"Down at the beach with the children."

"I promised to lend her the Goncourt. Don't forget to take it down when you go; it's there on the bookshelf over the small table." Clatter, clatter, clatter, bang! for the next five or eight minutes.

"Where is Victor going with the rockaway?"

"The rockaway? Victor?"

"Yes; down there in front. He seems to be getting ready to drive away somewhere."

"Call him." Clatter, clatter!

Robert uttered a shrill, piercing whistle which might have been heard back at the wharf.

"He won't look up."

Madame Lebrun flew to the window. She called "Victor!" She waved a handkerchief and called again. The young fellow below got into the vehicle and started the horse off at a gallop.

Madame Lebrun went back to the machine, crimson with annoyance. Victor was the younger son and brother—a *tête montée*,[1] with a temper which invited violence and a will which no ax could break.

"Whenever you say the word I'm read to thrash any amount of reason into him that he's able to hold."

"If your father had only lived!" Clatter, clatter, clatter, clatter, bang! It was a fixed belief with Madame Lebrun that the conduct of the universe and all things pertaining thereto would have been manifestly of a more intelligent and higher order had not Mon-

---

1 A hot head, as in "he is hot headed."

sieur Lebrun been removed to other spheres during the early years of their married life.

"What do you hear from Montel?" Montel was a middle-aged gentleman whose vain ambition and desire for the past twenty years had been to fill the void which Monsieur Lebrun's taking off had left in the Lebrun household. Clatter, clatter, bang, clatter!

"I have a letter somewhere," looking in the machine drawer and finding the letter in the bottom of the work-basket. "He says to tell you he will be in Vera Cruz[1] the beginning of next month"—clatter, clatter!—"and if you still have the intention of joining him"—bang! clatter, clatter, bang!

"Why didn't you tell me so before, mother? You know I wanted—" Clatter, clatter, clatter!

"Do you see Mrs. Pontellier starting back with the children? She will be in late to luncheon again. She never starts to get ready for luncheon till the last minute." Clatter, clatter! "Where are you going?"

"Where did you say the Goncourt was?"

IX

Every light in the hall was ablaze; every lamp turned as high as it could be without smoking the chimney or threatening explosion. The lamps were fixed at intervals against the wall, encircling the whole room. Some one had gathered orange and lemon branches, and with these fashioned graceful festoons between. The dark green of the branches stood out and glistened against the white muslin curtains which draped the windows, and which puffed, floated, and flapped at the capricious will of a stiff breeze that swept up from the Gulf.

It was Saturday night a few weeks after the intimate conversation held between Robert and Madame Ratignolle on their way from the beach. An unusual number of husbands, fathers, and friends had come down to stay over Sunday; and they were being suitably entertained by their families, with the material help of Madame Lebrun. The dining tables had all been removed to one end of the hall, and the chairs ranged about in rows and in clusters. Each little family group had had its say and exchanged its

---

1 Port city on the Gulf Coast of Mexico known for its role in the African slave trade.

domestic gossip earlier in the evening. There was now an apparent disposition to relax; to widen the circle of confidences and give a more general tone to the conversation.

Many of the children had been permitted to sit up beyond their usual bedtime. A small band of them were lying on their stomachs on the floor looking at the colored sheets of the comic papers which Mr. Pontellier had brought down. The little Pontellier boys were permitting them to do so, and making their authority felt.

Music, dancing, and a recitation or two were the entertainments furnished, or rather, offered. But there was nothing systematic about the programme, no appearance of prearrangement nor even premeditation.

At an early hour in the evening the Farival twins were prevailed upon to play the piano. They were girls of fourteen, always clad in the Virgin's colors, blue and white, having been dedicated to the Blessed Virgin at their baptism. They played a duet from "Zampa," and at the earnest solicitation of every one present followed it with the overture to "The Poet and the Peasant."

"*Allez vous-en! Sapristi!*" shrieked the parrot outside the door. He was the only being present who possessed sufficient candor to admit that he was not listening to these gracious performances for the first time that summer. Old Monsieur Farival, grandfather of the twins, grew indignant over the interruption, and insisted upon having the bird removed and consigned to regions of darkness. Victor Lebrun objected; and his decrees were as immutable as those of Fate. The parrot fortunately offered no further interruption to the entertainment, the whole venom of his nature apparently having been cherished up and hurled against the twins in that one impetuous outburst.

Later a young brother and sister gave recitations, which every one present had heard many times at winter evening entertainments in the city.

A little girl performed a skirt dance[1] in the center of the floor. The mother played her accompaniments and at the same time watched her daughter with greedy admiration and nervous apprehension. She need have had no apprehension. The child was mistress of the situation. She had been properly dressed for the

---

1 Invented in 1876 by Kate Vaughn, a member of the Gaiety Quartet, it combines ballet steps and acrobatic kicks into a Vaudeville form. The dance features a colorful, ruffled skirt that allowed just enough of the dancer's leg to peep out to be provocative.

occasion in black tulle[1] and black silk tights. Her little neck and arms were bare, and her hair, artificially crimped, stood out like fluffy black plumes over her head. Her poses were full of grace, and her little black-shod toes twinkled as they shot out and upward with a rapidity and suddenness which were bewildering.

But there was no reason why every one should not dance. Madame Ratignolle could not, so it was she who gaily consented to play for the others. She played very well, keeping excellent waltz time and infusing an expression into the strains which was indeed inspiring. She was keeping up her music on account of the children, she said; because she and her husband both considered it a means of brightening the home and making it attractive.

Almost every one danced but the twins, who could not be induced to separate during the brief period when one or the other should be whirling around the room in the arms of a man. They might have danced together, but they did not think of it.

The children were sent to bed. Some went submissively; others with shrieks and protests as they were dragged away. They had been permitted to sit up till after the ice-cream, which naturally marked the limit of human indulgence.

The ice-cream was passed around with cake—gold and silver cake arranged on platters in alternate slices; it had been made and frozen during the afternoon back of the kitchen by two black women, under the supervision of Victor. It was pronounced a great success—excellent if it had only contained a little less vanilla or a little more sugar, if it had been frozen a degree harder, and if the salt might have been kept out of portions of it. Victor was proud of his achievement, and went about recommending it and urging every one to partake of it to excess.

After Mrs. Pontellier had danced twice with her husband, once with Robert, and once with Monsieur Ratignolle, who was thin and tall and swayed like a reed in the wind when he danced, she went out on the gallery and seated herself on the low window-sill, where she commanded a view of all that went on in the hall and could look out toward the Gulf. There was a soft effulgence in the east. The moon was coming up, and its mystic shimmer was casting a million lights across the distant, restless water.

"Would you like to hear Mademoiselle Reisz play?" asked Robert, coming out on the porch where she was. Of course Edna would like to hear Mademoiselle Reisz play; but she feared it would be useless to entreat her.

---

1   A sheer material used in veils or ballet costumes.

"I'll ask her," he said. "I'll tell her that you want to hear her. She likes you. She will come." He turned and hurried away to one of the far cottages, where Mademoiselle Reisz was shuffling away. She was dragging a chair in and out of her room, and at intervals objecting to the crying of a baby, which a nurse in the adjoining cottage was endeavoring to put to sleep. She was a disagreeable little woman, no longer young, who had quarreled with almost every one, owing to a temper which was self-assertive and a disposition to trample upon the rights of others. Robert prevailed upon her without any too great difficulty.

She entered the hall with him during a lull in the dance. She made an awkward, imperious little bow as she went in. She was a homely woman, with a small weazened face and body and eyes that glowed. She had absolutely no taste in dress, and wore a batch of rusty black lace with a bunch of artificial violets pinned to the side of her hair.

"Ask Mrs. Pontellier what she would like to hear me play," she requested of Robert. She sat perfectly still before the piano, not touching the keys, while Robert carried her message to Edna at the window. A general air of surprise and genuine satisfaction fell upon every one as they saw the pianist enter. There was a settling down, and a prevailing air of expectancy everywhere. Edna was a trifle embarrassed at being thus signaled out for the imperious little woman's favor. She would not dare to choose, and begged that Mademoiselle Reisz would please herself in her selections.

Edna was what she herself called very fond of music. Musical strains, well rendered, had a way of evoking pictures in her mind. She sometimes liked to sit in the room of mornings when Madame Ratignolle played or practiced. One piece which that lady played Edna had entitled "Solitude."[1] It was a short, plaintive, minor strain. The name of the piece was something else, but she called it "Solitude." When she heard it there came before her imagination the figure of a man standing beside a desolate rock on the seashore. He was naked. His attitude was one of hopeless resignation as he looked toward a distant bird winging its flight away from him.

Another piece called to her mind a dainty young woman clad in an Empire gown, taking mincing dancing steps as she came down a long avenue between tall hedges. Again, another

---

1 Also the title of a short story by French writer Guy de Maupassant (1850-93) that Chopin translated. Her translation was published in *St. Louis Life*, 28 December 1895.

reminded her of children at play, and still another of nothing on earth but a demure lady stroking a cat.

The very first chords which Mademoiselle Reisz struck upon the piano sent a keen tremor down Mrs. Pontellier's spinal column. It was not the first time she had heard an artist at the piano. Perhaps it was the first time she was ready, perhaps the first time her being was tempered to take an impress of the abiding truth.

She waited for the material pictures which she thought would gather and blaze before her imagination. She waited in vain. She saw no pictures of solitude, of hope, of longing, or of despair. But the very passions themselves were aroused within her soul, swaying it, lashing it, as the waves daily beat upon her splendid body. She trembled, she was choking, and the tears blinded her.

Mademoiselle had finished. She arose, and bowing her stiff, lofty bow, she went away, stopping for neither thanks nor applause. As she passed along the gallery she patted Edna upon the shoulder.

"Well, how did you like my music?" she asked. The young woman was unable to answer; she pressed the hand of the pianist convulsively. Mademoiselle Reisz perceived her agitation and even her tears. She patted her again upon the shoulder as she said:

"You are the only one worth playing for. Those others? Bah!" and she went shuffling and sidling on down the gallery toward her room.

But she was mistaken about "those others." Her playing had aroused a fever of enthusiasm. "What passion!" "What an artist!" "I have always said no one could play Chopin[1] like Mademoiselle Reisz!" "That last prelude! Bon Dieu![2] It shakes a man!"

It was growing late, and there was a general disposition to disband. But some one, perhaps it was Robert, thought of a bath at that mystic hour and under that mystic moon.

X

At all events Robert proposed it, and there was not a dissenting voice. There was not one but was ready to follow when he led the way. He did not lead the way, however, he directed the way; and he himself loitered behind with the lovers, who had betrayed a

---

1 Frederic Chopin (1810-49), Polish pianist and composer.
2 Good God!

disposition to linger and hold themselves apart. He walked between them, whether with malicious or mischievous intent was not wholly clear, even to himself.

The Pontelliers and Ratignolles walked ahead; the women leaning upon the arms of their husbands. Edna could hear Robert's voice behind them, and could sometimes hear what he said. She wondered why he did not join them. It was unlike him not to. Of late he had sometimes held away from her for an entire day, redoubling his devotion upon the next and the next, as though to make up for hours that had been lost. She missed him the days when some pretext served to take him away from her, just as one misses the sun on a cloudy day without having thought much about the sun when it was shining.

The people walked in little groups toward the beach. They talked and laughed; some of them sang. There was a band playing down at Klein's hotel, and the strains reached them faintly, tempered by the distance. There were strange, rare odors abroad—a tangle of the sea smell and of weeds and damp, new-plowed earth, mingled with the heavy perfume of a field of white blossoms somewhere near. But the night sat lightly upon the sea and the land. There was no weight of darkness; there were no shadows. The white light of the moon had fallen upon the world like the mystery and the softness of sleep.

Most of them walked into the water as though into a native element. The sea was quiet now, and swelled lazily in broad billows that melted into one another and did not break except upon the beach in little foamy crests that coiled back like slow, white serpents.

Edna had attempted all summer to learn to swim. She had received instructions from both the men and women; in some instances from the children. Robert had pursued a system of lessons almost daily; and he was nearly at the point of discouragement in realizing the futility of his efforts. A certain ungovernable dread hung about her when in the water, unless there was a hand near by that might reach out and reassure her.

But that night she was like the little tottering, stumbling, clutching child, who of a sudden realizes its powers, and walks for the first time alone, boldly and with over-confidence. She could have shouted for joy. She did shout for joy, as with a sweeping stroke or two she lifted her body to the surface of the water.

A feeling of exultation overtook her, as if some power of significant import had been given her to control the working of her body and her soul. She grew daring and reckless, overestimating her strength. She wanted to swim far out, where no woman had swum before.

Her unlooked-for achievement was the subject of wonder, applause, and admiration. Each one congratulated himself that his special teachings had accomplished this desired end.

"How easy it is!" she thought. "It is nothing," she said aloud; "why did I not discover before that it was nothing. Think of the time I have lost splashing about like a baby!" She would not join the groups in their sports and bouts, but intoxicated with her newly conquered power, she swam out alone.

She turned her face seaward to gather in an impression of space and solitude, which the vast expanse of water, meeting and melting with the moonlit sky, conveyed to her excited fancy. As she swam she seemed to be reaching out for the unlimited in which to lose herself.

Once she turned and looked toward the shore, toward the people she had left there. She had not gone any great distance— that is, what would have been a great distance for an experienced swimmer. But to her unaccustomed vision the stretch of water behind her assumed the aspect of a barrier which her unaided strength would never be able to overcome.

A quick vision of death smote her soul, and for a second of time appalled and enfeebled her senses. But by an effort she rallied her staggering faculties and managed to regain the land.

She made no mention of her encounter with death and her flash of terror, except to say to her husband, "I thought I should have perished out there alone."

"You were not so very far, my dear; I was watching you," he told her.

Edna went at once to the bath-house, and she had put on her dry clothes and was ready to return home before the others had left the water. She started to walk away alone. They all called to her and shouted to her. She waved a dissenting hand, and went on, paying no further heed to their renewed cries which sought to detain her.

"Sometimes I am tempted to think that Mrs. Pontellier is capricious," said Madame Lebrun, who was amusing herself immensely and feared that Edna's abrupt departure might put an end to the pleasure.

"I know she is," assented Mr. Pontellier; "sometimes, not often."

Edna had not traversed a quarter of the distance on her way home before she was overtaken by Robert.

"Did you think I was afraid?" she asked him, without a shade of annoyance.

"No; I knew you weren't afraid."

"Then why did you come? Why didn't you stay out there with the others?"

"I never thought of it."

"Thought of what?"

"Of anything. What difference does it make?"

"I'm very tired," she uttered, complainingly.

"I know you are."

"You don't know anything about it. Why should you know? I never was so exhausted in my life. But it isn't unpleasant. A thousand emotions have swept through me to-night. I don't comprehend half of them. Don't mind what I'm saying; I am just thinking aloud. I wonder if I shall ever be stirred again as Mademoiselle Reisz's playing moved me to-night. I wonder if any night on earth will ever again be like this one. It is like a night in a dream. The people about me are like some uncanny, half-human beings. There must be spirits abroad to-night."

"There are," whispered Robert. "Didn't you know this was the twenty-eighth of August?"

"The twenty-eighth of August?"

"Yes. On the twenty-eighth of August, at the hour of midnight, and if the moon is shining—the moon must be shining—a spirit that has haunted these shores for ages rises up from the Gulf. With its own penetrating vision the spirit seeks some one mortal worthy to hold him company, worthy of being exalted for a few hours into realms of the semi-celestials.[1] His search has always hitherto been fruitless, and he has sunk back, disheartened, into the sea. But to-night he found Mrs. Pontellier. Perhaps he will never wholly release her from the spell. Perhaps she will never again suffer a poor, unworthy earthling to walk in the shadow of her divine presence."

"Don't banter me," she said, wounded at what appeared to be his flippancy. He did not mind the entreaty, but the tone with its delicate note of pathos was like a reproach. He could not explain; he could not tell her that he had penetrated her mood and understood. He said nothing except to offer her his arm, for, by her own admission, she was exhausted. She had been walking alone with her arms hanging limp, letting her white skirts trail along the dewy path. She took his arm, but she did not lean upon it. She

---

1 Partially heavenly or mythical beings.

let her hand lie listlessly, as though her thoughts were else-where—somewhere in advance of her body, and she was striving to overtake them.

Robert assisted her into the hammock which swung from the post before her door out to the trunk of a tree.

"Will you stay out here and wait for Mr. Pontellier?" he asked.

"I'll stay out here. Good-night."

"Shall I get you a pillow?"

"There's one here," she said, feeling about, for they were in the shadow.

"It must be soiled; the children have been tumbling it about."

"No matter." And having discovered the pillow, she adjusted it beneath her head. She extended herself in the hammock with a deep breath of relief. She was not a supercilious or an over-dainty woman. She was not much given to reclining in the hammock, and when she did so it was with no cat-like suggestion of volup-tuous ease, but with a beneficent repose which seemed to invade her whole body.

"Shall I stay with you till Mr. Pontellier comes?" asked Robert, seating himself on the outer edge of one of the steps and taking hold of the hammock rope which was fastened to the post.

"If you wish. Don't swing the hammock. Will you get my white shawl which I left on the window-sill over at the house?"

"Are you chilly?"

"No; but I shall be presently."

"Presently?" he laughed. "Do you know what time it is? How long are you going to stay out here?"

"I don't know. Will you get the shawl?"

"Of course I will," he said, rising. He went over to the house, walking along the grass. She watched his figure pass in and out of the strips of moonlight. It was past midnight. It was very quiet.

When he returned with the shawl she took it and kept it in her hand. She did not put it around her.

"Did you say I should stay till Mr. Pontellier came back?"

"I said you might if you wished to."

He seated himself again and rolled a cigarette, which he smoked in silence. Neither did Mrs. Pontellier speak. No multitude of words could have been more significant than those moments of silence, or more pregnant with the first-felt throbbings of desire.

When the voices of the bathers were heard approaching, Robert said good-night. She did not answer him. He thought she was asleep. Again she watched his figure pass in and out of the strips of moonlight as he walked away.

XI

"What are you doing out here, Edna? I thought I should find you in bed," said her husband, when he discovered her lying there. He had walked up with Madame Lebrun and left her at the house. His wife did not reply.

"Are you asleep?" he asked, bending down close to look at her.

"No." Her eyes gleamed bright and intense, with no sleepy shadows, as they looked into his.

"Do you know it is past one o'clock? Come on," and he mounted the steps and went into their room.

"Edna!" called Mr. Pontellier from within, after a few moments had gone by.

"Don't wait for me," she answered. He thrust his head through the door.

"You will take cold out there," he said, irritably. "What folly is this? Why don't you come in?"

"It isn't cold; I have my shawl."

"The mosquitoes will devour you."

"There are no mosquitoes."

She heard him moving about the room; every sound indicating impatience and irritation. Another time she would have gone in at his request. She would, through habit, have yielded to his desire; not with any sense of submission or obedience to his compelling wishes, but unthinkingly, as we walk, move, sit, stand, go through the daily treadmill of the life which has been portioned out to us.

"Edna, dear, are you not coming in soon?" he asked again, this time fondly, with a note of entreaty.

"No; I am going to stay out here."

"This is more than folly," he blurted out. "I can't permit you to stay out there all night. You must come in the house instantly."

With a writhing motion she settled herself more securely in the hammock. She perceived that her will had blazed up, stubborn and resistant. She could not at that moment have done other than denied and resisted. She wondered if her husband had ever spoken to her like that before, and if she had submitted to his command. Of course she had; she remembered that she had. But she could not realize why or how she should have yielded, feeling as she then did.

"Léonce, go to bed," she said. "I mean to stay out here. I don't wish to go in, and I don't intend to. Don't speak to me like that again; I shall not answer you."

Mr. Pontellier had prepared for bed, but he slipped on an extra garment. He opened a bottle of wine, of which he kept a small and select supply in a buffet of his own. He drank a glass of the wine and went out on the gallery and offered a glass to his wife. She did not wish any. He drew up the rocker, hoisted his slippered feet on the rail, and proceeded to smoke a cigar. He smoked two cigars; then he went inside and drank another glass of wine. Mrs. Pontellier again declined to accept a glass when it was offered to her. Mr. Pontellier once more seated himself with elevated feet, and after a reasonable interval of time smoked some more cigars.

Edna began to feel like one who awakens gradually out of a dream, a delicious, grotesque, impossible dream, to feel again the realities pressing into her soul. The physical need for sleep began to overtake her; the exuberance which had sustained and exalted her spirit left her helpless and yielding to the conditions which crowded her in.

The stillest hour of the night had come, the hour before dawn, when the world seems to hold its breath. The moon hung low, and had turned from silver to copper in the sleeping sky. The old owl no longer hooted, and the water-oaks had ceased to moan as they bent their heads.

Edna arose, cramped from lying so long and still in the hammock. She tottered up the steps, clutching feebly at the post before passing into the house.

"Are you coming in, Léonce?" she asked, turning her face toward her husband.

"Yes, dear," he answered, with a glance following a misty puff of smoke. "Just as soon as I have finished my cigar."

XII

She slept but a few hours. They were troubled and feverish hours, disturbed with dreams that were intangible, that eluded her, leaving only an impression upon her half-awakened senses of something unattainable. She was up and dressed in the cool of the early morning. The air was invigorating and steadied somewhat her faculties. However, she was not seeking refreshment or help from any source, either external or from within. She was blindly following whatever impulse moved her, as if she had placed herself in alien hands for direction, and freed her soul of responsibility.

Most of the people at that early hour were still in bed and asleep. A few, who intended to go over to the *Chênière* for mass, were moving about. The lovers, who had laid their plans the night before, were already strolling toward the wharf. The lady in black, with her Sunday prayer-book, velvet and gold-clasped, and her Sunday silver beads, was following them at no great distance. Old Monsieur Farival was up, and was more than half inclined to do anything that suggested itself. He put on his big straw hat, and taking his umbrella from the stand in the hall, followed the lady in black, never overtaking her.

The little negro girl who worked Madame Lebrun's sewing-machine was sweeping the galleries with long, absent-minded strokes of the broom. Edna sent her up into the house to awaken Robert.

"Tell him I am going to the *Chênière*. The boat is ready; tell him to hurry."

He had soon joined her. She had never sent for him before. She had never asked for him. She had never seemed to want him before. She did not appear conscious that she had done anything unusual in commanding his presence. He was apparently equally unconscious of anything extraordinary in the situation. But his face was suffused with a quiet glow when he met her.

They went together back to the kitchen to drink coffee. There was no time to wait for any nicety of service. They stood outside the window and the cook passed them their coffee and a roll, which they drank and ate from the window-sill. Edna said it tasted good. She had not thought of coffee nor of anything. He told her he had often noticed that she lacked forethought.

"Wasn't it enough to think of going to the *Chênière* and waking you up?" she laughed. "Do I have to think of everything?—as Léonce says when he's in a bad humor. I don't blame him; he'd never be in a bad humor if it weren't for me."

They took a short cut across the sands. At a distance they could see the curious procession moving toward the wharf—the lovers, shoulder to shoulder, creeping; the lady in black, gaining steadily upon them; old Monsieur Farival, losing ground inch by inch, and a young barefooted Spanish girl, with a red kerchief on her head and a basket on her arm, bringing up the rear.

Robert knew the girl, and he talked to her a little in the boat. No one present understood what they said. Her name was Mariequita. She had a round, sly, piquant face and pretty black eyes. Her hands were small, and she kept them folded over the handle of her basket. Her feet were broad and coarse. She did not strive to hide them. Edna looked at her feet, and noticed the sand and slime between her brown toes.

Beaudelet grumbled because Mariequita was there, taking up so much room. In reality he was annoyed at having old Monsieur Farival, who considered himself the better sailor of the two. But he would not quarrel with so old a man as Monsieur Farival, so he quarreled with Mariequita. The girl was deprecatory at one moment, appealing to Robert. She was saucy the next, moving her head up and down, making "eyes" at Robert and making "mouths" at Beaudelet.

The lovers were all alone. They saw nothing, they heard nothing. The lady in black was counting her beads for the third time. Old Monsieur Farival talked incessantly of what he knew about handling a boat, and of what Beaudelet did not know on the same subject.

Edna liked it all. She looked Mariequita up and down, from her ugly brown toes to her pretty black eyes, and back again.

"Why does she look at me like that?" inquired the girl of Robert.

"Maybe she thinks you are pretty. Shall I ask her?"

"No. Is she your sweetheart?"

"She's a married lady, and has two children."

"Oh! well! Francisco ran away with Sylvano's wife, who had four children. They took all his money and one of the children and stole his boat."

"Shut up!"

"Does she understand?"

"Oh, hush!"

"Are those two married over there—leaning on each other?"

"Of course not," laughed Robert.

"Of course not," echoed Mariequita, with a serious, confirmatory bob of the head.

The sun was high up and beginning to bite. The swift breeze seemed to Edna to bury the sting of it into the pores of her face and hands. Robert held his umbrella over her.

As they went cutting sidewise through the water, the sails bellied taut, with the wind filling and overflowing them. Old Monsieur Farival laughed sardonically at something as he looked at the sails, and Beaudelet swore at the old man under his breath.

Sailing across the bay to the *Chênière Caminada*, Edna felt as if she were being borne away from some anchorage which had held her fast, whose chains had been loosening—had snapped the night before when the mystic spirit was abroad, leaving her free to drift whithersoever she chose to set her sails. Robert spoke to her incessantly; he no longer noticed Mariequita. The girl had shrimps in her bamboo basket. They were covered with Spanish moss. She beat the moss down impatiently, and muttered to herself sullenly.

"Let us go to Grande Terre[1] to-morrow?" said Robert in a low voice.

"What shall we do there?"

"Climb up the hill to the old fort and look at the little wriggling gold snakes, and watch the lizards sun themselves."

She gazed away toward Grande Terre and thought she would like to be alone there with Robert, in the sun, listening to the ocean's roar and watching the slimy lizards writhe in and out among the ruins of the old fort.

"And the next day or the next we can sail to the Bayou Brulow,"[2] he went on.

"What shall we do there?"

"Anything—cast bait for fish."

"No; we'll go back to Grande Terre. Let the fish alone."

"We'll go wherever you like," he said. "I'll have Tonie come over and help me patch and trim my boat. We shall not need Beaudelet nor any one. Are you afraid of the pirogue?"[3]

"Oh, no."

"Then I'll take you some night in the pirogue when the moon shines. Maybe your Gulf spirit will whisper to you in which of these islands the treasures are hidden—direct you to the very spot, perhaps."

"And in a day we should be rich!" she laughed. "I'd give it all to you, the pirate gold and every bit of treasure we could dig up. I think you would know how to spend it. Pirate gold isn't a thing to be hoarded or utilized. It is something to squander and throw to the four winds, for the fun of seeing the golden specks fly."

"We'd share it, and scatter it together," he said. His face flushed.

They all went together up to the quaint little Gothic church of Our Lady of Lourdes,[4] gleaming all brown and yellow with paint in the sun's glare.

---

1 An island off the coast of Louisiana between Barataria Bay and the Gulf Coast.
2 A small village near Grand Isle, built on stilts because of the frequent hurricanes in the area.
3 A small, flat-bottomed boat similar to a canoe that is commonly used in Louisiana.
4 Catholic church on Grand Isle, built by a French nobleman, Baron d'Espinose. The tall, narrow church was located in the middle of the island and fashioned in Gothic style.

Only Beaudelet remained behind, tinkering at his boat, and Mariequita walked away with her basket of shrimps, casting a look of childish ill-humor and reproach at Robert from the corner of her eye.

XIII

A feeling of oppression and drowsiness overcame Edna during the service. Her head began to ache, and the lights on the altar swayed before her eyes. Another time she might have made an effort to regain her composure; but her one thought was to quit the stifling atmosphere of the church and reach the open air. She arose, climbing over Robert's feet with a muttered apology. Old Monsieur Farival, flurried, curious, stood up, but upon seeing that Robert had followed Mrs. Pontellier, he sank back into his seat. He whispered an anxious inquiry of the lady in black, who did not notice him or reply, but kept her eyes fastened upon the pages of her velvet prayer-book.

"I felt giddy and almost overcome," Edna said, lifting her hands instinctively to her head and pushing her straw hat up from her forehead. "I couldn't have stayed through the service." They were outside in the shadow of the church. Robert was full of solicitude.

"It was folly to have thought of going in the first place, let alone staying. Come over to Madame Antoine's;[1] you can rest there." He took her arm and led her away, looking anxiously and continuously down into her face.

How still it was, with only the voice of the sea whispering through the reeds that grew in the salt-water pools! The long line of little gray, weather-beaten houses nestled peacefully among the orange trees. It must always have been God's day on that low, drowsy island, Edna thought. They stopped, leaning over a jagged fence made of sea-drift, to ask for water. A youth, a mild-faced Acadian,[2] was drawing water from the cistern, which was nothing more than a rusty buoy, with an opening on one side, sunk in the ground. The water which the youth handed to them in a tin pail

---

1   A recurring character in Chopin's other fiction, specifically "At Chênière Caminada" (see below, 169).

2   The term from which Cajun is derived, i.e., a French Canadian from the Acadia region of Nova Scotia who settled in Louisiana after the Acadian Expulsion (see Appendix 278).

was not cold to taste, but it was cool to her heated face, and it greatly revived and refreshed her.

Madame Antoine's cot[1] was at the far end of the village. She welcomed them with all the native hospitality, as she would have opened her door to let the sunlight in. She was fat, and walked heavily and clumsily across the floor. She could speak no English, but when Robert made her understand that the lady who accompanied him was ill and desired to rest, she was all eagerness to make Edna feel at home and to dispose of her comfortably.

The whole place was immaculately clean, and the big, four-posted bed, snow-white, invited one to repose. It stood in a small side room which looked out across a narrow grass plot toward the shed, where there was a disabled boat lying keel upward.

Madame Antoine had not gone to mass. Her son Tonie had, but she supposed he would soon be back, and she invited Robert to be seated and wait for him. But he went and sat outside the door and smoked. Madame Antoine busied herself in the large front room preparing dinner. She was boiling mullets[2] over a few red coals in the huge fireplace.

Edna, left alone in the little side room, loosened her clothes, removing the greater part of them. She bathed her face, her neck and arms in the basin that stood between the windows. She took off her shoes and stockings and stretched herself in the very center of the high, white bed. How luxurious it felt to rest thus in a strange, quaint bed, with its sweet country odor of laurel lingering about the sheets and mattress! She stretched her strong limbs that ached a little. She ran her fingers through her loosened hair for a while. She looked at her round arms as she held them straight up and rubbed them one after the other, observing closely, as if it were something she saw for the first time, the fine, firm quality and texture of her flesh. She clasped her hands easily above her head, and it was thus she fell asleep.

She slept lightly at first, half awake and drowsily attentive to the things about her. She could hear Madame Antoine's heavy, scraping tread as she walked back and forth on the sanded floor. Some chickens were clucking outside the windows, scratching for bits of gravel in the grass. Later she half heard the voices of Robert and Tonie talking under the shed. She did not stir. Even her eyelids rested numb and heavily over her sleepy eyes. The voices went on—Tonie's slow, Acadian drawl, Robert's quick,

---

1 Cottage.
2 A small fish, used more often for bait than for food.

soft, smooth French. She understood French imperfectly unless directly addressed, and the voices were only part of the other drowsy, muffled sounds lulling her senses.

When Edna awoke it was with the conviction that she had slept long and soundly. The voices were hushed under the shed. Madame Antoine's step was no longer to be heard in the adjoining room. Even the chickens had gone elsewhere to scratch and cluck. The mosquito bar was drawn over her; the old woman had come in while she slept and let down the bar. Edna arose quietly from the bed, and looking between the curtains of the window, she saw by the slanting rays of the sun that the afternoon was far advanced. Robert was out there under the shed, reclining in the shade against the sloping keel of the overturned boat. He was reading from a book. Tonie was no longer with him. She wondered what had become of the rest of the party. She peeped out at him two or three times as she stood washing herself in the little basin between the windows.

Madame Antoine had laid some coarse, clean towels upon a chair, and had placed a box of *poudre de riz*[1] within easy reach. Edna dabbed the powder upon her nose and cheeks as she looked at herself closely in the little distorted mirror which hung on the wall above the basin. Her eyes were bright and wide awake and her face glowed.

When she had completed her toilet she walked into the adjoining room. She was very hungry. No one was there. But there was a cloth spread upon the table that stood against the wall, and a cover was laid for one, with a crusty brown loaf and a bottle of wine beside the plate. Edna bit a piece from the brown loaf, tearing it with her strong, white teeth. She poured some of the wine into the glass and drank it down. Then she went softly out of doors, and plucking an orange from the low-hanging bough of a tree, threw it at Robert, who did not know she was awake and up.

An illumination broke over his whole face when he saw her and joined her under the orange tree.

"How many years have I slept?" she inquired. "The whole island seems changed. A new race of beings must have sprung up, leaving only you and me as past relics. How many ages ago did Madame Antoine and Tonie die? and when did our people from Grand Isle disappear from the earth?"

He familiarly adjusted a ruffle upon her shoulder.

---

1   Face powder.

"You have slept precisely one hundred years. I was left here to guard your slumbers; and for one hundred years I have been out under the shed reading a book. The only evil I couldn't prevent was to keep a broiled fowl from drying up."

"If it has turned to stone, still will I eat it," said Edna, moving with him into the house. "But really, what has become of Monsieur Farival and the others?"

"Gone hours ago. When they found that you were sleeping they thought it best not to awake you. Any way, I wouldn't have let them. What was I here for?"

"I wonder if Léonce will be uneasy!" she speculated, as she seated herself at table.

"Of course not; he knows you are with me," Robert replied, as he busied himself among sundry pans and covered dishes which had been left standing on the hearth.

"Where are Madame Antoine and her son?" asked Edna.

"Gone to Vespers,[1] and to visit some friends, I believe. I am to take you back in Tonie's boat whenever you are ready to go."

He stirred the smoldering ashes till the broiled fowl began to sizzle afresh. He served her with no mean repast, dripping the coffee anew and sharing it with her. Madame Antoine had cooked little else than the mullets, but while Edna slept Robert had foraged the island. He was childishly gratified to discover her appetite, and to see the relish with which she ate the food which he had procured for her.

"Shall we go right away?" she asked, after draining her glass and brushing together the crumbs of the crusty loaf.

"The sun isn't as low as it will be in two hours," he answered.

"The sun will be gone in two hours."

"Well, let it go; who cares!"

They waited a good while under the orange trees, till Madame Antoine came back, panting, waddling, with a thousand apologies to explain her absence. Tonie did not dare to return. He was shy, and would not willingly face any woman except his mother.

It was very pleasant to stay there under the orange trees, while the sun dipped lower and lower, turning the western sky to flaming copper and gold. The shadows lengthened and crept out like stealthy, grotesque monsters across the grass.

Edna and Robert both sat upon the ground—that is, he lay upon the ground beside her, occasionally picking at the hem of her muslin gown.

---

1 Evening worship service.

Madame Antoine seated her fat body, broad and squat, upon a bench beside the door. She had been talking all the afternoon, and had wound herself up to the story-telling pitch.

And what stories she told them! But twice in her life she had left the *Chênière Caminada*, and then for the briefest span. All her years she had squatted and waddled there upon the island, gathering legends of the Baratarians[1] and the sea. The night came on, with the moon to lighten it. Edna could hear the whispering voices of dead men and the click of muffled gold.

When she and Robert stepped into Tonie's boat, with the red lateen sail, misty spirit forms were prowling in the shadows and among the reeds, and upon the water were phantom ships, speeding to cover.

XIV

The youngest boy, Etienne, had been very naughty, Madame Ratignolle said, as she delivered him into the hands of his mother. He had been unwilling to go to bed and had made a scene; whereupon she had taken charge of him and pacified him as well as she could. Raoul had been in bed and asleep for two hours.

The youngster was in his long white nightgown, that kept tripping him up as Madame Ratignolle led him along by the hand. With the other chubby fist he rubbed his eyes, which were heavy with sleep and ill humor. Edna took him in her arms, and seating herself in the rocker, began to coddle and caress him, calling him all manner of tender names, soothing him to sleep.

It was not more than nine o'clock. No one had yet gone to bed but the children.

Léonce had been very uneasy at first, Madame Ratignolle said, and had wanted to start at once for the *Chênière*. But Monsieur Farival had assured him that his wife was only overcome with sleep and fatigue, that Tonie would bring her safely back later in the day; and he had thus been dissuaded from crossing the bay. He had gone over to Klein's, looking up some cotton broker whom he wished to see in regard to securities, exchanges, stocks, bonds, or something of the sort, Madame Ratignolle did not remember what. He said he would not remain away late. She herself was suffering from heat and oppression, she said. She carried a bottle of salts and a large fan. She would not consent to

---

1 A group of Gulf islands off the coast of Louisiana, famous for pirate legends.

remain with Edna, for Monsieur Ratignolle was alone, and he detested above all things to be left alone.

When Etienne had fallen asleep Edna bore him into the back room, and Robert went and lifted the mosquito bar that she might lay the child comfortably in his bed. The quadroon had vanished. When they emerged from the cottage Robert bade Edna good-night.

"Do you know we have been together the whole livelong day, Robert—since early this morning?" she said at parting.

"All but the hundred years when you were sleeping. Good-night."

He pressed her hand and went away in the direction of the beach. He did not join any of the others, but walked alone toward the Gulf.

Edna stayed outside, awaiting her husband's return. She had no desire to sleep or to retire; nor did she feel like going over to sit with the Ratignolles, or to join Madame Lebrun and a group whose animated voices reached her as they sat in conversation before the house. She let her mind wander back over her stay at Grand Isle; and she tried to discover wherein this summer had been different from any and every other summer of her life. She could only realize that she herself—her present self—was in some way different from the other self. That she was seeing with different eyes and making the acquaintance of new conditions in herself that colored and changed her environment, she did not yet suspect.

She wondered why Robert had gone away and left her. It did not occur to her to think he might have grown tired of being with her the livelong day. She was not tired, and she felt that he was not. She regretted that he had gone. It was so much more natural to have him stay when he was not absolutely required to leave her.

As Edna waited for her husband she sang low a little song that Robert had sung as they crossed the bay. It began with "Ah! *Si tu savais*,"[1] and every verse ended with "*si tu savais.*"

Robert's voice was not pretentious. It was musical and true. The voice, the notes, the whole refrain haunted her memory.

---

1 If you (only) knew.

XV

When Edna entered the dining-room one evening a little late, as was her habit, an unusually animated conversation seemed to be going on. Several persons were talking at once, and Victor's voice was predominating, even over that of his mother. Edna had returned late from her bath, had dressed in some haste, and her face was flushed. Her head, set off by her dainty white gown, suggested a rich, rare blossom. She took her seat at table between old Monsieur Farival and Madame Ratignolle.

As she seated herself and was about to begin to eat her soup, which had been served when she entered the room, several persons informed her simultaneously that Robert was going to Mexico. She laid her spoon down and looked about her bewildered. He had been with her, reading to her all the morning, and had never even mentioned such a place as Mexico. She had not seen him during the afternoon; she had heard some one say he was at the house, upstairs with his mother. This she had thought nothing of, though she was surprised when he did not join her later in the afternoon, when she went down to the beach.

She looked across at him, where he sat beside Madame Lebrun, who presided. Edna's face was a blank picture of bewilderment, which she never thought of disguising. He lifted his eyebrows with the pretext of a smile as he returned her glance. He looked embarrassed and uneasy.

"When is he going?" she asked of everybody in general, as if Robert were not there to answer for himself.

"To-night!" "This very evening!" "Did you ever!" "What possesses him!" were some of the replies she gathered, uttered simultaneously in French and English.

"Impossible!" she exclaimed. "How can a person start off from Grand Isle to Mexico at a moment's notice, as if he were going over to Klein's or to the wharf or down to the beach?"

"I said all along I was going to Mexico; I've been saying so for years!" cried Robert, in an excited and irritable tone, with the air of a man defending himself against a swarm of stinging insects.

Madame Lebrun knocked on the table with her knife handle.

"Please let Robert explain why he is going, and why he is going to-night," she called out. "Really, this table is getting to be more and more like Bedlam[1] every day, with everybody talking at once.

---

1   Originally an insane asylum in London, but the term later came to
    mean an uproar or confusion.

Sometimes—I hope God will forgive me—but positively, sometimes I wish Victor would lose the power of speech."

Victor laughed sardonically as he thanked his mother for her holy wish, of which he failed to see the benefit to anybody, except that it might afford her a more ample opportunity and license to talk herself.

Monsieur Farival thought that Victor should have been taken out in mid-ocean in his earliest youth and drowned. Victor thought there would be more logic in thus disposing of old people with an established claim for making themselves universally obnoxious. Madame Lebrun grew a trifle hysterical; Robert called his brother some sharp, hard names.

"There's nothing much to explain, mother," he said; though he explained, nevertheless—looking chiefly at Edna—that he could only meet the gentleman whom he intended to join at Vera Cruz by taking such and such a steamer, which left New Orleans on such a day; that Beaudelet was going out with his lugger-load of vegetables that night, which gave him an opportunity of reaching the city and making his vessel in time.

"But when did you make up your mind to all this?" demanded Monsieur Farival.

"This afternoon," returned Robert, with a shade of annoyance.

"At what time this afternoon?" persisted the old gentleman, with nagging determination, as if he were cross-questioning a criminal in a court of justice.

"At four o'clock this afternoon, Monsieur Farival," Robert replied, in a high voice and with a lofty air, which reminded Edna of some gentleman on the stage.

She had forced herself to eat most of her soup, and now she was picking the flaky bits of a *court bouillon*[1] with her fork.

The lovers were profiting by the general conversation on Mexico to speak in whispers of matters which they rightly considered were interesting to no one but themselves. The lady in black had once received a pair of prayer-beads of curious workmanship from Mexico, with very special indulgence[2] attached to them, but she had never been able to ascertain whether the indulgence extended outside the Mexican border. Father Fochel of the

---

1 A richly flavored soup, traditionally including pieces of fish or other seafood.
2 A Catholic practice of having the punishment due to sin cancelled or reduced by a specific blessing or action.

Cathedral had attempted to explain it; but he had not done so to her satisfaction. And she begged that Robert would interest himself, and discover, if possible, whether she was entitled to the indulgence accompanying the remarkably curious Mexican prayer-beads.

Madame Ratignolle hoped that Robert would exercise extreme caution in dealing with the Mexicans, who, she considered, were a treacherous people, unscrupulous and revengeful. She trusted she did them no injustice in thus condemning them as a race. She had known personally but one Mexican, who made and sold excellent tamales, and whom she would have trusted implicitly, so soft-spoken was he. One day he was arrested for stabbing his wife. She never knew whether he had been hanged or not.

Victor had grown hilarious, and was attempting to tell an anecdote about a Mexican girl who served chocolate one winter in a restaurant in Dauphine Street. No one would listen to him but old Monsieur Farival, who went into convulsions over the droll story.

Edna wondered if they had all gone mad, to be talking and clamoring at that rate. She herself could think of nothing to say about Mexico or the Mexicans.

"At what time do you leave?" she asked Robert.

"At ten," he told her. "Beaudelet wants to wait for the moon."

"Are you all ready to go?"

"Quite ready. I shall only take a hand-bag, and shall pack my trunk in the city."

He turned to answer some question put to him by his mother, and Edna, having finished her black coffee, left the table.

She went directly to her room. The little cottage was close and stuffy after leaving the outer air. But she did not mind; there appeared to be a hundred different things demanding her attention indoors. She began to set the toilet-stand to rights, grumbling at the negligence of the quadroon, who was in the adjoining room putting the children to bed. She gathered together stray garments that were hanging on the backs of chairs, and put each where it belonged in closet or bureau drawer. She changed her gown for a more comfortable and commodious wrapper. She rearranged her hair, combing and brushing it with unusual energy. Then she went in and assisted the quadroon in getting the boys to bed.

They were very playful and inclined to talk—to do anything but lie quiet and go to sleep. Edna sent the quadroon away to her supper and told her she need not return. Then she sat and told the children a story. Instead of soothing it excited them, and added to their wakefulness. She left them in heated argument, speculating about the conclusion of the tale which their mother promised to finish the following night.

The little black girl came in to say that Madame Lebrun would like to have Mrs. Pontellier go and sit with them over at the house till Mr. Robert went away. Edna returned answer that she had already undressed, that she did not feel quite well, but perhaps she would go over to the house later. She started to dress again, and got as far advanced as to remove her *peignoir*. But changing her mind once more she resumed the *peignoir*, and went outside and sat down before her door. She was overheated and irritable, and fanned herself energetically for a while. Madame Ratignolle came down to discover what was the matter.

"All that noise and confusion at the table must have upset me," replied Edna, "and moreover, I hate shocks and surprises. The idea of Robert starting off in such a ridiculously sudden and dramatic way! As if it were a matter of life and death! Never saying a word about it all morning when he was with me."

"Yes," agreed Madame Ratignolle. "I think it was showing us all—you especially—very little consideration. It wouldn't have surprised me in any of the others; those Lebruns are all given to heroics. But I must say I should never have expected such a thing from Robert. Are you not coming down? Come on, dear; it doesn't look friendly."

"No," said Edna, a little sullenly. "I can't go to the trouble of dressing again; I don't feel like it."

"You needn't dress; you look all right; fasten a belt around your waist. Just look at me!"

"No," persisted Edna; "but you go on. Madame Lebrun might be offended if we both stayed away."

Madame Ratignolle kissed Edna good-night, and went away, being in truth rather desirous of joining in the general and animated conversation which was still in progress concerning Mexico and the Mexicans.

Somewhat later Robert came up, carrying his hand-bag.

"Aren't you feeling well?" he asked.

"Oh, well enough. Are you going right away?"

He lit a match and looked at his watch. "In twenty minutes," he said. The sudden and brief flare of the match emphasized the darkness for a while. He sat down upon a stool which the children had left out on the porch.

"Get a chair," said Edna.

"This will do," he replied. He put on his soft hat and nervously took it off again, and wiping his face with his handkerchief, complained of the heat.

"Take the fan," said Edna, offering it to him.

"Oh, no! Thank you. It does no good; you have to stop fanning some time, and feel all the more uncomfortable afterward."

"That's one of the ridiculous things which men always say. I have never known one to speak otherwise of fanning. How long will you be gone?"

"Forever, perhaps. I don't know. It depends upon a good many things."

"Well, in case it shouldn't be forever, how long will it be?"

"I don't know."

"This seems to me perfectly preposterous and uncalled for. I don't like it. I don't understand your motive for silence and mystery, never saying a word to me about it this morning." He remained silent, not offering to defend himself. He only said, after a moment:

"Don't part from me in an ill-humor. I never knew you to be out of patience with me before."

"I don't want to part in any ill-humor," she said. "But can't you understand? I've grown used to seeing you, to having you with me all the time, and your action seems unfriendly, even unkind. You don't even offer an excuse for it. Why, I was planning to be together, thinking of how pleasant it would be to see you in the city next winter."

"So was I," he blurted. "Perhaps that's the——" He stood up suddenly and held out his hand. "Good-by, my dear Mrs. Pontellier; good-by. You won't—I hope you won't completely forget me." She clung to his hand, striving to detain him.

"Write to me when you get there, won't you, Robert?" she entreated.

"I will, thank you. Good-by."

How unlike Robert! The merest acquaintance would have said something more emphatic than "I will, thank you; good-by," to such a request.

He had evidently already taken leave of the people over at the house, for he descended the steps and went to join Beaudelet, who was out there with an oar across his shoulder waiting for Robert. They walked away in the darkness. She could only hear Beaudelet's voice; Robert had apparently not even spoken a word of greeting to his companion.

Edna bit her handkerchief convulsively, striving to hold back and to hide, even from herself as she would have hidden from another, the emotion which was troubling—tearing—her. Her eyes were brimming with tears.

For the first time she recognized anew the symptoms of infatuation which she had felt incipiently as a child, as a girl in her earliest teens, and later as a young woman. The recognition did not lessen the reality, the poignancy of the revelation by any suggestion or promise of instability. The past was nothing to her; offered no lesson which she was willing to heed. The future was a mystery which she never attempted to penetrate. The present alone was significant; was hers, to torture her as it was doing then with the biting conviction that she had lost that which she had held, that she had been denied that which her impassioned, newly awakened being demanded.

XVI

"Do you miss your friend greatly?" asked Mademoiselle Reisz one morning as she came creeping up behind Edna, who had just left her cottage on her way to the beach. She spent much of her time in the water since she had acquired finally the art of swimming. As their stay at Grand Isle drew near its close, she felt that she could not give too much time to a diversion which afforded her the only real pleasurable moments that she knew. When Mademoiselle Reisz came and touched her upon the shoulder and spoke to her, the woman seemed to echo the thought which was ever in Edna's mind; or, better, the feeling which constantly possessed her.

Robert's going had some way taken the brightness, the color, the meaning out of everything. The conditions of her life were in no way changed, but her whole existence was dulled, like a faded garment which seems to be no longer worth wearing. She sought him everywhere—in others whom she induced to talk about him. She went up in the mornings to Madame Lebrun's room, braving the clatter of the old sewing-machine. She sat there and chatted at intervals as Robert had done. She gazed around the room at the pictures and photographs hanging upon the wall, and discovered in some corner an old family album, which she examined with the keenest interest, appealing to Madame Lebrun for enlightenment concerning the many figures and faces which she discovered between its pages.

There was a picture of Madame Lebrun with Robert as a baby, seated in her lap, a round-faced infant with a fist in his mouth. The eyes alone in the baby suggested the man. And that was he also in kilts, at the age of five, wearing long curls and holding a whip in his hand. It made Edna laugh, and she laughed, too, at the portrait in his first long trousers; while another interested her, taken when he left for college, looking thin, long-faced, with eyes full of fire, ambition and great intentions. But there was no recent picture, none which suggested the Robert who had gone away five days ago, leaving a void and wilderness behind him.

"Oh, Robert stopped having his pictures taken when he had to pay for them himself! He found wiser use for his money, he says," explained Madame Lebrun. She had a letter from him, written before he left New Orleans. Edna wished to see the letter, and Madame Lebrun told her to look for it either on the table or the dresser, or perhaps it was on the mantelpiece.

The letter was on the bookshelf. It possessed the greatest interest and attraction for Edna; the envelope, its size and shape, the post-mark, the handwriting. She examined every detail of the outside before opening it. There were only a few lines, setting forth that he would leave the city that afternoon, that he had packed his trunk in good shape, that he was well, and sent her his love and begged to be affectionately remembered to all. There was no special message to Edna except a postscript saying that if Mrs. Pontellier desired to finish the book which he had been reading to her, his mother would find it in his room, among other books there on the table. Edna experienced a pang of jealousy because he had written to his mother rather than to her.

Every one seemed to take for granted that she missed him. Even her husband, when he came down the Saturday following Robert's departure, expressed regret that he had gone.

"How do you get on without him, Edna?" he asked.

"It's very dull without him," she admitted. Mr. Pontellier had seen Robert in the city, and Edna asked him a dozen questions or more. Where had they met? On Carondelet Street, in the morning. They had gone "in" and had a drink and a cigar together. What had they talked about? Chiefly about his prospects in Mexico, which Mr. Pontellier thought were promising. How did he look? How did he seem—grave, or gay, or how? Quite cheerful, and wholly taken up with the idea of his trip, which Mr. Pontellier found altogether natural in a young fellow about to seek fortune and adventure in a strange, queer country.

Edna tapped her foot impatiently, and wondered why the children persisted in playing in the sun when they might be under the trees. She went down and led them out of the sun, scolding the quadroon for not being more attentive.

It did not strike her as in the least grotesque that she should be making of Robert the object of conversation and leading her husband to speak of him. The sentiment which she entertained for Robert in no way resembled that which she felt for her husband, or had ever felt, or ever expected to feel. She had all her life long been accustomed to harbor thoughts and emotions which never voiced themselves. They had never taken the form of struggles. They belonged to her and were her own, and she entertained the conviction that she had a right to them and that they concerned no one but herself. Edna had once told Madame Ratignolle that she would never sacrifice herself for her children, or for any one.

Then had followed a rather heated argument; the two women did not appear to understand each other or to be talking the same language. Edna tried to appease her friend, to explain. "I would give up the unessential; I would give my money, I would give my life for my children; but I wouldn't give myself. I can't make it more clear; it's only something which I am beginning to comprehend, which is revealing itself to me."

"I don't know what you would call the essential, or what you mean by the unessential," said Madame Ratignolle, cheerfully; "but a woman who would give her life for her children could do no more than that—your Bible tells you so. I'm sure I couldn't do more than that."

"Oh, yes you could!" laughed Edna.

She was not surprised at Mademoiselle Reisz's question the morning that lady, following her to the beach, tapped her on the shoulder and asked if she did not greatly miss her young friend.

"Oh, good morning, Mademoiselle; is it you? Why, of course I miss Robert. Are you going down to bathe?"

"Why should I go down to bathe at the very end of the season when I haven't been in the surf all summer," replied the woman, disagreeably.

"I beg your pardon," offered Edna, in some embarrassment, for she should have remembered that Mademoiselle Reisz's avoidance of the water had furnished a theme for much pleasantry. Some among them thought it was on account of her false hair, or the dread of getting the violets wet, while others attributed it to the natural aversion for water sometimes believed to accompany the artistic temperament. Mademoiselle offered Edna some chocolates in a paper bag, which she took from her pocket, by way

of showing that she bore no ill feeling. She habitually ate chocolates for their sustaining quality; they contained much nutriment
in small compass, she said. They saved her from starvation, as
Madame Lebrun's table was utterly impossible; and no one save
so impertinent a woman as Madame Lebrun could think of offering such food to people and requiring them to pay for it.

"She must feel very lonely without her son," said Edna, desir-
ing to change the subject. "Her favorite son, too. It must have
been quite hard to let him go."

Mademoiselle laughed maliciously.

"Her favorite son! Oh, dear! Who could have been imposing
such a tale upon you? Aline Lebrun lives for Victor, and for Victor
alone. She has spoiled him into the worthless creature he is. She
worships him and the ground he walks on. Robert is very well in
a way, to give up all the money he can earn to the family, and
keep the barest pittance for himself. Favorite son, indeed! I miss
the poor fellow myself, my dear. I liked to see him and to hear
him about the place—the only Lebrun who is worth a pinch of
salt. He comes to see me often in the city. I like to play to him.
That Victor! hanging would be too good for him. It's a wonder
Robert hasn't beaten him to death long ago."

"I thought he had great patience with his brother," offered
Edna, glad to be talking about Robert, no matter what was said.

"Oh! he thrashed him well enough a year or two ago," said
Mademoiselle. "It was about a Spanish girl, whom Victor considered that he had some sort of claim upon. He met Robert one day
talking to the girl, or walking with her, or bathing with her, or carrying her basket—I don't remember what;—and he became so
insulting and abusive that Robert gave him a thrashing on the
spot that has kept him comparatively in order for a good while.
It's about time he was getting another."

"Was her name Mariequita?" asked Edna.

"Mariequita—yes, that was it; Mariequita. I had forgotten.
Oh, she's a sly one, and a bad one, that Mariequita!"

Edna looked down at Mademoiselle Reisz and wondered how
she could have listened to her venom so long. For some reason
she felt depressed, almost unhappy. She had not intended to go
into the water; but she donned her bathing suit, and left Mademoiselle alone, seated under the shade of the children's tent. The
water was growing cooler as the season advanced. Edna plunged
and swam about with an abandon that thrilled and invigorated
her. She remained a long time in the water, half hoping that
Mademoiselle Reisz would not wait for her.

But Mademoiselle waited. She was very amiable during the walk back, and raved much over Edna's appearance in her bathing suit. She talked about music. She hoped that Edna would go to see her in the city, and wrote her address with the stub of a pencil on a piece of card which she found in her pocket.

"When do you leave?" asked Edna.

"Next Monday; and you?"

"The following week," answered Edna, adding, "It has been a pleasant summer, hasn't it, Mademoiselle?"

"Well," agreed Mademoiselle Reisz, with a shrug, "rather pleasant, if it hadn't been for the mosquitoes and the Farival twins."

XVII

The Pontelliers possessed a very charming home on Esplanade Street[1] in New Orleans. It was a large, double cottage, with a broad front veranda, whose round, fluted columns supported the sloping roof. The house was painted a dazzling white; the outside shutters, or jalousies, were green. In the yard, which was kept scrupulously neat, were flowers and plants of every description which flourishes in South Louisiana. Within doors the appointments[2] were perfect after the conventional type. The softest carpets and rugs covered the floors; rich and tasteful draperies hung at doors and windows. There were paintings, selected with judgment and discrimination, upon the walls. The cut glass, the silver, the heavy damask[3] which daily appeared upon the table were the envy of many women whose husbands were less generous than Mr. Pontellier.

Mr. Pontellier was very fond of walking about his house examining its various appointments and details, to see that nothing was amiss. He greatly valued his possessions, chiefly because they were his, and derived genuine pleasure from contemplating a painting, a statuette, a rare lace curtain—no matter what—after he had bought it and placed it among his household gods.[4]

---

1 A fashionable street on the edge of French Quarter in New Orleans.
2 Furnishings and decorations.
3 A heavy fabric.
4 Although some readers view this as a typographical error (i.e., "gods" for "goods") on Chopin's part, given Oscar's fondness for his material possessions, it seems likely that Chopin is making a clear point with this statement.

On Tuesday afternoons—Tuesday being Mrs. Pontellier's reception day[1]—there was a constant stream of callers—women who came in carriages or in the street cars, or walked when the air was soft and distance permitted. A light-colored mulatto boy,[2] in dress coat and bearing a diminutive silver tray for the reception of cards, admitted them. A maid, in white fluted cap, offered the callers liqueur, coffee, or chocolate, as they might desire. Mrs. Pontellier, attired in a handsome reception gown,[3] remained in the drawing-room the entire afternoon receiving her visitors. Men sometimes called in the evening with their wives.

This had been the programme which Mrs. Pontellier had religiously followed since her marriage, six years before. Certain evenings during the week she and her husband attended the opera or sometimes the play.

Mr. Pontellier left his home in the mornings between nine and ten o'clock, and rarely returned before half-past six or seven in the evening—dinner being served at half-past seven.

He and his wife seated themselves at table one Tuesday evening, a few weeks after their return from Grand Isle. They were alone together. The boys were being put to bed; the patter of their bare, escaping feet could be heard occasionally, as well as the pursuing voice of the quadroon, lifted in mild protest and entreaty. Mrs. Pontellier did not wear her usual Tuesday reception gown; she was in ordinary house dress. Mr. Pontellier, who was observant about such things, noticed it, as he served the soup and handed it to the boy in waiting.

"Tired out, Edna? Whom did you have? Many callers?" he asked. He tasted his soup and began to season it with pepper, salt, vinegar, mustard—everything within reach.

"There were a good many," replied Edna, who was eating her soup with evident satisfaction. "I found their cards when I got home; I was out."

"Out!" exclaimed her husband, with something like genuine consternation in his voice as he laid down the vinegar cruet and looked at her through his glasses. "Why, what could have taken you out on Tuesday? What did you have to do?"

---

1 A day set aside to entertain friends. On the protocol associated with visiting and receiving guests, see Appendix C.
2 Indication of an individual of mixed race. According to Louisiana law, a mulatto was half white and half black.
3 A dress specifically intended for day wear while receiving and entertaining visitors.

"Nothing. I simply felt like going out, and I went out."

"Well, I hope you left some suitable excuse," said her husband, somewhat appeased, as he added a dash of cayenne pepper to the soup.

"No, I left no excuse. I told Joe to say I was out, that was all."

"Why, my dear, I should think you'd understand by this time that people don't do such things; we've got to observe *les convenances*[1] if we ever expect to get on and keep up with the procession. If you felt that you had to leave home this afternoon, you should have left some suitable explanation for your absence.

"This soup is really impossible; it's strange that woman hasn't learned yet to make a decent soup. Any free-lunch stand in town serves a better one. Was Mrs. Belthrop here?"

"Bring the tray with the cards, Joe. I don't remember who was here."

The boy retired and returned after a moment, bringing the tiny silver tray, which was covered with ladies' visiting cards. He handed it to Mrs. Pontellier.

"Give it to Mr. Pontellier," she said.

Joe offered the tray to Mr. Pontellier, and removed the soup.

Mr. Pontellier scanned the names of his wife's callers, reading some of them aloud, with comments as he read.

"'The Misses Delasidas.' I worked a big deal in futures[2] for their father this morning; nice girls; it's time they were getting married. 'Mrs. Belthrop.' I tell you what it is, Edna; you can't afford to snub Mrs. Belthrop. Why, Belthrop could buy and sell us ten times over. His business is worth a good, round sum to me. You'd better write her a note. 'Mrs. James Highcamp.' Hugh! the less you have to do with Mrs. Highcamp, the better. 'Madame Laforcé.' Came all the way from Carrolton,[3] too, poor old soul. 'Miss Wiggs,' 'Mrs. Eleanor Boltons.'" He pushed the cards aside.

"Mercy!" exclaimed Edna, who had been fuming. "Why are you taking the thing so seriously and making such a fuss over it?"

"I'm not making any fuss over it. But it's just such seeming trifles that we've got to take seriously; such things count."

The fish was scorched. Mr. Pontellier would not touch it. Edna said she did not mind a little scorched taste. The roast was

---

1 Accepted conventions of behavior.
2 Buying or selling commodities at present prices based on delivery later.
3 Now a part of New Orleans, but a separate village in the 1800s, noted for its gardens and pleasant atmosphere. See Appendix D1.

in some way not to his fancy, and he did not like the manner in which the vegetables were served.

"It seems to me," he said, "we spend money enough in this house to procure at least one meal a day which a man could eat and retain his self-respect."

"You used to think the cook was a treasure," returned Edna, indifferently.

"Perhaps she was when she first came; but cooks are only human. They need looking after, like any other class of persons that you employ. Suppose I didn't look after the clerks in my office, just let them run things their own way; they'd soon make a nice mess of me and my business."

"Where are you going?" asked Edna, seeing that her husband arose from table without having eaten a morsel except a taste of the highly-seasoned soup.

"I'm going to get my dinner at the club. Good night." He went into the hall, took his hat and stick from the stand, and left the house.

She was somewhat familiar with such scenes. They had often made her very unhappy. On a few previous occasions she had been completely deprived of any desire to finish her dinner. Sometimes she had gone into the kitchen to administer a tardy rebuke to the cook. Once she went to her room and studied the cookbook during an entire evening, finally writing out a menu for the week, which left her harassed with a feeling that, after all, she had accomplished no good that was worth the name.

But that evening Edna finished her dinner alone, with forced deliberation. Her face was flushed and her eyes flamed with some inward fire that lighted them. After finishing her dinner she went to her room, having instructed the boy to tell any other callers that she was indisposed.

It was a large, beautiful room, rich and picturesque in the soft, dim light which the maid had turned low. She went and stood at an open window and looked out upon the deep tangle of the garden below. All the mystery and witchery of the night seemed to have gathered there amid the perfumes and the dusky and tortuous outlines of flowers and foliage. She was seeking herself and finding herself in just such sweet, half-darkness which met her moods. But the voices were not soothing that came to her from the darkness and the sky above and the stars. They jeered and sounded mournful notes without promise, devoid even of hope. She turned back into the room and began to walk to and fro down its whole length, without stopping, without resting. She carried in her hands a thin handkerchief, which she tore into ribbons, rolled into a ball, and flung from her. Once she stopped, and taking off her wedding ring, flung it upon the carpet. When she saw it lying there, she stamped her heel upon it, striving to crush it. But her small boot heel did not make an indenture, not a mark upon the little glittering circlet.

In a sweeping passion she seized a glass vase from the table and flung it upon the tiles of the hearth. She wanted to destroy something. The crash and clatter were what she wanted to hear.

A maid, alarmed at the din of breaking glass, entered the room to discover what was the matter.

"A vase fell upon the hearth," said Edna. "Never mind; leave it till morning."

"Oh! you might get some of the glass in your feet, ma'am," insisted the young woman, picking up bits of the broken vase that were scattered upon the carpet. "And here's your ring ma'am, under the chair."

Edna held out her hand, and taking the ring, slipped it upon her finger.

XVIII

The following morning Mr. Pontellier, upon leaving for his office, asked Edna if she would not meet him in town in order to look at some new fixtures for the library.

"I hardly think we need new fixtures, Léonce. Don't let us get anything new; you are too extravagant. I don't believe you ever think of saving or putting by."

"The way to become rich is to make money, my dear Edna, not to save it," he said. He regretted that she did not feel inclined to go with him and select new fixtures. He kissed her good-by, and told her she was not looking well and must take care of herself. She was unusually pale and very quiet.

She stood on the front veranda as he quitted the house, and absently picked a few sprays of jessamine[1] that grew upon a trellis near by. She inhaled the odor of the blossoms and thrust them into the bosom of her white morning gown. The boys were dragging along the banquette[2] a small "express wagon,"[3] which they had filled with blocks and sticks. The quadroon was following

---

1 Jasmine.
2 A raised sidewalk.
3 A child's toy wagon.

them with little quick steps, having assumed a fictitious animation and alacrity for the occasion. A fruit vender was crying his
wares in the street.

Edna looked straight before her with a self-absorbed expression upon her face. She felt no interest in anything about her. The
street, the children, the fruit vender, the flowers growing there
under her eyes, were all part and parcel of an alien world which
had suddenly become antagonistic.

She went back into the house. She had thought of speaking to
the cook concerning her blunders of the previous night; but Mr.
Pontellier had saved her that disagreeable mission, for which she
was so poorly fitted. Mr. Pontellier's arguments were usually convincing with those whom he employed. He left home feeling quite
sure that he and Edna would sit down that evening, and possibly
a few subsequent evenings, to a dinner deserving of the name.

Edna spent an hour or two in looking over some of her old
sketches. She could see their shortcomings and defects, which
were glaring in her eyes. She tried to work a little, but found she
was not in the humor. Finally she gathered together a few of the
sketches—those which she considered the least discreditable; and
she carried them with her when, a little later, she dressed and left
the house. She looked handsome and distinguished in her street
gown.[1] The tan of the seashore had left her face, and her forehead
was smooth, white, and polished beneath her heavy, yellow-
brown hair. There were a few freckles on her face, and a small,
dark mole near the under lip and one on the temple, half-hidden
in her hair.

As Edna walked along the street she was thinking of Robert.
She was still under the spell of her infatuation. She had tried to
forget him, realizing the inutility of remembering. But the
thought of him was like an obsession, ever pressing itself upon
her. It was not that she dwelt upon details of their acquaintance,
or recalled in any special or peculiar way his personality; it was
his being, his existence, which dominated her thought, fading
sometimes as if it would melt into the mist of the forgotten, reviv-
ing again with an intensity which filled her with an incomprehensible longing.

Edna was on her way to Madame Ratignolle's. Their intimacy,
begun at Grand Isle, had not declined, and they had seen each
other with some frequency since their return to the city. The
Ratignolles lived at no great distance from Edna's home, on the

---

1 A dress for day wear, appropriate for wearing outside.

corner of a side street, where Monsieur Ratignolle owned and conducted a drug store which enjoyed a steady and prosperous trade. His father had been in the business before him, and Monsieur Ratignolle stood well in the community and bore an enviable reputation for integrity and clear-headedness. His family lived in commodious apartments over the store, having an entrance on the side within the *porte cochère*.[1] There was something which Edna thought very French, very foreign, about their whole manner of living. In the large and pleasant salon which extended across the width of the house, the Ratignolles entertained their friends once a fortnight with a *soirée musicale*,[2] sometimes diversified by card-playing. There was a friend who played upon the 'cello. One brought his flute and another his violin, while there were some who sang and a number who performed upon the piano with various degrees of taste and agility. The Ratignolles' *soirées musicales* were widely known, and it was considered a privilege to be invited to them.

Edna found her friend engaged in assorting the clothes which had returned that morning from the laundry. She at once abandoned her occupation upon seeing Edna, who had been ushered without ceremony into her presence.

"'Cité can do it as well as I; it is really her business," she explained to Edna, who apologized for interrupting her. And she summoned a young black woman, whom she instructed, in French, to be very careful in checking off the list which she handed her. She told her to notice particularly if a fine linen handkerchief of Monsieur Ratignolle's, which was missing last week, had been returned; and to be sure to set to one side such pieces as required mending and darning.

Then placing an arm around Edna's waist, she led her to the front of the house, to the salon, where it was cool and sweet with the odor of great roses that stood upon the hearth in jars.

Madame Ratignolle looked more beautiful than ever there at home, in a negligé which left her arms almost wholly bare and exposed the rich, melting curves of her white throat.

"Perhaps I shall be able to paint your picture some day," said Edna with a smile when they were seated. She produced the roll of sketches and started to unfold them. "I believe I ought to work again. I feel as if I wanted to be doing something. What do you

---

1 An entry way for a carriage.
2 An evening party with music performance and appreciation as its focus.

think of them? Do you think it worth while to take it up again and study some more? I might study for a while with Laidpore."

She knew that Madame Ratignolle's opinion in such a matter would be next to valueless, that she herself had not alone decided, but determined; but she sought the words of praise and encouragement that would help her to put heart into her venture.

"Your talent is immense, dear!"

"Nonsense!" protested Edna, well pleased.

"Immense, I tell you," persisted Madame Ratignolle, surveying the sketches one by one, at close range, then holding them at arm's length, narrowing her eyes, and dropping her head on one side. "Surely, this Bavarian peasant is worthy of framing; and this basket of apples! never have I seen anything more lifelike. One might almost be tempted to reach out a hand and take one."

Edna could not control a feeling which bordered upon complacency at her friend's praise, even realizing, as she did, its true worth. She retained a few of the sketches, and gave all the rest to Madame Ratignolle, who appreciated the gift far beyond its value and proudly exhibited the pictures to her husband when he came up from the store a little later for his midday dinner.

Mr. Ratignolle was one of those men who are called the salt of the earth. His cheerfulness was unbounded, and it was matched by his goodness of heart, his broad charity, and common sense. He and his wife spoke English with an accent which was only discernible through its un-English emphasis and a certain carefulness and deliberation. Edna's husband spoke English with no accent whatever. The Ratignolles understood each other perfectly. If ever the fusion of two human beings into one has been accomplished on this sphere it was surely in their union.

As Edna seated herself at table with them she thought, "Better a dinner of herbs,"[1] though it did not take her long to discover that it was no dinner of herbs, but a delicious repast, simple, choice, and in every way satisfying.

Monsieur Ratignolle was delighted to see her, though he found her looking not so well as at Grand Isle, and he advised a tonic. He talked a good deal on various topics, a little politics, some city news and neighborhood gossip. He spoke with an animation and earnestness that gave an exaggerated importance to every syllable he uttered. His wife was keenly interested in every-

---

1 Proverbs 15:17: "Better is a dinner of herbs where love is, than a stalled ox and hatred therewith."

thing he said, laying down her fork the better to listen, chiming in, taking the words out of his mouth.

Edna felt depressed rather than soothed after leaving them. The little glimpse of domestic harmony which had been offered her, gave her no regret, no longing. It was not a condition of life which fitted her, and she could see in it but an appalling and hopeless ennui. She was moved by a kind of commiseration for Madame Ratignolle,—a pity for that colorless existence which never uplifted its possessor beyond the region of blind contentment, in which no moment of anguish ever visited her soul, in which she would never have the taste of life's delirium. Edna vaguely wondered what she meant by "life's delirium." It had crossed her thought like some unsought, extraneous impression.

XIX

Edna could not help but think that it was very foolish, very childish, to have stamped upon her wedding ring and smashed the crystal vase upon the tiles. She was visited by no more outbursts, moving her to such futile expedients. She began to do as she liked and to feel as she liked. She completely abandoned her Tuesdays at home, and did not return the visits of those who had called upon her. She made no ineffectual efforts to conduct her household *en bonne ménagère*,[1] going and coming as it suited her fancy, and, so far as she was able, lending herself to any passing caprice.

Mr. Pontellier had been a rather courteous husband so long as he met a certain tacit submissiveness in his wife. But her new and unexpected line of conduct completely bewildered him. It shocked him. Then her absolute disregard for her duties as a wife angered him. When Mr. Pontellier became rude, Edna grew insolent. She had resolved never to take another step backward.

"It seems to me the utmost folly for a woman at the head of a household, and the mother of children, to spend in an atelier[2] days which would be better employed contriving for the comfort of her family."

"I feel like painting," answered Edna. "Perhaps I shan't always feel like it."

"Then in God's name paint! but don't let the family go to the devil. There's Madame Ratignolle; because she keeps up her

---

1 Like a good wife.
2 An artist's studio or workroom.

music, she doesn't let everything else go to chaos. And she's more of a musician than you are a painter."

"She isn't a musician, and I'm not a painter. It isn't on account of painting that I let things go."

"On account of what, then?"

"Oh! I don't know. Let me alone; you bother me."

It sometimes entered Mr. Pontellier's mind to wonder if his wife were not growing a little unbalanced mentally. He could see plainly that she was not herself. That is, he could not see that she was becoming herself and daily casting aside that fictitious self which we assume like a garment with which to appear before the world.

Her husband let her alone as she requested, and went away to his office. Edna went up to her atelier—a bright room in the top of the house. She was working with great energy and interest, without accomplishing anything, however, which satisfied her even in the smallest degree. For a time she had the whole household enrolled in the service of art. The boys posed for her. They thought it amusing at first, but the occupation soon lost its attractiveness when they discovered that it was not a game arranged especially for their entertainment. The quadroon sat for hours before Edna's palette, patient as a savage, while the house-maid took charge of the children, and the drawing-room went undusted. But the house-maid, too, served her term as model when Edna perceived that the young woman's back and shoulders were molded on classic lines, and that her hair, loosened from its confining cap, became an inspiration. While Edna worked she sometimes sang low the little air, "*Ah! si tu savais!*"

It moved her with recollections. She could hear again the ripple of the water, the flapping sail. She could see the glint of the moon upon the bay, and could feel the soft, gusty beating of the hot south wind. A subtle current of desire passed through her body, weakening her hold upon the brushes and making her eyes burn.

There were days when she was very happy without knowing why. She was happy to be alive and breathing, when her whole being seemed to be one with the sunlight, the color, the odors, the luxuriant warmth of some perfect Southern day. She liked then to wander alone into strange and unfamiliar places. She discovered many a sunny, sleepy corner, fashioned to dream in. And she found it good to dream and to be alone and unmolested.

There were days when she was unhappy, she did not know why,—when it did not seem worth while to be glad or sorry, to be alive or dead; when life appeared to her like a grotesque pande-monium and humanity like worms struggling blindly toward inevitable annihilation. She could not work on such a day, nor weave fancies to stir her pulses and warm her blood.

XX

It was during such a mood that Edna hunted up Mademoiselle Reisz. She had not forgotten the rather disagreeable impression left upon her by their last interview; but she nevertheless felt a desire to see her—above all, to listen while she played upon the piano. Quite early in the afternoon she started upon her quest for the pianist. Unfortunately she had mislaid or lost Mademoiselle Reisz's card, and looking up her address in the city directory, she found that the woman lived on Bienville Street, some distance away. The directory which fell into her hands was a year or more old, however, and upon reaching the number indicated, Edna dis-covered that the house was occupied by a respectable family of mulattoes who had *chambres garnies*[1] to let. They had been living there for six months, and knew absolutely nothing of a Made-moiselle Reisz. In fact, they knew nothing of any of their neigh-bors; their lodgers were all people of the highest distinction, they assured Edna. She did not linger to discuss class distinctions with Madame Pouponne, but hastened to a neighboring grocery store, feeling sure that Mademoiselle would have left her address with the proprietor.

He knew Mademoiselle Reisz a good deal better than he wanted to know her, he informed his questioner. In truth, he did not want to know her at all, or anything concerning her—the most disagreeable and unpopular woman who ever lived in Bienville Street. He thanked heaven she had left the neighbor-hood, and was equally thankful that he did not know where she had gone.

Edna's desire to see Mademoiselle Reisz had increased tenfold since these unlooked-for obstacles had arisen to thwart it. She was wondering who could give her the information she sought, when it suddenly occurred to her that Madame Lebrun would be the one most likely to do so. She knew it was useless to ask Madame Ratignolle, who was on the most distant terms with the musician, and preferred to know nothing concerning her. She

---

1 Furnished rooms.

had once been almost as emphatic in expressing herself upon the subject as the corner grocer.

Edna knew that Madame Lebrun had returned to the city, for it was the middle of November. And she also knew where the Lebruns lived, on Chartres Street.

Their home from the outside looked like a prison, with iron bars before the door and lower windows. The iron bars were a relic of the old *régime*,[1] and no one had ever thought of dislodging them. At the side was a high fence enclosing the garden. A gate or door opening upon the street was locked. Edna rang the bell at this side garden gate, and stood upon the banquette, waiting to be admitted.

It was Victor who opened the gate for her. A black woman, wiping her hands upon her apron, was close at his heels. Before she saw them Edna could hear them in altercation, the woman—plainly an anomaly—claiming the right to be allowed to perform her duties, one of which was to answer the bell.

Victor was surprised and delighted to see Mrs. Pontellier, and he made no attempt to conceal either his astonishment or his delight. He was a dark-browed, good-looking youngster of nineteen, greatly resembling his mother, but with ten times her impetuosity. He instructed the black woman to go at once and inform Madame Lebrun that Mrs. Pontellier desired to see her. The woman grumbled a refusal to do part of her duty when she had not been permitted to do it all, and started back to her interrupted task of weeding the garden. Whereupon Victor administered a rebuke in the form of a volley of abuse, which, owing to its rapidity and incoherence, was all but incomprehensible to Edna. Whatever it was, the rebuke was convincing, for the woman dropped her hoe and went mumbling into the house.

Edna did not wish to enter. It was very pleasant there on the side porch, where there were chairs, a wicker lounge, and a small table. She seated herself, for she was tired from her long tramp; and she began to rock gently and smooth out the folds of her silk parasol. Victor drew up his chair beside her. He at once explained that the black woman's offensive conduct was all due to imperfect training, as he was not there to take her in hand. He had only come up from the island the morning before, and expected to return next day. He stayed all winter at the island; he lived there, and kept the place in order and got things ready for the summer visitors.

---

1 The old ruling class or the upper crust of society.

But a man needed occasional relaxation, he informed Mrs. Pontellier, and every now and again he drummed up a pretext to bring him to the city. My! but he had had a time of it the evening before! He wouldn't want his mother to know, and he began to talk in a whisper. He was scintillant with recollections. Of course, he couldn't think of telling Mrs. Pontellier all about it, she being a woman and not comprehending such things. But it all began with a girl peeping and smiling at him through the shutters as he passed by. Oh! but she was a beauty! Certainly he smiled back, and went up and talked to her. Mrs. Pontellier did not know him if she supposed he was one to let an opportunity like that escape him. Despite herself, the youngster amused her. She must have betrayed in her look some degree of interest or entertainment. The boy grew more daring, and Mrs. Pontellier might have found herself, in a little while, listening to a highly colored story but for the timely appearance of Madame Lebrun.

That lady was still clad in white, according to her custom of the summer. Her eyes beamed an effusive welcome. Would not Mrs. Pontellier go inside? Would she partake of some refreshment? Why had she not been there before? How was that dear Mr. Pontellier and how were those sweet children? Had Mrs. Pontellier ever known such a warm November?

Victor went and reclined on the wicker lounge behind his mother's chair, where he commanded a view of Edna's face. He had taken her parasol from her hands while he spoke to her, and he now lifted it and twirled it above him as he lay on his back. When Madame Lebrun complained that it was *so* dull coming back to the city; that she saw *so* few people now; that even Victor, when he came up from the island for a day or two, had *so* much to occupy him and engage his time; then it was that the youth went into contortions on the lounge and winked mischievously at Edna. She somehow felt like a confederate in crime, and tried to look severe and disapproving.

There had been but two letters from Robert, with little in them, they told her. Victor said it was really not worth while to go inside for the letters, when his mother entreated him to go in search of them. He remembered the contents, which in truth he rattled off very glibly when put to the test.

One letter was written from Vera Cruz and the other from the City of Mexico. He had met Montel, who was doing everything toward his advancement. So far, the financial situation was no improvement over the one he had left in New Orleans, but of course the prospects were vastly better. He wrote of the City of Mexico, the buildings, the people and their habits, the conditions of life which he found there. He sent his love to the family. He inclosed a check to his mother, and hoped she would affectionately remember him to all his friends. That was about the substance of the two letters. Edna felt that if there had been a message for her, she would have received it. The despondent frame of mind in which she had left home began again to overtake her, and she remembered that she wished to find Mademoiselle Reisz.

Madame Lebrun knew where Mademoiselle Reisz lived. She gave Edna the address, regretting that she would not consent to stay and spend the remainder of the afternoon, and pay a visit to Mademoiselle Reisz some other day. The afternoon was already well advanced.

Victor escorted her out upon the banquette, lifted her parasol, and held it over her while he walked to the car with her. He entreated her to bear in mind that the disclosures of the afternoon were strictly confidential. She laughed and bantered him a little, remembering too late that she should have been dignified and reserved.

"How handsome Mrs. Pontellier looked!" said Madame Lebrun to her son.

"Ravishing!" he admitted. "The city atmosphere has improved her. Some way she doesn't seem like the same woman."

XXI

Some people contended that the reason Mademoiselle Reisz always chose apartments up under the roof was to discourage the approach of beggars, peddlars and callers. There were plenty of windows in her little front room. They were for the most part dingy, but as they were nearly always open it did not make so much difference. They often admitted into the room a good deal of smoke and soot; but at the same time all the light and air that there was came through them. From her windows could be seen the crescent of the river, the masts of ships and the big chimneys of the Mississippi steamers. A magnificent piano crowded the apartment. In the next room she slept, and in the third and last she harbored a gasoline stove on which she cooked her meals when disinclined to descend to the neighboring restaurant. It was there also that she ate, keeping her belongings in a rare old buffet,[1] dingy and battered from a hundred years of use.

When Edna knocked at Mademoiselle Reisz's front room door and entered, she discovered that person standing beside the window, engaged in mending or patching an old prunella gaiter.[2] The little musician laughed all over when she saw Edna. Her laugh consisted of a contortion of the face and all the muscles of the body. She seemed strikingly homely, standing there in the afternoon light. She still wore the shabby lace and the artificial bunch of violets on the side of her head.

"So you remembered me at last," said Mademoiselle. "I had said to myself, 'Ah, bah! she will never come.'"

"Did you want me to come?" asked Edna with a smile.

"I had not thought much about it," answered Mademoiselle. The two had seated themselves on a little bumpy sofa which stood against the wall. "I am glad, however, that you came. I have the water boiling back there, and was just about to make some coffee. You will drink a cup with me. And how is *la belle dame*?[3] Always handsome! always healthy! always contented!" She took Edna's hand between her strong wiry fingers, holding it loosely without warmth, and executing a sort of double theme upon the back and palm.

"Yes," she went on; "I sometimes thought: 'She will never come. She promised as those women in society always do, without meaning it. She will not come.' For I really don't believe you like me, Mrs. Pontellier."

"I don't know whether I like you or not," replied Edna, gazing down at the little woman with a quizzical look.

The candor of Mrs. Pontellier's admission greatly pleased Mademoiselle Reisz. She expressed her gratification by repairing forthwith to the region of the gasoline stove and rewarding her guest with the promised cup of coffee. The coffee and the biscuit accompanying it proved very acceptable to Edna, who had declined refreshment at Madame Lebrun's and was now beginning to feel hungry. Mademoiselle set the tray which she brought in upon a small table near at hand, and seated herself once again on the lumpy sofa.

"I have had a letter from your friend," she remarked, as she poured a little cream into Edna's cup and handed it to her.

---

1 A piece of furniture used for storage, especially in a dining room.
2 A heavy piece of cloth used as leg or shoe coverings.
3 Beautiful lady.

"My friend?"

"Yes, your friend Robert. He wrote to me from the City of Mexico."

"Wrote to *you*?" repeated Edna in amazement, stirring her coffee absently.

"Yes, to me. Why not? Don't stir all the warmth out of your coffee; drink it. Though the letter might as well have been sent to you; it was nothing but Mrs. Pontellier from beginning to end."

"Let me see it," requested the young woman, entreatingly.

"No; a letter concerns no one but the person who writes it and the one to whom it is written."

"Haven't you just said it concerned me from beginning to end?"

"It was written about you, not to you. 'Have you seen Mrs. Pontellier? How is she looking?' he asks. 'As Mrs. Pontellier says,' or 'as Mrs. Pontellier once said.' 'If Mrs. Pontellier should call upon you, play for her that Impromptu of Chopin's, my favorite. I heard it here a day or two ago, but not as you play it. I should like to know how it affects her,' and so on, as if he supposed we were constantly in each other's society."

"Let me see the letter."

"Oh, no."

"Have you answered it?"

"No."

"Let me see the letter."

"No, and again, no."

"Then play the Impromptu for me."

"It is growing late; what time do you have to be home?"

"Time doesn't concern me. Your question seems a little rude. Play the Impromptu."

"But you have told me nothing of yourself. What are you doing?"

"Painting!" laughed Edna. "I am becoming an artist. Think of it!"

"Ah! an artist! You have pretensions, Madame."

"Why pretensions? Do you think I could not become an artist?"

"I do not know you well enough to say. I do not know your talent or your temperament. To be an artist includes much; one must possess many gifts—absolute gifts—which have not been acquired by one's own effort. And, moreover, to succeed, the artist must possess the courageous soul."

"What do you mean by the courageous soul?"

"Courageous, *ma foi!*[1] The brave soul. The soul that dares and defies."

"Show me the letter and play for me the Impromptu. You see that I have persistence. Does that quality count for anything in art?"

"It counts with a foolish old woman whom you have captivated," replied Mademoiselle, with her wriggling laugh.

The letter was right there at hand in the drawer of the little table upon which Edna had just placed her coffee cup. Mademoiselle opened the drawer and drew forth the letter, the topmost one. She placed it in Edna's hands, and without further comment arose and went to the piano.

Mademoiselle played a soft interlude. It was an improvisation. She sat low at the instrument, and the lines of her body settled into ungraceful curves and angles that gave it an appearance of deformity. Gradually and imperceptibly the interlude melted into the soft opening minor chords of the Chopin Impromptu.

Edna did not know when the Impromptu began or ended. She sat in the sofa corner reading Robert's letter by the fading light. Mademoiselle had glided from the Chopin into the quivering love-notes of Isolde's song,[2] and back again to the Impromptu with its soulful and poignant longing.

The shadows deepened in the little room. The music grew strange and fantastic—turbulent, insistent, plaintive and soft with entreaty. The shadows grew deeper. The music filled the room. It floated out upon the night, over the housetops, the crescent of the river, losing itself in the silence of the upper air.

Edna was sobbing, just as she had wept one midnight at Grand Isle when strange, new voices awoke in her. She arose in some agitation to take her departure. "May I come again, Mademoiselle?" she asked at the threshold.

"Come whenever you feel like it. Be careful; the stairs and landings are dark; don't stumble."

Mademoiselle reëntered and lit a candle. Robert's letter was on the floor. She stooped and picked it up. It was crumpled and damp with tears. Mademoiselle smoothed the letter out, restored it to the envelope, and replaced it in the table drawer.

---

1 My faith! Indeed!
2 The final song sung by Isolde in Richard Wagner's opera *Tristan und Isolde* (1865), commonly called "*Liebestod*" (love-death) as she is kneeling by her dead lover.

XXII

One morning on his way into town Mr. Pontellier stopped at the house of his old friend and family physician, Doctor Mandelet. The Doctor was a semi-retired physician, resting, as the saying is, upon his laurels. He bore a reputation for wisdom rather than skill—leaving the active practice of medicine to his assistants and younger contemporaries—and was much sought for in matters of consultation. A few families, united to him by bonds of friendship, he still attended when they required the services of a physician. The Pontelliers were among these.

Mr. Pontellier found the Doctor reading at the open window of his study. His house stood rather far back from the street, in the center of a delightful garden, so that it was quiet and peaceful at the old gentleman's study window. He was a great reader. He stared up disapprovingly over his eye-glasses as Mr. Pontellier entered, wondering who had the temerity to disturb him at that hour of the morning.

"Ah, Pontellier! Not sick, I hope. Come and have a seat. What news do you bring this morning?" He was quite portly, with a profusion of gray hair, and small blue eyes which age had robbed of much of their brightness but none of their penetration.

"Oh! I'm never sick, Doctor. You know that I come of tough fiber—of that old Creole race of Pontelliers that dry up and finally blow away. I came to consult—no, not precisely to consult—to talk to you about Edna. I don't know what ails her."

"Madame Pontellier not well?" marveled the Doctor. "Why, I saw her—I think it was a week ago—walking along Canal Street, the picture of health, it seemed to me."

"Yes, yes; she seems quite well," said Mr. Pontellier, leaning forward and whirling his stick between his two hands; "but she doesn't act well. She's odd, she's not like herself. I can't make her out, and I thought perhaps you'd help me."

"How does she act?" inquired the doctor.

"Well, it isn't easy to explain," said Mr. Pontellier, throwing himself back in his chair. "She lets the housekeeping go to the dickens."

"Well, well; women are not all alike, my dear Pontellier. We've got to consider—"

"I know that; I told you I couldn't explain. Her whole attitude—toward me and everybody and everything—has changed. You know I have a quick temper, but I don't want to quarrel or be rude to a woman, especially my wife; yet I'm driven to it, and feel like ten thousand devils after I've made a fool of myself. She's making it devilishly uncomfortable for me," he went on nervously. "She's got some sort of notion in her head concerning the eternal rights of women; and—you understand—we meet in the morning at the breakfast table."

The old gentleman lifted his shaggy eyebrows, protruded his thick nether lip, and tapped the arms of his chair with his cushioned finger-tips.

"What have you been doing to her, Pontellier?"

"Doing! *Parbleu!*"[1]

"Has she," asked the Doctor, with a smile, "has she been associating of late with a circle of pseudo-intellectual women[2]—super-spiritual superior beings? My wife has been telling me about them."

"That's the trouble," broke in Mr. Pontellier, "she hasn't been associating with any one. She has abandoned her Tuesdays at home, has thrown over all her acquaintances, and goes tramping about by herself, moping in the street-cars, getting in after dark. I tell you she's peculiar. I don't like it; I feel a little worried over it."

This was a new aspect for the Doctor. "Nothing hereditary?" he asked, seriously. "Nothing peculiar about her family antecedents, is there?"

"Oh, no, indeed! She comes of sound old Presbyterian Kentucky stock. The old gentleman, her father, I have heard, used to atone for his week-day sins with his Sunday devotions. I know for a fact, that his race horses literally ran away with the prettiest bit of Kentucky farming land I ever laid eyes upon. Margaret—you know Margaret—she has all the Presbyterianism undiluted. And the youngest is something of a vixen. By the way, she gets married in a couple of weeks from now."

"Send your wife up to the wedding," exclaimed the Doctor, foreseeing a happy solution. "Let her stay among her own people for a while; it will do her good."

"That's what I want her to do. She won't go to the marriage. She says a wedding is one of the most lamentable spectacles on earth. Nice thing for a woman to say to her husband!" exclaimed Mr. Pontellier, fuming anew at the recollection.

---

1 Idiomatic expression similar to "By Jove!"

2 Probably referring to women such as Charlotte Perkins Gilman and Elizabeth Cady Stanton (see Introduction, 14; Appendices B6 and B8), who were agitating for more rights for women.

"Pontellier," said the Doctor, after a moment's reflection, "let your wife alone for a while. Don't bother her, and don't let her bother you. Woman, my dear friend, is a very peculiar and delicate organism—a sensitive and highly organized woman, such as I know Mrs. Pontellier to be, is especially peculiar. It would require an inspired psychologist to deal successfully with them. And when ordinary fellows like you and me attempt to cope with their idiosyncrasies the result is bungling. Most women are moody and whimsical. This is some passing whim of your wife, due to some cause or causes which you and I needn't try to fathom. But it will pass happily over, especially if you let her alone. Send her around to see me."

"Oh! I couldn't do that; there'd be no reason for it," objected Mr. Pontellier.

"Then I'll go around and see her," said the Doctor. "I'll drop in to dinner some evening *en bon ami*."[1]

"Do! by all means," urged Mr. Pontellier. "What evening will you come? Say Thursday. Will you come Thursday?" he asked, rising to take his leave.

"Very well; Thursday. My wife may possibly have some engagement for me Thursday. In case she has, I shall let you know. Otherwise, you may expect me."

Mr. Pontellier turned before leaving to say:

"I am going to New York on business very soon. I have a big scheme on hand, and want to be on the field proper to pull the ropes and handle the ribbons.[2] We'll let you in on the inside if you say so, Doctor," he laughed.

"No, I thank you, my dear sir," returned the Doctor. "I leave such ventures to you younger men with the fever of life still in your blood."

"What I wanted to say," continued Mr. Pontellier, with his hand on the knob; "I may have to be absent a good while. Would you advise me to take Edna along?"

"By all means, if she wishes to go. If not, leave her here. Don't contradict her. The mood will pass, I assure you. It may take a month, two, three months—possibly longer, but it will pass; have patience."

"Well, good-by, *à jeudi*,"[3] said Mr. Pontellier, as he let himself out.

---

1 As a good friend.
2 Manage the reins, or be in control of the situation.
3 Until Thursday.

The Doctor would have liked during the course of conversation to ask, "Is there any man in the case?" but he knew his Creole too well to make such a blunder as that.

He did not resume his book immediately, but sat for a while meditatively looking out into the garden.

XXIII

Edna's father was in the city, and had been with them several days. She was not very warmly or deeply attached to him, but they had certain tastes in common, and when together they were companionable. His coming was in the nature of a welcome disturbance; it seemed to furnish a new direction for her emotions.

He had come to purchase a wedding gift for his daughter, Janet, and an outfit for himself in which he might make a creditable appearance at her marriage. Mr. Pontellier had selected the bridal gift, as every one immediately connected with him always deferred to his taste in such matters. And his suggestions on the question of dress—which too often assumes the nature of a problem—were of inestimable value to his father-in-law. But for the past few days the old gentleman had been upon Edna's hands, and in his society she was becoming acquainted with a new set of sensations. He had been a colonel in the Confederate army, and still maintained, with the title, the military bearing which had always accompanied it. His hair and mustache were white and silky, emphasizing the rugged bronze of his face. He was tall and thin, and wore his coats padded, which gave a fictitious breadth and depth to his shoulders and chest. Edna and her father looked very distinguished together, and excited a good deal of notice during their perambulations. Upon his arrival she began by introducing him to her atelier and making a sketch of him. He took the whole matter very seriously. If her talent had been tenfold greater than it was, it would not have surprised him, convinced as he was that he had bequeathed to all of his daughters the germs of a masterful capability, which only depended upon their own efforts to be directed toward successful achievement.

Before her pencil he sat rigid and unflinching, as he had faced the cannon's mouth in days gone by. He resented the intrusion of the children, who gaped with wondering eyes at him, sitting so stiff up there in their mother's bright atelier. When they drew near he motioned them away with an expressive action of the foot, loath to disturb the fixed lines of his countenance, his arms, or his rigid shoulders.

Edna, anxious to entertain him, invited Mademoiselle Reisz to meet him, having promised him a treat in her piano playing; but Mademoiselle declined the invitation. So together they attended a *soirée musicale* at the Ratignolle's. Monsieur and Madame Ratignolle made much of the Colonel, installing him as the guest of honor and engaging him at once to dine with them the following Sunday, or any day which he might select. Madame coquetted with him in the most captivating and naïve manner, with eyes, gestures, and a profusion of compliments, till the Colonel's old head felt thirty years younger on his padded shoulders. Edna marveled, not comprehending. She herself was almost devoid of coquetry.

There were one or two men whom she observed at the *soirée musicale*; but she would never have felt moved to any kittenish display to attract their notice—to any feline or feminine wiles to express herself toward them. Their personality attracted her in an agreeable way. Her fancy selected them, and she was glad when a lull in the music gave them an opportunity to meet her and talk with her. Often on the street the glance of strange eyes had lingered in her memory, and sometimes had disturbed her.

Mr. Pontellier did not attend these *soirées musicales*. He considered them *bourgeois*, and found more diversion at the club. To Madame Ratignolle he said the music dispensed at her *soirées* was too "heavy," too far beyond his untrained comprehension. His excuse flattered her. But she disapproved of Mr. Pontellier's club, and she was frank enough to tell Edna so.

"It's a pity Mr. Pontellier doesn't stay home more in the evenings. I think you would be more—well, if you don't mind my saying it—more united, if he did."

"Oh! dear no!" said Edna, with a blank look in her eyes. "What should I do if he stayed home? We wouldn't have anything to say to each other."

She had not much of anything to say to her father, for that matter; but he did not antagonize her. She discovered that he interested her, though she realized that he might not interest her long; and for the first time in her life she felt as if she were thoroughly acquainted with him. He kept her busy serving him and ministering to his wants. It amused her to do so. She would not permit a servant or one of the children to do anything for him which she might do herself. Her husband noticed, and thought it was the expression of a deep filial attachment which he had never suspected.

The Colonel drank numerous "toddies" during the course of the day, which left him, however, imperturbed. He was an expert at concocting strong drinks. He had even invented some, to which he had given fantastic names, and for whose manufacture he required diverse ingredients that it devolved upon Edna to procure for him.

When Doctor Mandelet dined with the Pontelliers on Thursday he could discern in Mrs. Pontellier no trace of that morbid condition which her husband had reported to him. She was excited and in a manner radiant. She and her father had been to the race course, and their thoughts when they seated themselves at table were still occupied with the events of the afternoon, and their talk was still of the track. The Doctor had not kept pace with turf affairs. He had certain recollections of racing in what he called "the good old times" when the Lecompte stables flourished, and he drew upon this fund of memories so that he might not be left out and seem wholly devoid of the modern spirit. But he failed to impose upon the Colonel, and was even far from impressing him with this trumped-up knowledge of bygone days. Edna had staked her father on his last venture, with the most gratifying results to both of them. Besides, they had met some very charming people, according to the Colonel's impressions. Mrs. Mortimer Merriman and Mrs. James Highcamp, who were there with Alcée Arobin, had joined them and had enlivened the hours in a fashion that warmed him to think of.

Mr. Pontellier himself had no particular leaning toward horse-racing, and was even rather inclined to discourage it as a pastime, especially when he considered the fate of that blue-grass farm in Kentucky. He endeavored, in a general way, to express a particular disapproval, and only succeeded in arousing the ire and opposition of his father-in-law. A pretty dispute followed, in which Edna warmly espoused her father's cause and the Doctor remained neutral.

He observed his hostess attentively from under his shaggy brows, and noted a subtle change which had transformed her from the listless woman he had known into a being who, for the moment, seemed palpitant with the forces of life. Her speech was warm and energetic. There was no repression in her glance or gesture. She reminded him of some beautiful, sleek animal waking up in the sun.

The dinner was excellent. The claret was warm and the champagne was cold, and under their beneficent influence the threatened unpleasantness melted and vanished with the fumes of the wine.

Mr. Pontellier warmed up and grew reminiscent. He told some amusing plantation experiences, recollections of old Iberville and his youth, when he hunted 'possum in company with some friendly darky; thrashed the pecan trees, shot the grosbec,[1] and roamed the woods and fields in mischievous idleness.

The Colonel, with little sense of humor and of the fitness of things, related a somber episode of those dark and bitter days, in which he had acted a conspicuous part and always formed a central figure. Nor was the Doctor happier in his selection, when he told the old, ever new and curious story of the waning of a woman's love, seeking strange, new channels, only to return to its legitimate source after days of fierce unrest. It was one of the many little human documents which had been unfolded to him during his long career as a physician. The story did not seem especially to impress Edna. She had one of her own to tell, of a woman who paddled away with her lover one night in a pirogue and never came back. They were lost amid the Baratarian Islands, and no one ever heard of them or found trace of them from that day to this. It was a pure invention. She said that Madame Antoine had related it to her. That, also, was an invention. Perhaps it was a dream she had had. But every glowing word seemed real to those who listened. They could feel the hot breath of the Southern night; they could hear the long sweep of the pirogue through the glistening moonlit water, the beating of birds' wings, rising startled from among the reeds in the salt-water pools; they could see the faces of the lovers, pale, close together, rapt in oblivious forgetfulness, drifting into the unknown.

The champagne was cold, and its subtle fumes played fantastic tricks with Edna's memory that night.

Outside, away from the glow of the fire and the soft lamplight, the night was chill and murky. The Doctor doubled his old-fashioned cloak across his breast as he strode home through the darkness. He knew his fellow-creatures better than most men; knew that inner life which so seldom unfolds itself to unanointed eyes. He was sorry he had accepted Pontellier's invitation. He was growing old, and beginning to need rest and an imperturbed spirit. He did not want the secrets of other lives thrust upon him.

---

1 A type of finch, more commonly spelled grosbeak.

"I hope it isn't Arobin," he muttered to himself as he walked. "I hope to heaven it isn't Alcée Arobin."

XXIV

Edna and her father had a warm, and almost violent dispute upon the subject of her refusal to attend her sister's wedding. Mr. Pontellier declined to interfere, to interpose either his influence or his authority. He was following Doctor Mandelet's advice, and letting her do as she liked. The Colonel reproached his daughter for her lack of filial kindness and respect, her want of sisterly affection and womanly consideration. His arguments were labored and unconvincing. He doubted if Janet would accept any excuse—forgetting that Edna had offered none. He doubted if Janet would ever speak to her again, and he was sure Margaret would not.

Edna was glad to be rid of her father when he finally took himself off with his wedding garments and his bridal gifts, with his padded shoulders, his Bible reading, his "toddies" and ponderous oaths.

Mr. Pontellier followed him closely. He meant to stop at the wedding on his way to New York and endeavor by every means which money and love could devise to atone somewhat for Edna's incomprehensible action.

"You are too lenient, too lenient by far, Léonce," asserted the Colonel. "Authority, coercion are what is needed. Put your foot down good and hard; the only way to manage a wife. Take my word for it."

The Colonel was perhaps unaware that he had coerced his own wife into her grave. Mr. Pontellier had a vague suspicion of it which he thought it needless to mention at that late day.

Edna was not so consciously gratified at her husband's leaving home as she had been over the departure of her father. As the day approached when he was to leave her for a comparatively long stay, she grew melting and affectionate, remembering his many acts of consideration and his repeated expressions of an ardent attachment. She was solicitous about his health and his welfare. She bustled around, looking after his clothing, thinking about heavy underwear, quite as Madame Ratignolle would have done under similar circumstances. She cried when he went away, calling him her dear, good friend, and she was quite certain she would grow lonely before very long and go to join him in New York.

But after all, a radiant peace settled upon her when she at last found herself alone. Even the children were gone. Old Madame Pontellier had come herself and carried them off to Iberville with their quadroon. The old madame did not venture to say she was afraid they would be neglected during Léonce's absence; she hardly ventured to think so. She was hungry for them—even a little fierce in her attachment. She did not want them to be wholly "children of the pavement," she always said when begging to have them for a space. She wished them to know the country, with its streams, its fields, its woods, its freedom, so delicious to the young. She wished them to taste something of the life their father had lived and known and loved when he, too, was a little child.

When Edna was at last alone, she breathed a big, genuine sigh of relief. A feeling that was unfamiliar but very delicious came over her. She walked all through the house, from one room to another, as if inspecting it for the first time. She tried the various chairs and lounges, as if she had never sat and reclined upon them before. And she perambulated around the outside of the house, investigating, looking to see if windows and shutters were secure and in order. The flowers were like new acquaintances; she approached them in a familiar spirit, and made herself at home among them. The garden walks were damp, and Edna called to the maid to bring out her rubber sandals. And there she stayed, and stooped, digging around the plants, trimming, picking dead, dry leaves. The children's little dog came out, interfering, getting in her way. She scolded him, laughed at him, played with him. The garden smelled so good and looked so pretty in the afternoon sunlight. Edna plucked all the bright flowers she could find, and went into the house with them, she and the little dog.

Even the kitchen assumed a sudden interesting character which she had never before perceived. She went in to give directions to the cook, to say that the butcher would have to bring much less meat, that they would require only half their usual quantity of bread, of milk and groceries. She told the cook that she herself would be greatly occupied during Mr. Pontellier's absence, and she begged her to take all thought and responsibility of the larder upon her own shoulders.

That night Edna dined alone. The candelabra, with a few candles in the center of the table, gave all the light she needed. Outside the circle of light in which she sat, the large dining-room looked solemn and shadowy. The cook, placed upon her mettle, served a delicious repast—a luscious tenderloin broiled *à point.*[1] The wine tasted good; the *marron glacé*[2] seemed to be just what she wanted. It was so pleasant, too, to dine in a comfortable *peignoir*.

She thought a little sentimentally about Léonce and the children, and wondered what they were doing. As she gave a dainty scrap or two to the doggie, she talked intimately to him about Etienne and Raoul. He was beside himself with astonishment and delight over these companionable advances, and showed his appreciation by his little quick, snappy barks and a lively agitation.

Then Edna sat in the library after dinner and read Emerson[3] until she grew sleepy. She realized that she had neglected her reading, and determined to start anew upon a course of improving studies, now that her time was completely her own to do with as she liked.

After a refreshing bath, Edna went to bed. And as she snuggled comfortably beneath the eiderdown a sense of restfulness invaded her, such as she had not known before.

XXV

When the weather was dark and cloudy Edna could not work. She needed the sun to mellow and temper her mood to the sticking point. She had reached a stage when she seemed to be no longer feeling her way, working, when in the humor, with sureness and ease. And being devoid of ambition, and striving not toward accomplishment, she drew satisfaction from the work in itself.

On rainy or melancholy days Edna went out and sought the society of the friends she had made at Grand Isle. Or else she stayed indoors and nursed a mood with which she was becoming too familiar for her own comfort and peace of mind. It was not despair; but it seemed to her as if life were passing by, leaving its promise broken and unfulfilled. Yet there were other days when she listened, was led on and deceived by fresh promises which her youth held out to her.

---

1 Cooked to perfection.
2 A candied chestnut.
3 Ralph Waldo Emerson (1803-82) was a leader in the American transcendentalist movement who wrote works such as *Nature* and "Self Reliance." See Appendix B1.

She went again to the races, and again. Alcée Arobin and Mrs. Highcamp called for her one bright afternoon in Arobin's drag.[1] Mrs. Highcamp was a worldly but unaffected, intelligent, slim, tall blonde woman in the forties, with an indifferent manner and blue eyes that stared. She had a daughter who served her as a pretext for cultivating the society of young men of fashion. Alcée Arobin was one of them. He was a familiar figure at the race course, the opera, the fashionable clubs. There was a perpetual smile in his eyes, which seldom failed to awaken a corresponding cheerfulness in any one who looked into them and listened to his good-humored voice. His manner was quiet, and at times a little insolent. He possessed a good figure, a pleasing face, not over-burdened with depth of thought or feeling; and his dress was that of the conventional man of fashion.

He admired Edna extravagantly, after meeting her at the races with her father. He had met her before on other occasions, but she had seemed to him unapproachable until that day. It was at his instigation that Mrs. Highcamp called to ask her to go with them to the Jockey Club[2] to witness the turf event of the season.

There were possibly a few track men out there who knew the race horse as well as Edna, but there was certainly none who knew it better. She sat between her two companions as one having authority to speak. She laughed at Arobin's pretensions, and deplored Mrs. Highcamp's ignorance. The race horse was a friend and intimate associate of her childhood. The atmosphere of the stables and the breath of the blue grass paddock revived in her memory and lingered in her nostrils. She did not perceive that she was talking like her father as the sleek geldings ambled in review before them. She played for very high stakes, and fortune favored her. The fever of the game flamed in her cheeks and eyes, and it got into her blood and into her brain like an intoxicant. People turned their heads to look at her, and more than one lent an attentive ear to her utterances, hoping thereby to secure the elusive but ever-desired "tip." Arobin caught the contagion of excitement which drew him to Edna like a magnet. Mrs. Highcamp remained, as usual, unmoved, with her indifferent stare and uplifted eyebrows.

Edna stayed and dined with Mrs. Highcamp upon being urged to do so. Arobin also remained and sent away his drag.

---

1 Horse-drawn coach.
2 In New Orleans, a club housed in a converted family mansion that was chartered in 1871 to promote horse racing. See Appendix D1.

The dinner was quiet and uninteresting, save for the cheerful efforts of Arobin to enliven things. Mrs. Highcamp deplored the absence of her daughter from the races, and tried to convey to her what she had missed by going to the "Dante reading"[1] instead of joining them. The girl held a geranium leaf up to her nose and said nothing, but looked knowing and noncommittal. Mr. Highcamp was a plain, bald-headed man, who only talked under compulsion. He was unresponsive. Mrs. Highcamp was full of delicate courtesy and consideration toward her husband. She addressed most of her conversation to him at table. They sat in the library after dinner and read the evening papers together under the drop-light;[2] while the younger people went into the drawing-room near by and talked. Miss Highcamp played some selections from Grieg[3] upon the piano. She seemed to have apprehended all of the composer's coldness and none of his poetry. While Edna listened she could not help wondering if she had lost her taste for music.

When the time came for her to go home, Mr. Highcamp grunted a lame offer to escort her, looking down at his slippered feet with tactless concern. It was Arobin who took her home. The car ride was long, and it was late when they reached Esplanade Street. Arobin asked permission to enter for a second to light his cigarette—his match safe[4] was empty. He filled his match safe, but did not light his cigarette until he left her, after she had expressed her willingness to go to the races with him again.

Edna was neither tired nor sleepy. She was hungry again, for the Highcamp dinner, though of excellent quality, had lacked abundance. She rummaged in the larder and brought forth a slice of "Gruyère"[5] and some crackers. She opened a bottle of beer which she found in the ice-box. Edna felt extremely restless and excited. She vacantly hummed a fantastic tune as she poked at the wood embers on the hearth and munched a cracker.

She wanted something to happen—something, anything; she did not know what. She regretted that she had not made Arobin

---

1   Dante Alighieri (c. 1265-1321) was an Italian poet most famous for his *Divine Comedy*, part of which is *Inferno*, a poem about hell. The implication is that going to the races was much more fun and entertaining than going to a reading with Dante as the subject.
2   A light suspended by a cord or chain.
3   Edvard Grieg (1843-1907) was a Norwegian composer.
4   A matchbox made of non-flammable material.
5   A hard cheese from Gruyères, Switzerland.

stay a half hour to talk over the horses with her. She counted the money she had won. But there was nothing else to do, so she went to bed, and tossed there for hours in a sort of monotonous agitation.

In the middle of the night she remembered that she had forgotten to write her regular letter to her husband; and she decided to do so next day and tell him about her afternoon at the Jockey Club. She lay wide awake composing a letter which was nothing like the one which she wrote next day. When the maid awoke her in the morning Edna was dreaming of Mr. Highcamp playing the piano at the entrance of a music store on Canal Street, while his wife was saying to Alcée Arobin, as they boarded an Esplanade Street car:

"What a pity that so much talent has been neglected! but I must go."

When, a few days later, Alcée Arobin again called for Edna in his drag, Mrs. Highcamp was not with him. He said they would pick her up. But as that lady had not been apprised of his intention of picking her up, she was not at home. The daughter was just leaving the house to attend the meeting of a branch Folk Lore Society,[1] and regretted that she could not accompany them. Arobin appeared nonplused, and asked Edna if there were any one else she cared to ask.

She did not deem it worth while to go in search of any of the fashionable acquaintances from whom she had withdrawn herself. She thought of Madame Ratignolle, but knew that her fair friend did not leave the house, except to take a languid walk around the block with her husband after nightfall. Mademoiselle Reisz would have laughed at such a request from Edna. Madame Lebrun might have enjoyed the outing, but for some reason Edna did not want her. So they went alone, she and Arobin.

The afternoon was intensely interesting to her. The excitement came back upon her like a remittent fever. Her talk grew familiar and confidential. It was no labor to become intimate with Arobin. His manner invited easy confidence. The preliminary stage of becoming acquainted was one which he always endeavored to ignore when a pretty and engaging woman was concerned.

He stayed and dined with Edna. He stayed and sat beside the wood fire. They laughed and talked; and before it was time to go he was telling her how different life might have been if he had

---

1 A local organization, founded in 1892 and still in existence today, that fosters research and support for all aspects of folklore.

known her years before. With ingenuous frankness he spoke of what a wicked, ill-disciplined boy he had been, and impulsively drew up his cuff to exhibit upon his wrist the scar from a saber cut which he had received in a duel outside of Paris when he was nineteen. She touched his hand as she scanned the red cicatrice[1] on the inside of his white wrist. A quick impulse that was somewhat spasmodic impelled her fingers to close in a sort of clutch upon his hand. He felt the pressure of her pointed nails in the flesh of his palm.

She arose hastily and walked toward the mantel.

"The sight of a wound or scar always agitates and sickens me," she said. "I shouldn't have looked at it."

"I beg your pardon," he entreated, following her; "it never occurred to me that it might be repulsive."

He stood close to her, and the effrontery in his eyes repelled the old, vanishing self in her, yet drew all her awakening sensuousness. He saw enough in her face to impel him to take her hand and hold it while he said his lingering good night.

"Will you go to the races again?" he asked.

"No," she said. "I've had enough of the races. I don't want to lose all the money I've won, and I've got to work when the weather is bright, instead of—"

"Yes; work; to be sure. You promised to show me your work. What morning may I come up to your atelier? To-morrow?"

"No!"

"Day after?"

"No, no."

"Oh, please don't refuse me! I know something of such things. I might help you with a stray suggestion or two."

"No. Good night. Why don't you go after you have said good night? I don't like you," she went on in a high, excited pitch, attempting to draw away her hand. She felt that her words lacked dignity and sincerity, and she knew that he felt it.

"I'm sorry you don't like me. I'm sorry I offended you. How have I offended you? What have I done? Can't you forgive me?" And he bent and pressed his lips upon her hand as if he wished never more to withdraw them.

"Mr. Arobin," she complained, "I'm greatly upset by the excitement of the afternoon; I'm not myself. My manner must have misled you in some way. I wish you to go, please." She spoke in a monotonous, dull tone. He took his hat from the table, and

---

1 A scar, more commonly spelled cicatrix.

stood with eyes turned from her, looking into the dying fire. For a moment or two he kept an impressive silence.

"Your manner has not misled me, Mrs. Pontellier," he said finally. "My own emotions have done that. I couldn't help it. When I'm near you, how could I help it? Don't think anything of it, don't bother, please. You see, I go when you command me. If you wish me to stay away, I shall do so. If you let me come back, I—oh! you will let me come back?"

He cast one appealing glance at her, to which she made no response. Alcée Arobin's manner was so genuine that it often deceived even himself.

Edna did not care or think whether it were genuine or not. When she was alone she looked mechanically at the back of her hand which he had kissed so warmly. Then she leaned her head down on the mantelpiece. She felt somewhat like a woman who in a moment of passion is betrayed into an act of infidelity, and realizes the significance of the act without being wholly awakened from its glamour. The thought was passing vaguely through her mind, "What would he think?"

She did not mean her husband; she was thinking of Robert Lebrun. Her husband seemed to her now like a person whom she had married without love as an excuse.

She lit a candle and went up to her room. Alcée Arobin was absolutely nothing to her. Yet his presence, his manners, the warmth of his glances, and above all the touch of his lips upon her hand had acted like a narcotic upon her.

She slept a languorous sleep, interwoven with vanishing dreams.

XXVI

Alcée Arobin wrote Edna an elaborate note of apology, palpitant with sincerity. It embarrassed her; for in a cooler, quieter moment it appeared to her absurd that she should have taken his action so seriously, so dramatically. She felt sure that the significance of the whole occurrence had lain in her own self-consciousness. If she ignored his note it would give undue importance to a trivial affair. If she replied to it in a serious spirit it would still leave in his mind the impression that she had in a susceptible moment yielded to his influence. After all, it was no great matter to have one's hand kissed. She was provoked at his having written the apology. She answered in as light and bantering a spirit as she fancied it deserved, and said she would be glad to have him look in upon her at work whenever he felt the inclination and his business gave him the opportunity.

He responded at once by presenting himself at her home with all his disarming naïveté. And then there was scarcely a day which followed that she did not see him or was not reminded of him. He was prolific in pretexts. His attitude became one of good-humored subservience and tacit adoration. He was ready at all times to submit to her moods, which were as often kind as they were cold. She grew accustomed to him. They became intimate and friendly by imperceptible degrees, and then by leaps. He sometimes talked in a way that astonished her at first and brought the crimson into her face; in a way that pleased her at last, appealing to the animalism that stirred impatiently within her.

There was nothing which so quieted the turmoil of Edna's senses as a visit to Mademoiselle Reisz. It was then, in the presence of that personality which was offensive to her, that the woman, by her divine art, seemed to reach Edna's spirit and set it free.

It was misty, with heavy, lowering atmosphere, one afternoon, when Edna climbed the stairs to the pianist's apartments under the roof. Her clothes were dripping with moisture. She felt chilled and pinched as she entered the room. Mademoiselle was poking at a rusty stove that smoked a little and warmed the room indifferently. She was endeavoring to heat a pot of chocolate on the stove. The room looked cheerless and dingy to Edna as she entered. A bust of Beethoven,[1] covered with a hood of dust, scowled at her from the mantelpiece.

"Ah! here comes the sunlight!" exclaimed Mademoiselle, rising from her knees before the stove. "Now it will be warm and bright enough; I can let the fire alone."

She closed the stove door with a bang, and approaching, assisted in removing Edna's dripping mackintosh.[2]

"You are cold; you look miserable. The chocolate will soon be hot. But would you rather have a taste of brandy? I have scarcely touched the bottle which you brought me for my cold." A piece of red flannel was wrapped around Mademoiselle's throat; a stiff neck compelled her to hold her head on one side.

"I will take some brandy," said Edna, shivering as she removed her gloves and overshoes. She drank the liquor from the glass as a man would have done. Then flinging herself upon the uncom-

1 Ludwig van Beethoven, German composer (1770-1827).
2 A raincoat.

fortable sofa she said, "Mademoiselle, I am going to move away from my house on Esplanade Street."

"Ah!" ejaculated the musician, neither surprised nor especially interested. Nothing ever seemed to astonish her very much. She was endeavoring to adjust the bunch of violets which had become loose from its fastening in her hair. Edna drew her down upon the sofa, and taking a pin from her own hair, secured the shabby artificial flowers in their accustomed place.

"Aren't you astonished?"

"Passably. Where are you going? to New York? to Iberville? to your father in Mississippi? where?"

"Just two steps away," laughed Edna, "in a little four-room house around the corner. It looks so cozy, so inviting and restful, whenever I pass by; and it's for rent. I'm tired looking after that big house. It never seemed like mine, anyway—like home. It's too much trouble. I have to keep too many servants. I am tired bothering with them."

"That is not your true reason, *ma belle*.[1] There is no use in telling me lies. I don't know your reason, but you have not told me the truth." Edna did not protest or endeavor to justify herself.

"The house, the money that provides for it, are not mine. Isn't that enough reason?"

"They are your husband's," returned Mademoiselle, with a shrug and a malicious elevation of the eyebrows.

"Oh! I see there is no deceiving you. Then let me tell you: It is a caprice. I have a little money of my own from my mother's estate, which my father sends me by driblets. I won a large sum this winter on the races, and I am beginning to sell my sketches. Laidpore is more and more pleased with my work; he says it grows in force and individuality. I cannot judge of that myself, but I feel that I have gained in ease and confidence. However, as I said, I have sold a good many through Laidpore. I can live in the tiny house for little or nothing, with one servant. Old Celestine, who works occasionally for me, says she will come stay with me and do my work. I know I shall like it, like the feeling of freedom and independence."

"What does your husband say?"

"I have not told him yet. I only thought of it this morning. He will think I am demented, no doubt. Perhaps you think so."

Mademoiselle shook her head slowly. "Your reason is not yet clear to me," she said.

---

1 My lady.

Neither was it quite clear to Edna herself; but it unfolded itself as she sat for a while in silence. Instinct had prompted her to put away her husband's bounty in casting off her allegiance. She did not know how it would be when he returned. There would have to be an understanding, an explanation. Conditions would some way adjust themselves, she felt; but whatever came, she had resolved never again to belong to another than herself.

"I shall give a grand dinner before I leave the old house!" Edna exclaimed. "You will have to come to it, Mademoiselle. I will give you everything that you like to eat and to drink. We shall sing and laugh and be merry for once." And she uttered a sigh that came from the very depths of her being.

If Mademoiselle happened to have received a letter from Robert during the interval of Edna's visits, she would give her the letter unsolicited. And she would seat herself at the piano and play as her humor prompted her while the young woman read the letter.

The little stove was roaring; it was red-hot, and the chocolate in the tin sizzled and sputtered. Edna went forward and opened the stove door, and Mademoiselle rising, took a letter from under the bust of Beethoven and handed it to Edna.

"Another! so soon!" she exclaimed, eyes filled with delight. "Tell me, Mademoiselle, does he know that I see his letters?"

"Never in the world! He would be angry and would never write to me again if he thought so. Does he write to you? Never a line. Does he send you a message? Never a word. It is because he loves you, poor fool, and is trying to forget you, since you are not free to listen to him or to belong to him."

"Why do you show me his letters, then?"

"Haven't you begged for them? Can I refuse you anything? Oh! you cannot deceive me," and Mademoiselle approached her beloved instrument and began to play. Edna did not at once read the letter. She sat holding it in her hand, while the music penetrated her whole being like an effulgence, warming and brightening the dark places of her soul. It prepared her for joy and exultation.

"Oh!" she exclaimed, letting the letter fall to the floor. "Why did you not tell me?" She went and grasped Mademoiselle's hands up from the keys. "Oh! unkind! malicious! Why did you not tell me?"

"That he was coming back? No great news, *ma foi*. I wonder he did not come long ago."

"But when, when?" cried Edna, impatiently. "He does not say when."

"He says 'very soon.' You know as much about it as I do; it is all in the letter."

"But why? Why is he coming? Oh, if I thought—" and she snatched the letter from the floor and turned the pages this way and that way, looking for the reason, which was left untold.

"If I were young and in love with a man," said Mademoiselle, turning on the stool and pressing her wiry hands between her knees as she looked down at Edna, who sat on the floor holding the letter, "it seems to me he would have to be some *grand esprit*; a man with lofty aims and ability to reach them; one who stood high enough to attract the notice of his fellow-men. It seems to me if I were young and in love I should never deem a man of ordinary caliber worthy of my devotion."

"Now it is you who are telling lies and seeking to deceive me, Mademoiselle; or else you have never been in love, and know nothing about it. Why," went on Edna, clasping her knees and looking up into Mademoiselle's twisted face, "do you suppose a woman knows why she loves? Does she select? Does she say to herself: 'Go to! Here is a distinguished statesman with presidential possibilities; I shall proceed to fall in love with him.' Or, 'I shall set my heart upon this musician, whose fame is on every tongue?' Or, 'This financier, who controls the world's money markets?'"

"You are purposely misunderstanding me, *ma reine*.[1] Are you in love with Robert?"

"Yes," said Edna. It was the first time she had admitted it, and a glow overspread her face, blotching it with red spots.

"Why?" asked her companion. "Why do you love him when you ought not to?"

Edna, with a motion or two, dragged herself on her knees before Mademoiselle Reisz, who took the glowing face between her two hands.

"Why? Because his hair is brown and grows away from his temples; because he opens and shuts his eyes, and his nose is a little out of drawing; because he has two lips and a square chin, and a little finger which he can't straighten from having played baseball too energetically in his youth. Because—"

---

1 My queen.

"Because you do, in short," laughed Mademoiselle. "What will you do when he comes back?" she asked.

"Do? Nothing, except feel glad and happy to be alive."

She was already glad and happy to be alive at the mere thought of his return. The murky, lowering sky, which had depressed her a few hours before, seemed bracing and invigorating as she splashed through the streets on her way home.

She stopped at a confectioner's and ordered a huge box of bonbons for the children in Iberville. She slipped a card in the box, on which she scribbled a tender message and sent an abundance of kisses.

Before dinner in the evening Edna wrote a charming letter to her husband, telling him of her intention to move for a while into the little house around the block, and to give a farewell dinner before leaving, regretting that he was not there to share it, to help her out with the menu and assist her in entertaining the guests. Her letter was brilliant and brimming with cheerfulness.

XXVII

"What is the matter with you?" asked Arobin that evening. "I never found you in such a happy mood." Edna was tired by that time, and was reclining on the lounge before the fire.

"Don't you know the weather prophet has told us we shall see the sun pretty soon?"

"Well, that ought to be reason enough," he acquiesced. "You wouldn't give me another if I sat here all night imploring you." He sat close to her on a low tabouret,[1] and as he spoke his fingers lightly touched the hair that fell a little over her forehead. She liked the touch of his fingers through her hair, and closed her eyes sensitively.

"One of these days," she said, "I'm going to pull myself together for a while and think—try to determine what character of a woman I am; for, candidly, I don't know. By all the codes which I am acquainted with, I am a devilishly wicked specimen of the sex. But some way I can't convince myself that I am. I must think about it."

"Don't. What's the use? Why should you bother thinking about it when I can tell you what manner of woman you are." His

---

1   A round seat or stool without arms or legs, similar to a footstool or ottoman.

fingers strayed occasionally down to her warm, smooth cheeks and firm chin, which was growing a little full and double.

"Oh, yes! You will tell me that I am adorable; everything that is captivating. Spare yourself the effort."

"No; I shan't tell you anything of the sort, though I shouldn't be lying if I did."

"Do you know Mademoiselle Reisz?" she asked irrelevantly.

"The pianist? I know her by sight. I've heard her play."

"She says queer things sometimes in a bantering way that you don't notice at the time and you find yourself thinking about afterward."

"For instance?"

"Well, for instance, when I left her to-day, she put her arms around me and felt my shoulder blades, to see if my wings were strong, she said. 'The bird that would soar above the level plain of tradition and prejudice must have strong wings. It is a sad spectacle to see the weaklings bruised, exhausted, fluttering back to earth.'"

"Whither would you soar?"

"I'm not thinking of any extraordinary flights. I only half comprehend her."

"I've heard she's partially demented," said Arobin.

"She seems to me wonderfully sane," Edna replied.

"I'm told she's extremely disagreeable and unpleasant. Why have you introduced her at a moment when I desired to talk of you?"

"Oh! talk of me if you like," cried Edna, clasping her hands beneath her head; "but let me think of something else while you do."

"I'm jealous of your thoughts to-night. They're making you a little kinder than usual; but some way I feel as if they were wandering, as if they were not here with me." She only looked at him and smiled. His eyes were very near. He leaned upon the lounge with an arm extended across her, while the other hand still rested upon her hair. They continued silently to look into each other's eyes. When he leaned forward and kissed her, she clasped his head, holding his lips to hers.

It was the first kiss of her life to which her nature had really responded. It was a flaming torch that kindled desire.

XXVIII

Edna cried a little that night after Arobin left her. It was only one phase of the multitudinous emotions which had assailed her. There was with her an overwhelming feeling of irresponsibility. There was the shock of the unexpected and the unaccustomed. There was her husband's reproach looking at her from the external things around her which he had provided for her external existence. There was Robert's reproach making itself felt by a quicker, fiercer, more overpowering love, which had awakened within her toward him. Above all, there was understanding. She felt as if a mist had been lifted from her eyes, enabling her to look upon and comprehend the significance of life, that monster made up of beauty and brutality. But among the conflicting sensations which assailed her, there was neither shame nor remorse. There was a dull pang of regret because it was not the kiss of love which had inflamed her, because it was not love which had held this cup of life to her lips.

XXIX

Without even waiting for an answer from her husband regarding his opinion or wishes in the matter, Edna hastened her preparations for quitting her home on Esplanade Street and moving into the little house around the block. A feverish anxiety attended her every action in that direction. There was no moment of deliberation, no interval of repose between the thought and its fulfillment. Early upon the morning following those hours passed in Arobin's society, Edna set about securing her new abode and hurrying her arrangements for occupying it. Within the precincts of her home she felt like one who has entered and lingered within the portals of some forbidden temple in which a thousand muffled voices bade her begone.

Whatever was her own in the house, everything which she had acquired aside from her husband's bounty, she caused to be transported to the other house, supplying simple and meager deficiencies from her own resources.

Arobin found her with rolled sleeves, working in company with the house-maid when he looked in during the afternoon. She was splendid and robust, and had never appeared handsomer than in the old blue gown, with a red silk handkerchief knotted at random around her head to protect her hair from the dust. She was mounted upon a high step-ladder, unhooking a picture from the wall when he entered. He had found the front door open, and had followed his ring by walking in unceremoniously.

"Come down!" he said. "Do you want to kill yourself?" She greeted him with affected carelessness, and appeared absorbed in her occupation.

If he had expected to find her languishing, reproachful, or indulging in sentimental tears, he must have been greatly surprised.

He was no doubt prepared for any emergency, ready for any one of the foregoing attitudes, just as he bent himself easily and naturally to the situation which confronted him.

"Please come down," he insisted, holding the ladder and looking up at her.

"No," she answered; "Ellen is afraid to mount the ladder. Joe is working over at the 'pigeon house'—that's the name Ellen gives it, because it's so small and looks like a pigeon house—and some one has to do this."

Arobin pulled off his coat, and expressed himself ready and willing to tempt fate in her place. Ellen brought him one of her dust-caps, and went into contortions of mirth, which she found it impossible to control, when she saw him put it on before the mirror as grotesquely as he could. Edna herself could not refrain from smiling when she fastened it at his request. So it was he who in turn mounted the ladder, unhooking pictures and curtains, and dislodging ornaments as Edna directed. When he had finished he took off his dust-cap and went out to wash his hands.

Edna was sitting on the tabouret, idly brushing the tips of a feather duster along the carpet when he came in again.

"Is there anything more you will let me do?" he asked.

"That is all," she answered. "Ellen can manage the rest." She kept the young woman occupied in the drawing-room, unwilling to be left alone with Arobin.

"What about the dinner?" he asked; "the grand event, the *coup d'état?*"[1]

"It will be day after to-morrow. Why do you call it the '*coup d'état?*' Oh! it will be very fine; all my best of everything—crystal, silver and gold, Sèvres, flowers, music, and champagne to swim in. I'll let Léonce pay the bills. I wonder what he'll say when he sees the bills."

---

1 Crowning achievement.

"And you ask me why I call it a *coup d'état*?" Arobin had put on his coat, and he stood before her and asked if his cravat[1] was plumb. She told him it was, looking no higher than the tip of his collar.

"When do you go to the 'pigeon house?'—with all due acknowledgment to Ellen."

"Day after to-morrow, after the dinner. I shall sleep there."

"Ellen, will you very kindly get me a glass of water?" asked Arobin. "The dust in the curtains, if you will pardon me for hinting such a thing, has parched my throat to a crisp."

"While Ellen gets the water," said Edna, rising, "I will say good-by and let you go. I must get rid of this grime, and I have a million things to do and think of."

"When shall I see you?" asked Arobin, seeking to detain her, the maid having left the room.

"At the dinner, of course. You are invited."

"Not before?—not to-night or to-morrow morning or to-morrow noon or night? or the day after morning or noon? Can't you see yourself, without my telling you, what an eternity it is?"

He had followed her into the hall and to the foot of the stairway, looking up at her as she mounted with her face half turned to him.

"Not an instant sooner," she said. But she laughed and looked at him with eyes that at once gave him courage to wait and made it torture to wait.

XXX

Though Edna had spoken of the dinner as a very grand affair, it was in truth a very small affair and very select, in so much as the guests invited were few and were selected with discrimination. She had counted upon an even dozen seating themselves at her round mahogany board, forgetting for the moment that Madame Ratignolle was to the last degree *souffrante*[2] and unpresentable, and not foreseeing that Madame Lebrun would send a thousand regrets at the last moment. So there were only ten, after all, which made a cozy, comfortable number.

There were Mr. and Mrs. Merriman, a pretty, vivacious little woman in the thirties; her husband, a jovial fellow, something of a shallow-pate,[3] who laughed a good deal at other people's witti-

---

1   A scarf or band worn around the neck instead of a tie.
2   Suffering.
3   A simpleton or featherbrain; someone flighty or airheaded.

cisms, and had thereby made himself extremely popular. Mrs. Highcamp had accompanied them. Of course, there was Alcée Arobin; and Mademoiselle Reisz had consented to come. Edna had sent her a fresh bunch of violets with black lace trimmings for her hair. Monsieur Ratignolle brought himself and his wife's excuses. Victor Lebrun, who happened to be in the city, bent upon relaxation, had accepted with alacrity. There was a Miss Mayblunt, no longer in her teens, who looked at the world through lorgnettes[1] and with the keenest interest. It was thought and said that she was intellectual; it was suspected of her that she wrote under a *nom de guerre*.[2] She had come with a gentleman by the name of Gouvernail,[3] connected with one of the daily papers, of whom nothing special could be said, except that he was observant and seemed quiet and inoffensive. Edna herself made the tenth, and at half-past eight they seated themselves at table, Arobin and Monsieur Ratignolle on either side of their hostess.

Mrs. Highcamp sat between Arobin and Victor Lebrun. Then came Mrs. Merriman, Mr. Gouvernail, Miss Mayblunt, Mr. Merriman, and Mademoiselle Reisz next to Monsieur Ratignolle.

There was something extremely gorgeous about the appearance of the table, an effect of splendor conveyed by a cover of pale yellow satin under strips of lace-work. There were wax candles in massive brass candelabra, burning softly under yellow silk shades; full, fragrant roses, yellow and red, abounded. There were silver and gold, as she had said there would be, and crystal which glittered like the gems which the women wore.

The ordinary stiff dining chairs had been discarded for the occasion and replaced by the most commodious and luxurious which could be collected throughout the house. Mademoiselle Reisz, being exceedingly diminutive, was elevated upon cushions, as small children are sometimes hoisted at table upon bulky volumes.

"Something new, Edna?" exclaimed Miss Mayblunt, with lorgnette directed toward a magnificent cluster of diamonds that sparkled, that almost sputtered, in Edna's hair, just over the center of her forehead.

---

1 Eyeglasses that have a handle on them and are brought up to the eyes rather than worn on the head.

2 Pseudonym.

3 Another of Chopin's recurring characters, who reappears in "A Respectable Woman" (see below, 183).

"Quite new; 'brand' new, in fact; a present from my husband. It arrived this morning from New York. I may as well admit that this is my birthday, and that I am twenty-nine. In good time I expect you to drink my health. Meanwhile, I shall ask you to begin with this cocktail, composed—would you say 'composed?'" with an appeal to Miss Mayblunt—"composed by my father in honor of Sister Janet's wedding."

Before each guest stood a tiny glass that looked and sparkled like a garnet gem.

"Then, all things considered," spoke Arobin, "it might not be amiss to start out by drinking the Colonel's health in the cocktail which he composed, on the birthday of the most charming of women—the daughter whom he invented."

Mr. Merriman's laugh at this sally was such a genuine outburst and so contagious that it started the dinner with an agreeable swing that never slackened.

Miss Mayblunt begged to be allowed to keep her cocktail untouched before her, just to look at. The color was marvelous! She could compare it to nothing she had ever seen, and the garnet lights which it emitted were unspeakably rare. She pronounced the Colonel an artist, and stuck to it.

Monsieur Ratignolle was prepared to take things seriously: the mets,[1] the entre-mets,[2] the service, the decorations, even the people. He looked up from his pompono[3] and inquired of Arobin if he were related to the gentleman of that name who formed one of the firm of Laitner and Arobin, lawyers. The young man admitted that Laitner was a warm personal friend, who permitted Arobin's name to decorate the firm's letterheads and to appear upon a shingle that graced Perdido Street.

"There are so many inquisitive people and institutions abounding," said Arobin, "that one is really forced as a matter of convenience these days to assume the virtue of an occupation if he has it not."

Monsieur Ratignolle stared a little, and turned to ask Mademoiselle Reisz if she considered the symphony concerts up to the standard which had been set the previous winter. Mademoiselle Reisz answered Monsieur Ratignolle in French, which Edna thought a little rude, under the circumstances, but characteristic.

---

1 A dish or delicacy.
2 A dessert or side dish.
3 More commonly "pompano," a fish found off the southern Atlantic or Gulf coasts.

Mademoiselle had only disagreeable things to say of the symphony concerts, and insulting remarks to make of all the musicians of New Orleans, singly and collectively. All her interest seemed to be centered upon the delicacies placed before her.

Mr. Merriman said that Mr. Arobin's remark about inquisitive people reminded him of a man from Waco[1] the other day at the St. Charles Hotel—but as Mr. Merriman's stories were always lame and lacking point, his wife seldom permitted him to complete them. She interrupted him to ask if he remembered the name of the author whose book she had bought the week before to send to a friend in Geneva. She was talking "books" with Mr. Gouvernail and trying to draw from him his opinion upon current literary topics. Her husband told the story of the Waco man privately to Miss Mayblunt, who pretended to be greatly amused and to think it extremely clever.

Mrs. Highcamp hung with languid but unaffected interest upon the warm and impetuous volubility of her left-hand neighbor, Victor Lebrun. Her attention was never for a moment withdrawn from him after seating herself at table; and when he turned to Mrs. Merriman, who was prettier and more vivacious than Mrs. Highcamp, she waited with easy indifference for an opportunity to reclaim his attention. There was the occasional sound of music, of mandolins, sufficiently removed to be an agreeable accompaniment rather than an interruption to the conversation. Outside the soft, monotonous splash of a fountain could be heard; the sound penetrated into the room with the heavy odor of jessamine that came through the open windows.

The golden shimmer of Edna's satin gown spread in rich folds on either side of her. There was a soft fall of lace encircling her shoulders. It was the color of her skin, without the glow, the myriad living tints that one may sometimes discover in vibrant flesh. There was something in her attitude, in her whole appearance when she leaned her head against the high-backed chair and spread her arms, which suggested the regal woman, the one who rules, who looks on, who stands alone.

But as she sat there amid her guests, she felt the old ennui overtaking her; the hopelessness which so often assailed her, which came upon her like an obsession, like something extraneous, independent of volition. It was something which announced itself; a chill breath that seemed to issue from some vast cavern wherein discords wailed. There came over her the acute longing

1 A city in Texas.

which always summoned into her spiritual vision the presence of the beloved one, overpowering her at once with a sense of the unattainable.

The moments glided on, while a feeling of good fellowship passed around the circle like a mystic cord, holding and binding these people together with jest and laughter. Monsieur Ratignolle was the first to break the pleasant charm. At ten o'clock he excused himself. Madame Ratignolle was waiting for him at home. She was *bien souffrante*,[1] and she was filled with vague dread, which only her husband's presence could allay.

Mademoiselle Reisz arose with Monsieur Ratignolle, who offered to escort her to the car. She had eaten well; she had tasted the good, rich wines, and they must have turned her head, for she bowed pleasantly to all as she withdrew from table. She kissed Edna upon the shoulder, and whispered: "*Bonne nuit, ma reine; soyez sage.*"[2] She had been a little bewildered upon rising, or rather, descending from her cushions, and Monsieur Ratignolle gallantly took her arm and led her away.

Mrs. Highcamp was weaving a garland of roses, yellow and red. When she had finished the garland, she laid it lightly upon Victor's black curls. He was reclining far back in the luxurious chair, holding a glass of champagne to the light.

As if a magician's wand had touched him, the garland of roses transformed him into a vision of Oriental beauty. His cheeks were the color of crushed grapes, and his dusky eyes glowed with a languishing fire.

"*Sapristi!*" exclaimed Arobin.

But Mrs. Highcamp had one more touch to add to the picture. She took from the back of her chair a white silken scarf, with which she had covered her shoulders in the early part of the evening. She draped it across the boy in graceful folds, and in a way to conceal his black, conventional evening dress. He did not seem to mind what she did to him, only smiled, showing a faint gleam of white teeth, while he continued to gaze with narrowing eyes at the light through his glass of champagne.

"Oh! to be able to paint in color rather than in words!" exclaimed Miss Mayblunt, losing herself in a rhapsodic dream as she looked at him.

---

1 Suffering a lot.
2 Good night, my queen; be good.

"'There was a graven image of Desire
Painted with red blood on a ground of gold.'"[1]

murmured Gouvernail, under his breath.

The effect of the wine upon Victor was to change his accustomed volubility into silence. He seemed to have abandoned himself to a reverie, and to be seeing pleasing visions in the amber bead.

"Sing," entreated Mrs. Highcamp. "Won't you sing to us?"

"Let him alone," said Arobin.

"He's posing," offered Mr. Merriman; "let him have it out."

"I believe he's paralyzed," laughed Mrs. Merriman. And leaning over the youth's chair, she took the glass from his hand and held it to his lips. He sipped the wine slowly, and when he had drained the glass she laid it upon the table and wiped his lips with her little filmy handkerchief.

"Yes, I'll sing for you," he said, turning in his chair toward Mrs. Highcamp. He clasped his hands behind his head, and looking up at the ceiling began to hum a little, trying his voice like a musician tuning an instrument. Then, looking at Edna, he began to sing:

"Ah! si tu savais!"

"Stop!" she cried, "don't sing that. I don't want you to sing it," and she laid her glass so impetuously and blindly upon the table as to shatter it against a caraffe. The wine spilled over Arobin's legs and some of it trickled down upon Mrs. Highcamp's black gauze gown. Victor had lost all idea of courtesy, or else he thought his hostess was not in earnest, for he laughed and went on:

"Ah! si tu savais
Ce que tes yeux me disent"—[2]

"Oh! you mustn't! you mustn't," exclaimed Edna, and pushing back her chair she got up, and going behind him placed her hand over his mouth. He kissed the soft palm that pressed upon his lips.

"No, no, I won't, Mrs. Pontellier. I didn't know you meant it," looking up at her with caressing eyes. The touch of his lips was like a pleasing sting to her hand. She lifted the garland of roses from his head and flung it across the room.

1 From the poem "A Cameo," by Algernon Charles Swinburne (1837-1909). See Appendix B3.
2 If you only knew / what your eyes are telling me.

"Come, Victor; you've posed long enough. Give Mrs. High-camp her scarf."

Mrs. Highcamp undraped the scarf from about him with her own hands. Miss Mayblunt and Mr. Gouvernail suddenly conceived the notion that it was time to say good night. And Mr. and Mrs. Merriman wondered how it could be so late.

Before parting from Victor, Mrs. Highcamp invited him to call upon her daughter, who she knew would be charmed to meet him and talk French and sing French songs with him. Victor expressed his desire and intention to call upon Miss Highcamp at the first opportunity which presented itself. He asked if Arobin were going his way. Arobin was not.

The mandolin players had long since stolen away. A profound stillness had fallen upon the broad, beautiful street. The voices of Edna's disbanding guests jarred like a discordant note upon the quiet harmony of the night.

XXXI

"Well?" questioned Arobin, who had remained with Edna after the others had departed.

"Well," she reiterated, and stood up, stretching her arms, and feeling the need to relax her muscles after having been so long seated.

"What next?" he asked.

"The servants are all gone. They left when the musicians did. I have dismissed them. The house has to be closed and locked, and I shall trot around to the pigeon house, and shall send Celestine over in the morning to straighten things up."

He looked around, and began to turn out some of the lights.

"What about upstairs?" he inquired.

"I think it is all right; but there may be a window or two unlatched. We had better look; you might take a candle and see. And bring me my wrap and hat on the foot of the bed in the middle room."

He went up with the light, and Edna began closing doors and windows. She hated to shut in the smoke and the fumes of the wine. Arobin found her cape and hat, which he brought down and helped her to put on.

When everything was secured and the lights put out, they left through the front door, Arobin locking it and taking the key, which he carried for Edna. He helped her down the steps.

"Will you have a spray of jessamine?" he asked, breaking off a few blossoms as he passed.

"No; I don't want anything."

She seemed disheartened, and had nothing to say. She took his arm, which he offered her, holding up the weight of her satin train with the other hand. She looked down, noticing the black line of his leg moving in and out so close to her against the yellow shimmer of her gown. There was the whistle of a railway train somewhere in the distance, and the midnight bells were ringing. They met no one in their short walk.

The "pigeon-house" stood behind a locked gate, and a shallow *parterre*[1] that had been somewhat neglected. There was a small front porch, upon which a long window and the front door opened. The door opened directly into the parlor; there was no side entry. Back in the yard was a room for servants, in which old Celestine had been ensconced.

Edna had left a lamp burning low upon the table. She had succeeded in making the room look habitable and homelike. There were some books on the table and a lounge near at hand. On the floor was a fresh matting, covered with a rug or two; and on the walls hung a few tasteful pictures. But the room was filled with flowers. These were a surprise to her. Arobin had sent them, and had had Celestine distribute them during Edna's absence. Her bedroom was adjoining, and across a small passage were the dining-room and kitchen.

Edna seated herself with every appearance of discomfort.

"Are you tired?" he asked.

"Yes, and chilled, and miserable. I feel as if I had been wound up to a certain pitch—too tight—and something inside of me had snapped." She rested her head against the table upon her bare arm.

"You want to rest," he said, "and to be quiet. I'll go; I'll leave you and let you rest."

"Yes," she replied.

He stood up beside her and smoothed her hair with his soft, magnetic hand. His touch conveyed to her a certain physical comfort. She could have fallen quietly asleep there if he had continued to pass his hand over her hair. He brushed the hair upward from the nape of her neck.

---

1 A small garden.

"I hope you will feel better and happier in the morning," he said. "You have tried to do too much in the past few days. The dinner was the last straw; you might have dispensed with it."

"Yes," she admitted; "it was stupid."

"No, it was delightful; but it has worn you out." His hand had strayed to her beautiful shoulders, and he could feel the response of her flesh to his touch. He seated himself beside her and kissed her lightly upon the shoulder.

"I thought you were going away," she said, in an uneven voice.

"I am, after I have said good night."

"Good night," she murmured.

He did not answer, except to continue to caress her. He did not say good night until she had become supple to his gentle, seductive entreaties.

XXXII

When Mr. Pontellier learned of his wife's intention to abandon her home and take up her residence elsewhere, he immediately wrote her a letter of unqualified disapproval and remonstrance. She had given reasons which he was unwilling to acknowledge as adequate. He hoped she had not acted upon her rash impulse; and he begged her to consider first, foremost, and above all else, what people would say. He was not dreaming of scandal when he uttered this warning; that was a thing which would never have entered into his mind to consider in connection with his wife's name or his own. He was simply thinking of his financial integrity. It might get noised about that the Pontelliers had met with reverses, and were forced to conduct their *ménage*[1] on a humbler scale than heretofore. It might do incalculable mischief to his business prospects.

But remembering Edna's whimsical turn of mind of late, and foreseeing that she had immediately acted upon her impetuous determination, he grasped the situation with his usual promptness and handled it with his well-known business tact and cleverness.

The same mail which brought to Edna his letter of disapproval carried instructions—the most minute instructions—to a well-known architect concerning the remodeling of his home, changes which he had long contemplated, and which he desired carried forward during his temporary absence.

---

1 Household.

Expert and reliable packers and movers were engaged to convey the furniture, carpets, pictures—everything movable, in short—to places of security. And in an incredibly short time the Pontellier house was turned over to the artisans. There was to be an addition—a small snuggery;[1] there was to be frescoing,[2] and hardwood flooring was to be put into such rooms as had not yet been subjected to this improvement.

Furthermore, in one of the daily papers appeared a brief notice to the effect that Mr. and Mrs. Pontellier were contemplating a summer sojourn abroad, and that their handsome residence on Esplanade Street was undergoing sumptuous alterations, and would not be ready for occupancy until their return. Mr. Pontellier had saved appearances!

Edna admired the skill of his maneuver, and avoided any occasion to balk his intentions. When the situation as set forth by Mr. Pontellier was accepted and taken for granted, she was apparently satisfied that it should be so.

The pigeon-house pleased her. It at once assumed the intimate character of a home, while she herself invested it with a charm which it reflected like a warm glow. There was with her a feeling of having descended in the social scale, with a corresponding sense of having risen in the spiritual. Every step which she took toward relieving herself from obligations added to her strength and expansion as an individual. She began to look with her own eyes; to see and to apprehend the deeper undercurrents of life. No longer was she content to "feed upon opinion" when her own soul had invited her.

After a little while, a few days, in fact, Edna went up and spent a week with her children in Iberville. They were delicious February days, with all the summer's promise hovering in the air.

How glad she was to see the children! She wept for very pleasure when she felt their little arms clasping her; their hard, ruddy cheeks pressed against her own glowing cheeks. She looked into their faces with hungry eyes that could not be satisfied with looking. And what stories they had to tell their mother! About the pigs, the cows, the mules! About riding to the mill behind Gluglu; fishing back in the lake with their Uncle Jasper; picking pecans with Lidie's little black brood, and hauling chips in their express wagon. It was a thousand times more fun to haul real chips for

1   A small room.
2   Painting.

old lame Susie's real fire than to drag painted blocks along the banquette on Esplanade Street!

She went with them herself to see the pigs and the cows, to look at the darkies laying the cane, to thrash the pecan trees, and catch fish in the back lake. She lived with them a whole week long, giving them all of herself, and gathering and filling herself with their young existence. They listened, breathless, when she told them the house in Esplanade Street was crowded with workmen, hammering, nailing, sawing, and filling the place with clatter. They wanted to know where their bed was; what had been done with their rocking-horse; and where did Joe sleep, and where had Ellen gone, and the cook? But, above all, they were fired with a desire to see the little house around the block. Was there any place to play? Were there any boys next door? Raoul, with pessimistic foreboding, was convinced that there were only girls next door. Where would they sleep, and where would papa sleep? She told them the fairies would fix it all right.

The old Madame was charmed with Edna's visit, and showered all manner of delicate attentions upon her. She was delighted to know that the Esplanade Street house was in a dismantled condition. It gave her the promise and pretext to keep the children indefinitely.

It was with a wrench and a pang that Edna left her children. She carried away with her the sound of their voices and the touch of their cheeks. All along the journey homeward their presence lingered with her like the memory of a delicious song. But by the time she had regained the city the song no longer echoed in her soul. She was again alone.

XXXIII

It happened sometimes when Edna went to see Mademoiselle Reisz that the little musician was absent, giving a lesson or making some small necessary household purchase. The key was always left in a secret hiding-place in the entry, which Edna knew. If Mademoiselle happened to be away, Edna would usually enter and wait for her return.

When she knocked at Mademoiselle Reisz's door one afternoon there was no response; so unlocking the door, as usual, she entered and found the apartment deserted, as she had expected. Her day had been quite filled up, and it was for a rest, for a refuge, and to talk about Robert, that she sought out her friend.

She had worked at her canvas—a young Italian character study—all the morning, completing the work without the model; but there had been many interruptions, some incident to her modest housekeeping, and others of a social nature.

Madame Ratignolle had dragged herself over, avoiding the too public thorough-fares, she said. She complained that Edna had neglected her much of late. Besides, she was consumed with curiosity to see the little house and the manner in which it was conducted. She wanted to hear all about the dinner party; Monsieur Ratignolle had left *so* early. What had happened after he left? The champagne and grapes which Edna sent over were *too* delicious. She had so little appetite; they had refreshed and toned her stomach. Where on earth was she going to put Mr. Pontellier in that little house, and the boys? And then she made Edna promise to go to her when her hour of trial overtook her.

"At any time—any time of the day or night, dear," Edna assured her.

Before leaving Madame Ratignolle said:

"In some way you seem to me like child, Edna. You seem to act without a certain amount of reflection which is necessary in this life. That is the reason I want to say you mustn't mind if I advise you to be a little careful while you are living here alone. Why don't you have some one come and stay with you? Wouldn't Mademoiselle Reisz come?"

"No; she wouldn't wish to come, and I shouldn't want her always with me."

"Well, the reason—you know how evil-minded the world is—some one was talking of Alcée Arobin visiting you. Of course, it wouldn't matter if Mr. Arobin had not such a dreadful reputation. Monsieur Ratignolle was telling me that his attentions alone are considered enough to ruin a woman's name."

"Does he boast of his successes?" asked Edna, indifferently, squinting at her picture.

"No, I think not. I believe he is a decent fellow as far as that goes. But his character is so well known among the men. I shan't be able to come back and see you; it was very, very imprudent to-day."

"Mind the step!" cried Edna.

"Don't neglect me," entreated Madame Ratignolle; "and don't mind what I said about Arobin, or having some one to stay with you."

"Of course not," Edna laughed. "You may say anything you like to me." They kissed each other good-by. Madame Ratignolle had not far to go, and Edna stood on the porch a while watching her walk down the street.

Then in the afternoon Mrs. Merriman and Mrs. Highcamp had made their "party call."[1] Edna felt that they might have dispensed with the formality. They had also come to invite her to play *vingt-et-un*[2] one evening at Mrs. Merriman's. She was asked to go early, to dinner, and Mr. Merriman or Mr. Arobin would take her home. Edna accepted in a half-hearted way. She sometimes felt very tired of Mrs. Highcamp and Mrs. Merriman.

Late in the afternoon she sought refuge with Mademoiselle Reisz, and stayed there alone, waiting for her, feeling a kind of repose invade her with the very atmosphere of the shabby, unpretentious little room.

Edna sat at the window, which looked out over the house-tops and across the river.

The window frame was filled with pots of flowers, and she sat and picked the dry leaves from a rose geranium. The day was warm, and the breeze which blew from the river was very pleasant. She removed her hat and laid it on the piano. She went on picking the leaves and digging around the plants with her hat pin. Once she thought she heard Mademoiselle Reisz approaching. But it was a young black girl, who came in, bringing a small bundle of laundry, which she deposited in the adjoining room, and went away.

Edna seated herself at the piano, and softly picked out with one hand the bars of a piece of music which lay open before her. A half-hour went by. There was the occasional sound of people going and coming in the lower hall. She was growing interested in her occupation of picking out the aria, when there was a second rap at the door. She vaguely wondered what these people did when they found Mademoiselle's door locked.

"Come in," she called, turning her face toward the door. And this time it was Robert Lebrun who presented himself. She attempted to rise; she could not have done so without betraying the agitation which mastered her at sight of him, so she fell back upon the stool, only exclaiming, "Why, Robert!"

He came and clasped her hand, seemingly without knowing what he was saying or doing.

---

1 A follow-up visit after a party to thank the host and/or hostess.
2 Literally "twenty-one," a card game from France similar to blackjack.

"Mrs. Pontellier! How do you happen—oh! how well you look! Is Mademoiselle Reisz not here? I never expected to see you."

"When did you come back?" asked Edna in an unsteady voice, wiping her face with her handkerchief. She seemed ill at ease on the piano stool, and he begged her to take the chair by the window. She did so, mechanically, while he seated himself on the stool.

"I returned day before yesterday," he answered, while he leaned his arm on the keys, bringing forth a crash of discordant sound.

"Day before yesterday!" she repeated, aloud; and went on thinking to herself, "day before yesterday," in a sort of an uncomprehending way. She had pictured him seeking her at the very first hour, and he had lived under the same sky since day before yesterday; while only by accident had he stumbled upon her. Mademoiselle must have lied when she said, "Poor fool, he loves you."

"Day before yesterday," she repeated, breaking off a spray of Mademoiselle's geranium; "then if you had not met me here to-day you wouldn't—when—that is, didn't you mean to come and see me?"

"Of course, I should have gone to see you. There have been so many things—" he turned the leaves of Mademoiselle's music nervously. "I started in at once yesterday with the old firm. After all there is as much chance for me here as there was there—that is, I might find it profitable some day. The Mexicans were not very congenial."

So he had come back because the Mexicans were not congenial; because business was as profitable here as there; because of any reason, and not because he cared to be near her. She remembered the day she sat on the floor, turning the pages of his letter, seeking the reason which was left untold.

She had not noticed how he looked—only feeling his presence; but she turned deliberately and observed him. After all, he had been absent but a few months, and was not changed. His hair—the color of hers—waved back from his temples in the same way as before. His skin was not more burned than it had been at Grand Isle. She found in his eyes, when he looked at her for one silent moment, the same tender caress, with an added warmth and entreaty which had not been there before—the same glance which had penetrated to the sleeping places of her soul and awakened them.

A hundred times Edna had pictured Robert's return, and imagined their first meeting. It was usually at her home, whither

he had sought her out at once. She always fancied him expressing or betraying in some way his love for her. And here, the reality
was that they sat ten feet apart, she at the window, crushing geranium leaves in her hand and smelling them, he twirling around
on the piano stool, saying:

"I was very much surprised to hear of Mr. Pontellier's
absence; it's a wonder Mademoiselle Reisz did not tell me; and
your moving—mother told me yesterday. I should think you
would have gone to New York with him, or to Iberville with the
children, rather than be bothered here with housekeeping. And
you are going abroad, too, I hear. We shan't have you at Grand
Isle next summer; it won't seem—do you see much of Mademoiselle Reisz? She often spoke of you in the few letters she
wrote."

"Do you remember that you promised to write to me when
you went away?" A flush overspread his whole face.

"I couldn't believe that my letters would be of any interest to
you."

"That is an excuse; it isn't the truth." Edna reached for her hat
on the piano. She adjusted it, sticking the hat pin through the
heavy coil of hair with some deliberation.

"Are you not going to wait for Mademoiselle Reisz?" asked
Robert.

"No; I have found when she is absent this long, she is liable
not to come back till late." She drew on her gloves, and Robert
picked up his hat.

"Won't you wait for her?" asked Edna.

"Not if you think she will not be back till late," adding, as if
suddenly aware of some discourtesy in his speech, "and I should
miss the pleasure of walking home with you." Edna locked the
door and put the key back in its hiding-place.

They went together, picking their way across muddy streets
and sidewalks encumbered with the cheap display of small
tradesmen. Part of the distance they rode in the car, and after dis-
embarking, passed the Pontellier mansion, which looked broken
and half torn asunder. Robert had never known the house, and
looked at it with interest.

"I never knew you in your home," he remarked.

"I am glad you did not."

"Why?" She did not answer. They went on around the corner,
and it seemed as if her dreams were coming true after all, when
he followed her into the little house.

"You must stay and dine with me, Robert. You see I am all

alone, and it is so long since I have seen you. There is so much I want to ask you."

She took off her hat and gloves. He stood irresolute, making some excuse about his mother who expected him; he even muttered something about an engagement. She struck a match and lit the lamp on the table; it was growing dusk. When he saw her face in the lamp-light, looking pained, with all the soft lines gone out of it, he threw his hat aside and seated himself.

"Oh! you know I want to stay if you will let me!" he exclaimed. All the softness came back. She laughed, and went and put her hand on his shoulder.

"This is the first moment you have seemed like the old Robert. I'll go tell Celestine." She hurried away to tell Celestine to set an extra place. She even sent her off in search of some added delicacy which she had not thought of for herself. And she recommended great care in dripping the coffee and having the omelet done to a proper turn.

When she reëntered, Robert was turning over magazines, sketches, and things that lay upon the table in great disorder. He picked up a photograph, and exclaimed:

"Alcée Arobin! What on earth is his picture doing here?"

"I tried to make a sketch of his head one day," answered Edna, "and he thought the photograph might help me. It was at the other house. I thought it had been left there. I must have packed it up with my drawing materials."

"I should think you would give it back to him if you have finished with it."

"Oh! I have a great many such photographs. I never think of returning them. They don't amount to anything." Robert kept on looking at the picture.

"It seems to me—do you think his head worth drawing? Is he a friend of Mr. Pontellier's? You never said you knew him."

"He isn't a friend of Mr. Pontellier's; he's a friend of mine. I always knew him—that is, it is only of late that I know him pretty well. But I'd rather talk about you, and know what you have been seeing and doing and feeling out there in Mexico." Robert threw aside the picture.

"I've been seeing the waves and the white beach of Grande Isle; the quiet, grassy street of the *Chênière*; the old fort at Grande Terre. I've been working like a machine, and feeling like a lost soul. There was nothing interesting."

She leaned her head upon her hand to shade her eyes from the light.

"And what have you been seeing and doing and feeling all these days?" he asked.

"I've been seeing the waves and the white beach of Grand Isle; the quiet, grassy street of the *Chênière Caminada*; the old sunny fort at Grande Terre. I've been working with a little more comprehension than a machine, and still feeling like a lost soul. There was nothing interesting."

"Mrs. Pontellier, you are cruel," he said, with feeling, closing his eyes and resting his head back in his chair. They remained in silence till old Celestine announced dinner.

XXXIV

The dining-room was very small. Edna's round mahogany would have almost filled it. As it was there was but a step or two from the little table to the kitchen, to the mantel, the small buffet, and the side door that opened out on the narrow brick-paved yard.

A certain degree of ceremony settled upon them with the announcement of dinner. There was no return to personalities. Robert related incidents of his sojourn in Mexico, and Edna talked of events likely to interest him, which had occurred during his absence. The dinner was of ordinary quality, except for the few delicacies which she had sent out to purchase. Old Celestine, with a bandana *tignon*[1] twisted about her head, hobbled in and out, taking a personal interest in everything; and she lingered occasionally to talk patois[2] with Robert, whom she had known as a boy.

He went out to a neighboring cigar stand to purchase cigarette papers, and when he came back he found that Celestine had served the black coffee in the parlor.

"Perhaps I shouldn't have come back," he said. "When you are tired of me, tell me to go."

"You never tire me. You must have forgotten the hours and hours at Grand Isle in which we grew accustomed to each other and used to being together."

"I have forgotten nothing at Grand Isle," he said, not looking at her, but rolling a cigarette. His tobacco pouch, which he laid upon the table, was a fantastic embroidered silk affair, evidently the handiwork of a woman.

---

1   A head-covering that female slaves were required by law to wear during the antebellum era.

2   A non-standard dialect.

"You used to carry your tobacco in a rubber pouch," said Edna, picking up the pouch and examining the needlework.

"Yes; it was lost."

"Where did you buy this one? In Mexico?"

"It was given to me by a Vera Cruz girl; they are very generous," he replied, striking a match and lighting his cigarette.

"They are very handsome, I suppose, those Mexican women; very picturesque, with their black eyes and their lace scarfs."

"Some are; others are hideous. Just as you find women everywhere."

"What was she like—the one who gave you the pouch? You must have known her very well."

"She was very ordinary. She wasn't of the slightest importance. I knew her well enough."

"Did you visit at her house? Was it interesting? I should like to know and hear about the people you met, and the impressions they made on you."

"There are some people who leave impressions not so lasting as the imprint of an oar upon the water."

"Was she such a one?"

"It would be ungenerous for me to admit that she was of that order and kind." He thrust the pouch back in his pocket, as if to put away the subject with the trifle which had brought it up.

Arobin dropped in with a message from Mrs. Merriman, to say that the card party was postponed on account of the illness of one of her children.

"How do you do, Arobin?" said Robert, rising from the obscurity.

"Oh! Lebrun. To be sure! I heard yesterday you were back. How did they treat you down in Mexique?"

"Fairly well."

"But not well enough to keep you there. Stunning girls, though, in Mexico. I thought I should never get away from Vera Cruz when I was down there a couple of years ago."

"Did they embroider slippers and tobacco pouches and hatbands and things for you?" asked Edna.

"Oh! my! no! I didn't get so deep in their regard. I fear they made more impression on me than I made on them."

"You were less fortunate than Robert, then."

"I am always less fortunate than Robert. Has he been imparting tender confidences?"

"I've been imposing myself long enough," said Robert, rising, and shaking hands with Edna. "Please convey my regards to Mr. Pontellier when you write."

He shook hands with Arobin and went away.

"Fine fellow, that Lebrun," said Arobin when Robert had gone. "I never heard you speak of him."

"I knew him last summer at Grand Isle," she replied. "Here is that photograph of yours. Don't you want it?"

"What do I want with it? Throw it away." She threw it back on the table.

"I'm not going to Mrs. Merriman's," she said. "If you see her, tell her so. But perhaps I had better write. I think I shall write now, and say that I am sorry her child is sick, and tell her not to count on me."

"It would be a good scheme," acquiesced Arobin. "I don't blame you; stupid lot!"

Edna opened the blotter, and having procured paper and pen, began to write the note. Arobin lit a cigar and read the evening paper, which he had in his pocket.

"What is the date?" she asked. He told her.

"Will you mail this for me when you go out?"

"Certainly." He read to her little bits out of the newspaper, while she straightened things on the table.

"What do you want to do?" he asked, throwing aside the paper. "Do you want to go out for a walk or a drive or anything? It would be a fine night to drive."

"No; I don't want to do anything but just be quiet. You go away and amuse yourself. Don't stay."

"I'll go away if I must; but I shan't amuse myself. You know that I only live when I am near you."

He stood up to bid her good night.

"Is that one of the things you always say to women?"

"I have said it before, but I don't think I ever came so near meaning it," he answered with a smile. There were no warm lights in her eyes; only a dreamy, absent look.

"Good night. I adore you. Sleep well," he said, and he kissed her hand and went away.

She stayed alone in a kind of reverie—a sort of stupor. Step by step she lived over every instant of the time she had been with Robert after he had entered Mademoiselle Reisz's door. She recalled his words, his looks. How few and meager they had been for her hungry heart! A vision—a transcendently seductive vision of a Mexican girl arose before her. She writhed with a jealous pang. She wondered when he would come back. He had not said he would come back. She had been with him, had heard his voice and touched his hand. But some way he had seemed nearer to her off there in Mexico.

XXXV

The morning was full of sunlight and hope. Edna could see before her no denial—only the promise of excessive joy. She lay in bed awake, with bright eyes full of speculation. "He loves you, poor fool." If she could but get that conviction firmly fixed in her mind, what mattered about the rest? She felt she had been childish and unwise the night before in giving herself over to despondency. She recapitulated the motives which no doubt explained Robert's reserve. They were not insurmountable; they would not hold if he really loved her; they could not hold against her own passion, which he must come to realize in time. She pictured him going to his business that morning. She even saw how he was dressed; how he walked down one street, and turned the corner of another; saw him bending over his desk, talking to people who entered the office, going to his lunch, and perhaps watching for her on the street. He would come to her in the afternoon or evening, sit and roll his cigarette, talk a little, and go away as he had done the night before. But how delicious it would be to have him there with her! She would have no regrets, nor seek to penetrate his reserve if he still chose to wear it.

Edna ate her breakfast only half dressed. The maid brought her a delicious printed scrawl from Raoul, expressing his love, asking her to send him some bonbons, and telling her they had found that morning ten tiny white pigs all lying in a row beside Lidie's big white pig.

A letter also came from her husband, saying he hoped to be back early in March, and then they would get ready for that journey abroad which he had promised her so long, which he felt now fully able to afford; he felt able to travel as people should, without any thought of small economies—thanks to his recent speculations in Wall Street.

Much to her surprise she received a note from Arobin, written at midnight from the club. It was to say good morning to her, to hope that she had slept well, to assure her of his devotion, which he trusted she in some faintest manner returned.

All these letters were pleasing to her. She answered the children in a cheerful frame of mind, promising them bonbons, and congratulating them upon their happy find of the little pigs.

She answered her husband with friendly evasiveness,—not with any fixed design to mislead him, only because all sense of reality had gone out of her life; she had abandoned herself to Fate, and awaited the consequences with indifference.

To Arobin's note she made no reply. She put it under Celestine's stove-lid.

Edna worked several hours with much spirit. She saw no one but a picture dealer, who asked her if it were true that she was going abroad to study in Paris.

She said possibly she might, and he negotiated with her for some Parisian studies to reach him in time for the holiday trade in December.

Robert did not come that day. She was keenly disappointed. He did not come the following day, nor the next. Each morning she awoke with hope, and each night she was a prey to despondency. She was tempted to seek him out. But far from yielding to the impulse, she avoided any occasion which might throw her in his way. She did not go to Mademoiselle Reisz's nor pass by Madame Lebrun's, as she might have done if he had still been in Mexico.

When Arobin, one night, urged her to drive with him, she went—out to the lake, on the Shell Road.[1] His horses were full of mettle, and even a little unmanageable. She liked the rapid gait at which they spun along, and the quick, sharp sound of the horses' hoofs on the hard road. They did not stop anywhere to eat or to drink. Arobin was not needlessly imprudent. But they ate and they drank when they regained Edna's little dining-room—which was comparatively early in the evening.

It was late when he left her. It was getting to be more than a passing whim with Arobin to see her and be with her. He had detected the latent sensuality, which unfolded under his delicate sense of her nature's requirements like a torpid, torrid, sensitive blossom.

There was no despondency when she fell asleep that night; nor was there hope when she awoke in the morning.

XXXVI

There was a garden out in the suburbs; a small, leafy corner, with a few green tables under the orange trees. An old cat slept all day

---

1   A road paved with shells that ran alongside the New Basin Canal out to Lake Ponchartrain; its hard surface made it popular for Sunday drives and racing.

on the stone step in the sun, and an old *mulatresse*[1] slept her idle hours away in her chair at the open window, till some one happened to knock on one of the green tables. She had milk and cream cheese to sell, and bread and butter. There was no one who could make such excellent coffee or fry a chicken so golden brown as she.

The place was too modest to attract the attention of people of fashion, and so quiet as to have escaped the notice of those in search of pleasure and dissipation. Edna had discovered it accidentally one day when the high-board gate stood ajar. She caught sight of a little green table, blotched with the checkered sunlight that filtered through the quivering leaves overhead. Within she had found the slumbering *mulatresse*, the drowsy cat, and a glass of milk which reminded her of the milk she had tasted in Iberville.

She often stopped there during her perambulations; sometimes taking a book with her, and sitting an hour or two under the trees when she found the place deserted. Once or twice she took a quiet dinner there alone, having instructed Celestine beforehand to prepare no dinner at home. It was the last place in the city where she would have expected to meet any one she knew.

Still she was not astonished when, as she was partaking of a modest dinner late in the afternoon, looking into an open book, stroking the cat, which had made friends with her—she was not greatly astonished to see Robert come in at the tall garden gate.

"I am destined to see you only by accident," she said, shoving the cat off the chair beside her. He was surprised, ill at ease, almost embarrassed at meeting her thus so unexpectedly.

"Do you come here often?" he asked.

"I almost live here," she said.

"I used to drop in very often for a cup of Catiche's good coffee. This is the first time since I came back."

"She'll bring you a plate, and you will share my dinner. There's always enough for two—even three." Edna had intended to be indifferent and as reserved as he when she met him; she had reached the determination by a laborious train of reasoning, incident to one of her despondent moods. But her resolve melted when she saw him before her, seated there beside her in the little garden, as if a designing Providence had led him into her path.

---

1 The feminine form of mulatto: a woman of color who was half white and half black; a racial designation under Louisiana law.

"Why have you kept away from me, Robert?" she asked, closing the book that lay open upon the table.

"Why are you so personal, Mrs. Pontellier? Why do you force me to idiotic subterfuges?" he exclaimed with sudden warmth. "I suppose there's no use telling you I've been very busy, or that I've been sick, or that I've been to see you and not found you at home. Please let me off with any one of these excuses."

"You are the embodiment of selfishness," she said. "You save yourself something—I don't know what—but there is some selfish motive, and in sparing yourself you never consider for a moment what I think, or how I feel your neglect and indifference. I suppose this is what you would call unwomanly; but I have got into a habit of expressing myself. It doesn't matter to me, and you may think me unwomanly if you like."

"No; I only think you cruel, as I said the other day. Maybe not intentionally cruel; but you seem to be forcing me into disclosures which can result in nothing; as if you would have me bare a wound for the pleasure of looking at it, without the intention or power of healing it."

"I'm spoiling your dinner, Robert; never mind what I say. You haven't eaten a morsel."

"I only came in for a cup of coffee." His sensitive face was all disfigured with excitement.

"Isn't this a delightful place?" she remarked. "I am so glad it has never actually been discovered. It is so quiet, so sweet, here. Do you notice there is scarcely a sound to be heard? It's so out of the way; and a good walk from the car. However, I don't mind walking. I always feel so sorry for women who don't like to walk; they miss so much—so many rare little glimpses of life; and we women learn so little of life on the whole.

"Catiche's coffee is always hot. I don't know how she manages it, here in the open air. Celestine's coffee gets cold bringing it from the kitchen to the dining-room. Three lumps! How can you drink it so sweet? Take some of the cress with your chop; it's so biting and crisp. Then there's the advantage of being able to smoke with your coffee out here. Now, in the city—aren't you going to smoke?"

"After a while," he said, laying a cigar on the table.

"Who gave it to you?" she laughed.

"I bought it. I suppose I'm getting reckless; I bought a whole box." She was determined not to be personal again and make him uncomfortable.

The cat made friends with him, and climbed into his lap when he smoked his cigar. He stroked her silky fur, and talked a little about her. He looked at Edna's book, which he had read; and he told her the end, to save her the trouble of wading through it, he said.

Again he accompanied her back to her home; and it was after dusk when they reached the little "pigeon-house." She did not ask him to remain, which he was grateful for, as it permitted him to stay without the discomfort of blundering through an excuse which he had no intention of considering. He helped her to light the lamp; then she went into her room to take off her hat and to bathe her face and hands.

When she came back Robert was not examining the pictures and magazines as before; he sat off in the shadow, leaning his head back on the chair as if in a reverie. Edna lingered a moment beside the table, arranging the books there. Then she went across the room to where he sat. She bent over the arm of his chair and called his name.

"Robert," she said, "are you asleep?"

"No," he answered, looking up at her.

She leaned over and kissed him—a soft, cool, delicate kiss, whose voluptuous sting penetrated his whole being—then she moved away from him. He followed, and took her in his arms, just holding her close to him. She put her hand up to his face and pressed his cheek against her own. The action was full of love and tenderness. He sought her lips again. Then he drew her down upon the sofa beside him and held her hand in both of his.

"Now you know," he said, "now you know what I have been fighting against since last summer at Grand Isle; what drove me away and drove me back again."

"Why have you been fighting against it?" she asked. Her face glowed with soft lights.

"Why? Because you were not free; you were Léonce Pontellier's wife. I couldn't help loving you if you were ten times his wife; but so long as I went away from you and kept away I could help telling you so." She put her free hand up to his shoulder, and then against his cheek, rubbing it softly. He kissed her again. His face was warm and flushed.

"There in Mexico I was thinking of you all the time, and longing for you."

"But not writing to me," she interrupted.

"Something put into my head that you cared for me; and I lost my senses. I forgot everything but a wild dream of your some way becoming my wife."

"Your wife!"

"Religion, loyalty, everything would give way if only you cared."

"Then you must have forgotten that I was Léonce Pontellier's wife."

"Oh! I was demented, dreaming of wild, impossible things, recalling men who had set their wives free, we have heard of such things."

"Yes, we have heard of such things."

"I came back full of vague, mad intentions. And when I got here—"

"When you got here you never came near me!" She was still caressing his cheek.

"I realized what a cur I was to dream of such a thing, even if you had been willing."

She took his face between her hands and looked into it as if she would never withdraw her eyes more. She kissed him on the forehead, the eyes, the cheeks, and the lips.

"You have been a very, very foolish boy, wasting your time dreaming of impossible things when you speak of Mr. Pontellier setting me free! I am no longer one of Mr. Pontellier's possessions to dispose of or not. I give myself where I choose. If he were to say, 'Here, Robert, take her and be happy; she is yours,' I should laugh at you both."

His face grew a little white. "What do you mean?" he asked.

There was a knock at the door. Old Celestine came in to say that Madame Ratignolle's servant had come around the back way with a message that Madame had been taken sick and begged Mrs. Pontellier to go to her immediately.

"Yes, yes," said Edna, rising; "I promised. Tell her yes—to wait for me. I'll go back with her."

"Let me walk over with you," offered Robert.

"No," she said; "I will go with the servant." She went into her room to put on her hat, and when she came in again she sat once more upon the sofa beside him. He had not stirred. She put her arms about his neck.

"Good-by, my sweet Robert. Tell me good-by." He kissed her with a degree of passion which had not before entered into his caress, and strained her to him.

"I love you," she whispered, "only you; no one but you. It was you who awoke me last summer out of a life-long, stupid dream. Oh! you have made me so unhappy with your indifference. Oh! I have suffered, suffered! Now you are here we shall love each other, my Robert. We shall be everything to each other. Nothing else in the world is of any consequence. I must go to my friend; but you will wait for me? No matter how late; you will wait for me, Robert?"

"Don't go; don't go! Oh! Edna, stay with me," he pleaded. "Why should you go? Stay with me, stay with me."

"I shall come back as soon as I can; I shall find you here." She buried her face in his neck, and said good-by again. Her seductive voice, together with his great love for her, had enthralled his senses, had deprived him of every impulse but the longing to hold her and keep her.

XXXVII

Edna looked in at the drug store. Monsieur Ratignolle was putting up a mixture himself, very carefully, dropping a red liquid into a tiny glass. He was grateful to Edna for having come; her presence would be a comfort to his wife. Madame Ratignolle's sister, who had always been with her at such trying times, had not been able to come up from the plantation, and Adèle had been inconsolable until Mrs. Pontellier so kindly promised to come to her. The nurse had been with them at night for the past week, as she lived a great distance away. And Dr. Mandelet had been coming and going all the afternoon. They were then looking for him any moment.

Edna hastened upstairs by a private stairway that led from the rear of the store to the apartments above. The children were all sleeping in a back room. Madame Ratignolle was in the salon, whither she had strayed in her suffering impatience. She sat on the sofa, clad in an ample white *peignoir*, holding a handkerchief tight in her hand with a nervous clutch. Her face was drawn and pinched, her sweet blue eyes haggard and unnatural. All her beautiful hair had been drawn back and plaited. It lay in a long braid on the sofa pillow, coiled like a golden serpent. The nurse, a comfortable looking *Griffe*[1] woman in white apron and cap, was urging her to return to her bedroom.

"There is no use, there is no use," she said at once to Edna. "We must get rid of Mandelet; he is getting too old and careless. He said he would be here at half-past seven; now it must be eight. See what time it is, Joséphine."

---

1 A person of color who was designated as three-quarters black and one-quarter white under Louisiana law.

The woman was possessed of a cheerful nature, and refused to take any situation too seriously, especially a situation with which she was so familiar. She urged Madame to have courage and patience. But Madame only set her teeth hard into her under lip, and Edna saw the sweat gather in beads on her white forehead. After a moment or two she uttered a profound sigh and wiped her face with the handkerchief rolled in a ball. She appeared exhausted. The nurse gave her a fresh handkerchief, sprinkled with cologne water.

"This is too much!" she cried. "Mandelet ought to be killed! Where is Alphonse? Is it possible I am to be abandoned like this—neglected by every one?"

"Neglected, indeed!" exclaimed the nurse. Wasn't she there? And here was Mrs. Pontellier leaving, no doubt, a pleasant evening at home to devote to her? And wasn't Monsieur Ratignolle coming that very instant through the hall? And Joséphine was quite sure she had heard Doctor Mandelet's coupé.[1] Yes, there it was, down at the door.

Adèle consented to go back to her room. She sat on the edge of a little low couch next to her bed.

Doctor Mandelet paid no attention to Madame Ratignolle's upbraidings. He was accustomed to them at such times, and was too well convinced of her loyalty to doubt it.

He was glad to see Edna, and wanted her to go with him into the salon and entertain him. But Madame Ratignolle would not consent that Edna should leave her for an instant. Between agonizing moments, she chatted a little, and said it took her mind off her sufferings.

Edna began to feel uneasy. She was seized with a vague dread. Her own like experiences seemed far away, unreal, and only half remembered. She recalled faintly an ecstasy of pain, the heavy odor of chloroform, a stupor which had deadened sensation, and an awakening to find a little new life to which she had given being, added to the great unnumbered multitude of souls that come and go.

She began to wish she had not come; her presence was not necessary. She might have invented a pretext for staying away; she might even invent a pretext now for going. But Edna did not go. With an inward agony, with a flaming, outspoken revolt against the ways of Nature, she witnessed the scene [of] torture.

---

1 A four-wheeled horse-drawn carriage that seats two people, with an outside seat for the driver.

She was still stunned and speechless with emotion when later she leaned over her friend to kiss her and softly say good-by. Adèle, pressing her cheek, whispered in an exhausted voice: "Think of the children, Edna. Oh think of the children! Remember them!"

XXXVIII

Edna still felt dazed when she got outside in the open air. The Doctor's coupé had returned for him and stood before the *porte cochère*. She did not wish to enter the coupé, and told Doctor Mandelet she would walk; she was not afraid, and would go alone. He directed his carriage to meet him at Mrs. Pontellier's, and he started to walk home with her.

Up—away up, over the narrow street between the tall houses, the stars were blazing. The air was mild and caressing, but cool with the breath of spring and the night. They walked slowly, the Doctor with a heavy, measured tread and his hands behind him; Edna, in an absent-minded way, as she had walked one night at Grand Isle, as if her thoughts had gone ahead of her and she was striving to overtake them.

"You shouldn't have been there, Mrs. Pontellier," he said. "That was no place for you. Adèle is full of whims at such times. There were a dozen women she might have had with her, unimpressionable women. I felt that it was cruel, cruel. You shouldn't have gone."

"Oh, well!" she answered, indifferently. "I don't know that it matters after all. One has to think of the children some time or other; the sooner the better."

"When is Léonce coming back?"

"Quite soon. Some time in March."

"And you are going abroad?"

"Perhaps—no, I am not going. I'm not going to be forced into doing things. I don't want to go abroad. I want to be let alone. Nobody has any right—except children, perhaps—and even then, it seems to me—or it did seem—" She felt that her speech was voicing the incoherency of her thoughts, and stopped abruptly.

"The trouble is," sighed the Doctor, grasping her meaning intuitively, "that youth is given up to illusions. It seems to be a provision of Nature; a decoy to secure mothers for the race. And Nature takes no account of moral consequences, of arbitrary conditions which we create, and which we feel obliged to maintain at any cost."

"Yes," she said. "The years that are gone seem like dreams—if one might go on sleeping and dreaming—but to wake up and find—oh! well! perhaps it is better to wake up after all, even to suffer, rather than to remain a dupe to illusions all one's life."

"It seems to me, my dear child," said the Doctor at parting, holding her hand, "you seem to me to be in trouble. I am not going to ask for your confidence. I will only say that if ever you feel moved to give it to me, perhaps I might help you. I know I would understand, and I tell you there are not many who would—not many, my dear."

"Some way I don't feel moved to speak of things that trouble me. Don't think I am ungrateful or that I don't appreciate your sympathy. There are periods of despondency and suffering which take possession of me. But I don't want anything but my own way. That is wanting a good deal, of course, when you have to trample upon the lives, the hearts, the prejudices of others—but no matter—still, I shouldn't want to trample upon the little lives. Oh! I don't know what I'm saying, Doctor. Good night. Don't blame me for anything."

"Yes, I will blame you if you don't come and see me soon. We will talk of things you never have dreamt of talking about before. It will do us both good. I don't want you to blame yourself, whatever comes. Good night, my child."

She let herself in at the gate, but instead of entering she sat upon the step of the porch. The night was quiet and soothing. All the tearing emotion of the last few hours seemed to fall away from her like a somber, uncomfortable garment, which she had but to loosen to be rid of. She went back to that hour before Adèle had sent for her; and her senses kindled afresh in thinking of Robert's words, the pressure of his arms, and the feeling of his lips upon her own. She could picture at that moment no greater bliss on earth than possession of the beloved one. His expression of love had already given him to her in part. When she thought that he was there at hand, waiting for her, she grew numb with the intoxication of expectancy. It was so late; he would be asleep perhaps. She would awaken him with a kiss. She hoped he would be asleep that she might arouse him with her caresses.

Still, she remembered Adèle's voice whispering, "Think of the children; think of them." She meant to think of them; that determination had driven into her soul like a death wound—but not to-night. To-morrow would be time to think of everything.

Robert was not waiting for her in the little parlor. He was

nowhere at hand. The house was empty. But he had scrawled on a piece of paper that lay in the lamplight:

"I love you. Good-by—because I love you."

Edna grew faint when she read the words. She went and sat on the sofa. Then she stretched herself out there, never uttering a sound. She did not sleep. She did not go to bed. The lamp sputtered and went out. She was still awake in the morning, when Celestine unlocked the kitchen door and came in to light the fire.

XXXIX

Victor, with hammer and nails and scraps of scantling,[1] was patching a corner of one of the galleries. Mariequita sat near by, dangling her legs, watching him work, and handing him nails from the tool-box. The sun was beating down upon them. The girl had covered her head with her apron folded into a square pad. They had been talking for an hour or more. She was never tired of hearing Victor describe the dinner at Mrs. Pontellier's. He exaggerated every detail, making it appear a veritable Lucillean feast. The flowers were in tubs, he said. The champagne was quaffed from huge golden goblets. Venus rising from the foam[2] could have presented no more entrancing a spectacle than Mrs. Pontellier, blazing with beauty and diamonds at the head of the board, while the other women were all of them youthful houris,[3] possessed of incomparable charms.

She got it into her head that Victor was in love with Mrs. Pontellier, and he gave her evasive answers, framed so as to confirm her belief. She grew sullen and cried a little, threatening to go off and leave him to his fine ladies. There were a dozen men crazy about her at the *Chênière*; and since it was the fashion to be in love with married people, why, she could run away any time she liked to New Orleans with Célina's husband.

Célina's husband was a fool, a coward, and a pig, and to prove it to her, Victor intended to hammer his head into a jelly the next time he encountered him. This assurance was very consoling to Mariequita. She dried her eyes, and grew cheerful at the prospect.

---

1 Small pieces of lumber.
2 *The Birth of Venus* is a famous Renaissance painting by Sandro Botticelli (c. 1445-1510) and depicts the goddess Venus rising from the water.
3 Beautiful women.

They were still talking of the dinner and the allurements of city life when Mrs. Pontellier herself slipped around the corner of the house. The two youngsters stayed dumb with amazement before what they considered to be an apparition. But it was really she in flesh and blood, looking tired and a little travel-stained.

"I walked up from the wharf," she said, "and heard the hammering. I supposed it was you, mending the porch. It's a good thing. I was always tripping over those loose planks last summer. How dreary and deserted everything looks!"

It took Victor some little time to comprehend that she had come in Beaudelet's lugger, that she had come alone, and for no purpose but to rest.

"There's nothing fixed up yet, you see. I'll give you my room; it's the only place."

"Any corner will do," she assured him.

"And if you can stand Philomel's cooking," he went on, "though I might try to get her mother while you are here. Do you think she would come?" turning to Mariequita.

Mariequita thought that perhaps Philomel's mother might come for a few days, and money enough.

Beholding Mrs. Pontellier make her appearance, the girl had at once suspected a lovers' rendezvous. But Victor's astonishment was so genuine, and Mrs. Pontellier's indifference so apparent, that the disturbing notion did not lodge long in her brain. She contemplated with the greatest interest this woman who gave the most sumptuous dinners in America, and who had all the men in New Orleans at her feet.

"What time will you have dinner?" asked Edna. "I'm very hungry; but don't get anything extra."

"I'll have it ready in little or no time," he said, bustling and packing away his tools. "You may go to my room to brush up and rest yourself. Mariequita will show you."

"Thank you," said Edna. "But, do you know, I have a notion to go down to the beach and take a good wash and even a little swim, before dinner?"

"The water is too cold!" they both exclaimed. "Don't think of it."

"Well, I might go down and try—dip my toes in. Why, it seems to me the sun is hot enough to have warmed the very depths of the ocean. Could you get me a couple of towels? I'd better go right away, so as to be back in time. It would be a little too chilly if I waited till this afternoon."

Mariequita ran over to Victor's room, and returned with some towels, which she gave to Edna.

"I hope you have fish for dinner," said Edna, as she started to walk away; "but don't do anything extra if you haven't."

"Run and find Philomel's mother," Victor instructed the girl. "I'll go to the kitchen and see what I can do. By Gimminy! Women have no consideration! She might have sent me word."

Edna walked on down to the beach rather mechanically, not noticing anything special except that the sun was hot. She was not dwelling upon any particular train of thought. She had done all the thinking which was necessary after Robert went away, when she lay awake upon the sofa till morning.

She had said over and over to herself: "To-day it is Arobin; to-morrow it will be some one else. It makes no difference to me, it doesn't matter about Léonce Pontellier—but Raoul and Etienne!" She understood now clearly what she had meant long ago when she said to Adèle Ratignolle that she would give up the unessential, but she would never sacrifice herself for her children.

Despondency had come upon her there in the wakeful night, and had never lifted. There was no one thing in the world that she desired. There was no human being whom she wanted near her except Robert; and she even realized that the day would come when he, too, and the thought of him would melt out of her existence, leaving her alone. The children appeared before her like antagonists who had overcome her; who had overpowered and sought to drag her into the soul's slavery for the rest of her days. But she knew a way to elude them. She was not thinking of these things when she walked down to the beach.

The water of the Gulf stretched out before her, gleaming with the million lights of the sun. The voice of the sea is seductive, never ceasing, whispering, clamoring, murmuring, inviting the soul to wander in abysses of solitude. All along the white beach, up and down, there was no living thing in sight. A bird with a broken wing was beating the air above, reeling, fluttering, circling disabled down, down to the water.

Edna had found her old bathing suit still hanging, faded, upon its accustomed peg.

She put it on, leaving her clothing in the bath-house. But when she was there beside the sea, absolutely alone, she cast the unpleasant, pricking garments from her, and for the first time in her life she stood naked in the open air, at the mercy of the sun, the breeze that beat upon her, and the waves that invited her.

How strange and awful it seemed to stand naked under the sky! how delicious! She felt like some new-born creature, opening its eyes in a familiar world that it had never known.

The foamy wavelets curled up to her white feet, and coiled like serpents about her ankles. She walked out. The water was chill, but she walked on. The water was deep, but she lifted her white body and reached out with a long, sweeping stroke. The touch of the sea is sensuous, enfolding the body in its soft, close embrace.

She went on and on. She remembered the night she swam far out, and recalled the terror that seized her at the fear of being unable to regain the shore. She did not look back now, but went on and on, thinking of the blue-grass meadow that she had traversed when a little child, believing that it had no beginning and no end.

Her arms and legs were growing tired.

She thought of Léonce and the children. They were a part of her life. But they need not have thought that they could possess her, body and soul. How Mademoiselle Reisz would have laughed, perhaps sneered, if she knew! "And you call yourself an artist! What pretensions, Madame! The artist must possess the courageous soul that dares and defies."

Exhaustion was pressing upon and overpowering her.

"Good-by—because, I love you." He did not know; he did not understand. He would never understand. Perhaps Doctor Mandelet would have understood if she had seen him—but it was too late; the shore was far behind her, and her strength was gone.

She looked into the distance, and the old terror flamed up for an instant, then sank again. Edna heard her father's voice and her sister Margaret's. She heard the barking of an old dog that was chained to the sycamore tree. The spurs of the cavalry officer clanged as he walked across the porch. There was the hum of bees, and the musky odor of pinks[1] filled the air.

---

1 Sweet-scented flowers that are members of the dianthus family, which includes sweet william, baby's breath, and carnations.

OTHER FICTION

From *At Fault* (1890)

[Prior to writing *The Awakening*, Kate Chopin authored two other novels: *At Fault*, a love story set in Natchitoches Parish, and *Young Dr. Gosse and Theo*, which Chopin destroyed after numerous unsuccessful attempts to publish it. *At Fault* pits the Catholic prohibition of divorce against the compelling need to escape from a toxic relationship. The widowed Thérèse Lafirme leases the forested areas of her property to a lumber company, which brings outsider David Hosmer to town as the mill's manager. The two fall in love but are unable to pursue a relationship as a result of his divorce. One of the sub-plots of the novel involves a summer flirtation between a local Creole, Grégoire, and Hosmer's niece, Melicent. Although the affair ultimately ends badly, its beginnings illustrate the innocence of young love set against the backdrop of the lush, humid beauty of rural Louisiana.]

Chapter 3: In the Pirogue

"You got to set mighty still in this pirogue,"[1] said Grégoire, as with a long oar-stroke he pulled out into mid stream.

"Yes, I know," answered Melicent complacently, arranging herself opposite him in the long narrow boat, all sense of danger which the situation might arouse being dulled by the attractiveness of a new experience. Her resemblance to Hosmer ended with height and slenderness of figure, olive tinted skin, and eyes and hair which were of that dark brown often miscalled black; but unlike his, her face was awake with an eagerness to know and test the novelty and depth of unaccustomed sensation. She had thus far lived an unstable existence, free from the weight of responsibilities, with a notion lying somewhere deep in her consciousness that the world must one day be taken seriously; but that contingency was yet too far away to disturb the harmony of her days.

She had eagerly responded to her brother's suggestion of spending a summer with him in Louisiana. Hitherto, having passed her summers in North, West, or East as alternating caprice prompted, she was ready at a word to fit her humor to the novelty of a season at the South. She enjoyed in advance the startling effect which her announced intention produced upon her inti-

---

1 A small, flat-bottomed boat similar to a canoe common in Louisiana.

mate circle at home; thinking that her whim deserved the distinction of eccentricity with which they chose to invest it. But Melicent was chiefly moved by the prospect of uninterrupted sojourn with her brother, whom she loved blindly, and to whom she attributed qualities of mind and heart which she thought the world had discovered to use against him.

"You got to set mighty still in this pirogue."

"Yes, I know; you told me so before," and she laughed.

"W'at are you laughin' at?" asked Grégoire with amused but uncertain expectancy.

"Laughing at you. Grégoire; how can I help it?" laughing again.

"Betta wait tell I do somethin' funny, I reckon. Ain't this a putty sight?" he added, referring to the dense canopy of an overarching tree, beneath which they were gliding, and whose extreme branches dipped quite into the slow moving water.

The scene had not attracted Melicent. For she had been engaged in observing her companion rather closely; his personality holding her with a certain imaginative interest.

The young man whom she so closely scrutinized was slightly undersized, but of close and brawny build. His hands were not so refinedly white as those of certain office bred young men of her acquaintance, yet they were not coarsened by undue toil: it being somewhat an axiom with him to so nothing that an available "nigger" might do for him.

Close fitting, high-heeled boots of fine quality encased his feet, in whose shapeliness he felt a pardonable pride; for a young man's excellence was often measured in the circle which he had frequented, by the possession of such a foot. A peculiar grace in the dance and a talent for bold repartée were further characteristics which had made Grégoire's departure keenly felt among certain belles of upper Red River. His features were handsome, of sharp and refined cut; and his eyes black and brilliant as eyes of an alert and intelligent animal sometimes are. Melicent could not reconcile his voice to her liking; it was too softly low and feminine, and carried a note of pleading or *pathos*, unless he argued with his horse, his dog or a "nigger," at which times, though not unduly raised, it acquired a biting quality that served the purpose of relieving him from further form of insistence.

He pulled rapidly and in silence down the bayou, that was now so entirely sheltered from the open light of the sky by the meeting branches above, as to seem a dim leafy tunnel fashioned by man's ingenuity. There were no perceptible banks, for the water spread out on either side of them, further than they could follow in flashings through the rank underbrush. The dull splash of some object falling into the water, or the wild call of a lonely bird were the only sounds that broke upon the stillness, beside the monotonous dipping of the oars and the occasional low undertones of their own voices. When Grégoire called the girl's attention to an object nearby, she fancied it was the protruding stump of a decaying tree; but reaching for his revolver and taking quiet aim, he drove a ball into the black up-turned nozzle that sent it below the surface with an angry splash.

"Will he follow us?" she asked, mildly agitated.

"Oh no; he's glad 'nough to get out o' the way. You betta put down yo' veil," he added a moment later.

Before she could ask a reason—for it was not her fashion to obey at word of command—the air was filled with the doleful hum of a gray swarm of mosquitoes, which attacked them fiercely.

"You didn't tell me the bayou was the refuge of such savage creatures," she said, fastening her veil closely about face and neck, but not before she had felt the sharpness of their angry sting.

"I reckoned you'd 'a knowed all about it: seems like you know everything." After a short interval he added, "you betta take yo' veil off."

She was amused at Grégoire's authoritative tone and she said to him laughing, yet obeying his suggestion, which carried a note of command: "you shall tell me always, why I should do things."

"All right," he replied; "because they ain't any mo' mosquitoes; because I want you to see somethin' worth seein' afta while; and because I like to look at you," which he was doing, with the innocent boldness of a forward child. "Ain't that 'nough reasons?"

"More than enough," she replied shortly.

The rank and clustering vegetation had become denser as they went on, forming an impenetrable tangle on either side, and pressing so closely above that they often needed to lower their heads to avoid the blow of some drooping branch. Then a sudden and unlooked for turn in the bayou carried them out upon the far-spreading waters of the lake, with the broad canopy of the open sky above them.

"Oh," cried Melicent, in surprise. Her exclamation was like a sigh of relief which comes at the removal of some pressure from body or brain.

The wildness of the scene caught upon her erratic fancy, speeding it for a quick moment into the realms of romance. She was an Indian maiden of the far past, fleeing and seeking with her dusky lover some wild and solitary retreat on the borders of this lake, which offered them no seeming foot-hold save such as they would hew themselves with axe or tomahawk. Here and there, a grim cypress lifted its head above the water, and spread wide its moss-covered arms inviting refuge to the great black-winged buzzards that circled over and about in mid-air. Nameless voices— weird sounds that awake in a Southern forest at twilight's approach,—were crying a sinister welcome to the settling gloom.

"This is a place that can make a man sad, I tell you," said Grégoire, resting his oars, and wiping the moisture from his forehead. "I wouldn't want to be yere alone, not fur any money."

"It is an awful place," replied Melicent with a little appreciative shudder; adding "do you consider me a bodily protection?" and feebly smiling into his face.

"Oh; I ain't fraid o' any thing I can see and on'erstan'. I can han'le mos' any thing thet's got a body. But they do tell some mighty queer tales bout this lake an' the pin hills yonda."

"Queer—how?"

"W'y, ole McFarlane's buried up there on the hill; an' they's folks round yere says he walks about o' nights; can't res' in his grave fur the niggas he's killed."

"Gracious! And who was old McFarlane?"

"The meanest w'ite man that ever lived, seems like. Used to own this place long befo' the Lafirmes got it. They say he's the person that Mrs. W'at's her name wrote about in *Uncle Tom's Cabin*."[1]

"Legree? I wonder if it could be true?" Melicent asked with interest.

"Thet's w'at they all say: ask any body."

---

1 Harriet Beecher Stowe's most famous work, *Uncle Tom's Cabin* (1852), earned her the appellation of "the little lady who started this big war" from Abraham Lincoln. A legend persists in Natchitoches Parish that Stowe modeled the character of Simon Legree after Robert McAlpin, a local slave owner who was widely known for his cruelty to his slaves. According to affidavits held by the Cammie G. Henry Research Center at Northwestern State University, she did so in retaliation after McAlpin unceremoniously evicted her and her party from his home.

"You'll take me to his grave, won't you Grégoire," she entreated.

"Well, not this evenin'—I reckon not. It'll have to be broad day, an' the sun shinin' mighty bright w'en I take you to old McFarlane's grave."

They had retraced their course and again entered the bayou, from which the light had now nearly vanished, making it needful that they watch carefully to escape the hewn logs that floated in numbers upon the water.

"I didn't suppose you were ever sad Grégoire," Melicent said gently.

"Oh my! yes;" with frank acknowledgment. "You ain't never seen me w'en I was real lonesome. 'Tain't so bad sence you come. But times w'en I git to thinkin' 'bout home, I'm boun' to cry— seems like I can't he'p it."

"Why did you ever leave home?" she asked sympathetically.

"You see w'en father died, fo' year ago, mother she went back to France, t'her folks there; she never could stan' this country— an' lef' us boys to manage the place. Hec, he took charge the firs' year an' run it in debt. Placide an' me did'n' have no betta luck the next year. Then the creditors come up from New Orleans an' took holt. That's the time I packed my duds an' lef'."

"And you came here?"

"No not at firs'. You see the Santien boys had a putty hard name in the country. Aunt Thérèse, she'd fallen out with father years ago 'bout the way, she said, he was bringin' us up. Father, he wasn't the man to take nothin' from nobody. Never lowed any of us to come down yere. I was in Texas, goin' to the devil I reckon, w'en she sent for me, an' yere I am."

"And here you ought to stay, Grégoire."

"Oh, they ain't no betta woman in the worl' then Aunt Thérèse, w'en you do like she wants. See 'em yonda waintin' fur us? Reckon they thought we was drowned."

"At Chênière Caminada" (1893)

[Kate Chopin created an imaginary community in the real locations of Natchitoches Parish and other Louisiana places, and populated them with characters who recur with some frequency across her body of work. Tonie, the protagonist of "At Chênière Caminada," is one of those characters. In this story, Tonie suffers a broken heart and nearly succumbs to it, until an unexpected turn of events sets his world right again, illustrating Chopin's unconventional view of love and romantic entanglements. The protagonist of this story reappears in a minor capacity in *The Awakening* as the owner of the small boat that takes Robert away from Grand Isle.]

There was no clumsier looking fellow in church that Sunday morning than Antoine Bocaze—the one they called Tonie. But Tonie did not really care if he were clumsy or not. He felt that he could speak intelligibly to no woman save his mother; but since he had no desire to inflame the hearts of any of the island maidens, what difference did it make?

He knew there was no better fisherman on the Chênière Caminada than himself, if his face was too long and bronzed, his limbs too unmanageable and his eyes too earnest—almost too honest.

It was a midsummer day, with a lazy, scorching breeze blowing from the Gulf straight into the church windows. The ribbons on the young girls' hats fluttered like the wings of birds, and the old women clutched the flapping ends of the veils that covered their heads.

A few mosquitoes, floating through the blistering air, with their nipping and humming fretted the people to a certain degree of attention and consequent devotion. The measured tones of the priest at the altar rose and fell like a song: "Credo in unum Deum patrem omnipotentem"[1] he chanted. And then the people all looked at one another, suddenly electrified.

Some one was playing upon the organ whose notes no one on the whole island was able to awaken; whose tones had not been heard during the many months since a passing stranger had one day listlessly dragged his fingers across its idle keys. A long, sweet strain of music floated down from the loft and filled the church.

It seemed to most of them—it seemed to Tonie standing there beside his old mother—that some heavenly being must have descended upon the Church of Our Lady of Lourdes and chosen this celestial way of communicating with its people.

But it was no creature from a different sphere; it was only a young lady from Grand Isle. A rather pretty young person with blue eyes and nut-brown hair, who wore a dotted lawn of fine texture and fashionable make, and a white Leghorn sailor-hat.

Tonie saw her standing outside of the church after mass, receiving the priest's voluble praises and thanks for her graceful service.

---

1 Beginning of a Latin prayer, recited during the Catholic mass: I believe in one God, the Father Almighty.

She had come over to mass from Grand Isle in Baptiste Beaudelet's lugger,[1] with a couple of young men, and two ladies who kept a pension over there. Tonie knew these two ladies—the widow Lebrun and her old mother—but he did not attempt to speak with them; he would not have known what to say. He stood aside gazing at the group, as others were doing, his serious eyes fixed earnestly upon the fair organist.

Tonie was late at dinner that day. His mother must have waited an hour for him, sitting patiently with her coarse hands folded in her lap, in that little still room with its "brick-painted" floor, its gaping chimney and homely furnishings.

He told her that he had been walking—walking he hardly knew where, and he did not know why. He must have tramped from one end of the island to the other; but he brought her no bit of news or gossip. He did not know if the Cotures had stopped for dinner with the Avendettes; whether old Pierre François was worse, or better, or dead, or if lame Philibert was drinking again this morning. He knew nothing; yet he had crossed the village, and passed every one of its small houses that stood close together in a long jagged line facing the sea; they were gray and battered by time and the rude buffets of the salt sea winds.

He knew nothing though the Cotures had all bade him "good day" as they filed into Avendette's, where a steaming plate of crab gumbo was waiting for each. He had heard some woman screaming, and others saying it was because old Pierre François had just passed away. But he did not remember this, nor did he recall the fact that lame Philibert had staggered against him when he stood absently watching a "fiddler" sidling across the sun-baked sand. He could tell his mother nothing of all this; but he said he had noticed that the wind was fair and must have driven Baptiste's boat, like a flying bird, across the water.

Well, that was something to talk about, and old Ma'me Antoine, who was fat, leaned comfortably upon the table after she had helped Tonie to his courtbouillon,[2] and remarked that she found Madame was getting old. Tonie thought that perhaps she was aging and her hair was getting whiter. He seemed glad to talk about her, and reminded his mother of old Madame's kindness and sympathy at the time his father and brothers had per-

---

1 A small boat used for fishing or sailing that has two or three masts, each with a sail. Beaudelet is also mentioned in *The Awakening*.
2 Literally "short boil," this aromatic base is used for making soups or sauces for fish or chicken.

ished. It was when he was a little fellow, ten years before, during a squall in Barataria Bay.

Ma'me Antoine declared that she could never forget that sympathy, if she lived till Judgment Day; but all the same she was sorry to see that Madame Lebrun was also not so young or fresh as she used to be. Her chances of getting a husband were surely lessening every year; especially with the young girls around her, budding each spring like flowers to be plucked. The one who had played upon the organ was Mademoiselle Duvigné, Claire Duvigné, a great belle, the daughter of the famous lawyer who lived in New Orleans, on Rampart street. Ma'me Antoine had found that out during the ten minutes she and others had stopped after mass to gossip with the priest.

"Claire Duvigné," muttered Tonie, not even making a pretense to taste his courtbouillon, but picking little bits from the half loaf of crusty brown bread that lay beside his plate. "Claire Duvigné; that is a pretty name. Don't you think so, mother? I can't think of anyone on the Chênière who has so pretty a one, nor at Grand Isle, either, for that matter. And you say she lives on Rampart street?"

It appeared to him a matter of great importance that he should have his mother repeat all that the priest had told her.

II

Early the following morning Tonie went out in search of lame Philibert, than whom there was no cleverer workman on the island when he could be caught sober.

Tonie had tried to work on his big lugger that lay bottom upward under the shed, but it had seemed impossible. His mind, his hands, his tools refused to do their office, and in sudden desperation he desisted. He found Philibert and set him to work in his own place under the shed. Then he got into his small boat with the red lateen-sail and went over to Grand Isle.

There was no one at hand to warn Tonie that he was acting the part of a fool. He had, singularly, never felt those premonitory symptoms of love which afflict the greater portion of mankind before they reach the age which he had attained. He did not at first recognize this powerful impulse that had, without warning, possessed itself of his entire being. He obeyed it without a struggle, as naturally as he would have obeyed the dictates of hunger and thirst.

Tonie left his boat at the wharf and proceeded at once to Mme. Lebrun's pension, which consisted of a group of plain, stoutly built cottages that stood in mid island, about half a mile from the sea.

The day was bright and beautiful with soft, velvety gusts of wind blowing from the water. From a cluster of orange trees a flock of doves ascended, and Tonie stopped to listen to the beating of their wings and follow their flight toward the water oaks whither he himself was moving.

He walked with a dragging, uncertain step through the yellow, fragrant camomile, his thoughts traveling before him. In his mind was always the vivid picture of the girl as it had stamped itself there yesterday, connected in some mystical way with that celestial music which had thrilled him and was vibrating yet in his soul.

But she did not look the same to-day. She was returning from the beach when Tonie first saw her, leaning upon the arm of one of the men who had accompanied her yesterday. She was dressed differently—in a dainty blue cotton gown. Her companion held a big white sunshade over them both. They had exchanged hats and were laughing with great abandonment.

Two young men walked behind them and were trying to engage her attention. She glanced at Tonie, who was leaning against a tree when the group passed by; but of course she did not know him. She was speaking English, a language which he hardly understood.

There were other young people gathered under the water oaks—girls who were, many of them, more beautiful than Mlle. Duvigné; but for Tonie they simply did not exist. His whole universe had suddenly become converted into a glamorous background for the person of Mlle. Duvigné, and the shadowy figures of men who were about her.

Tonie went to Mme. Lebrun and told her he would bring her oranges next day from the Chênière. She was well pleased, and commissioned him to bring her other things from the stores there, which she could not procure at Grand Isle. She did not question his presence, knowing that these summer days were idle ones for the Chênière fishermen. Nor did she seem surprised when he told her that his boat was at the wharf, and would be there every day at her service. She knew his frugal habits, and supposed he wished to hire it, as others did. He intuitively felt that this could be the only way.

And that is how it happened that Tonie spent so little of his time at the Chênière Caminada that summer. Old Ma'me Antoine grumbled enough about it. She herself had been twice in her life to Grand Isle and once to Grand Terre, and each time had been more than glad to get back to the Chênière. And why Tonie should want to spend his days, and even his nights, away from home, was a thing she could not comprehend, especially as he would have to be away the whole winter; and meantime there was much work to be done at his own hearthside and in the company of his own mother. She did not know that Tonie had much, much more to do at Grand Isle than at the Chênière Caminada.

He had to see how Claire Duvigné sat upon the gallery in the big rocking chair that she kept in motion by the impetus of her slender, slippered foot; turning her head this way and that way to speak to the men who were always near her. He had to follow her lithe motions at tennis or croquet, that she often played with the children under the trees. Some days he wanted to see how she spread her bare, white arms, and walked out to meet the foam-crested waves. Even here there were men with her. And then at night, standing alone like a still shadow under the stars, did he not have to listen to her voice when she talked and laughed and sang? Did he not have to follow her slim figure whirling through the dance, in the arms of men who must have loved her and wanted her as he did. He did not dream that they could help it more than he could help it. But the days when she stepped into his boat, the one with the red lateen sail, and sat for hours within a few feet of him, were days that he would have given up for nothing else that he could think of.

III

There were always others in her company at such times, young people with jests and laughter on their lips. Only once she was alone.

She had foolishly brought a book with her, thinking she would want to read. But with the breath of the sea stinging her she could not read a line. She looked precisely as she had looked the day he first saw her, standing outside of the church at Chênière Caminada.

She laid the book down in her lap, and let her soft eyes sweep dreamily along the line of the horizon where the sky and water met. Then she looked straight at Tonie, and for the first time spoke directly to him.

She called him Tonie, as she had heard others do, and questioned him about his boat and his work. He trembled, and answered her vaguely and stupidly. She did not mind, but spoke to him anyhow, satisfied to talk herself when she found that he could not or would not. She spoke French, and talked about the Chênière Caminada, its people and its church. She talked of the day she had played upon the organ there, and complained of the instrument being woefully out of tune.

Tonie was perfectly at home in the familiar task of guiding his boat before the wind that bellied its taut, red sail. He did not seem clumsy and awkward as when he sat in church. The girl noticed that he appeared as strong as an ox.

As she looked at him and surprised one of his shifting glances, a glimmer of the truth began to dawn faintly upon her. She remembered how she had encountered him daily in her path, with his earnest, devouring eyes always seeking her out. She recalled—but there was no need to recall anything. There are women whose perception of passion is very keen; they are the women who most inspire it.

A feeling of complacency took possession of her with this conviction. There was some softness and sympathy mingled with it. She would have liked to lean over and pat his big, brown hand, and tell him she felt sorry and would have helped it if she could. With this belief he ceased to be an object of complete indifference in her eyes. She had thought, awhile before, of having him turn about and take her back home. But now it was really piquant to pose for an hour longer before a man—even a rough fisherman—to whom she felt herself to be an object of silent and consuming devotion. She could think of nothing more interesting to do on shore.

She was incapable of conceiving the full force and extent of his infatuation. She did not dream that under the rude, calm exterior before her a man's heart was beating clamorously, and his reason yielding to the savage instinct of his blood.

"I hear the Angelus[1] ringing at Chênière, Tonie," she said. "I didn't know it was so late; let us go back to the island." There had been a long silence which her musical voice interrupted.

Tonie could now faintly hear the Angelus bell himself. A vision of the church came with it, the odor of incense and the sound of the organ. The girl before him was again that celestial being whom Our Lady of Lourdes had once offered to his immortal vision.

It was growing dusk when they landed at the pier, and frogs had begun to croak among the reeds in the pools. There were two

---

1 Bells ringing at dawn, noon, and dusk, calling the Catholic faithful to the recitation of a devotional prayer in memory of the incarnation.

of Mlle. Duvigné's usual attendants anxiously awaiting her return. But she chose to let Tonie assist her out of the boat. The touch of her hand fired his blood again.

She said to him very low and half-laughing, "I have no money tonight, Tonie; take this instead," pressing into his palm a delicate silver chain, which she had worn twined about her bare wrist. It was purely a spirit of coquetry that prompted the action, and a touch of the sentimentality which most women possess. She had read in some romance of a young girl doing something like that.

As she walked away between her two attendants she fancied Tonie pressing the chain to his lips. But he was standing quite still, and held it buried in his tightly-closed hand; wanting to hold as long as he might the warmth of the body that still penetrated the bauble when she thrust it into his hand.

He watched her retreating figure like a blotch against the fading sky. He was stirred by a terrible, an overmastering regret, that he had not clasped her in his arms when they were out there alone, and sprung with her into the sea. It was what he had vaguely meant to do when the sound of the Angelus had weakened and palsied his resolution. Now she was going from him, fading away into the mist with those figures on either side of her, leaving him alone. He resolved within himself that if ever again she were out there on the sea at his mercy, she would have to perish in his arms. He would go far, far out where the sound of no bell could reach him. There was some comfort for him in the thought.

But as it happened, Mlle. Duvigné never went out alone in the boat with Tonie again.

IV

It was one morning in January. Tonie had been collecting a bill from one of the fishmongers at the French Market, in New Orleans, and had turned his steps toward St. Philip street. The day was chilly; a keen wind was blowing. Tonie mechanically buttoned his rough, warm coat and crossed over into the sun.

There was perhaps not a more wretched-hearted being in the whole district, that morning, than he. For months the woman he so hopelessly loved had been lost to his sight. But all the more she dwelt in his thoughts, preying upon his mental and bodily forces until his unhappy condition became apparent to all who knew him. Before leaving his home for the winter fishing grounds he had opened his whole heart to his mother, and told her of the trouble that was killing him. She hardly expected that he would ever come back to her when he went away. She feared that he would not, for he had spoken wildly of the rest and peace that could only come to him with death.

That morning when Tonie had crossed St. Philip street he found himself accosted by Madame Lebrun and her mother. He had not noticed them approaching, and, moreover, their figures in winter garb appeared unfamiliar to him. He had never seen them elsewhere than at Grand Isle and the Chênière during the summer. They were glad to meet him, and shook his hand cordially. He stood as usual a little helplessly before them. A pulse in his throat was beating and almost choking him, so poignant were the recollections which their presence stirred up.

They were staying in the city this winter, they told him. They wanted to hear the opera as often as possible, and the island was really too dreary with everyone gone. Madame Lebrun had left her son there to keep order and superintend repairs, and so on.

"You are both well?" stammered Tonie.

"In perfect health, my dear Tonie," Madame Lebrun replied. She was wondering at his haggard eyes and thin, gaunt cheeks; but possessed too much tact to mention them.

"And—the young lady who used to go sailing—is she well?" he inquired lamely.

"You mean Mlle. Favette? She was married just after leaving Grand Isle."

"No; I mean the one you called Claire—Mamzelle Duvigné— is she well?"

Mother and daughter exclaimed together: "Impossible! You haven't heard? Why, Tonie," madame continued, "Mlle. Duvigné died three weeks ago! But that was something sad, I tell you ... Her family heartbroken ... Simply from a cold caught by standing in thin slippers, waiting for her carriage after the opera.... What a warning!"

The two were talking at once. Tonie kept looking from one to the other. He did not know what they were saying, after madame had told him, "Elle est morte."[1]

As in a dream he finally heard that they said good-bye to him, and sent their love to his mother.

He stood still in the middle of the banquette[2] when they had left him, watching them go toward the market. He could not stir.

---

1 She is dead.
2 A raised sidewalk.

Something had happened to him—he did not know what. He wondered if the news was killing him.

Some women passed by, laughing coarsely. He noticed how they laughed and tossed their heads. A mockingbird was singing in a cage which hung from a window above his head. He had not heard it before.

Just beneath the window was the entrance to a bar-room. Tonie turned and plunged through its swinging doors. He asked the bartender for whisky. The man thought he was already drunk, but pushed the bottle toward him nevertheless. Tonie poured a great quantity of the fiery liquor into a glass and swallowed it at a draught. The rest of the day he spent among the fishermen and Barataria[1] oystermen; and that night he slept soundly and peacefully until morning.

He did not know why it was so; he could not understand. But from that day he felt that he began to live again, to be once more a part of the moving world about him. He would ask himself over and over again why it was so, and stay bewildered before this truth that he could not answer or explain, and which he began to accept as a holy mystery.

One day in early spring Tonie sat with his mother upon a piece of drift-wood close to the sea.

He had returned that day to the Chênière Caminada. At first she thought he was like his former self again, for all his old strength and courage had returned. But she found that there was a new brightness in his face which had not been there before. It made her think of the Holy Ghost descending and bringing some kind of light to a man.

She knew that Mademoiselle Duvigné was dead, and all along had feared that this knowledge would be the death of Tonie. When she saw him come back to her like a new being, at once she dreaded that he did not know. All day the doubt had been fretting her, and she could bear the uncertainty no longer.

"You know, Tonie—that young lady whom you cared for—well, some one read it to me in the papers—she died last winter." She had tried to speak as cautiously as she could.

"Yes, I know she is dead. I am glad."

It was the first time he had said this in words, and it made his heart beat quicker.

---

1 Bay in the Gulf of Mexico near Grand Isle, believed to have been the base for the pirate Jean Lafitte (c. 1776-c. 1823).

Ma'me Antoine shuddered and drew aside from him. To her it was somehow like murder to say such a thing.

"What do you mean? Why are you glad?" she demanded, indignantly.

Tonie was sitting with his elbows on his knees. He wanted to answer his mother, but it would take time; he would have to think. He looked out across the water that glistened gem-like with the sun upon it, but there was nothing there to open his thought. He looked down into his open palm and began to pick at the callous flesh that was hard as a horse's hoof. Whilst he did this his ideas began to gather and take form.

"You see, while she lived I could never hope for anything," he began, slowly feeling his way. "Despair was the only thing for me. There were always men about her. She walked and sang and danced with them. I knew it all the time, even when I didn't see her. But I saw her often enough. I knew that some day one of them would please her and she would give herself to him—she would marry him. That thought haunted me like an evil spirit."

Tonie passed his hand across his forehead as if to sweep away anything of the horror that might have remained there.

"It kept me awake at night," he went on. "But that was not so bad; the worst torture was to sleep, for then I would dream that it was all true.

"Oh, I could see her married to one of them—his wife—coming year after year to Grand Isle and bringing her little children with her! I can't tell you all that I saw—all that was driving me mad! But now"—and Tonie clasped his hands together and smiled as he looked again across the water—"she is where she belongs; there is no difference up there; the curé has often told us there is no difference between men. It is with the soul that we approach each other there. Then she will know who has loved her best. That is why I am so contented. Who knows what may happen up there?"

Ma'me Antoine could not answer. She only took her son's big, rough hand and pressed it against her.

"And now, ma mère,"[1] he exclaimed, cheerfully, rising, "I shall go light the fire for your bread; it is a long time since I have done anything for you," and he stooped and pressed a warm kiss on her withered old cheek.

With misty eyes she watched him walk away in the direction of the big brick oven that stood open-mouthed under the lemon trees.

---

1 My mother.

"Madame Célestin's Divorce," from *Bayou Folk* (1894)

[Never one to shy away from taboo subjects, in "Madame Célestin's Divorce" Chopin examines a burgeoning relationship between a lovely married woman and her would-be suitor, a well-regarded attorney. Rather than having Madame Célestin follow the path that Edna chooses in *The Awakening*, Chopin instead creates a more conventional ending for this story. Despite the fact that the protagonist dallies with the idea of renouncing her marriage vows to a no-account, albeit charming, husband, she ultimately chooses the conventional, womanly path.]

Madame Célestin always wore a neat and snugly fitting calico wrapper when she went out in the morning to sweep her small gallery. Lawyer Paxton thought she looked very pretty in the gray one that was made with a graceful Watteau[1] fold at the back: and with which she invariably wore a bow of pink ribbon at the throat. She was always sweeping her gallery when lawyer Paxton passed by in the morning on his way to his office in St. Denis Street.

Sometimes he stopped and leaned over the fence to say good-morning at his ease; to criticise or admire her rosebushes; or, when he had time enough, to hear what she had to say. Madame Célestin usually had a good deal to say. She would gather up the train of her calico wrapper in one hand, and balancing the broom gracefully in the other, would go tripping down to where the lawyer leaned, as comfortably as he could, over her picket fence.

Of course she had talked to him of her troubles. Every one knew Madame Célestin's troubles.

"Really, madame," he told her once, in his deliberate, calculating, lawyer-tone, "it's more than human nature—woman's nature—should be called upon to endure. Here you are, working your fingers off"—she glanced down at two rosy finger-tips that showed through the rents in her baggy doeskin gloves—"taking in sewing; giving music lessons; doing God knows what in the way of manual labor to support yourself and those two little ones"—Madame Célestin's pretty face beamed with satisfaction at this enumeration of her trials.

"You right, Judge. Not a picayune,[2] not one, not one, have I lay my eyes on in the pas' fo' months that I can say Célestin give it to me or sen' it to me."

---

1 A hat with a shallow crown and an up-turned back brim trimmed with flowers.
2 A coin of small value, generally worth about a nickel.

"The scoundrel!" muttered lawyer Paxton in his beard.

"An' *pourtant*,"[1] she resumed, "they say he 's making money down roun' Alexandria w'en he wants to work."

"I dare say you have n't seen him for months?" suggested the lawyer.

"It 's good six month' since I see a sight of Célestin," she admitted.

"That 's it, that 's what I say; he has practically deserted you; fails to support you. It wouldn't surprise me a bit to learn that he has ill treated you."

"Well, you know, Judge," with an evasive cough, "a man that drinks—w'at can you expec'? An' if you would know the promises he has made me! Ah, if I had as many dolla' as I had promise from Célestin, I would n' have to work, *je vous garantis*."[2]

"And in my opinion, madame, you would be a foolish woman to endure it longer, when the divorce court is there to offer you redress."

"You spoke about that befo', Judge; I 'm goin' think about that divo'ce. I believe you right."

Madame Célestin thought about the divorce and talked about it, too; and lawyer Paxton grew deeply interested in the theme.

"You know, about that divo'ce, Judge," Madame Célestin was waiting for him that morning, "I been talking to my family an' my frien's, an' it 's me that tells you, they all plumb agains' that divo'ce."

"Certainly, to be sure; that 's to be expected, madame, in this community of Creoles. I warned you that you would meet with opposition, and would have to face it and brave it."

"Oh, don't fear, I 'm going to face it! Maman says it 's a disgrace like it 's neva been in the family. But it 's good for Maman to talk, her. W'at trouble she ever had? She says I mus' go by all means consult with Père Duchéron—it 's my confessor, you undastan'—Well, I 'll go, Judge, to please Maman. But all the confessor' in the worl' ent goin' make me put up with that conduc' of Célestin any longa."

A day or two later, she was there waiting for him again. "You know, Judge, about that divo'ce."

"Yes, yes," responded the lawyer, well pleased to trace a new determination in her brown eyes and in the curves of her pretty mouth. "I suppose you saw Père Duchéron and had to brave it out with him, too."

---

1 However.
2 I guarantee you!

"Oh, fo' that, a perfec' sermon, I assho you. A talk of giving scandal an' bad example that I thought would neva en'! He says, fo' him, he wash' his hands; I mus' go see the bishop."

"You won't let the bishop dissuade you, I trust," stammered the lawyer more anxiously than he could well understand.

"You don't know me yet, Judge," laughed Madame Célestin with a turn of the head and a flirt of the broom which indicated that the interview was at an end.

"Well, Madame Célestin! And the bishop!" Lawyer Paxton was standing there holding to a couple of the shaky pickets. She had not seen him. "Oh, it's you, Judge?" and she hastened towards him with an *empressement*[1] that could not but have been flattering.

"Yes, I saw Monseigneur," she began. The lawyer had already gathered from her expressive countenance that she had not wavered in her determination. "Ah, he's a eloquent man. It's not a mo' eloquent man in Natchitoches parish. I was fo'ced to cry, the way he talked to me about my troubles; how he undastan's them, an' feels for me. It would move even you, Judge, to hear how he talk' about that step I want to take; its danga, its temptation. How it is the duty of a Catholic to stan' everything till the las' extreme. An' that life of retirement an' self-denial I would have to lead,—he tole me all that."

"But he hasn't turned you from your resolve, I see," laughed the lawyer complacently.

"For that, no," she returned emphatically. "The bishop don't know w'at it is to be married to a man like Célestin, an' have to endu' that conduc' like I have to endu' it. The Pope himse'f can't make me stan' that any longer, if you say I got the right in the law to sen' Célestin sailing."

A noticeable change had come over lawyer Paxton. He discarded his work-day coat and began to wear his Sunday one to the office. He grew solicitous as to the shine of his boots, his collar, and the set of his tie. He brushed and trimmed his whiskers with a care that had not before been apparent. Then he fell into a stupid habit of dreaming as he walked the streets of the old town. It would be very good to take unto himself a wife, he dreamed. And he could dream of no other than pretty Madame Célestin filling that sweet and sacred office as she filled his thoughts, now. Old Natchitoches would not hold them comfort-

---

1 Extreme attentiveness or concern.

ably, perhaps; but the world was surely wide enough to live in, outside of Natchitoches town.

His heart beat in a strangely irregular manner as he neared Madame Célestin's house one morning, and discovered her behind the rosebushes, as usual plying her broom. She had finished the gallery and steps and was sweeping the little brick walk along the edge of the violet border.

"Good-morning, Madame Célestin."

"Ah, it 's you, Judge? Good-morning." He waited. She seemed to be doing the same. Then she ventured, with some hesitancy, "You know, Judge, about that divo'ce. I been thinking,—I reckon you betta neva mine about that divo'ce." She was making deep rings in the palm of her gloved hand with the end of the broom-handle, and looking at them critically. Her face seemed to the lawyer to be unusually rosy; but maybe it was only the reflection of the pink bow at the throat. "Yes, I reckon you need n' mine. You see, Judge, Célestin came home las' night. An' he 's promise me on his word an' honor he 's going to turn ova a new leaf."

"A Respectable Woman" (1894)

["A Respectable Woman" develops the character of Gouvernail, who is featured at Edna's sumptuous farewell dinner in *The Awakening*, as well as in her 1895 story, "Athènaïse." A central figure here, Gouvernail at first annoys, then intrigues, and finally tempts Mrs. Baroda, who ultimately removes herself from his presence rather than risk becoming embroiled in a scandalous affair. Chopin illustrates a more conventional response to extra-marital temptation in this story, although the last line leaves the reader questioning Mrs. Baroda's decision to invite Gouvernail back into her home.]

Mrs. Baroda was a little provoked to learn that her husband expected his friend, Gouvernail, up to spend a week or two on the plantation.

They had entertained a good deal during the winter; much of the time had also been passed in New Orleans in various forms of mild dissipation. She was looking forward to a period of unbroken rest, now, and undisturbed tête-a-tête with her husband, when he informed her that Gouvernail was coming up to stay a week or two.

This was a man she had heard much of but never seen. He had been her husband's college friend; was now a journalist, and in no sense a Society man or "a man about town," which were, perhaps, some of the reasons she had never met him. But she had unconsciously formed an image of him in her mind. She pictured him tall, slim, cynical; with eye-glasses, and his hands in his pockets; and she did not like him. Gouvernail was slim enough, but he wasn't very tall nor very cynical; neither did he wear eye-glasses nor carry his hands in his pockets. And she rather liked him when he first presented himself.

But why she liked him she could not explain satisfactorily to herself when she partly attempted to do so. She could discover in him none of those brilliant and promising traits which Gaston, her husband, had often assured her that he possessed. On the contrary, he sat rather mute and receptive before her chatty eagerness to make him feel at home and in face of Gaston's frank and wordy hospitality. His manner was as courteous toward her as the most exacting woman could require; but he made no direct appeal to her approval or even esteem.

Once settled at the plantation he seemed to like to sit upon the wide portico in the shade of one of the big Corinthian pillars,[1] smoking his cigar lazily and listening attentively to Gaston's experience as a sugar planter.

"This is what I call living," he would utter with deep satisfaction, as the air that swept across the sugar field caressed him with its warm and scented velvety touch. It pleased him also to get on familiar terms with the big dogs that came about him, rubbing themselves sociably against his legs. He did not care to fish, and displayed no eagerness to go out and kill grosbecs[2] when Gaston proposed doing so.

Gouvernail's personality puzzled Mrs. Baroda, but she liked him. Indeed, he was a lovable, inoffensive fellow. After a few days, when she could understand him no better than at first, she gave over being puzzled and remained piqued. In this mood she left her husband and her guest, for the most part, alone together. Then finding that Gouvernail took no manner of exception to her action, she imposed her society upon him, accompanying him in his idle strolls to the mill and walks along the batture.[3] She persistently sought to penetrate the reserve in which he had unconsciously enveloped himself.

---

1 A style of pillar in Greek-influenced architecture.
2 In Creole French, a finch or grosbeak.
3 The elevated shore of a river subject to periodic flooding.

"When is he going—your friend?" she one day asked her husband. "For my part, he tires me frightfully."

"Not for a week yet, dear. I can't understand; he gives you no trouble."

"No. I should like him better if he did; if he were more like others, and I had to plan somewhat for his comfort and enjoyment."

Gaston took his wife's pretty face between his hands and looked tenderly and laughingly into her troubled eyes. They were making a bit of toilet sociably together in Mrs. Baroda's dainty dressing-room.

"You are full of surprises, ma belle," he said to her. "Even I can never count upon how you are going to act under given conditions." He kissed her and turned to fasten his cravat before the mirror.

"Here you are," he went on, "taking poor Gouvernail seriously and making a commotion over him, the last thing he would desire or expect."

"Commotion!" she hotly resented. "Nonsense! How can you say such a thing? Commotion, indeed! But, you know, you said he was clever."

"So he is. But the poor fellow is run down by overwork now. That's why I asked him here to take a rest."

"You used to say he was a man of ideas," she retorted, unconciliated. "I expected him to be interesting, at least. I'm going to the city in the morning to have my spring gowns fitted. Let me know when Mr. Gouvernail is gone [sic] I shall be at my Aunt Octavie's."

That night she went and sat alone upon a bench that stood beneath a live oak tree at the edge of the gravel walk.

She had never known her thoughts or her intentions to be so confused. She could gather nothing from them but the feeling of a distinct necessity to quit her home in the morning.

Mrs. Baroda heard footsteps crunching the gravel; but could discern in the darkness only the approaching red point of a lighted cigar. She knew it was Gouvernail, for her husband did not smoke. She hoped to remain unnoticed, but her white gown revealed her to him. He threw away his cigar and seated himself upon the bench beside her; without a suspicion that she might object to his presence.

"Your husband told me to bring this to you, Mrs. Baroda," he said, handing her a filmy, white scarf with which she sometimes enveloped her head and shoulders. She accepted the scarf from him with a murmur of thanks, and let it lie in her lap.

He made some commonplace observation upon the baneful effect of the night air at the season. Then as his gaze reached out into the darkness, he murmured, half to himself:

"'Night of south winds—night of the large few stars!
Still nodding night—'"[1]

She made no reply to this apostrophe to the night, which indeed, was not addressed to her.

Gouvernail was in no sense a diffident man, for he was not a self-conscious one. His periods of reserve were not constitutional, but the result of moods. Sitting there beside Mrs. Baroda, his silence melted for the time.

He talked freely and intimately in a low, hesitating drawl that was not unpleasant to hear. He talked of the old college days when he and Gaston had been a good deal to each other; of the days of keen and blind ambitions and large intentions. Now there was left with him, at least, a philosophic acquiescence to the existing order—only a desire to be permitted to exist, with now and then a little whiff of genuine life, such as he was breathing now.

Her mind only vaguely grasped what he was saying. Her physical being was for the moment predominant. She was not thinking of his words, only drinking in the tones of his voice. She wanted to reach out her hand in the darkness and touch him with the sensitive tips of her fingers upon the face or the lips. She wanted to draw close to him and whisper against his cheek—she did not care what—as she might have done if she had not been a respectable woman.

The stronger the impulse grew to bring herself near him, the further, in fact, did she draw away from him. As soon as she could do so without an appearance of too great rudeness, she rose and left him there alone.

Before she reached the house, Gouvernail had lighted a fresh cigar and ended his apostrophe to the night.

Mrs. Baroda was greatly tempted that night to tell her husband—who was also her friend—of this folly that had seized her. But she did not yield to the temptation. Beside being a respectable woman she was a very sensible one; and she knew there are some battles in life which a human being must fight alone.

---

1 From Walt Whitman's epic poem "Song of Myself" (from *Leaves of Grass*, 1855).

When Gaston arose in the morning, his wife had already departed. She had taken an early morning train to the city. She did not return till Gouvernail was gone from under her roof.

There was some talk of having him back during the summer that followed. That is, Gaston greatly desired it; but this desire yielded to his wife's strenuous opposition.

However, before the year ended, she proposed, wholly from herself, to have Gouvernail visit them again. Her husband was surprised and delighted with the suggestion coming from her.

"I am glad, chère amie, to know that you have finally overcome your dislike for him; truly he did not deserve it."

"Oh," she told him laughingly, after pressing a long, tender kiss upon his lips, "I have overcome everything! you will see. This time I shall be very nice to him."

"An Egyptian Cigarette" (1897)

["An Egyptian Cigarette" is unique among Chopin's fiction, as it presents an allegory of sorts that depicts the loss of a lover as a visceral experience. Much of the story is recounted from the perspective of a hallucinating narrator who describes her dream in vivid, sensory detail. The character in the dream relates the emotional impact of losing an emotionally detached lover who carelessly announces his permanent departure. After she returns to herself, the narrator discards the Egyptian cigarettes that led to the disturbing hallucination, noting that she is "a little worse for the dream."]

My friend, the Architect, who is something of a traveler, was showing us various curios which he had gathered during a visit to the Orient.

"Here is something for you," he said, picking up a small box and turning it over in his hand. "You are a cigarette-smoker; take this home with you. It was given to me in Cairo by a species of fakir,[1] who fancied I had done him a good turn."

The box was covered with glazed, yellow paper, so skillfully gummed as to appear to be all one piece. It bore no label, no stamp—nothing to indicate its contents.

"How do you know they are cigarettes?" I asked, taking the box and turning it stupidly around as one turns a sealed letter and speculates before opening it.

---

1 A spiritual counselor in the Muslim tradition.

"I only know what he told me," replied the Architect, "but it is easy enough to determine the question of his integrity." He handed me a sharp, pointed paper-cutter, and with it I opened the lid as carefully as possible.

The box contained six cigarettes, evidently hand-made. The wrappers were of pale-yellow paper, and the tobacco was almost the same color. It was of finer cut than the Turkish or ordinary Egyptian, and threads of it stuck out at either end.

"Will you try one now, Madam?" asked the Architect, offering to strike a match.

"Not now and not here," I replied, "after the coffee, if you will permit me to slip into your smoking-den. Some of the women here detest the odor of cigarettes."

The smoking-room lay at the end of a short, curved passage. Its appointments were exclusively Oriental. A broad, low window opened out upon a balcony that overhung the garden. From the divan upon which I reclined, only the swaying tree-tops could be seen. The maple leaves glistened in the afternoon sun. Beside the divan was a low stand which contained the complete paraphernalia of a smoker. I was feeling quite comfortable, and congratulated myself upon having escaped for a while the incessant chatter of the women that reached me faintly.

I took a cigarette and lit it, placing the box upon the stand just as the tiny clock, which was there, chimed in silvery strokes the hour of five.

I took one long inspiration of the Egyptian cigarette. The gray-green smoke arose in a small puffy column that spread and broadened, that seemed to fill the room. I could see the maple leaves dimly, as if they were veiled in a shimmer of moonlight. A subtle, disturbing current passed through my whole body and went to my head like the fumes of disturbing wine. I took another deep inhalation of the cigarette.

★ ★ ★ ★ ★

"Ah! the sand has blistered my cheek! I have lain here all day with my face in the sand. Tonight, when the everlasting stars are burning, I shall drag myself to the river."

He will never come back.

Thus far I followed him; with flying feet; with stumbling feet; with hands and knees, crawling; and outstretched arms, and here I have fallen in the sand.

The sand has blistered my cheek; it has blistered all my body, and the sun is crushing me with hot torture. There is shade beneath yonder cluster of palms.

I shall stay here in the sand till the hour and the night comes.

I laughed at the oracles and scoffed at the stars when they told that after the rapture of life I would open my arms inviting death, and the waters would envelop me.

Oh! how the sand blisters my cheek! and I have no tears to quench the fire. The river is cool and the night is not far distant.

I turned from the gods and said: "There is but one; Barajas is my god." That was when I decked myself with lilies and wove flowers into a garland and held him close in the frail, sweet fetters.

He will never come back. He turned upon his camel as he rode away. He turned and looked at me crouching here and laughed, showing his gleaming white teeth.

Whenever he kissed me and went away he always came back again. Whenever he flamed with fierce anger and left me with stinging words, he always came back. But to-day he neither kissed me nor was he angry. He only said:

"Oh! I am tired of fetters, and kisses, and you. I am going away. You will never see me again. I am going to the great city where men swarm like bees. I am going beyond, where the monster stones are rising heavenward in a monument for the unborn ages. Oh! I am tired. You will see me no more."

And he rode away on his camel. He smiled and showed his cruel white teeth as he turned to look at me crouching here.

How slow the hours drag! It seems to me that I have lain here for days in the sand, feeding upon despair. Despair is bitter and it nourishes resolve.

I hear the wings of a bird flapping above my head, flying low, in circles.

The sun is gone.

The sand has crept between my lips and teeth and under my parched tongue.

If I raise my head, perhaps I shall see the evening star.

Oh! the pain in my arms and legs! My body is sore and bruised as if broken. Why can I not rise and run as I did this morning? Why must I drag myself thus like a wounded serpent, twisting and writhing?

The river is near at hand. I hear it—I see it—Oh! the sand! Oh! the shine! How cool! how cold!

The water! the water! In my eyes, my ears, my throat! It stran-
gles me! Help! will the gods not help me?

Oh! the sweet rapture of rest! There is music in the Temple.
And here is fruit to taste. Bardja came with the music—The
moon shines and the breeze is soft—A garland of flowers—let us
go into the King's garden and look at the blue lily, Bardja.

* * * * *

The maple leaves looked as if a silvery shimmer enveloped
them. The gray-green smoke no longer filled the room. I could
hardly lift the lids of my eyes. The weight of centuries seemed to
suffocate my soul that struggled to escape, to free itself and
breathe.

I had tasted the depths of human despair.

The little clock upon the stand pointed to a quarter past five.
The cigarettes still reposed in the yellow box. Only the stub of the
one I had smoked remained. I had laid it in the ash tray.

As I looked at the cigarettes in their pale wrappers, I wondered
what other visions they might hold for me; what might I not find
in their mystic fumes? Perhaps a vision of celestial peace; a dream
of hopes fulfilled; a taste of rapture, such as had not entered into
my mind to conceive.

I took the cigarettes and crumpled them between my hands. I
walked to the window and spread my palms wide. The light
breeze caught up the golden threads and bore them writhing and
dancing far out among the maple leaves.

My friend, the Architect, lifted the curtain and entered, bringing me a second cup of coffee.

"How pale you are!" he exclaimed, solicitously. "Are you not
feeling well?"

"A little the worse for a dream," I told him.

"The Storm: A Sequel to 'At the 'Cadian Ball'" (1898)

[In her most overt depiction of adultery and extramarital sex,
Chopin offers here a non-judgmental view of the resolution of an
unrequited passion. In the earlier story, Calixta loves the upper-
class Alcée, but he marries a woman of his own class, a conventional beauty who is sexually distant but an appropriate choice
for a wife. Heart-broken, Calixta consents to marry Bobinôt who
is her peer and in love with her. Despite their marriages to other
people, Calixta's and Alcée's feelings remain unresolved until the

fateful afternoon described in "The Storm." Chopin's sensuous language and provocative ending suggest that there may be worse choices than committing adultery.]

I

The leaves were so still that even Bibi thought it was going to rain. Bobinôt, who was accustomed to converse on terms of perfect equality with his little son, called the child's attention to certain sombre clouds that were rolling with sinister intention from the west, accompanied by a sullen, threatening roar. They were at Friedheimer's store and decided to remain there till the storm had passed. They sat within the door on two empty kegs. Bibi was four years old and looked very wise.

"Mama'll be 'fraid, yes," he suggested with blinking eyes.

"She'll shut the house. Maybe she got Sylvie helpin' her this evenin'," Bobinôt responded reassuringly.

"No; she ent got Sylvie. Sylvie was helpin' her yistiday," piped Bibi.

Bobinôt arose and going across to the counter purchased a can of shrimps, of which Calixta was very fond. Then he returned to his perch on the keg and sat stolidly holding the can of shrimps while the storm burst. It shook the wooden store and seemed to be ripping great furrows in the distant field. Bibi laid his little hand on his father's knee and was not afraid.

II

Calixta, at home, felt no uneasiness for their safety. She sat at a side window sewing furiously on a sewing machine. She was greatly occupied and did not notice the approaching storm. But she felt very warm and often stopped to mop her face on which the perspiration gathered in beads. She unfastened her white sacque[1] at the throat. It began to grow dark, and suddenly realizing the situation she got up hurriedly and went about closing windows and doors.

Out on the small front gallery she had hung Bobinôt's Sunday clothes to air and she hastened out to gather them before the rain fell. As she stepped outside, Alcée Laballière rode in at the gate. She had not seen him very often since her marriage, and never

---

1 A loose-fitting gown that fastens at the neck.

alone. She stood there with Bobinôt's coat in her hands, and the big rain drops began to fall. Alcée rode his horse under the shelter of a side projection where the chickens had huddled and there were plows and a harrow piled up in the corner.

"May I come and wait on your gallery till the storm is over, Calixta?" he asked.

"Come 'long in, M'sieur Alcée."

His voice and her own startled her as if from a trance, and she seized Bobinôt's vest. Alcée, mounting to the porch, grabbed the trousers and snatched Bibi's braided jacket that was about to be carried away by a sudden gust of wind. He expressed an intention to remain outside, but it was soon apparent that he might as well have been out in the open: the water beat in upon the boards in driving sheets, and he went inside, closing the door after him. It was even necessary to put something beneath the door to keep the water out.

"My! what a rain! It's good two years sence it rain' like that," exclaimed Calixta as she rolled up a piece of bagging and Alcée helped her to thrust it beneath the crack.

She was a little fuller of figure than five years before when she married; but she had lost nothing of her vivacity. Her blue eyes still retained their melting quality; and her yellow hair, dishevelled by the wind and rain, kinked more stubbornly than ever about her ears and temples.

The rain beat upon the low, shingled roof with a force and clatter that threatened to break an entrance and deluge them there. They were in the dining room—the sitting room—the general utility room. Adjoining was her bed room, with Bibi's couch along side her own. The door stood open, and the room with its white, monumental bed, its closed shutters, looked dim and mysterious.

Alcée flung himself into a rocker and Calixta nervously began to gather up from the floor the lengths of a cotton sheet which she had been sewing.

"If this keeps up, *Dieu sait*[1] if the levees goin' to stan it!" she exclaimed.

"What have you got to do with the levees?"

"I got enough to do! An' there's Bobinôt with Bibi out in that storm—if he only didn' left Friedheimer's!"

"Let us hope, Calixta, that Bobinôt's got sense enough to come in out of a cyclone."

---

1 God knows.

She went and stood at the window with a greatly disturbed look on her face. She wiped the frame that was clouded with moisture. It was stiflingly hot. Alcée got up and joined her at the window, looking over her shoulder. The rain was coming down in sheets obscuring the view of far-off cabins and enveloping the distant wood in a gray mist. The playing of the lightning was incessant. A bolt struck a tall chinaberry tree at the edge of the field. It filled all visible space with a blinding glare and the crash seemed to invade the very boards they stood upon.

Calixta put her hands to her eyes, and with a cry, staggered backward. Alcée's arm encircled her, and for an instant he drew her close and spasmodically to him.

"*Bonté!*"[1] she cried, releasing herself from his encircling arm and retreating from the window, "the house'll go next! If I only knew w'ere Bibi was!" She would not compose herself; she would not be seated. Alcée clasped her shoulders and looked into her face. The contact of her warm, palpitating body when he had unthinkingly drawn her into his arms, had aroused all the old-time infatuation and desire for her flesh.

"Calixta," he said, "don't be frightened. Nothing can happen. The house is too low to be struck, with so many tall trees standing about. There! aren't you going to be quiet? say, aren't you?" He pushed her hair back from her face that was warm and steaming. Her lips were as red and moist as pomegranate seed. Her white neck and a glimpse of her full, firm bosom disturbed him powerfully. As she glanced up at him the fear in her liquid blue eyes had given place to a drowsy gleam that unconsciously betrayed a sensuous desire. He looked down into her eyes and there was nothing for him to do but to gather her lips in a kiss. It reminded him of Assumption.

"Do you remember—in Assumption, Calixta?" he asked in a low voice broken by passion. Oh! she remembered; for in Assumption he had kissed her and kissed and kissed her; until his senses would well nigh fail, and to save her he would resort to a desperate flight. If she was not an immaculate dove in those days, she was still inviolate; a passionate creature whose very defenselessness had made her defense, against which his honor forbade him to prevail. Now—well, now—her lips seemed in a manner free to be tasted, as well as her round, white throat and her whiter breasts.

1 Goodness!

They did not heed the crashing torrents, and the roar of the elements made her laugh as she lay in his arms. She was a revelation in that dim, mysterious chamber; as white as the couch she lay upon. Her firm, elastic flesh that was knowing for the first time its birthright, was like a creamy lily that the sun invites to contribute its breath and perfume to the undying life of the world.

The generous abundance of her passion, without guile or trickery, was like a white flame which penetrated and found response in depths of his own sensuous nature that had never yet been reached.

When he touched her breasts they gave themselves up in quivering ecstasy, inviting his lips. Her mouth was a fountain of delight. And when he possessed her, they seemed to swoon together at the very borderland of life's mystery.

He stayed cushioned upon her, breathless, dazed, enervated, with his heart beating like a hammer upon her. With one hand she clasped his head, her lips lightly touching his forehead. The other hand stroked with a soothing rhythm his muscular shoulders.

The growl of the thunder was distant and passing away. The rain beat softly upon the shingles, inviting them to drowsiness and sleep. But they dared not yield.

The rain was over; and the sun was turning the glistening green world into a palace of gems. Calixta, on the gallery, watched Alcée ride away. He turned and smiled at her with a beaming face; and she lifted her pretty chin in the air and laughed aloud.

III

Bobinôt and Bibi, trudging home, stopped without at the cistern[1] to make themselves presentable.

"My! Bibi, w'at will yo' mama say! You ought to be ashame'. You oughta' put on those good pants. Look at 'em! An' that mud on yo' collar! How you got that mud on yo' collar, Bibi? I never saw such a boy!" Bibi was the picture of pathetic resignation. Bobinôt was the embodiment of serious solicitude as he strove to remove from his own person and his son's the signs of their tramp

---

1 Receptacle for holding rain water.

over heavy roads and through wet fields. He scraped the mud off Bibi's bare legs and feet with a stick and carefully removed all traces from his heavy brogans. Then, prepared for the worst—the meeting with an over-scrupulous housewife, they entered cautiously at the back door.

Calixta was preparing supper. She had set the table and was dripping coffee at the hearth. She sprang up as they came in.

"Oh, Bobinôt! You back! My! but I was uneasy. W'ere you been during the rain? An' Bibi? he ain't wet? he ain't hurt?" She had clasped Bibi and was kissing him effusively. Bobinôt's explanations and apologies which he had been composing all along the way, died on his lips as Calixta felt him to see if he were dry, and seemed to express nothing but satisfaction at their safe return.

"I brought you some shrimps, Calixta," offered Bobinôt, hauling the can from his ample side pocket and laying it on the table.

"Shrimps! Oh, Bobinôt! you too good fo' anything!" and she gave him a smacking kiss on the cheek that resounded. "*J'vous réponds*,[1] we'll have a feas' to night! umph-umph!"

Bobinôt and Bibi began to relax and enjoy themselves, and when the three seated themselves at table they laughed much and so loud that anyone might have heard them as far away as Laballière's.

IV

Alcée Laballière wrote to his wife, Clarisse, that night. It was a loving letter, full of tender solicitude. He told her not to hurry back, but if she and the babies liked it at Biloxi, to stay a month longer. He was getting on nicely; and though he missed them, he was willing to bear the separation a while longer—realizing that their health and pleasure were the first things to be considered.

V

As for Clarisse, she was charmed upon receiving her husband's letter. She and the babies were doing well. The society was agreeable; many of her old friends and acquaintances were at the

---

1 Slang; I'll tell you what!

bay. And the first free breath since her marriage seemed to restore the pleasant liberty of her maiden days. Devoted as she was to her husband, their intimate conjugal life was something which she was more than willing to forego for a while.

So the storm passed and every one was happy.

POETRY

[Kate Chopin's first publications were not short stories, but a song and a variety of poems. Although her fiction is clearly far stronger than her poetry, some of the same themes that she develops in her fiction can also be seen in the poems presented here. Her poetry develops her feelings about being a woman in a society that does not seem to acknowledge a woman's right to her own feelings, including sexual feelings. While not all of the poems are full of despair, they tend to be downhearted and imply that a woman is not granted the same rights of a sexual being as a man.]

"A Fancy" (1892)

Happily naught came of it.
'Twas but a fancy born of fate and wishing.
But I thought all the same of it.
Now that the wishing's dead,
I find that naught remains of it.
Fancy and fate are fled.

"To Mrs B_____" (1896)

Your greeting filled me with distress.
I've pondered long and sore to guess
What 't would express.

Ah, Lady fair! can you not see:
From gentlemen of high degree
I always flee!

"To A Lady at the Piano" — "Mrs. R" (1896)

I do not know you out upon the street
    Where people meet.
We talk as women talk; shall I confess?
    I know you less!
I hear you play, and touched by a wondrous spell
    I know you well!

"A Document in Madness" (1898)

There's an ecstasy of madness
Where the March hares dwell;
A delirium of gladness
Too deep to tell.

The Moon has gone a-maying
And the Sun's so far!
'O! What's the use of staying
with a blinking star!

Let us join hands this instant—
and fly a-top the hill
and whether near or distant—
We'll ne'er stop still

Till we find the Moon that's Maying
And the sun so far,
That lift us here a-praying
To a blinking star.

"The Haunted Chamber" (1899)

Of course 'twas an excellent story to tell
Of a fair, frail, passionate woman who fell.
It may have been false, it may have been true.
That was nothing to me—it was less to you.
But with bottle between us, and clouds of smoke
From your last cigar, 'twas more of a joke
Than a matter of sin or a matter of shame
That a woman had fallen, and nothing to blame,
So far as you or I could discover,
But her beauty, her blood and an ardent lover.
But when you were gone and the lights were low
And the breeze came in with the moon's pale glow,
The far, faint voice of a woman, I heard,
'Twas but a wail, and it spoke no word.
It rose from the depths of some infinite gloom
And its tremulous anguish filled the room.
Yet the woman was dead and could not deny,
But women forever will whine and cry.

So now I must listen the whole night through
To the torment with which I had nothing to do—
But women forever will whine and cry
And men forever must listen—and sigh—...

"A day with a splash of sunlight" (1899)

A day with a splash of sunlight,
Some mist and a little rain.
A life with a dash of love-light,
Some dreams and a touch of pain.
To love a little and then to die!
To live a little and never know why!

[Like many writers of her time, Kate Chopin kept copious journals and diaries, as well as detailed account books of the disposition of her manuscripts. The selections presented here illustrate some of her personal thoughts on women and love, as well as her translation of Guy de Maupassant, a French short-story writer whom Chopin greatly admired. Some of her non-fiction essays were published in her hometown St. Louis newspapers as a result of her literary celebrity.

"Emancipation. A Life Fable" is an allegory tracing the development of an animal that is given every care and consideration but is caged. Despite the seeming advantages of being so well cared for, the animal is tempted away by light and freedom. "A Solitude" provides the reader with a glimpse into Chopin's perspective on the human tendency to escape from the "isolation of self." In "Is Love Divine?," Chopin provides a rather unconventional definition of love, but she is asked the question by an interviewer because, "as a novelist, [she] should know what love is." Finally, in "Reflection," she compares individuals who are spared the need for inner reflection as they avoid growing "weary ... [and] fall[ing] out of rank and sink[ing] by the wayside to be left contemplating the moving procession." In the end, however, Chopin's more personal writings encourage reflection and stillness because of the enlightenment that can result.]

"Emancipation. A Life Fable" (1869-70)

There was once an animal born into this world, and opening his eyes upon Life, he saw above and about him confining walls, and before him were bars of iron through which came air and light from without; this animal was born in a cage.

Here he grew, and throve in strength and beauty under the care of an invisible protecting hand. Hungering, food was ever at hand. When he thirsted water was brought, and when he felt the need to rest, there was provided a bed of straw upon which to lie; and here he found it good, licking his handsome flanks, to bask in the sun beam that he thought existed but to lighten his home.

Awaking one day from his slothful rest, lo! the door of his cage stood open: accident had opened it. In the corner he crouched, wondering and fearingly. Then slowly did he approach the door, dreading the unaccustomed, and would have closed it, but for such a task his limbs were purposeless. So out the opening he thrust his head, to see the canopy of the sky grow broader, and the world waxing wider.

Back to his corner but not to rest, for the spell of the Unknown was over him, and again and again he goes to the open door, seeing each time more Light.

Then one time standing in the flood of it; a deep in-drawn breath—a bracing of strong limbs, and with a bound he was gone.

On he rushes, in his mad flight, heedless that he is wounding and tearing his sleek sides—seeing, smelling, touching of all things; even stopping to put his lips to the noxious pool, thinking it may be sweet.

Hungering there is no food but such as he must seek and oft-times fight for; and his limbs are weighted before he reaches the water that is good to his thirsting throat.

So does he live, seeking, finding, joying and suffering. The door which accident had opened is opened still, but the cage remains forever empty!

"Solitude" (1895)

It was after a jovial "stag" dinner that one of the party, a friend of long standing, proposed to me to accompany him in a walk up the Avenue of the Champs Elysées.[1]

We strolled very leisurely under the trees that were but beginning to put forth leaves. No sound could be heard save the confused and continued rumble of Paris. A cool breeze was blowing, and a legion of stars besprinkled the black heavens like powdered gold.

"I know not why it is," began my companion, "but here, at night, I breathe more freely than anywhere else. Here, my thoughts seem to expand, and there comes to me at times a sort of spiritual illumination, like a promise of the revelation of hidden things."

At intervals shadowy couples flitted by us. Upon a bench which we passed a man and woman were seated, and so closely interlaced in each other's arms to give the impression of a single dark figure.

"Poor things!" muttered my friend, "they inspire me with pro-

---

1 Called "the most beautiful avenue in the world" by the French, this stretch of city street in Paris is known for its high-end boutique shopping and restaurants.

found pity, seeking like the rest of us—like all creatures—to escape the isolation of self."

"For a long time," he continued, "I have endured the anguish of having discovered and understood the solitude in which I live. And I know that nothing can end it; nothing! Whatever we may do or attempt, despite the embraces and transports of love, the hunger of the lips, we are always alone.

"I have dragged you out tonight in the vain hope of a moment's escape from the horrible solitude which overpowers me. But what is the use! I speak and you answer me, and still each of us is alone; side by side but alone.

"You may think me a little mad, but since I have realized solitude of my being I feel as if I were sinking day by day into some boundless subterranean depths, with no one near me, no other living soul to clasp my outstretched, groping hands. There are noises, there are voices and cries in the darkness. I strive to reach them, but I can never discover whence they come, in the darkness, in this life which engulfs me.

"Others besides myself have known this atrocious suffering. Musset[1] disclosed something of it when he wrote:

'Who comes? Who calls? No one!
I am alone. It is the hour which sounds.
O, Solitude! O, Poverty!'

"But with Musset it was a mood, not an abiding horror as with me. He was a poetry who peopled life with phantoms and dreams. He was never really alone as I am.

"And Flaubert—Gustave Flaubert[2]—one of the unhappiest because one of the most lucid of men, says despondingly: 'We are all in a desert where no one person understands another.'

"No, we do not understand one another, try as we may. Do you know what is happening yonder among those stars flying like grains of fire across the heavens? Do you know any better what passes within the soul of another man? We know less of it, because thought is unfathomable.

---

1 French poet, dramatist, and novelist Albert de Musset (1810-57).
2 French novelist (1821-80) best known for writing *Madame Bovary*, to which *The Awakening* is frequently compared by critics.

"Can you conceive of anything more fearful than this incessant contact with beings whom we are unable to penetrate? I never feel more alone than when I have opened my heart to some friend. He is there before me. I see his bright eyes fixed upon me. But do I know the soul behind them? What does he think as he listens to me? He hates me, perhaps, or despises or mocks me. He judges, scoffs, condemns me; thinks me commonplace or stupid. How can I know that he thinks? How know whether he cares for me as I for him? What a mystery is the unfathomed thought of a human being; the hidden, free thought that we can neither know nor lead nor direct nor subdue! And I, myself, desire as I may, to open all the portals of my soul, the wish is vain. I still keep in the very depths that sanctuary self where no other soul penetrates.

"Do you think me mad? Are you asking yourself, 'what ails him tonight?' Oh, if some day you could come and say to me. 'I understand you,' it would make me happy for a moment perhaps.

"It is, above all, women who make me sensible of my solitude. Horrors! How I have suffered through them! Because they, oftener than men, have deceived me with the illusion that I am not alone.

"You must have known delicious moments spent in the company of some being whose charm of feature, whose hair, whose glances were maddening. But after each embrace the isolation grows, and how poignant it is. And after the rapturous union which must, it would seem, blend two souls into one being, how, more than ever before do you feel yourself alone—alone!

"And yet, after all, there is nothing better in the world than to spend an evening beside a well-beloved woman, without speaking, almost completely happy, through the single sensation of her presence. Let us not ask for more.

"As for me, now that I have closed my soul, my thoughts, my beliefs, my loves remain closed within it. Knowing myself condemned to hideous solitude, I keep my opinions. What are opinions to me! What are strife and pleasure and beliefs! Why should I be interested in what I cannot share with another! My invisible thought remains unsolved. Do you understand?"

We had ascended the long avenue as far as l'Arc de Triomphe de l'Etoile,[1] and we descended to la Place de la Concorde[2]—for

---

1 The world's largest triumphal arch, located at one end of the Champs Elysées. Commissioned by Napoleon Bonaparte (1769-1821), it was completed in 1833 and is a well-known Parisian landmark.

2 Largest *place* in Paris; marks the beginning of the Champs Elysées.

he had said all this slowly—this and much more which I have forgotten—the granite obelisk[1] stood before us, its long Egyptian
profile lost amid the stars. He stopped and suddenly extended an
arm toward the exiled monument.

"There," he said, "we are all like that stone." And he quitted
me without a further word.

Was he drunk? Was he mad? Was he wise? I do not know.
Sometimes I think he was right. Sometimes it seems to me that
he had lost his mind.

from "Is Love Divine?
The Question Answered by Three Ladies
Well Known in St. Louis Society" (1898)

Mrs. Kate Chopin,

Who has written stories of Southern life and as a novelist should
know what love is:
It is as difficult to distinguish between the divine love and the
natural, animal love, as it is to explain just why we love at all. In
a discussion of this character between two women in my new
novel[2] I have made my heroine say: "Why is it I love this man? Is
it because his hair is brown, growing high on his temples; because
his eyes droop a bit at the corners, or because his nose is just so
much out of drawing?"

One really never knows the exact, definite thing which excites
love for any one person, and one can never truly know whether
this love is the result of circumstance or whether it is predestina-
tion. I am inclined to think that love springs from animal instinct,
and therefore is, in a measure, divine. One can never resolve to
love this man, this woman or child, and then carry out the resolution unless one feels irresistibly drawn by an indefinable
current of magnetism. This subject allows an immense field for
discussion and profound thought, and one could scarcely voice a
definite opinion in a ten minutes [sic] talk. But I am sure we all
feel that love—true, pure love, is an uncontrollable emotion that
allows of no analysation [sic] and no vivisection.

---

1 A tall, narrow, four-sided monument tapering to a pyramid shaped top,
  first used in Egyptian architecture. A 75-foot red granite obelisk has
  stood in the Place de la Concorde since 1836.
2 Probably referring to *The Awakening*, which would be published in
  1899.

"Reflection" (1899)

Some people are born with a vital and responsive energy. It not only enables them to keep abreast of the time, it qualifies them to furnish in their own personality a good bit of the motive power to the mad pace. They are fortunate beings. They do not need to apprehend the significance of things. They do not grow weary nor miss step, nor do they fall out of rank and sink by the wayside to be left contemplating the moving procession.

Ah! That moving procession that has left me by the road-side! Its fantastic colors are more brilliant and beautiful than the sun on the undulating waters. What matter if souls and bodies are falling beneath the feet of the ever-pressing multitude! it moves with the majestic rhythm of the spheres. Its discordant classes sweep upward in one harmonious tone that blends with the music of other worlds—to complete God's orchestra.

It is greater than the stars—that moving procession of human energy; greater than the palpitating earth and the things growing thereon. Oh! I could weep at being left by the wayside; left with the grass and the clouds and a few dumb animals. True, I feel at home in the society of these symbols of life's immutability. In the procession I should feel the crushing feet, clashing discords, the ruthless hands and stifling breath. I could not hear the rhythm of the march.

Salve![1] ye dumb hearts. Let us be still and wait by the road-side.

---

1 Latin; be well; be in good health.

Appendix A: Contemporary Reviews

[The following reviews were published during Chopin's lifetime and give the reader an overall sense of the critical reception of *The Awakening*.]

1. From Frances Porcher, *The Mirror* [St. Louis] (4 May 1899): 6

Of an already successful writer's first novel one should not write, perhaps, while the spell of the book is upon one; it is something to be "dreamed upon," like a piece of wedding-cake for luck on one's first marriage-proposal, or anything upon which hangs some importance of decision. And so, because we admire Kate Chopin's other work immensely and delight in her ever-growing fame and are proud that she is "one-of-us St. Louisans," one dislikes to acknowledge a wish that she had not written her novel.

Not because it is not bright with her own peculiar charm of style, not because there is missing any touch of effect or lacking any beauty of description—but—well, it is one of the books of which we feel—"cui bono?"[1] it absorbs and interests, then makes one wonder, for the moment, with a little sick feeling, if all women are like the one, and that isn't a pleasant reflection after you have thoroughly taken in this character study whose "awakening" gives title to Mrs. Chopin's novel.

One would fain beg the gods, in pure cowardice, for sleep unending rather than to know what an ugly, cruel, loathsome monster Passion can be when, like a tiger, it slowly stretches its graceful length and yawns and finally awakens. This is the kind of an awakening that impresses the reader in Mrs. Chopin's heroine. I do not believe it impressed the heroine herself that way. I think, like the tiger, she hated to be balked of her desire and that was about the worst of it to her.

***

Had *Edna Pontellier* awakened to the gentle touch of Love, pure and simple, none could have judged her over-harshly, but her love was of the kind that savors in spirit of the sensual and devilish; it was a demon which awoke, not a misdirected wondering god.

Had she refused to live with her husband and accept his generosity after discovering that her heart was not his, she would have only been truer to herself and the real spirit of marriage, but she would not have gone to the man she loved, even then. Still, in her soul, she would have

---

1 Latin; literally "who benefits?"

been faithful to the ideals of that love and held it holy for its own sake—if it had been Love that had awakened.

On the contrary, she gave herself up to a purely sensual enjoyment, which the passion of another man offered her, and so played the wanton in her soul.

It is not a pleasant picture of soul-dissection, take it anyway you like; and so, though she finally kills herself, or rather lets herself drown to death, one feels that it is not in the desperation born of an over-burdened heart, torn by complicating duties but rather because she realizes that something is due to her children, that she cannot get away from, and she is too weak to face the issue. Besides which, and this is the stronger feeling, she has offered herself wholly to the man, who loves her too well to take her at her word; "she realizes that the day would come when he, too, and the thought of him, would melt out of her existence" [163], she has awakened to know the shifting, treacherous, fickle deeps of her own soul in which lies, alert and strong and cruel, the fiend called Passion that is all animal and all of the earth, earthy. It is better to lie down in the green waves and sink down in close embraces of old ocean, and so she does.

There is no fault to find with the telling of the story; there are no blemishes in its art, but it leaves one sick of human nature and so one feels—*cui bono*!

2. From the *St. Louis Daily Globe-Democrat* (13 May 1899): 5

The appearance of a new novel by Kate Chopin, of St. Louis, is an event of interest to St. Louisanans. The appearance of a book such as "The Awakening" by this St. Louis lady, is fraught with especial interest, and that interest carries with it surprise. Whether that surprise is pleasant or the reverse, depends largely on the view point of the reader. It is hardly the kind of a book some people would look for from her.

★★★

It is not a healthy book; if it points any particular moral or teaches any lesson, the fact is not apparent. But there is no denying the fact that it deals with existent conditions, and without attempting solution, handles a problem that obtrudes itself only too frequently in the social life of people with whom the question of food and clothing is not the all absorbing one. Mrs. Pontellier does not love her husband. The poison of passion seems to have entered her system, with her mother's milk. That she is violently in love with Robert Lebrun is made very apparent to the reader in the first chapter, though she does not seem to realize the fact herself. She is all heart, and entirely without balance. Naturally she lets her love for the young man, who also loves her, make her miserable. This is at a summer boarding house in Louisiana, and much of the story is brought out while a lot of people are bathing, or on the way to the beach or returning in the moonlight.

★★★

There are some pretty bits of description of Louisiana Creole life, and there are two or three minor characters in the book that are drawn with a deft hand. After reading the whole story, it can not be said that either of the principal characters claims admiration or sympathy. It is a morbid book, and the thought suggests itself that the author herself would probably like nothing better than ... [text incomplete].

3. From C.L. Deyo, *St. Louis Post-Dispatch* (20 May 1899): 3

There may be many opinions touching other aspects of Mrs. Chopin's novel "The Awakening," but all must concede its flawless art. The delicacy of touch of rare skill in construction, the subtle understanding of motive, the searching vision into the recesses of the heart—these are known to readers of "Bayou Folk" and "A Night in Acadie." But in this new work power appears, power born of confidence. There is no uncertainty in the lines, so surely and firmly drawn. Complete mastery is apparent on every page. Nothing is wanting to make a complete artistic whole. In delicious English, quick with life, never a word too much, simple and pure, the story proceeds with classic severity through a labyrinth of doubt and temptation and dumb despair.

It is not a tragedy, for it lacks the high motive of a tragedy. The woman, not quite brave enough, declines to a lower plane and does not commit a sin ennobled by love. But it is terribly tragic. Compassion, not pity, is excited, for pity is for those who sin, and Edna Pontellier only offended—weakly, passively, vainly offended.

"The Awakening" is not for the young person; not because the young person would be harmed by reading it; but because the young person wouldn't understand it, and everybody knows that the young person's understanding should be scrupulously respected. It is for seasoned souls, for those who have lived, who have ripened under the gracious or ungracious sun of experience and learned that realities do not show themselves on the outside of things where they can be seen and heard, weighed, measured and valued like the sugar commerce, but treasured within the heart, hidden away, never to be known perhaps save when exposed by temptation or called out by occasions of great pith and moment. No, the book is not for the young person, nor, indeed, for the old person who has no relish for unpleasant truths. For such there is much that is very improper in it, not to say positively unseemly. A fact, no matter how essential, which we have all agreed shall not be acknowledged, is as good as no fact at all. And it is disturbing—even indelicate—to mention it as something which, perhaps, does play an important part in the life behind the mask.

It is the life and not the mask that is the subject of the story.

***

It is sad and mad and bad, but it is all consummate art. The theme is difficult, but it is handled with a cunning craft. The work is more than unusual. It is unique. The integrity of its art is that of well-knit individuality at one with itself, with nothing superfluous to weaken the impression of a perfect whole.

4. From G.B., *St. Louis Post-Dispatch* (21 May 1899): 6

The ultimate element of the creature is self-love, in contradistinction to the universal love of the creative principle.

This self-love manifests in many ways, which for convenience may be divided into three forms—as instinctive love, under control of the subjective or unconscious mind; as reasonable love, under control of the objective or conscious mind; and as emotional love, in the debatable zone.

Instinctive love appears as passion, is involuntary and unerring.

The repression or stimulation of the passions begets emotional or artificial love.

Reasonable love is that form of self-love which has been called enlightened selfishness, which Christ commended as the love of one's neighbor, which is under the dominion of the will and is therefore unequal to the idea.

If the premise is correct, then is Kate Chopin's "Awakening" a work of genius, in that it states a universal principle in particular terms.

Edna's love of her husband, Pontellier, was reasonable, as such was an honest effort to love her neighbor as herself without relinquishing her inalienable rights, and like all such efforts it failed.

Edna's passion for Robert was involuntary, and its gratification would have satisfied the demands of that phase of her experience. Under repression her passion became perverted into a sensual sanction of Arobin. It was neither hot or cold, and as John of Patmos,[1] wrote of the Laodiceans,[2] "I would ye had been hot or cold, but

---

1 The author of the book of Revelation in the Christian Scriptures. The author, who calls himself "John," was exiled to Patmos, a Greek island, where he wrote this book.

2 Early Christians whom John of Patmos directly rebukes in Revelation because of their lukewarm faith, warning them of dire spiritual consequences should they not repent.

because ye have been lukewarm and neither cold nor hot I will spew thee out of my mouth."

The glaring defect of the book greets one on the title page, which rumor says was furnished by the intelligent publishers.

Life is a succession of awakenings.

From the dawn of consciousness to the eve of senility we are continually arriving.

Edna thought she had solved the riddle, and apprehending wantonness she fled. These publishers thereupon indorsed her error and called it "The" instead of "An Awakening."

The science of the human soul and its operations is instinctive in Kate Chopin. In her creations she commits unutterable crimes against polite society, but in the essentials of her art she never blunders.

Like most of her work, however, "The Awakening" is too strong drink for moral babes, and should be labeled "poison."

5. From the *Chicago Times-Herald* (1 June 1899): 9

***

Kate Chopin, author of those delightful sketches, "A Night in Acadie" had made a new departure in her long story, "The Awakening" (Stone, Chicago). The many admirers whom she has won by her earlier work will be surprised—perhaps disagreeably—by this latest venture. That the book is strong and that Miss Chopin has a keen knowledge of certain phases of feminine character will not be denied. But it was not necessary for a writer of so great refinement and poetic grace to enter the overworked field of sex fiction.

***

This is not a pleasant story, but the contrast between the heroine and another character who is devoted to her husband and family saves it from utter gloom, and gives the reader a glimpse of the real Miss Chopin, who is at her best as a creator of sweet and lovable characters.

6. New Orleans *Times-Democrat* (18 June 1899): 14-15

Perhaps, however, had poor, silly Edna Pontellier possessed a Planchette[1] [hero of another novel reviewed on some page, who tries to find out if there is an after-life] she might have found a higher rule of life than that which she worked out by her own unaided reflections upon "her position in the world as a human being," and "her relations as an individual to the world within and about her" [52].

---

1 A small triangular board that was believed to spell out subconscious or supernatural messages.

By the way, "The Awakening" does not strike one as a very happy title for the story Mrs. Chopin tells. A woman of twenty-eight, a wife and twice a mother, who in pondering upon her relation to the world about her, fails to perceive that her relation of a mother to her children is far more important than the gratification of which experience has taught her is by its very nature, evanescent, can hardly be said to be fully awake. This unhappy Edna's awakening seems to have been confined entirely to the senses, while reason, judgment and all the higher faculties and perceptions, whose office it is to weigh and criticize impulse and govern conduct, fell into slumber deep as that of the seven sleepers. It gives one a distinct shock to see Edna's crude mental operations, of which we are compelled to judge chiefly by results—characterized as "perhaps more wisdom than the Holy Ghost is usually pleased to vouchsafe to any woman["] [52]. The assumption that such a course as that pursued by Edna has any sort of divine sanction cannot be too strongly protested against. In a civilized society the right of the individual to indulge all his caprices is, and must be, subject to many restricted clauses, and it cannot for a moment be admitted that a woman who has willingly accepted the love and devotion of a man, even without an equal love on her part—who has become his wife and the mother of his children—had not incurred a moral obligation which peremptorily forbids her from wantonly severing her relations with him, and entering openly upon the independent existence of an unmarried woman. It is not altogether clear that this is the doctrine Mrs. Chopin intends to teach, but neither is it clear that it is not. Certainly there is throughout the story an undercurrent of sympathy for Edna, and nowhere a single note of censure of her totally unjustifiable conduct.

7. *Public Opinion* [New York] 26 (22 June 1899): 794

"The Awakening" by Kate Chopin is a feeble reflection of Bourget,[1] theme and manner of treatment both suggesting the French novelist. We very much doubt the possibility of a woman of "solid old Presbyterian Kentucky stock" being at all like Mrs. Edna Pontellier who has a long list of lesser loves, and one absorbing passion, but gives herself only to the man for whom she felt the least affection. If the author had secured our sympathy for this unpleasant person it would not have been a small victory, but we are well satisfied when Mrs. Pontellier deliberately swims out to her death in the waters of the gulf.

---

1 French novelist and critic (1852-1935) who wrote psychological novels and essays. He authored a sequence of essays tracing the sources of early twentieth-century literary pessimism to the works of writers such as Gustave Flaubert and Charles Baudelaire.

8. *Literature* 4 (23 June 1899): 570

One cannot refrain from regret that so beautiful a style and so much refinement of taste have been spent by Miss [*sic*] Chopin on an essentially vulgar story. The peculiarities of Creole life and temperament, and the sensuous atmosphere of life in New Orleans and at summer resorts on the Gulf, are happily sketched and outlined in the dramatic tale, and emphasis is laid upon the freedom of the Creole from false modesty and the pleasant social relation which inhere among Creole circles. A Creole husband as a rule entirely trusts his wife and is incapable of jealousy, for the reason that the right hand is not jealous of the left, nor the head of the heart. Nevertheless, Léonce Pentellier [*sic*], the Creole husband in the story, having married a beautiful Kentuckian, is less fortunate than most of his compatriots in having excellent reason for jealousy. His wife, having married him in reaction from a fancied love affair of her girlhood, does not find marriage and motherhood a cable strong enough to keep her from forming other attachments, and the story of these and her final awakening has little to redeem it from the commonplace, nor is it strong enough to condone the character of its revelations. The awakening itself is tragic, as might have been anticipated, and the waters of the gulf close appropriately over the one who has drifted from all right moorings, and has not the grace to repent.

9. From the *Boston Beacon* 16 (24 June 1899): 4

The Awakening, by Kate Chopin, is emphatically not a book for very young people; in it the author skims over some very thin ice, but it is a book that might be read by match-makers with profit. It reveals the dreadful consequences of marriage without real love, tracing the struggle of a woman's inborn sense of duty and right to be herself, against the conditions into which she was ignorantly inveigled and which then made it immoral before the world for her to act out herself and seek her affinity.... The pure affection of her lover saves the heroine from irrevocable disgrace by a very narrow margin, but it is a powerful stroke on the part of the author to secure a strong artistic effect. In thus dealing with the subject the author emphasizes the immorality of a marriage of convenience. Nor is this the only point the author makes. There is an evident effort to illustrate without prudery—very much without prudery—that the normal woman is capable without sin of experiencing a full awakening of the entire human nature. One closes the volume, wondering what good, clever old R. Mandelet[1]

---

1 A character in *The Awakening* in whom Edna attempts to confide shortly before her final swim.

would have said to justify his telling the heroine not to blame herself, whatever came.

10. From the *Los Angeles Sunday Times* (25 June 1899): 12

It is rather difficult to decide whether Mrs. Kate Chopin, the author of "The Awakening," tried in that novel merely to make an intimate, analytical study of the character of a selfish, capricious, woman, or whether she wanted to preach to the doctrine of the right of the individual to have what he wants no matter whether or not it may be good for him. It is true that the woman in the book who wanted her own way comes to an untimely end in the effort to get what she wants, or rather, in the effort to gratify every whim that moves her capricious soul, but there are sentences here and there through the book that indicate the author's desire to hint her belief that her heroine had the right of the matter and that if the woman had only been able to make other people "understand" things as she did she would not have had to drown herself in the blue waters of the Mexican Gulf.... And as the biography of one individual out of that large section of femininity which may be classified as "fool women", the book is a strong and graceful piece of work. It is like one of Aubrey Beardsley's[1] hideous but haunting pictures with their disfiguring leer of sensuality, but yet carrying a distinguishing strength and grace and individuality. The book shows a searching insight into the motives of the "fool woman" order of being, the woman who learns nothing by experience and has not a large enough circle of vision to see beyond her own immediate desires. In many ways, it is unhealthily introspective and morbid in feeling, as the story of that sort of woman must inevitably be. The evident powers of the author are employed on a subject that is unworthy of them, and when she writes another book it is to be hoped that she will choose a theme more healthful and sweeter of smell.

11. Sibert [Willa Cather], *Pittsburgh Leader* (8 July 1899): 6

A creole "Bovary"[2] is this little novel of Miss [*sic*] Chopin's. Not that the heroine is creole exactly, or that Miss Chopin is.

---

1 Aubrey Vincent Beardsley (1872-98) was a British artist and author. His drawings emphasized the grotesque, the decadent, and the erotic. He is closely associated with the aesthetic movement, along with Oscar Wilde and James A. McNeill Whistler.

2 Cather is referring to Gustave Flaubert's *Madame Bovary* (1857), to which Chopin's *The Awakening* has frequently been compared.

Flaubert—save the mark!—but the theme is similar to that which occupied Flaubert. There was, indeed, no need that a second "Madame Bovary" should be written, but an author's choice of themes is frequently as inexplicable as his choice of a wife. It is governed by some innate temperamental bias that cannot be diagrammed. This is particularly so in women who write, and I shall not attempt to say what Miss Chopin has devoted so exquisite and sensitive, well-governed a style to so trite and sordid a theme. She writes much better than it is ever given to most people to write and hers is a genuinely literary style; of so great elegance or solidity; but light, flexible, subtle and capable of producing telling effects directly and simply. The story she has to tell in the present instance is new neither in matter nor treatment. "Edna Pontellier," a Kentucky girl, who, like "Emma Bovary," had been in love with innumerable dream heroes before she was out of short skirts, married "Leonce Pontellier" as a sort of reaction from a vague and visionary passion for a tragedian whose unresponsive picture she used to kiss. She acquired the habit of liking her husband in time, and even of liking her children. Though we are not justified in presuming that she ever threw articles from her dressing table at them, as the charming "Emma" had a winsome habit of doing, we are told that "she would sometimes gather them passionately to her heart; she would sometimes forget them" [58]. At a creole watering place, which is admirably and deftly sketched by Miss Chopin, "Edna" met "Robert Lebrun," son of the landlady, who dreamed of a fortune awaiting him in Mexico while he occupied a petty clerical position in New Orleans. "Robert" made it his business to be agreeable to his mother's boarders, and "Edna," not being a creole, much against his wish and will, took him seriously. "Robert" went to Mexico, but found that fortunes were no easier to make there than in New Orleans. He returns and does not even call to pay his respect to her. She encounters him at the home of a friend and takes him home with her. She wheedles him into staying with her for dinner, and we are told she sent the maid off "in search of some delicacy she had not thought of for herself, and the recommended great care in the dripping of the coffee and having the omelet done to a turn" [147].

Only a few pages back we were informed that the husband "M. Pontellier" had cold soup and burnt fish for his dinner. Such is life. The lover of course disappointed her, was a coward, and ran away from his responsibilities before they began. He was afraid to begin a chapter with so serious and limited a woman. She remembered the sea where she had first met "Robert." Perhaps from the same motives which threw "Anna Keraninna"[1] [sic] under the engine

1 *Anna Karenina*, a novel by Russian writer Leo Tolstoy (1828-1910).

wheels, she threw herself into the sea, swam until she was tired and then let go.

"She looked into the distance, and for a moment the old terror flamed up, then sank again. She heard her father's voice, and her sister Margaret's. She heard the barking of an old dog that was chained to the sycamore tree. The spurs of the cavalry officer clanged as he walked across the porch. There was a hum of bees, and the musky odor of pinks filled the air." [164]

"Edna Pontellier" and "Emma Bovary" are studies in the same feminine type; one a finished and complete portrayal; the other a hasty sketch, but the theme is essentially the same. Both women belong to a class, not large, but forever clamoring in our ears, that demands more romance out of life than God put into it. Mr. G. Barnard [*sic*] Shaw[1] would say that they are victims of the over idealization of love. They are the spoil of the poets, the Iphigenias[2] of sentiment. The unfortunate feature of their disease is that it attacks only few women of brains, at least of rudimentary brains, but whose development is one-sided: women of strong and fine intuitions, but without the faculty of observation, comparison, reasoning about things. Probably, for emotional people, the most convenient thing about being able to think is that it occasionally give them a rest from feeling. Now with women of the "Bovary" type, this relaxation recreation is impossible. They are not critics of life, but, in the most personal sense, partakers of life. They receive impressions through the fancy. With them everything begins with fancy, and passions rise in the brain rather than in the blood, the poor, neglected, limited, one-sided brain that might do so much better things than badgering itself into frantic endeavors to love. For these are the people who pay with their blood for the fine ideals of the poets, as Marie Delclasse [*sic*] paid for Dumas' great creation, "Marguerite Gautier."[3] These people really expect the passion of love to fill and gratify every need of life, whereas nature only intended that it should

---

1   Irish playwright (1856-1950), winner of the Nobel Prize for Literature, and co-founder of the London School of Economics.

2   In Greek mythology, Iphigenia was the daughter of Agamemnon and Clytemnestra who was sacrificed to appease the goddess Artemis prior to the Trojan War.

3   Marguerite Gautier is the main character in Alexandre Dumas's tragic novel *The Lady of the Camellias* (1848). A kept woman, she dies at the end of the novel. Marguerite is loosely based on Marie Duplessis (1824-47) (not Delclasse, as Cather calls her), a French courtesan who may have been a lover of Dumas and of the composer Franz Liszt.

meet one of many demands. They insist upon making it stand for all the emotional pleasures of life and art: expecting an individual and self-limited passion to yield infinite variety, pleasure and distraction, to contribute to their lives what the arts and the pleasurable exercise of the intellect gives to less limited and less intense idealists. So this passion, when set up against Shakespeare, Balzac, Wagner, Raphael,[1] fails them. They have staked everything on one hand, and they lose. They have driven the blood until it will drive no further, they have played their nerves up to the point where any relaxation short of absolute annihilation is impossible. Every idealist abuses his nerves, and every sentimentalist brutally abuses them. And in the end, the nerves get even. Nobody ever cheats them, really. Then "the awakening" comes. Sometimes it comes in the form of arsenic as it came to "Emma Bovary," sometimes it is carbolic acid taken covertly in the police station, a goal to which unbalanced idealism not infrequently leads. "Edna Pontellier," fanciful and romantic to the last, chose the season of summer night and went down with the sound of her first lover's spurs in her ears, and the scent of pinks about her. And next time I hope that Miss Chopin will devote that flexible, iridescent style of hers to a better cause.

12. William Morton Payne, *The Dial* 37 (1 August 1899): 75

"The Awakening" by Mrs. Kate Chopin is a story in which, with no other accessories than the trivial details of everyday life in and about New Orleans, there is worded out a poignant spiritual tragedy. The story is familiar enough. A woman is married without knowing what it is to love. Her husband is kind but commonplace. He cares over much for the conventions of life: she, finding them a bar to the free development of her wayward personality, casts them off when "the awakening" comes to her, and discovers, too late, that she has cast off the anchor which alone could have saved her from shipwreck. It is needless to say that the agency by which she becomes awakened is provided by another man. But he proves strong enough to resist temptation, while she is too weak to think of atoning for her fault. To her distraught thinking, self-destruction is the only way out, and the tragedy is accomplished in picturesque fashion. The story is a simple one, not without charm, but not altogether wholesome in its tendency.

---

1 Honoré de Balzac (1799-1850) was a French realist novelist; Richard Wagner (1813-83) was a German composer and conductor best known for his operas; Raphael (1483-1520), an artist of the high Renaissance, is considered, along with Michelangelo and Leonardo da Vinci, to be one of the most notable artists of this period.

13. *The Nation* 69 (3 August 1899): 96

"The Awakening" is the sad story of a Southern lady who wanted to do what she wanted to. From wanting to, she did, with disastrous consequences: but as she swims out to sea in the end, it is to be hoped that her example may lie forever undredged. It is with high expectation that we open the volume, remembering the author's agreeable short stories, and with real disappointment that we close it. The recording reviewer drops a tear over one more clever author gone wrong. Mrs. Chopin's accustomed fine workmanship is here, the hinted effects, the well-expended epithet, the pellucid style: and, so far as construction goes, the writer shows herself as competent to write a novel as a sketch. The tint and air of Creole New Orleans and the Louisiana seacoast are conveyed to the reader with subtle skill, and among the secondary characters are several that are lifelike. But we cannot see that literature or the criticism of life is helped by the detailed history of the manifold and contemporary love affairs of a wife and mother. Had she lived by Prof. William James's[1] advice to do one thing a day one does not want to do (in Creole society, two would perhaps be better), flirted less and looked after her children more, or even assisted at more *accouchements*—her *chef d'oeuvre* in self-denial—we need not have been put to the unpleasantness of reading about her and the temptations she trumped for herself.

14. *Boston Herald* (12 August 1899): 7

That short, crisp and breezy style which has been the charm of Mrs. Kate Chopin's short stories is also the charm of "The Awakening" (Stone), her first novel the sad story of a woman who wanted to do just what she wanted to. The disastrous consequences which attend her unwise actions are set forth with rare skill, even to the end where she swims out to sea and loses everything forever. Mrs. Chopin has brought much of that Creole and Louisiana atmosphere which has always been the peculiar flavor of her other stories into the narrative of the love affairs of a wife and mother. Many of her minor characters are evidently drawn from real life. If Mrs. Pontellier had been more content with her life, had flirted less and desired less and had thought less of herself and more of others, she might have dreamed on and never awakened to the illusions of love and happiness. There were

---

1 Pioneer of American psychology and philosophy (1842-1910), as well as a medical doctor. A prolific writer in his own right, he was the brother of novelist Henry James.

days when she was very happy without knowing why, and others when she was perfectly miserable without knowing why; in fact, the story is a presentation of her moods and her power of creating tortures for herself. And, while it is related with all the fine mechanism of genius, it is most unpleasant in its bearings and not exactly profitable reading. So far as construction and plot are concerned, Mrs. Chopin shows quite as marked ability in the writing of a novel as she has in her sketches, and we only regret that she has not chosen a more agreeable theme. The raptures in love affairs after matrimony are not altogether commendable for fiction, except as stepping-stones to better conditions.

15. *Indianapolis Journal* (14 August 1899): 4

This is a story of Southern life by Kate Chopin, author of "Bayou Folks," etc. The scenes of the story are laid in New Orleans and Grand isle, a popular summer resort. The heroine, Mrs. Pontellier, a weak and emotional but interesting young married woman, is unhappy without knowing why, and naughty without intending wrong. She is foolish enough to grow indifferent to a husband who worships her and to fall in love with a young man who is scarcely worth it. The other characters are Southern summer resort people. It is a society story of the conventional, frivolous sort, and for that very reason readable. "The Awakening" is when Mrs. Pontellier discovers that she loves another man than her husband, and from that moment, owing to her emotional nature, the story moves to a tragic ending. It is not a healthy story, yet it is clever and one feels while reading it that he is moving among real people and events. The ending is abrupt and gives the reader somewhat the impression of being left hanging in midair.

16. *The Congregationalist* [Boston] 84.34 (24 August 1899): 256

Kate Chopin is the author of The Awakening [H.S. Stone & Co. $1.50]. It is a languorous passionate story of New Orleans and vicinity, hinging on the gradual yielding of a wife to the attractions of other men than her husband. It is a brilliant piece of writing, but unwholesome in its influence. We cannot commend it.

Appendix B: Background, Sources, and Contexts

[The selections in this section establish the major philosophical and social issues that shaped *The Awakening*. These texts influenced Chopin's world view and, by extension, her body of writing. Those mentioned in *The Awakening* serve to illuminate the themes presented in the novel. Algernon Charles Swinburne (1837-1909) was a Victorian poet who wrote "A Cameo" in 1889. One of the guests at Edna's dinner party quotes a passage from the poem, which describes lush desire. At another point in the novel, Edna Pontellier falls asleep while reading American poet Ralph Waldo Emerson (1803-82), which could constitute Chopin's critique of his philosophy. In "Self-Reliance," Emerson's notion of self, which incorporates a vision of human freedom that is unconsciously defined as male, is essentially unavailable to Edna. Richard von Krafft-Ebing (1840-1902), an Austro-German psychiatrist, in *Psychopathia Sexualis* discusses the common beliefs of that time about women's sexuality, which Edna's affair in *The Awakening* contradicts. English philosopher and sociologist Herbert Spencer's (1820-1903) *Essays on Education and Kindred Subjects* describes the type of moral education that should be presented to children and argues that one area that is lacking is teaching people to be good parents. This essay reflects the notion of that time that women's primary duty was that of mother, a notion that chafes Edna. The pieces by Gilman and Stanton (see Introduction, 14) both reflect the major social issues that influenced Chopin, including women's economic dependence in marriage, the role of wives in supporting class structures, and the "new woman" question. The short contemporary articles illuminate the ongoing beliefs held by some of the more vocal women during that time of the need for change, especially in divorce laws. American sociologist and economist Thorstein Veblen's (1857-1929) theories about the upper class illustrate many of the beliefs held by the characters in *The Awakening*.]

1. From Ralph Waldo Emerson, "Self-Reliance," *Essays: First Series*, new ed. (Boston: J. Munroe, 1841)

I READ THE OTHER DAY SOME VERSES written by an eminent painter which were original and not conventional. Always the soul hears an admonition in such lines, let the subject be what it may. The sentiment they instill is of more value than any thought they may contain. To believe your own thought, to believe that what is true for you in your private heart is true for all men,—that is genius.

★★★

Trust thyself: every heart vibrates to that iron string. Accept the place the divine providence has found for you, the society of your contemporaries, the connection of events. Great men have always done so, and confided themselves childlike to the genius of their age, betraying their perception that the Eternal was stirring at their heart, working through their hands, predominating in all their being. And we are now men, and must accept in the highest mind the same transcendent destiny; and not pinched in a corner, not cowards fleeing before a revolution, but redeemers and benefactors, pious aspirants to be noble clay under the Almighty effort let us advance on Chaos and the dark.

What pretty oracles nature yields us on this text in the face and behavior of children, babes, and even brutes. That divided and rebel mind, that distrust of a sentiment because our arithmetic has computed the strength and means opposed to our purpose, these have not. Their mind being whole, their eye is as yet unconquered, and when we look in their faces, we are disconcerted. Infancy conforms to nobody; all conform to it; so that one babe commonly makes four or five out of the adults who prattle and pray to it. So God has armed youth and puberty and manhood no less with its own piquancy and charm, and made it enviable and gracious and its claims not to be put by, if it will stand by itself.

★★★

These are the voices which we hear in solitude, but they grow faint and inaudible as we enter into the world. Society everywhere is in a conspiracy against the manhood of every one of its members. Society is a joint-stock company, in which the members agree for the better securing of his bread to each shareholder, to surrender the liberty and culture of the eater. The virtue in most request is conformity. Self-reliance is its aversion. It loves not realities and creators, but names and customs.

Whoso would be a man, must be a non-conformist. He who would gather immortal palms must not be hindered by the name of goodness, but must explore if it be goodness. Nothing is at last sacred but the integrity of your own mind. Absolve you to yourself, and you shall have the suffrage of the world. I remember an answer which when quite young I was prompted to make a valued adviser who was wont to importune me with the dear old doctrines of the church. On my saying, What have I to do with the sacredness of traditions, if I live wholly from within? my friend suggested,—"But these impulses may be from below, not from above." I replied, "They do not seem to me to be such; but if I am the devil's child, I will live then from the devil." No law can be sacred to me but that of my nature. Good and bad are but names very readily transferable to that or this; the only right is what is after my constitution; the only wrong what is against it. A man is to carry himself in the presence of all opposition as if every thing were titular and ephemeral but he. I am ashamed to think how easily we capitulate to badges and names, to large societies and dead institutions. Every decent and well-spoken individual affects and sways me more than is right. I ought to go upright and vital, and speak the rude truth in all ways.

***

For non-conformity the world whips you with its displeasure. And therefore a man must know how to estimate a sour face. The bystanders look askance on him in the public street or in the friend's parlor. If this aversion had its origin in the contempt and resistance like his own he might well go home with a sad countenance; but the sour face of the multitude, like their sweet faces, have no deep cause—disguise no god, but are put on and off as the wind blows and a newspaper directs. Yet is the discontent of the multitude more formidable than that of the senate and the college. It is easy enough for a firm man who knows the world to brook the rage of the cultivated classes. Their rage is decorous and prudent, for they are timid, as being very vulnerable themselves. But when to their feminine rage the indignation of the people is added, when the ignorant and the poor are aroused, when the unintelligent brute force that lies at the bottom of society is made to growl and mow, it needs the habit of magnanimity and religion to treat it godlike as a trifle of no concernment.

The other terror that scares us from self-trust is our consistency; a reverence for our past act or word because the eyes of others have no other data for computing our orbit than our past acts, and we are loath to disappoint them.

But why should you keep your head over your shoulder? Why drag about this monstrous corpse of your memory, lest you contradict somewhat you have stated in this or that public place? Suppose you should contradict yourself; what then? It seems to be a rule of wisdom never to rely on your memory alone, scarcely even in acts of pure memory, but to bring the past for judgment into the thousand-eyed present, and live ever in a new day. Trust your emotion. In your metaphysics you have denied personality to the Deity, yet when the devout motions of the soul come, yield to them heart and life, though they should clothe God with shape and color. Leave your theory, as Joseph his coat in the hands of the harlot, and flee.[1]

---

1 In the Old Testament, Joseph was the favorite of his father, who had given him a coat of many colors. His jealous brothers sold him into slavery, but he later became very powerful and led his family into Egypt.

A foolish consistency is the hobgoblin of little minds, adored by little statesmen and philosophers and divines. With consistency a great soul has simply nothing to do. He may as well concern himself with his shadow on the wall. Out upon your guarded lips! Sew them up with pocketthread, do. Else if you would be a man speak what you think today in words as hard as cannon balls, and tomorrow speak what tomorrow thinks in hard words again, though it contradict every thing you said today. Ah, then, exclaim the aged ladies, you shall be sure to be misunderstood! Misunderstood! It is a right fool's word. Is it so bad then to be misunderstood? Pythagoras[1] was misunderstood, and Socrates[2] and Jesus, and Luther,[3] and Copernicus,[4] and Galileo,[5] and Newton,[6] and every pure and wise spirit that ever took flesh. To be great is to be misunderstood.

***

I hope in these days we have heard the last of conformity and consistency. Let the words be gazetted and ridiculous henceforward.

***

The magnetism which all original action exerts is explained when we inquire the reason of self-trust. Who is the Trustee? What is the aboriginal Self, on which a universal reliance may be grounded? What is the nature and power of that science-baffling star, without parallax, without calculable elements, which shoots a ray of beauty even into trivial and impure actions, if the least mark of independence appear? The inquiry leads us to that source, at once the essence of genius, the essence of virtue, and the essence of life, which we call Spontaneity or Instinct. We denote this primary wisdom as Intuition, whilst all later teachings are tuitions. In that deep force, the last fact behind which analysis cannot go, all things find their common origin. For the sense of being which in calm hours rises, we know not how, in the soul, is not diverse from things, from space, from light, from time, from man, but one with them and preceedeth obviously from the same source whence their life and being also preceedeth. We at first share the life

---

1 Ancient Greek philosopher and mathematician (570-c. 500 BCE).
2 Ancient Greek philosopher (c. 469-399 BCE).
3 Martin Luther (1483-1546) was a German priest who challenged the authority of the Catholic Church and began the Protestant Reformation.
4 Nicolaus Copernicus (1473-1543) was a Polish-born mathematician and astronomer who first theorized that the Sun and not the earth was the center of the universe.
5 Galileo Galilei (1564-1642) was an Italian physicist and astronomer who championed Copernicus' idea about the sun being the center of the universe.
6 Sir Isaac Newton (1643-1727) was an English physicist, astronomer, and mathematician famous for his theories about gravity and motion.

by which things exist and afterwards see them as appearances in nature and forget that we have shared their cause. Here is the fountain of action and the fountain of thought. Here are the lungs of that inspiration which giveth man wisdom, of that inspiration of man which cannot be denied without impiety and atheism. We lie in the lap of immense intelligence, which makes us organs of its activity and receivers of its truth. When we discern justice, when we discern truth, we do nothing of ourselves, but allow a passage to its beams. If we ask whence this comes, if we seek to pry into the soul that causes—all metaphysics, all philosophy is at fault. Its presence or absence is all we can affirm. Every man discerns between the voluntary acts of his mind and his involuntary perceptions. And to his involuntary perceptions he knows a perfect respect is due. He may err in the expression of them, but he knows that these things are so, like day and night, not to be disputed. All my willful actions and acquisitions are but roving;—the most trivial reverie, the faintest native emotion, are domestic and divine. Thoughtless people contradict as readily the statement of perceptions as of opinions, or rather much more readily; for they do not distinguish between perception and notion. They fancy that I choose to see this or that thing. But perception is not whimsical, but fatal. If I see a trait, my children will see it after me, and in course of time all mankind,—although it may chance that no one has seen it before me. For my perception of it is as much a fact as the sun.

***

And now at last the highest truth on this subject remains unsaid; probably cannot be said; for all that we say is the far off remembering of the intuition. That thought, by what I can now nearest approach to say it, is this. When good is near you, when you have life in yourself,—it is not by any known or appointed way; you shall not discern the footprints of another; you shall not see the face of man; you shall not hear any name;—the way, the thought, the good, shall be wholly strange and new. It shall exclude all other being. You take the way from man, not to man. All persons that ever existed are its fugitive ministers. There shall be no fear in it. Fear and hope are alike beneath it. It asks nothing. There is somewhat low even in hope. We are then in vision. There is nothing that can be called gratitude, nor properly joy. The soul is raised over passion. It seeth identity and eternal causation. It is a perceiving that Truth and Right are. Hence it becomes a Tranquillity out of the knowing that all things go well. Vast spaces of nature; the Atlantic Ocean, the South Sea; vast intervals of time, years, centuries, are of no account. This which I think and feel underlay that former state of life and circumstances, as it does underlie my present and will always all circumstances, and what is called life and what is called death.

Life only avails, not the having lived.

***

I must be myself. I cannot break myself any longer for you, or you. If you can love me for what I am, we shall be the happier. If you cannot, I will still seek to deserve that you should. I must be myself. I will not hide my tastes or aversions. I will so trust that what is deep is holy, that I will do strongly before the sun and moon whatever inly rejoices me and the heart appoints. If you are noble, I will love you; if you are not, I will not hurt you and myself by hypocritical attentions. If you are true, but not in the same truth with me, cleave to your companions; I will seek my own. I do this not selfishly but humbly and truly. It is alike your interest, and mine, and all men's, however long we have dwelt in lies, to live in truth. Does this sound harsh today? You will soon love what is dictated by your nature as well as mine, and if we follow the truth it will bring us out safe at last—But so may you give these friends pain. Yes, but I cannot sell my liberty and my power, to save their sensibility. Besides, all persons have their moments of reason, when they look out into the region of absolute truth; then will they justify me and do the same thing.

***

Insist on yourself; never imitate. Your own gift you can present every moment with the cumulative force of a whole life's cultivation; but of the adopted talent of another you have only an extemporaneous half possession. That which each can do best, none but his Maker can teach him. No man yet knows what it is, nor can, till that person has exhibited it. Where is the master who could have taught Shakespeare? Where is the master who could have instructed Franklin,[1] or Washington,[2] or Bacon,[3] or Newton? Every great man is an unique. The Scipionism of Scipio[4] is precisely that part he could not borrow. If anybody will tell me whom the great man imitates in the original crisis when he performs a great act, I will tell him who else than himself can teach him. Shakespeare will never be made by the study of Shakespeare. Do that which is assigned thee and thou canst not hope too much or dare too much.

***

1 Benjamin Franklin (1706-90) was an American statesman and diplomat.
2 George Washington (1732-99), American revolutionary general and first American president.
3 Sir Francis Bacon (1561-1626) was an English statesman and writer who originated the scientific method.
4 Scipio Africanus / Scipio the Elder (235-183 BCE) was a Roman statesman and general in the Second Punic War, best known for defeating Hannibal.

Society never advances. It recedes as fast on one side as it gains on the other. Its progress is only apparent like the workers of a treadmill. It undergoes continual changes; it is barbarous, it is civilized, it is christianized, it is rich, it is scientific; but this change is not amelioration. For every thing that is given something is taken.

***

The civilized man has built a coach, but has lost the use of his feet. He is supported on crutches, but lacks so much support of the muscle. He has got a fine Geneva watch, but he has lost the skill to tell the hour by the sun. A Greenwich nautical almanac[1] he has, and so being sure of the information when he wants it, the man in the street does not know a star in the sky. The solstice he does not observe; the equinox he knows as little; and the whole bright calendar of the year is without a dial in his mind. His notebooks impair his memory; his libraries overload his wit; the insurance-office increases the number of accidents; and it may be a question whether machinery does not encumber; whether we have not lost by refinement some energy, by a Christianity entrenched in establishments and forms some vigor of wild virtue. For every stoic was a stoic; but in Christendom where is the Christian?

***

Society is a wave. The wave moves onward, but the water of which it is composed does not. The same particle does not rise from the valley to the ridge. Its unity is only phenomenal. The persons who make up a nation today, die, and their experience with them.

And so the reliance on Property, including the reliance on governments which protect it, is the want of self-reliance. Men have looked away from themselves and at things so long that they have come to esteem what they call the soul's progress, namely, the religious, learned and civil institutions as guards of property, and they depreciate assaults on property. They measure their esteem of each other by what each has, and not by what each is. But a cultivated man becomes ashamed of what he has, out of a new respect for his being. Especially he hates what he has if he see that it is accidental,—came to him by inheritance, or gift, or crime; then he feels that it is not having; it does not belong to him, has no root in him, and merely lies there because no revolution or no robber takes it away. But that which a man is, does always by necessity acquire, and what the man acquires, is permanent and living property, which does not wait the beck of rulers, or mobs,

---

1 An almanac used in the 1700s by most countries to help their sailors navigate through the oceans. Greenwich in London is a center of Maritime history and the location of Greenwich Mean Time.

or revolutions, or fire, or storm, or bankruptcies, but perpetually renews itself wherever the man is put.

***

Ask nothing of men, and, in the endless mutation, thou only firm column must presently appear the upholder of all that surrounds thee. He who knows that power is in the soul, that he is weak only because he has looked for good out of him and elsewhere, and, so perceiving, throws himself unhesitatingly on his thought, instantly rights himself, stands in the erect position, commands his limbs, works miracles; just as a man who stands on his feet is stronger than a man who stands on his head.

***

Nothing can bring you peace but yourself. Nothing can bring you peace but the triumph of principles.

2. Algernon Swinburne, "A Cameo," *Poems and Ballads* (New York: R. Worthington, 1866)

> There was a graven image of Desire
> > Painted with red blood on a ground of gold
> > Passing between the young men and the old,
> And by him Pain, whose body shone like fire,
> And Pleasure with gaunt hands that grasped their hire.
> > Of his left wrist, with fingers clenched and cold,
> > The insatiable Satiety kept hold,
> Walking with feet unshod that pashed the mire.
> The senses and the sorrows and the sins,
> > And the strange loves the suck the breasts of Hate
> Till lips and teeth bite in their sharp indenture,
> Followed like beasts with flap of wings and fins.
> > Death stood aloof behind a gaping grate,
> Upon whose lock was written *Peradventure*.

3. From Richard von Krafft-Ebing, *Psychopathia Sexualis: with Especial Reference to Contrary Sexual Instinct: a Medico-legal Study*, 1886, Trans. Charles Gilbert Chaddock (Philadelphia: F.A. Davis, 1886)

Platonic love is a platitude, a misnomer for "kindred spirits."

Since love implies the presence of sexual desire it can only exist between persons of different sex capable of sexual intercourse. When these conditions are wanting or destroyed, it is replaced by friendship.

The sexual functions of man exercise a very marked influence upon the development and preservation of character.

★★★

Man has beyond doubt the stronger sexual appetite of the two. From the period of pubescence he is instinctively drawn towards woman. His love is sensual, and his choice is strongly prejudiced in favour of physical attractions. A mighty impulse of nature makes him aggressive and impetuous in his courtship. Yet the law of nature does not wholly fill his psychic being. Having won the prize, his love is temporarily eclipsed by other vital and social interests.

Woman, however, if physically and mentally normal, and properly educated, has but little sensual desire. If it were otherwise, marriage and family would be empty words.

★★★

[S]exual consciousness is stronger in woman than in man. Her need of love is great; it is continual not periodical, but her love is more spiritual than sensual. Man primarily loves woman as his wife, and then as the mother of his children; the first place in woman's heart belongs to the father of her child, the second to him as husband. Woman is influenced in her choice more by mental than by physical qualities. As mother she divides her love between offspring and husband. Sensuality is merged in the mother's love. Thereafter the wife accepts marital intercourse not so much as a sensual gratification as a proof of her husband's affection.

Woman loves with her whole soul. To woman love is life, to man it is the joy of life. Misfortune in love bruises the heart of man; but it ruins the life of woman and wrecks her happiness. It is really a psychological question worthy of consideration whether woman can truly love twice in her life. Woman's mind certainly inclines more to monogamy than that of man.

★★★

From the fact that by nature man plays the aggressive *rôle* in sexual life, he is exposed to the danger of overstepping the limits set by law and morality.

The unfaithfulness of the wife, as compared with that of the husband, is morally of much wider bearing, and should always meet with severer punishment at the hands of the law. The unfaithful wife not only dishonours herself, but also her husband and her family, not to speak of the possible uncertainty of paternity.

Natural instincts and social position are frequent causes of disloyalty in man (the husband), whilst the wife is surrounded by many protecting influences.

Sexual intercourse is of different import to the spinster and to the bachelor. Society claims of the latter modesty, but exacts of the former chastity as well. Modern civilization conceded only to the wife that exalted position, in which woman sexually furthers the moral interests of society.

The ultimate aim, the ideal, of woman, even when she is dragged in the mire of vice, ever is and will be marriage. Woman, as *Mantegazza*[1] properly observes, seeks not only gratification of sensual desires, but also protection and support for herself and her offspring. No matter how sensual many may be, unless also thoroughly depraved, he seeks for a consort only that woman whose chastity he cannot doubt.

***

Woman far surpasses man in the natural psychology of love, partly because evolution and training have made love her proper element, and partly because she is animated by more refined feelings *(Mantegazza)*.

Even the best of breeding concedes to man that he looks upon woman mainly as a means by which to satisfy the craving of his natural instinct, though it confines him only to the woman of his choice. Thus civilization establishes a binding social contract which is called marriage, and grants by legal statutes protection and support to the wife and her issue.

***

A particular species of excessive sexual urge may be found in females in whom a most impulsive desire for sexual intercourse with certain men imperatively demands gratification. No doubt "unrequited love" for another man may often affect the married woman who does not either psychically or physically (because of impotence of the husband) experience connubial satisfaction; but the normal, untainted wife guided by ethical reason knows how to conquer herself.

***

... A young woman, mother of three children, with a blameless past, but daughter of a lunatic, tells her husband one day openly that she is in love with a certain young man and that she would kill herself if her intimate relations with him were interfered with. She begs permission to live with him for six months in order to quench the fire of her passion, when she would return to her family again. Husband and children have no place in her heart with her present love. The husband took her to a foreign country and placed her there under medical treatment.

This pathological love of married women for other men is a phenomenon in the domain of *psychopathia sexualis* which sadly stands in need of scientific explanation. The author has had the opportunity of observing

---

1   Paolo Mantegazza (1831-1910) was an Italian writer (among other professions) who wrote about the physiology of love and sexual relations.

five cases belonging to this category. The pathological conditions were paroxysmal, in one case repeatedly recurrent; but always sharply distinct from the unaffected, healthy period, during which deep sorrow and contrition over the occurrence were manifested. But it was the sorrow over an unavoidable fatality caused by psychically abnormal conditions.

Whilst the pathological conditions lasted, absolute indifference, even hatred, prevailed towards husband and children; and an utter want of understanding of the bearings and consequences of the scandalous behaviour, jeopardizing the honour and dignity of wife and family, were noticeable.

★★★

In this condition there is perverse emotional colouring of the sexual ideas. Ideas physiologically and psychologically accompanied by feelings of disgust, give rise to pleasurable sexual feelings; and the abnormal association finds expression in passionate, uncontrollable emotion. The practical results are perverse acts (perversion of the sexual instinct). This is more easily the case if the pleasurable feelings, increased to passionate intensity, inhibit any opposing ideas with corresponding feelings of disgust; or the influence of such opposing conceptions may be rendered impossible on account of the absence or loss of all ideas or morality, aesthetics and law. This loss, however, is only too frequently found where the wellspring of ethical ideas and feelings (a normal sexual instinct) has been poisoned from the beginning.

4. From Mary A. Livermore, Amelia E. Barr, and Rose Terry Cooke, "Women's Views of Divorce," *North American Review* 150 (1890): 115-17, 120-21, 126-27

Mary A. Livermore[1]

★★★

The question of marriage and divorce laws, and their reformation, is one in which women are vitally interested, for they are generally the deepest sufferers from the laws' immoral and unequal action, and for them there is the least redress. Whatever legislation may be undertaken, whether by concerted State action or through a national constitutional amendment, concerns both sexes equally, and both should have equal inference in directing it. Very many of the evils that have sprung up in the marriage relation have originated in the fact that one sex has been the sole dictator of laws of marriage and divorce, and women have never been consulted as to their wisdom, or their adaptability to women's own circumstances, or their approval of them.

---

1 American journalist (1820-1905) who was a staunch advocate for women's rights.

The husband has legal control of the person of the wife; her services belong to him, and have no money value. She is expected to work for food, shelter, and clothing, and is thus made a pauperized dependent on her husband. Whatever gains accrue from her unpaid labor become his property. If she has leisure and ability to engage in money-making employments after performing the household labor, many of the States of the Union give her earnings also to the husband. Four women of prominence in literary and professional life, whose names would be familiar to most of my readers, have been compelled to apply to the courts for protection against the husbands who would have robbed them of their earnings, while they were charged with the maintenance and education of the children. The impecunious condition of wives, not alone among those whose husbands are men of small incomes, but among many whose means are ample, is one of the most fruitful sources of restlessness and unhappiness in married life, and is one of the underlying causes of frequent divorce.

Only six of the United States allow the married mother to be an equal owner and guardian of the minor children with their father. In all other States the father is their sole owner and guardian. If the mother has no ownership in her little children, whom she wins in the valley of death, at the risk of her own life, she is, indeed, pauperized, most abject, most wretched. Ah, if men were not, in most instances, better than the laws they have made for women, this would be Pandemonium itself! A wife and mother should always be mistress of herself, and never the slave of another, not even when that other is her husband and the slavery is founded on her undying love.

***

Amelia E. Barr[1]

***

In a woman adultery is rarely a calculating offence. It is said, "The women who deliberates is lost." The truth is, women are lost because they do not deliberate. Thackeray[2] had the profoundest insight into a woman's heart when he made the miserable wife of Barnes Newcome[3] leave her husband and home in an hour when she had no such intention. Cruelly tempted, perplexed and bewildered, when passion is stronger than reason, women do not think of consequences, but go, blindfold, headlong to their ruin. Are such women likely to be kept moral by any legal enactment? As well try to deter or encourage them

---

1 British-American novelist (1831-1919).

2 William Makepeace Thackeray (1811-63) was an English novelist primarily known for his satirical work about English society, *Vanity Fair* (1848).

3 A character in Thackeray's novel *The Newcomes* (1855).

by the laws of gravitation. Prohibition never yet prevented crime: of what value is it, then, as punishment?

***

What is the effect of divorce on the integrity of the family? It is disintegrating. It is disastrous. The home is no longer sacred; the world has made a thoroughfare through it. Its effect upon the family is so evil that this cause alone may be depended upon to restrain divorce. For the paternal and the maternal love does not die with the conjugal love. A father and mother who would not fear the disabilities of divorce for themselves will bear a great deal ere they cast its stigma upon their sons and daughters. Yet when a family has come to a point where its heads are at two, where love is dead, and dislike or indifference brings for the ill words and ill deeds, divorce—so far as the family is concerned—has already taken place. It is even highly probable that the children will find the dissolution of a wretched condition some influence more favorable to their happiness and development. Nothing, at any rate, can be worse for them than a situation in which they must either become passionate partisans or else practice a constant indifference and a public deception....

Rose Terry Cooke[1]

***

But if divorce for any reason is degrading and demoralizing to a man, what must it be to a woman? For her the whole world has no mercy; there is no forgetfulness of her sin, even if she repent in the bitterness of death; and deeper woe than the world's scorn awaits her, for I believe the worst woman on earth cannot be forever separated from her children without agony sooner or later. In the first whirl of passion she may forget them, but passion flies like summer tempest and leaves devastation along its track. Her children's sweet, innocent eyes must forever haunt her; their frighted and saddened calls ring forever in her ear; and she will know in the blackness of despair that she has committed woman's unpardonable sin, for which society will allow her no place for repentance, though she seek it carefully and with tears of blood.

***

But when the mother goes, worse want ensures; then indeed their home is gone; their hearts are full to overflowing with earth's worst nostalgia; there are no fond kisses for those quivering lips at night; no sleep-songs to lull their wakeful weariness; no soothing of their sharp childish woes, "as one whom his mother comforteth"; no cool, soft hand on the forehead hot with fever or aching with fatigue. Oh! worst of all earth's

---

1 American writer (1827-92).

innumerable losses, no mother! Nor can any tell them the sweet story that she is in heaven awaiting them, or lead them to deck the sleeping-place of her dear dead body. She is worse than dead: she is divorced!

The family is the unit that is the germ of the state, the seed of civilization: where divorce so rends it and scatters its fragments abroad, can any philosophy, or any stupidity, or the crassest ignorance, deny that divorce destroys and obliterates its integrity?

As far as my knowledge extends there is no country and no church where "absolute prohibition of divorce" exists. The lofty stand-point of the Roman Church permits an absolute separation of the two parties for certain reason, without power of remarriage; ...

5. From Elizabeth Cady Stanton, "The Solitude of Self," *Address to the U.S. Congressional Committee of the Judiciary Hearing, 18 January 1892*

The point I wish plainly to bring before you on this occasion is the individuality of each human soul; our Protestant idea, the right of individual conscience and judgment; our republican idea, individual citizenship. In discussing the rights of woman, we are to consider, first, what belongs to her as an individual, in a world of her own, the arbiter of her own destiny, an imaginary Robinson Crusoe,[1] with her woman Friday[2] on a solitary island. Her rights under such circumstances are to use all her faculties for her own safety and happiness.

Secondly, if we consider her as a citizen, as a member of a great nation, she must have the same rights as all other members, according to the fundamental principles of our government.

Thirdly, viewed as a woman, an equal factor in civilization, her rights and duties are still the same; individual happiness and development.

Fourthly, it is only the incidental relations of life, such as mother, wife, sister, daughter, that may involve some special duties and training. In the usual discussion in regard to woman's sphere, such men as Herbert Spencer,[3] Frederic Harrison[4] and Grant Allen,[5] uniformly subordinate her rights and duties as an individual, as a citizen, as a woman, to the necessities of these incidental relations, neither of which a large class of women may ever assume. In discussing the sphere of man, we do not decide his rights as an individual, as a citizen, as a man,

---

1 Character in *Robinson Crusoe* by Daniel Defoe (1659-1731), first published in 1719, who is a castaway lost for 28 years.

2 Friday was a male character in *Robinson Crusoe* who escapes prison and becomes Crusoe's companion.

3 See Appendix B2.

4 British lawyer and historian (1831-1923).

5 Canadian-born writer (1848-99).

by his duties as a father, a husband, a brother or a son, relations he may never fill. Moreover, he would be better fitted for these very relations, and whatever special work he might choose to do to earn his bread, by the complete development of all his faculties as an individual.

Just so with woman. The education that will fit her to discharge the duties in the largest sphere of human usefulness will best fit her for whatever special work she may be compelled to do.

The isolation of every human soul, and the necessity of self-dependence, must give each individual the right to choose his own surroundings.

The strongest reason for giving woman all the opportunities for higher education, for the full development of her faculties, forces of mind and body; for giving her the most enlarged freedom of thought and action; a complete emancipation from all forms of bondage, of custom, dependence, superstition; from all the crippling influences of fear—is the solitude and personal responsibility of her own individual life. The strongest reason why we ask for woman a voice in the government under which she lives; in the religion she is asked to believe; equality in social life, where she is the chief factor; a place in the trades and professions, where she may earn her bread, is because of her birthright to self-sovereignty; because, as an individual, she must rely on herself. No matter how much women prefer to lean, to be protected and supported, nor how much men desire to have them to do so, they must make the voyage of life alone, and for safety in an emergency, they must know something of the laws of navigation. To guide our own craft, we must be captain, pilot, engineer; with chart and compass to stand at the wheel; to watch the winds and waves, and know when to take in the sail, and to read the signs in the firmament over all. It matters not whether the solitary voyager is man or woman; nature, having endowed them equally, leaves them to their own skill and judgment in the hour of danger, and, if not equal to the occasion, alike they perish.

To appreciate the importance of fitting every human soul for independent action, think for a moment of the immeasurable solitude of self. We come into the world alone, unlike all who have gone before us; we leave it alone, under circumstances peculiar to ourselves. No mortal ever has been, no mortal ever will be like the soul just launched on the sea of life. There can never again be just such a combination of prenatal influences; never again just such environments as make up the infancy, youth and manhood of this one. Nature never repeats herself, and the possibilities of one human soul will never be found in another. No one has ever found two blades of ribbon grass alike, and no one will ever find two human beings alike. Seeing, then, what must be the infinite diversity in human character, we can in a measure appreciate the loss to a nation when any large class of the people is uneducated and unrepresented in the government.

To throw obstacles in the way of a complete education is like putting out the eyes; to deny the rights of property, like cutting off the hands. To deny political equality is to rob the ostracised of all self-respect; of credit in the market place; of recompense in the world of work; of a voice in those who make and administer the law; a choice in the jury before whom they are tried, and in the judge who decides their punishment. Shakespeare's play of "Titus Andronicus"[1] contains a terrible satire on woman's position in the 19th century. Rude men (the play tells us) seized the king's daughter, cut out her tongue, cut off her hands, and then bade her go call for water and wash her hands. What a picture of woman's position. Robbed of her natural rights, handicapped by law and custom at every turn, yet compelled to fight her own battles and in the emergencies of life to fall back on herself for protection.

The girl of sixteen, thrown on the world to support herself, to make her own place in society, to resist the temptations that surround her and maintain a spotless integrity, must do all this by native force or superior education. She does not acquire this power by being trained to trust others and distrust herself. If she wearies of the struggle, finding it hard work to swim up stream, and allows herself to drift with the current, she will find plenty of company, but not one to share her misery in the hour of her deepest humiliation. If she tries to retrieve her position, to conceal the past, her life is hedged about with fears lest willing hands should tear the veil from what she fain would hide. Young and friendless, she knows the bitter solitude of self.

How the little courtesies of life on the surface of society, deemed so important from man towards woman, fade into utter insignificance in view of the deeper tragedies in which she must play her part alone, where no human aid is possible!

The young wife and mother, at the head of some establishment, with a kind husband to shield her from the adverse winds of life, with wealth, fortune and position, has a certain harbor of safety, secure against the ordinary ills of life. But to manage a household, have a desirable influence in society, keep her friends and the affections of her husband, train her children and servants well, she must have rare common sense, wisdom, diplomacy, and a knowledge of human nature. To do all this, she needs the cardinal virtues and the strong points of character that the most successful statesman possesses. An uneducated woman trained to dependence, with no resources in herself, must make a failure of any position in life. But society says women do not need a knowledge of the world, the liberal training that experience in public life must give, all the advantages of collegiate education, but when for the lack of all this, the woman's happiness is wrecked, alone she bears her humiliation; and the

---

1 Tragedy by Shakespeare, probably written in the early 1590s.

solitude of the weak and the ignorant is indeed pitiable. In the wild chase for the prizes of life, they are ground to powder.

***

Nothing strengthens the judgment and quickens the conscience like individual responsibility; nothing adds such dignity to character as the recognition of one's self-sovereignty; the right to an equal place, everywhere conceded; a place earned by personal merit, not an artificial attainment by inheritance, wealth, family and position. Seeing, then, that the responsibilities of life rest equally on man and woman, that their destiny is the same, they need the same preparation for time and eternity. The talk of sheltering woman from the fierce storms of life is the sheerest mockery, for they beat on her from every point of the compass, just as they do on man, and with more fatal results, for he has been trained to protect himself, to resist, and to conquer. Such are the facts in human experience, the responsibilities of individual sovereignty. Rich and poor, intelligent and ignorant, wise and foolish, virtuous and vicious, man and woman; it is ever the same, each soul must depend wholly on itself.

Whatever the theories may be of woman's dependence on man, in the supreme moments of her life, he cannot bear her burdens. Alone she goes to the gates of death to give life to every man that is born into the world; no one can share her fears, no one can mitigate her pangs; and if her sorrow is greater than she can bear, alone she passes beyond the gates into the vast unknown.

***

What special school training could have prepared these women for this sublime moment in their lives? In times like this, humanity rises above all college curriculums, and recognizes nature as the greatest of all teachers in the hour of danger and death. Women are already the equals of men in the whole realm of thought, in art, science, literature and government. With telescopic vision they explore the starry firmament and bring back the history of the planetary spheres. With chart and compass they pilot ships across the mighty deep, and with skillful fingers send electric messages around the world. In galleries of art the beauties of nature and the virtues of humanity are immortalized by them on canvas, and by their inspired touch dull blocks of marble are transformed into angels of light. In music they speak again the language of Mendelssohn,[1] Beethoven,[2] Chopin,[3] Schumann,[4] and

---

1 Felix Mendelssohn (1809–47) was a German composer and pianist.
2 Ludwig van Beethoven (1770-1827) was a German composer and pianist.
3 Frederic Chopin (1810-49) was a Polish composer and pianist.
4 Franz Schumann (1810-56) was a German composer and critic.

are worthy interpreters of their great thoughts. The poetry and novels of the century are theirs, and they have touched the keynote of reform, in religion, politics and social life. They fill the editor's and professor's chair, and plead at the bar of justice; walk the wards of the hospital, and speak from the pulpit and the platform. Such is the type of womanhood that an enlightened public sentiment welcomes to-day, and such the triumph of the facts of life over the false theories of the past.

Is it, then, consistent to hold the developed woman of this day within the same narrow political limits as the dame with the spinning-wheel and knitting-needle occupied in the past? No! no! Machinery has taken the labors of woman, as well as man, on its tireless shoulders, the loom and the spinning wheel are but dreams of the past; the pen, the brush, the easel, the chisel, have taken their places, while the hopes and ambitions of women are essentially changed.

We see reason sufficient in the outer conditions of human beings for individual liberty and development, but when we consider the self-dependence of every human soul we see the need of courage, judgment and the exercise of every faculty of mind and body, strengthened and developed by use, in woman.

Whatever may be said of man's protecting power in ordinary conditions, amid all the terrible disasters by land and sea, in the supreme moments of danger, alone woman must ever meet the horrors of the situation. The Angel of Death even makes no royal pathway for her. Man's love and sympathy enter only into the sunshine of our lives. In that solemn solitude of self, that links us with the immeasurable and the eternal, each soul lives alone forever. A recent writer says:

I remember once, in crossing the Atlantic, to have gone upon the deck of the ship at midnight, when a dense black cloud enveloped the sky, and the great deep was roaring madly under the lashes of demoniac winds. My feeling was not of danger or fear (which is a base surrender of the immortal soul) but of utter desolation and loneliness; a little speck of life shut in by a tremendous darkness. Again I remember to have climbed the slopes of the Swiss Alps, up beyond the point where vegetation ceases, and the stunted conifers no longer struggle against the unfeeling blasts. Around me lay a huge confusion of rocks, out of which the gigantic ice peaks shot into the measureless blue of the heavens; and again my only feeling was the awful solitude.

And yet, there is a solitude which each and every one of us has always carried with him, more inaccessible than the ice-cold mountains, more profound than the midnight sea; the solitude of self. Our inner being which we call ourself, no eye nor touch of man or angel has ever pierced. It is more hidden than the caves of the gnome; the sacred adytum[1] of the oracle; the hidden chamber of Eleusinian mystery,[2] for to it only Omniscience is permitted to enter.

Such is individual life. Who, I ask you, can take, dare take on himself the rights, the duties, the responsibilities of another human soul?

6. From "Wife Who Retains Her Maiden Name and Won't Obey," *St. Louis Post-Dispatch*, 14 May 1895

When Miss Lydia Kingsmill Commander married Rev. Herbert Newton Casson ... [s]he remained Miss Lydia Kingsmill. She made no promises of obedience. She read a statement of her position; the groom likewise read a statement setting forth his ideas of advanced matrimony ... united, yet with names unchanged.

***

... [T]he bride and groom have written and made public the following separate and joint statements:

The Conditions

"Having been joined together in the holy estate of matrimony according to the ideas advanced so-called, that we both entertain, we respond to the invitation to place on record our views with regard to union of hearts and lives in this age of enlightenment. We were agreed before our marriage that anything that fell short of soul-union was desecration. For the woman to give herself to the man in return for her support was to us a revolting idea. The rule that the woman change her name we regarded as another mark of the servitude of the wife to the husband; the very identity of the woman is lost and the name and title of the wife marks her degraded condition matrimonially, in that anyone can tell at once whether or not the woman is married and whose property she is. We were agreed that the equality of the sexes demanded that the woman retain her own name as an absolutely indisputable possession. With all this thoroughly understood between us, we agreed to unite our lives as man and wife."

By civil ceremony, then, there were married the Rev. Herbert N. Casson and Miss Lydia Kingsmill Commander. When the words were pronounced by the Judge who performed the ceremony, "By the power of the authority vested in me, I pronounce you man and wife,"

---

1 An inner sanctum; the most holy place in any house of worship.
2 Greek initiation ceremony to honor Demeter, the Greek goddess of the harvest, and Persephone, Greek queen of the underworld and daughter of Demeter and Zeus.

there walked from the hall, not the Rev. and Mrs. Herbert N. Casson, but Rev. Herbert N. Casson and Mrs. Lydia Kingsmill Commander. Both were equal when they walked to the hall. That equality was preserved when they left it and will be to the finish of the chapter.

***

The Bride's Statement

"... [E]ach should preserve his or her own individuality, developing all that lies within the nature to its highest capabilities, neither demanding aught of the other, but each seeking the welfare and happiness of the other.

"Believing that such affinity of heart and mind and soul does exist between us ... promising to share with him whatsoever the changes and chances of life may bring ... so long, and only so long, as love shall bind our hearts, and our souls are blended as one.

"Self-reverent each and reverencing each distinct in individualities, yet like each other, even as those who love."

The Groom's Statement

"... Marriage is ... not the destruction of individuality, but the union of liberty and co-operation. I do not, by virtue of this ceremony, claim any right which love does not freely give.

"I wish to marry a free-hearted woman, not a slave.

"... unless love is spontaneous and free it is not love."

***

"I pledge myself never to let this marriage interfere with the life work she has chosen....

"I will help her to make herself. Her own, to keep or give, to live and learn and be all that develops highest womanhood.

"... free from the objectionable thralldom that modern marriage usually means to the woman...."

7. From Charlotte Perkins Gilman, *Women and Economics* (Boston: Small, Maynard, 1898)

IX

THE main justification for the subjection of women, which is commonly advanced, is the alleged advantage to motherhood resultant from her extreme specialization to the uses of maternity under this condition.

There are two weak points in this position. One is that the advantage to motherhood cannot be proved: the other, that it is not the uses of maternity to which she is specialized, but the uses of sex-indulgence. So far from the economic dependence of women working in the interests of motherhood, it is the steadily acting cause of a pathological maternity and a decreasing birth-rate....

***

To meet this, it is necessary to show that our highly specialized motherhood is not so advantageous as believed; that it is below rather than above the efficacy of motherhood in other species; that its deficiency is due to the sexuo-economic relation; that the restoration of economic freedom to the female will improve motherhood; and, finally, to indicate in some sort the lines of social and individual development along which this improvement may be "practically" manifested.

***

There does not appear, in the care and education of the child as given by the mother, any special superiority in human maternity. Measuring woman first in direct comparison of her reproductive processes with those of other animals, she does not fulfill this function so easily or so well as they. Measuring her educative processes by interpersonal comparison, the few admittedly able mothers with the many painfully unable ones, she seems more lacking, if possible, than in the other branch. The gain in human education thus far has not been acquired or distributed through the mother, but through men and single women; and there is nothing in the achievements of human motherhood to prove that it is for the advantage of the race to have women give all their time to it. Giving all their time to it does not improve it either in quantity or quality. The woman who works is usually a better reproducer than the woman who does not. And the woman who does not work is not proportionately a better educator.

An extra-terrestrial sociologist, studying human life and hearing for the first time of our so-called "maternal sacrifice" as a means of benefiting the species, might be touched and impressed by the idea. "How beautiful!" he would say. "How exquisitely pathetic and tender! One-half of humanity surrendering all other human interests and activities to concentrate its time, strength, and devotion upon the functions of maternity! To bear and rear the majestic race to which they can never fully belong! To live vicariously forever, through their sons, the daughters being only another vicarious link! What a supreme and magnificent martyrdom!" And he would direct his researches toward discovering what system was used to develop and perfect this sublime consecration of half the race to the perpetuation of the other half. He would view with intense and pathetic interest the endless procession of girls, born human as their brothers were, but marked down at once as "female— abortive type—only use to produce males." He would expect to see this "sex sacrificed to reproductive necessities," yet gifted with human consciousness and intelligence, rise grandly to the occasion, and strive to fit itself in every way for its high office. He would expect to find society commiserating the sacrifice, and honoring above all the glorious creature whose life was to be sunk utterly in the lives of others, and using every force properly to rear and fully to fit these functionaries for their noble office. Alas for the extra-terrestrial sociologist and his natural expectations! After exhaustive study, finding nothing of these things, he would return to Mars or Saturn or wherever he came from, marveling within himself at the vastness of the human paradox.

If the position of woman is to be justified by the doctrine of maternal sacrifice, surely society, or the individual, or both, would make some preparation for it. No such preparation is made. Society recognizes no such function. Premiums have been sometimes paid for large numbers of children, but they were paid to the fathers of them. The elaborate social machinery which constitutes our universal marriage market has no department to assist or advance motherhood. On the contrary, it is directly inimical to it, so that in our society life motherhood means direct loss, and is avoided by the social devotee. And the individual? Surely here right provision will be made. Young women, glorying in their prospective duties, their sacred and inalienable office, their great sex-martyrdom to race-advantage, will be found solemnly preparing for this work. What do we find? We find our young women reared in an attitude which is absolutely unconscious of and often injurious to their coming motherhood,—an irresponsible, indifferent, ignorant class of beings, so far as motherhood is concerned. They are fitted to attract the other sex for economic uses or, at most, for mutual gratification, but not for motherhood. They are reared in unbroken ignorance of their supposed principal duties, knowing nothing of these duties till they enter upon them.

This is as though all men were to be soldiers with the fate of nations in their hands; and no man told or taught a word of war or military service until he entered the battle-field! The education of young women has no department of maternity. It is considered indelicate to give this consecrated functionary any previous knowledge of her sacred duties. This most important and wonderful of human functions is left from age to age in the hands of absolutely untaught women. It is tacitly supposed to be fulfilled by the mysterious working of what we call "the divine instinct of maternity." Maternal instinct is a very respectable and useful instinct common to most animals. It is "divine" and "holy" only as all the laws of nature are divine and holy; and it is such only when it works to the right fulfillment of its use. If the race-preservative processes are to be held more sacred than the self-preservative processes, we must admit all the functions and faculties of reproduction to the same degree of reverence,—the passion of the male for the female as well as the passion of the mother for her young. And if, still further, we are to honor the race-preservative processes most in their highest and latest development, which is the only comparison to be made on a natural basis, we should place the great, disinterested, social function of education far above the second-selfishness of individual maternal functions. Maternal instinct, merely as an instinct, is unworthy of our superstitious reverence. It should be measured only as a means to an end, and valued in proportion to its efficacy.

★★★

Before a man enters a trade, art, or profession, he studies it. He qualifies himself for the duties he is to undertake. He would be held a presuming impostor if he engaged in work he was not fitted to do, and his failure would mark him instantly with ridicule and reproach. In the more important professions, especially in those dealing with what we call "matters of life and death," the shipmaster or pilot, doctor or druggist, is required not only to study his business, but to pass an examination under those who have already become past masters, and obtain a certificate or a diploma or some credential to show that he is fit to be intrusted with the direct responsibility for human life.

Women enter a position which gives into their hands direct responsibility for the life or death of the whole human race with neither study nor experience, with no shadow of preparation or guarantee of capability. So far as they give it a thought, they fondly imagine that this mysterious "maternal instinct" will see them through. Instruction, if needed, they will pick up when the time comes: experience they will acquire as the children appear. "I guess I know how to bring up children!" cried the resentful old lady who was being advised: "I've buried seven!" The record of untrained instinct as a maternal faculty in the human race is to be read on the rows and rows of little gravestones which crowd our cemeteries. The experience gained by practising on the child is frequently buried with it.

No, the maternal sacrifice theory will not bear examination. As a sex specialized to reproduction, giving up all personal activity, all honest independence, all useful and progressive economic service for her glorious consecration to the uses of maternity, the human female has little to show in the way of results which can justify her position. Neither the enormous percentage of children lost by death nor the low average health of those who survive, neither physical nor mental progress, give any proof of race advantage from the maternal sacrifice....

★★★

Worse than the check set upon the physical activities of women has been the restriction of their power to think and judge for themselves. The extended use of the human will and its decisions is conditioned upon free, voluntary action. In her rudimentary position, woman was denied the physical freedom which underlies all knowledge, she was denied the mental freedom which is the path to further wisdom, she was denied the moral freedom of being mistress of her own action and of learning by the merciful law of consequences what was right and what was wrong; and she has remained, perforce, undeveloped in the larger judgment of ethics.

Her moral sense is large enough, morbidly large, because in this tutelage she is always being praised or blamed for her conduct. She lives in a forcing-bed of sensitiveness to moral distinctions, but the broad judgment that alone can guide and govern this sensitiveness she has not. Her contribution to moral progress has added to the anguish of the world the fierce sense of sin and shame, the desperate desire to do right, the fear of wrong; without giving it the essential help of a practical wisdom and a regulated will. Inheriting with each generation the accumulating forces of our social nature, set back in each generation by the conditions of the primitive human female, women have become vividly self-conscious centers of moral impulse, but poor guides as to the conduct which alone can make that impulse useful and build the habit of morality into the constitution of the race.

Recognizing her intense feeling on moral lines, and seeing in her the rigidly preserved virtues of faith, submission, and self-sacrifice,—qualities which in the Dark Ages were held to be the first of virtues,—we have agreed of late years to call woman the moral superior of man. But the ceaseless growth of human life, social life, has developed in him new virtues, later, higher, more needful; and the moral nature of woman, as maintained in this rudimentary stage by her economic dependence, is a continual check to the progress of the human soul. The main feature of her life—the restriction of her range of duty to the love and service of her own immediate family—acts upon us continually as a retarding influence, hindering the expansion of the spirit of social love and service on which our very lives depend. It keeps the moral standard of the patriarchal era still before us, and blinds our eyes to the full duty of man.

An intense self-consciousness, born of the ceaseless contact of close personal relation; an inordinate self-interest, bred by the constant personal attention and service of this relation; a feverish, torturing, moral sensitiveness, without the width and clarity of vision of a full-grown moral sense; a thwarted will, used to meek surrender, cunning evasion, or futile rebellion; a childish, wavering, short-range judgment, handicapped by emotion; a measureless devotion to one's own sex relatives, and a maternal passion swollen with the full strength of the great social heart, but denied social expression,—such psychic qualities as these, born in us all, are the inevitable result of the sexuo-economic relation.

It is not alone upon woman, and, through her, upon the race, that the ill-effects may be observed. Man, as master, has suffered from his position also. The lust for power and conquest, natural to the male of any species, has been fostered in him to an enormous degree by this cheap and easy lordship. His dominance is not that of one chosen as best fitted to rule or of one ruling by successful competition with "foemen worthy of his steel"; but it is a sovereignty based on the accident of sex, and holding over such helpless and inferior dependents as could not question or oppose. The easy superiority that needs no striving to maintain it; the temptation to cruelty always begotten by irresponsible power; the pride and self-will which surely accompany it,—these qualities have been bred into the souls of men by their side of the relation. When man's place was maintained by brute force, it made him more brutal: when his place was maintained by purchase, by the power of economic necessity, then he grew into the merciless use of such power as distinguishes him to-day.

Another giant evil engendered by this relation is what we call selfishness. Social life tends to reduce this feeling, which is but a belated individualism; but the sexuo-economic relation fosters and develops it. To have a whole human creature consecrated to his direct personal service, to pleasing and satisfying him in every way possible,—this has kept man selfish beyond the degree incidental to our stage of social growth. Even in our artificial society life men are more forbearing and considerate, more polite and kind, than they are at home. Pride, cruelty, and selfishness are the vices of the master; and these have been kept strong in the bosom of the family through the false position of woman. And every human soul is born, an impressionable child, into the close presence of these conditions. Our men must live in the ethics of a civilized, free, industrial, democratic age; but they are born and trained in the moral atmosphere of a primitive patriarchate. No wonder that we are all somewhat slow to rise to the full powers and privileges of democracy, to feel full social honor and social duty, while every soul of us is reared in this stronghold of ancient and outgrown emotions,—the economically related family.

So we may trace from the sexuo-economic relation of our species not only definite evils in psychic development, bred severally in men and women, and transmitted indifferently to their offspring, but the innate perversion of character resultant from the moral miscegenation of two so diverse souls,—the unfailing shadow and distortion which has darkened and twisted the spirit of man from its beginnings. We have been injured in body and in mind by the too dissimilar traits inherited from our widely separated parents, but nowhere is the injury more apparent than in its ill effects upon the moral nature of the race.

Yet here, as in the other evil results of the sexuo-economic relation, we can see the accompanying good that made the condition necessary in its time; and we can follow the beautiful results of our present changes with comforting assurance. A healthy, normal moral sense will be ours, freed from its exaggerations and contradictions; and, with that clear perception, we shall no longer conceive of the ethical process as something outside of and against nature, but as the most natural thing in the world.

Where now we strive and agonize after impossible virtues, we shall then grow naturally and easily into those very qualities; and we shall not even think of them as especially commendable. Where our progress hitherto has been warped and hindered by the retarding influence of surviving rudimentary forces, it will flow on smoothly and rapidly when both men and women stand equal in economic relation. When the mother of the race is free, we shall have a better world, by the easy right of birth and by the calm, slow, friendly forces of social evolution.

8. From Thorstein Veblen, *Theory of the Leisure Class* (New York: Macmillan, 1899)

Chapter IV: "Conspicuous Consumption"

In what has been said of the evolution of the vicarious leisure class and its differentiation from the general body of the working classes, reference has been made to a further division of labour,—that between different servant classes. One portion of the servant class, chiefly those persons whose occupation is vicarious leisure, come to undertake a new, subsidiary range of duties—the vicarious consumption of goods. The most obvious form in which this consumption occurs is seen in the wearing of liveries and the occupation of spacious servants' quarters. Another, scarcely less obtrusive or less effective form of vicarious consumption, and a much more widely prevalent one, is the consumption of food, clothing, dwelling, and furniture by the lady and the rest of the domestic establishment.

★★★

With the disappearance of servitude, the number of vicarious consumers attached to any one gentleman tends, on the whole, to decrease. The like is of course true, and perhaps in a still higher degree, of the number of dependents who perform vicarious leisure for him. In a general way, though not wholly nor consistently, these two groups coincide. The dependent who was first delegated for these duties was the wife, or the chief wife; and, as would be expected, in the later development of the institution, when the number of persons by whom these duties are customarily performed gradually narrows, the wife remains the last. In the higher grades of society a large volume of both these kinds of service is required; and here the wife is of course still assisted in the work by a more or less numerous corps of menials. But as we descend the social scale, the point is presently reached where the duties of vicarious leisure and consumption devolve upon the wife alone. In the communities of the Western culture, this point is at present found among the lower middle class.

And here occurs a curious inversion. It is a fact of common observation that in this lower middle class there is no pretence of leisure on the part of the head of household. Through force of circumstances it has fallen into disuse. But the middle-class wife still carries on the business of vicarious leisure, for the good name of the household and its master. In descending the social scale in any modern industrial community, the primary fact—the conspicuous leisure of the master of the household—disappears at a relatively high point. The head of the middle-class household has been reduced by economic circumstances to turn his hand to gaining a livelihood by occupations which often partake largely of the character of industry, as in the case of the ordinary business man of to-day. But the derivative fact—the vicarious leisure and consumption rendered by the wife, and the auxiliary vicarious performance of leisure by menials—remains in vogue as a conventionality which the demands of reputability will not suffer to be slighted. It is by no means an uncommon spectacle to find a man applying himself to work with the utmost assiduity, in order that his wife may in due form render for him that degree of vicarious leisure which the common sense of the time demands.

The leisure rendered by the wife in such cases is, of course, not a simple manifestation of idleness or indolence. It almost invariably occurs disguised under some form of work or household duties or social amenities, which prove on analysis to serve little or no ulterior end beyond showing that she does not and need not occupy herself with anything that is gainful or that is of substantial use. As has already been noticed under the head of manners, the greater part of the customary round of domestic cares to which the middle-class housewife gives her time and effort is of this character. Not that the results of her attention to household matters, of a decorative and mundificatory[1] character, are not pleasing to the sense of men trained in middle-class proprieties; but the taste to which these effects of household adornment and tidiness appeal is a taste which has been formed under the selective guidance of a canon of property that demands just these evidences of wasted effort. The effects are pleasing to us chiefly because we have been taught to find them pleasing. There goes into these domestic duties much solicitude for proper combination of form and colour, and for other ends that are to be classed as aesthetic in the proper sense of the term; and it is

---

1 Pertaining to cleansing or purifying.

not denied that effects having some substantial aesthetic value are sometimes attained. Pretty much all that is here insisted on is that, as regards these amenities of life, the housewife's efforts are under the guidance of traditions that have been shaped by the law of conspicuously wasteful expenditure of time and substance. If beauty or comfort is achieved,— and it is a more or less fortuitous circumstance if they are,—they must be achieved by means and methods that commend themselves to the great economic law of wasted effort. The more reputable, "presentable" portion of middle-class household paraphernalia are, on the one hand, items of conspicuous consumption, and on the other hand, apparatus for putting in evidence the vicarious leisure rendered by the housewife.

The requirement of vicarious consumption at the hands of the wife continues in force even at a lower point in the pecuniary scale than the requirement of vicarious leisure. At a point below which little if any pretence of wasted effort, in ceremonial cleanness and the like, is observable and where there is assuredly no conscious attempt at ostensible leisure, decency still requires the wife to consume some goods conspicuously for the reputability of the household and its head. So that, as the latter-day outcome of this evolution of an archaic institution, the wife, who was at the outset the drudge and chattel of the man, both in fact and in theory,—the producer of goods for him to consume—has become the ceremonial consumer of goods which he produces. But she still quite unmistakably remains his chattel in theory; for the habitual rendering of vicarious leisure and consumption is the abiding mark of the unfree servant.

This vicarious consumption practiced by the household of the middle and lower classes can not be counted as a direct expression of the leisure-class scheme of life, since the household of this pecuniary grade does not belong with the leisure class. It is rather that the leisure-class scheme of life here comes to an expression at the second remove. The leisure class stands at the head of the social structure in point of reputability; and its manner of life and its standards of worth therefore afford the norm of reputability for the community. The observance of these standards, in some degree of approximation, becomes incumbent upon all classes lower in the scale. In modern civilized communities the lines of demarcation between social classes have grown vague and transient, and wherever this happens the norm of reputability imposed by the upper class extends its coercive influence with but slight hindrance down through the social structure of the lowest strata. The result is that the members of each stratum accept as their ideal of decency the scheme of life in vogue in the next higher stratum, and bend their energies to live up to that ideal. On pain of forgetting their good name and their self-respect in case of failure, they must conform to the accepted code, at least in appearance.

As has been seen in the discussing of woman's status under the heads of Vicarious Leisure and Vicarious Consumption, it has in the course of economic development become the office of the woman to consume vicariously for the head of the household; and her apparel is contributed with this object in view. It has come about that obviously productive labour is in a peculiar degree derogatory to respectable women, and therefore special pains should be taken in the construction of women's dress, to impress upon the beholder the fact (often indeed a fiction) that the wearer does not and can not habitually engage in useful work. Prosperity requires respectable women to abstain more consistently from useful effort and to make more of a show of leisure than the men of the same social classes. It grates painfully on our nerves to contemplate the necessity of any well-bred woman's earning a livelihood by useful work. It is not "woman's sphere." Her sphere is within the household, which she should "beautify," and of which she should be the "chief ornament." The male head of the household is not currently spoken of as its ornament. This feature taken in conjunction with the other fact that propriety requires more unremitting attention to expensive display in the dress and other paraphernalia of women, goes to enforce the view already implied in what has gone before. By virtue of its descent from a patriarchal past, our social system makes it the woman's function in an especial degree to put in evidence her household's ability to pay. According to the modern civilized scheme of life, the good name of the household to which she belongs should be the special care of the woman; and the system of honorific expenditure and conspicuous leisure by which this good name is chiefly sustained is therefore the woman's sphere. In the ideal scheme, as it tends to realize itself in the life of the higher pecuniary classes, this attention to conspicuous waste of substance and effort should normally be the sole economic function of the woman.

At the stage of economic development at which the women were still in the full sense the property of the men, the performance of conspicuous leisure and consumption came to be part of the services required of them. The women being not their own masters, obvious expenditure and leisure on their part would redound to the credit of their master rather than on their own credit; and therefore the more expensive and the more obviously unproductive the women of the household are, the more creditable and more effective for the purpose of the reputability of the household or its head will their life be. So much so that the women have been required not only to afford evidence of a life of leisure, but even to disable themselves for useful activity.

To apply this generalization to women's dress, and put the matter in concrete terms: the high heel, the skirt, the impracticable bonnet, the corset, and the general disregard of the wearer's comfort which is an obvious feature of all civilized women's apparel, are so many items of evidence to the effect that in the modern civilized scheme of life the woman is still, in theory, the economic dependent of the man,—that, perhaps in a highly idealized sense, she still is the man's chattel. The homely reason for all this conspicuous leisure and attire on the part of women lies in the fact that they are servants to whom, in the differentiation of economic functions, has been delegated the office of putting in evidence their master's ability to pay.

There is a marked similarity in these respects between the apparel of women and that of domestic servants, especially liveried servants. In both there is a very elaborate show of unnecessary expensiveness, and in both cases there is also a notable disregard of the physical comfort of the wearer. But the attire of the lady goes farther in its elaborate insistence on the idleness, if not on the physical infirmity of the wearer, than does that of the domestic. And this is as it should be; for in theory, according to the ideal scheme of the pecuniary culture, the lady of the house is the chief menial of the household.

★★★

The fact has already been remarked upon incidentally in the course of the discussion of the growth of economic institutions generally, and in particular in speaking of vicarious leisure and of dress, that the position of women in the modern economic scheme is more widely and more consistently at variance with the promptings of the instinct of workmanship than is the position of the men of the same classes. It is also apparently true that the woman's temperament includes a large share of this instinct that approves peace and disapproves futility. It is therefore not a fortuitous circumstance that the women of modern industrial communities show a livelier sense of the discrepancy between the accepted scheme of life and the exigencies of the economic situation.

The several phases of the "woman question" have brought out in intelligible form the extent to which the life of women in modern society, and in the polite circles especially, is regulated by a body of common sense formulated under the economic circumstances of an earlier phase of development. It is still felt that woman's life, in its civil, economic, and social bearing, is essentially and normally a vicarious life, the merit or demerit of which is, in the nature of things, to be imputed to some other individual who stands in some relation of ownership or tutelage of the woman. So, for instance, any action on the part of a woman which traverses an injunction of the accepted schedule of proprieties is felt to reflect immediately upon the honour of the man whose woman she is. There may of course be some sense of incongruity in the mind of any one passing an opinion of this kind on the woman's frailty or perversity; but the common-sense judgment of the community in such matters is, after all, delivered without much hesitation, and few men would question the legitimacy of their sense of an outraged tutelage in any case that might arise. On the other hand, relatively little discredit attaches to a woman through the evil deeds of the man with whom her life is associated.

The good and beautiful scheme of life, then—that is to say the scheme to which we are habituated—assigns to the woman a "sphere" ancillary to the activity of the man; and it is felt that any departure from the traditions of her assigned round of duties is unwomanly. If the question is as to civil rights or the suffrage, our common sense in the matter—that is to say the logical deliverance of our general scheme of life upon the point in question—says that the woman should be represented in the body politic and before the law, not immediately in her own person, but through the mediation of the head of the household to which she belongs. It is unfeminine in her to aspire to a self-direction, self-centered life; and our common sense tells us that her direct participation in the affairs of the community, civil or industrial, is a menace to that social order which expresses our habits of thought as they have been formed under the guidance of the traditions of the pecuniary culture. "All this fume and forth of 'emancipating woman from the slavery of man' and so on, is, to use the chaste and expressive language of Elizabeth Cady Stanton[1] inversely, 'utter rot.' The social relations of the sexes are fixed by nature. Our entire civilisation—that is whatever is good in it—is based on the home." The "home" is the household with male head. This view, but commonly expressed even more chastely, is the prevailing view of the woman's status, not only among the common run of the men of civilised communities, but among the women as well. Women have a very alert sense of what the scheme of proprieties requires, and while it is true that many of them are ill at ease under the details which the code imposes, there are few who do not recognise that the existing moral order, of necessity and by the divine right of prescription, places the woman in a position ancillary to the man. In the last analysis, according to her own sense of what is good and beautiful, the woman's life is, and in theory must be, an expression of the man's life at the second remove.

But in spite of this pervading sense of what is the good and natural place for the woman, there is also perceptible an incipient development of sentiment to the effect that this whole arrangement of tutelage and vicarious life and imputation of merit and demerit is somehow a mistake. Or, at least, that even if it may be a natural

---

1 See the Introduction (14) and Appendix B6.

growth and a good arrangement in its time and place, and in spite of its patent aesthetic value, still it does not adequately serve the more everyday ends of life in a modern industrial community. Even that large and substantial body of well-bred, upper and middle-class women to whose dispassionate, matronly sense of the traditional proprieties this relation of status commends itself as fundamentally and eternally right—even these, whose attitude is conservative, commonly find some slight discrepancy in detail between things as they are and as they should be in this respect. But that less manageable body of modern women who, by force of youth, education or temperament, are in some degree out of touch with the traditions of status received from the barbarian culture, and in whom there is, perhaps, an undue reversion to the impulse of self-expression and workmanship,—these are touched with a sense of grievance too vivid to leave them at rest.

In this "New-Woman" movement,—as these blind and incoherent efforts to rehabilitate the woman's pre-glacial standing have been named,—there are at least two elements discernible, both of which are of an economic character. These two elements or motives are expressed by the double watchword, "Emancipation" and "Work." Each of these words is recognised to stand for something in the way of a wide-spread sense of grievance. The prevalence of the sentiment is recognised even by people who do not see that there is any real ground for a grievance in the situation as it stands to-day. It is among the women of the well-to-do classes, in the communities which are farthest advanced in industrial development, that this sense of a grievance to be redressed is most alive and finds most frequent expression. That is to say, in other words, there is a demand, more or less serious, for emancipation from all relation of status, tutelage, or vicarious life; and the revulsion asserts itself especially among the class of women upon whom the scheme of life handed down from the régime of status imposes with least mitigation a vicarious life, and in those communities whose economic development has departed farthest from the circumstances to which this traditional scheme is adapted. The demand comes from that portion of womankind which is excluded by the canons of good repute from all effectual work, and which is closely reserved for a life of leisure and conspicuous consumption.

More than one critic of this new-woman movement has misapprehended its motive. The case of the American "new woman" has lately been summed up with some warmth by a popular observer of social phenomena: "she is petted by her husband, the most devoted and hardworking of husbands in the world.... She is the superior of her husband in education, and in almost every respect. She is surrounded by the most numerous and delicate attentions. Yet she is not satisfied.... The Anglo-Saxon 'new woman' is the most ridiculous production of modern times, and destined to be the most ghastly failure of the century." Apart from the deprecation—perhaps well placed—which is contained in this presentment, it adds nothing but obscurity to the woman question. The grievance of the new woman is made up of those things which this typical characterization of the movement urges as reason why she should be content. She is petted, and is permitted, or even required, to consume largely and conspicuously—vicariously for her husband or other natural guardian. She is exempted, or debarred, from vulgarly useful employment—in order to perform leisure vicariously for the good repute of her natural (pecuniary) guardian. These offices are the conventional marks of the un-free, at the same time that they are compatible with the human impulse to purposeful activity. But the woman is endowed with her share—which there is reason to believe is more than an even share—of the instinct of workmanship, to which futility of life or of expenditure is obnoxious. She must unfold her life activity in response to the direct, unmediated stimuli of the economic enforcement with which she is in contact. The impulse is perhaps stronger upon the woman than upon the man to live her own life in her own way and to enter the industrial process of the community at something nearer than the second remove....

9. From Herbert Spencer, *Essays on Education and Kindred Subjects* (New York: E.P. Dutton, 1914)

from *"Moral Education"*

The greatest defect in our programmes of education is entirely overlooked. While much is being done in the detailed improvement of our systems in respect both of matter and manner, the most pressing desideratum has not yet been even recognised as a desideratum. To prepare the young for the duties of life is tacitly admitted to be the end which parents and schoolmasters should have in view; and happily, the value of the things taught, and the goodness of the methods followed in teaching them, are now ostensibly judged by their fitness to this end. The propriety of substituting for an exclusively classical training, a training in which the modern languages shall have a share, is argued on this ground. The necessity of increasing the amount of science is urged for like reasons. But though some care is taken to fit youth of both sexes for society and citizenship, no care whatever is taken to fit them for the position of parents. While it is seen that for the purpose of gaining a livelihood, an elaborate preparation is needed, it appears to be thought that for the bringing up of children, no preparation whatever is needed. While many years are spent by a boy in gaining knowledge of which the chief value is that it constitutes "the education of a gentleman;" and while many years are spent by a girl in those decorative acquirements which fit her for evening parties; not an hour is spent by either in preparation for that gravest of all responsibilities—the management of a family. Is it that this responsibility is but a remote contingency? On the contrary, it is sure to devolve on nine out of ten. Is it that the discharge of it is easy? Certainly not: of all functions which the adult has to fulfill, this is the most difficult. Is it that each may be trusted by self-instruction to fit himself, or herself, for the office of parent? No: not only is the need for such self-instruction unrecognised, but the complexity of the subject renders it the one of all others in which self-instruction is least likely to succeed. No rational plea can be put forward for leaving the Art of Education out of our *curriculum*. Whether as bearing on the happiness of parents themselves, or whether as affecting the characters and lives of their children and remote descendants, we must admit that a knowledge of the right methods of juvenile culture, physical, intellectual, and moral, is a knowledge of extreme importance. This topic should be the final one in the course of instruction passed through by each man and woman. As physical maturity is marked by the ability to produce offspring, so mental maturity is marked by the ability to train those offspring. *The subject which involves all other subjects, and therefore the subject in which education should culminate, is the Theory and Practice of Education.*

In the absence of this preparation, the management of children, and more especially the moral management, is lamentably bad. Parents either never think about the matter at all, or else their conclusions are crude and inconsistent. In most cases, and especially on the part of mothers, the treatment adopted on every occasion is that which the impulse of the moment prompts: it springs not from any reasoned-out conviction as to what will most benefit the child, but merely expresses the dominant parental feelings, whether good or ill; and varies from hour to hour as these feelings vary. Or if the dictates of passion are supplemented by any definite doctrines and methods, they are those handed down from the past, or those suggested by the remembrances of childhood, or those adopted from nurses and servants—methods devised not by the enlightenment, but by the ignorance, of the time.

★ ★ ★ ★ ★

We are not among those who believe in Lord Palmerston's[1] dogma, that "all children are born good." On the whole, the opposite dogma, untenable as it is, seems to us less wide of the truth. Nor do we agree

---

1 Henry John Temple (1784-1865) was a two-time prime minister of Great Britain (1855-58, 1859-65).

with those who think that, by skilful discipline, children may be made altogether what they should be. Contrariwise, we are satisfied that though imperfections of nature may be diminished by wise management, they cannot be removed by it. The notion that an ideal humanity might be forthwith produced by a perfect system of education, is near akin to that implied in the poems of Shelley,[1] that would mankind give up their old institutions and prejudices, all the evils in the world would at once disappear: neither notion being acceptable to such as have dispassionately studied human affairs.

Nevertheless, we may fitly sympathise with those who entertain these too sanguine hopes. Enthusiasm, pushed even to fanaticism, is a useful motive-power—perhaps an indispensable one. It is clear that the ardent politician would never undergo the labours and make the sacrifices he does, did he not believe that the reform he fights for is the one thing needful. But for his conviction that drunkenness is the root of all social evils, the teetotaler would agitate far less energetically. In philanthropy, as in other things, great advantage results from division of labour; and that there may be division of labour, each class of philanthropists must be more or less subordinated to its function—must have an exaggerated faith in its work. Hence, of those who regard education, intellectual or moral, as the panacea, we may say that their undue expectations are not without use; and that perhaps it is part of the beneficent order of things that their confidence cannot be shaken.

Even were it true, however, that by some possible system of moral control, children could be moulded into the desired form; and even could every parent be indoctrinated with this system, we should still be far from achieving the object in view. It is forgotten that the carrying out of any such system presupposes, on the part of adults, a degree of intelligence, of goodness, of self-control, possessed by no one. The error made by those who discuss questions of domestic discipline, lies in ascribing all the faults and difficulties to the children, and none to the parents. The current assumption respecting family government, as respecting national government, is, that the virtues are with the rulers and the vices with the ruled. Judging by educational theories, men and women are entirely transfigured in their relations to offspring. The citizens we do business with, the people we meet in the world, we know to be very imperfect creatures. In the daily scandals, in the quarrels of friends, in bankruptcy disclosures, in lawsuits, in police reports, we have constantly thrust before us the pervading selfishness, dishonesty, brutality. Yet when we criticise nursery-management and canvass the misbehaviour of juveniles, we

---

1 Percy Bysshe Shelley (1792-1822) was an English Romantic poet.

habitually take for granted that these culpable persons are free from moral delinquency in the treatment of their boys and girls! So far is this from the truth, that we do not hesitate to blame parental misconduct for a great part of the domestic disorder commonly ascribed to the perversity of children. We do not assert this of the more sympathetic and self-restrained, among whom we hope most of our readers may be classed; but we assert it of the mass. What kind of moral culture is to be expected from a mother who, time after time, angrily shakes her infant because it will not suck; which we once saw a mother do? How much sense of justice is likely to be instilled by a father who, on having his attention drawn by a scream to the fact that his child's finger is jammed between the window-sash and sill, begins to beat the child instead of releasing it? Yet that there are such fathers is testified to us by an eye-witness. Or, to take a still stronger case, also vouched for by direct testimony—what are the educational prospects of the boy who, on being taken home with a dislocated thigh, is saluted with a castigation? It is true that these are extreme instances—instances exhibiting in human beings that blind instinct which impels brutes to destroy the weakly and injured of their own race. But extreme though they are, they typify feelings and conduct daily observable in many families. Who has not repeatedly seen a child slapped by nurse or parent for a fretfulness probably resulting from bodily derangement? Who, when watching a mother snatch up a fallen little one, has not often traced, both in the rough manner and in the sharply-uttered exclamation—"You stupid little thing!"—an irascibility foretelling endless future squabbles? Is there not in the harsh tones in which a father bids his children be quiet, evidence of a deficient fellow-feeling with them? Are not the constant, and often quite needless, thwartings that the young experience—the injunctions to sit still, which an active child cannot obey without suffering great nervous irritation, the commands not to look out of the window when travelling by railway, which on a child of any intelligence entails serious deprivation—are not these thwartings, we ask, signs of a terrible lack of sympathy? The truth is, that the difficulties of moral education are necessarily of dual origin—necessarily result from the combined faults of parents and children. If hereditary transmission is a law of nature, as every naturalist knows it to be, and as our daily remarks and current proverbs admit it to be; then, on the average of cases, the defects of children mirror the defects of their parents;—on the average of cases, we say, because, complicated as the results are by the transmitted traits of remoter ancestors, the correspondence is not special but only general. And if, on the average of cases, this inheritance of defects exists, then the evil passions which parents have to check in their children, imply like evil passions in themselves: hidden, it may be, from the public eye, or perhaps obscured by other feelings, but still there. Evidently, therefore, the general practice of any ideal system of discipline is hopeless: parents are not good enough.

***

From *"On Manners and Fashion"*

What folly, then, underlies the whole system of our grand dinners, our "at homes," our evening parties—assemblages made up of many who never met before, many others who just bow to each other, many others who though familiar feel mutual indifference, with just a few real friends lost in the general mass! You need but look round at the artificial expressions of face, to see at once how it is. All have their disguises on; and how can there be sympathy between masks? No wonder that in private every one exclaims against the stupidity of these gatherings. No wonder that hostesses get them up rather because they must than because they wish. No wonder that the invited go less from the expectation of pleasure than from fear of giving offence. The whole thing is a gigantic mistake—an organised disappointment.

And then note, lastly, that in this case, as in all others, when an organisation has become effete and inoperative for its legitimate purpose, it is employed for quite other ones—quite opposite ones. What is the usual plea put in for giving and attending these tedious assemblies? "I admit that they are stupid and frivolous enough," replies every man to your criticisms; "but then, you know, one must keep up one's connections." And could you get from his wife a sincere answer, it would be—"Like you, I am sick of these frivolities; but then, we must get our daughters married." The one knows that there is a profession to push, a practice to gain, a business to extend: or parliamentary influence, or county patronage, or votes, or office, to be got: position, berths, favours, profit. The other's thoughts run upon husbands and settlements, wives and dowries. Worthless for their ostensible purpose of daily bringing human beings into pleasurable relations with each other, these cumbrous appliances of our social intercourse are now perseveringly kept in action with a view to the pecuniary and matrimonial results which they indirectly produce.

Who then shall say that the reform of our system of observances is unimportant? When we see how this system induces fashionable extravagance, with its entailed bankruptcy and ruin—when we mark how greatly it limits the amount of social intercourse among the less wealthy classes—when we find that many who most need to be disciplined by mixing with the refined are driven away by it, and led into dangerous and often fatal courses—when we count up the many minor evils it inflicts, the extra work which its costliness entails on all professional and mercantile men, the damage to public taste in dress and decoration by the setting up of its absurdities as standards for imitation, the injury to health indicated in the faces of its devotees at the close of the London season, the mortality of milliners and the like, which its sudden exigencies yearly involve;—and when to all these we add its fatal sin, that it blights, withers up, and kills, that high enjoyment it professedly ministers to—that enjoyment which is a chief end of our hard struggling in life to obtain—shall we not conclude that to reform our system of etiquette and fashion, is an aim yielding to few in urgency?

There needs, then, a protestantism in social usages. Forms that have ceased to facilitate and have become obstructive—whether political, religious, or other—have ever to be swept away; and eventually are so swept away in all cases. Signs are not wanting that some change is at hand.

***

The young convention-breaker eventually finds that he pays too heavily for his nonconformity. Hating, for example, everything that bears about it any remnant of servility, he determines, in the ardour of his independence, that he will uncover to no one. But what he means simply as a general protest, he finds that ladies interpret into a personal disrespect. Though he sees that, from the days of chivalry downwards, these marks of supreme consideration paid to the other sex have been but a hypocritical counterpart to the actual subjection in which men have held them—a pretended submission to compensate for a real domination; and though he sees that when the true dignity of women is recognised, the mock dignities given to them will be abolished; yet he does not like to be thus misunderstood, and so hesitates in his practice.

In other cases, again, his courage fails him. Such of his unconventionalities as can be attributed only to eccentricity, he has no qualms about: for, on the whole, he feels rather complimented than otherwise in being considered a disregarder of public opinion. But when they are liable to be put down to ignorance, to ill-breeding, or to poverty, he becomes a coward. However clearly the recent innovation of eating some kinds of fish with knife and fork proves the fork-and-bread practice to have had little but caprice for its basis, yet he dares not wholly ignore that practice while fashion partially maintains it. Though he thinks that a silk handkerchief is quite as appropriate for drawing-room use as a white cambric one, he is not altogether at ease in acting out his opinion. Then, too, he begins to perceive that his resistance to prescription brings round disadvantageous results which he had not calculated upon. He had expected that it would save him from a great deal of social intercourse of a frivolous kind—that it would offend the fools, but not the sensible people; and so would serve as a self-acting test by which those worth knowing would be separated from those not worth knowing. But the fools prove to be so greatly in the majority that, by offending them, he closes against himself nearly all the avenues through which the sensible people are to be reached. Thus he finds, that his nonconformity is frequently misinterpreted; that there are but few directions in which he dares to carry it consistently out; that the annoyances and disadvantages which it brings upon him are greater than he anticipated; and that the chances of his doing any good are very remote. Hence he gradually loses resolution, and lapses, step by step, into the ordinary routine of observances.

Abortive as individual protests thus generally turn out, it may possibly be that nothing effectual will be done until there arises some organised resistance to this invisible despotism, by which our modes and habits are dictated. It may happen, that the government of Manners and Fashion will be rendered less tyrannical, as the political and religious governments have been, by some antagonistic union. Alike in Church and State, men's first emancipations from excess of restriction were achieved by numbers, bound together by a common creed or a common political faith. What remained undone while there were but individual schismatics or rebels, was effected when there came to be many acting in concert. It is tolerably clear that these earliest install-ments of freedom could not have been obtained in any other way; for so long as the feeling of personal independence was weak and the rule strong, there could never have been a sufficient number of separate dis-sentients to produce the desired results. Only in these later times, during which the secular and spiritual controls have been growing less coercive, and the tendency towards individual liberty greater, has it become possible for smaller and smaller sects and parties to fight against established creeds and laws; until now men may safely stand even alone in their antagonism.

Appendix C: Etiquette and Social Customs

[The selections in this Appendix reflect the very rigorous etiquette and social customs enforced on women, especially upper-class women, in Chopin's era. These rules dictated everything from the types of visits women were expected to make and the length of time between visits, to types of clothing that should be worn on specific occasions, and women's duties on various social occasions. These sources also describe some of the more common social events, such as the dinners and horse races that Edna and her circle of friends in *The Awakening* attend with some regularity.]

1. From *The Elite Directory of St. Louis Society* (St. Louis: St. Louis Herald, 1877), 101-04

Complete Calling Code

First Calls

***

Lovers of literature, music, or art, may at pleasure, or on any occasion, call on any other of like taste without regard to local divisions [of the city]; and without ceremony, to form a personal acquaintance.

***

Return Calls

I

First calls should be returned as early as practicable. Thirty days is very ample time for this important courtesy.

II

In case illness, excessive occupation, or other just cause renders it impossible or very difficult to return a call in person within the proper time, a card or note of friendship and regret may be sent by post or messenger. This will continue the acquaintance until a call in person can be made, or an invitation to a reception or other entertainment given.

The usual hours for calling are from two to five P.M. An evening visit by a lady implies some degree of social acquaintance, and should never be made as first call, except under special circumstances. From seven to nine in the evening are the usual hours for gentlemen to call; and there is nothing more delightful in society than calls by husbands and wives, or brothers and sisters together, during the evening hours, on their acquaintances and friends.

Cards

Plain engraved cards are always in good taste. In making visits, always send in or leave your card. At receptions the usher takes your card. At other times, if the person called upon is not at home you turn down the right hand upper corner of the card, to indicate that you came in person. If the visit is intended for the various members of a family, you either give several cards, or leave one with the entire right end folded over. The choice is immaterial.

2. From *Blunders in Behavior Corrected* (New York: Garrett, Dick, and Fitzgerald, 1880)

COMMANDS should never be given in a commanding tone. A gentleman requests, he does not command. We are not to assume so much importance, whatever our station, as to give orders in the "imperative mood," nor are we ever justified in thrusting the consciousness of servitude on any one. The blunder of commanding sternly is most frequently committed by those who have themselves but just escaped servitude, and we should not exhibit to others a weakness so unbecoming.

CONTROL OF TEMPER.—It is very unbecoming to exhibit petulance, or angry feeling, though it is indulged in so largely in almost every circle. The true gentleman does not suffer his countenance to be easily ruffled; and we only look paltry when we suffer temper to hurry us into ill-judged expressions of feeling. "He that is soon angry dealeth foolishly."[1]

***

---

1   From the Hebrew scriptures, Proverbs 14:17.

DINING AT HOME.—When you invite several friends to dine with you, have your dinner ready within a short time after the hour named, but not punctually to a moment, that any who have not arrived may not feel slighted at your having commenced dinner. Do not invite, at the same time, persons who are not on terms with each other, though it is a delicate matter, always, to take into consideration other people's differences. Among kindred it is often advisable to pursue an opposite course—for many a friendship, among relatives, is renewed at another table, where petty differences are, of course, to be forgotten. Study the tastes of your guests; and if there is any particular dish which your visitors will prefer, set it before them, and with the remark, "I think I noticed you to prefer this or that;" or, "I think you are partial to so-and-so, I therefore obtained it for you." If you go out of your way to humor your friend you are not to be too modest to let him know it, though you are not to exaggerate your attention, and make him feel that you burden him with attentions.

★★★

FRIENDSHIP AND ACQUAINTANCE are to be distinguished from each other in worldly affairs. Acquaintances sometimes become the depositories of secrets which should be even guardedly told to friends. Be wary how you treat a mere acquaintance, that you do not place your affairs in his hands, and on the slightest rupture regret having reposed in him too much confidence. Acquaintances made at convivial meetings are generally as hollow as the meetings themselves. Under the temptations of hospitality men confide in each other more than wisdom would dictate, and the "evening's diversions" do not always "bear the morning's reflections."

3. From James S. Zacharie, *New Orleans Guide* (New Orleans: New Orleans News, 1885)

The social manners and customs of New Orleans, a mixture of the French, Spanish and English, are somewhat different from those of other parts of the United States, and, as their peculiarities are rigidly adhered to, a few words on this subject may be found useful.

★★★

Balls and Parties. The season of balls and parties begins about the 15th of December and lasts until Ash-Wednesday, the first day of Lent. For these entertainments, which being at 9 P.M., formal written or engraved invitations are sent, which should be accepted or declined, in writing.

★★★

Dinners. In the Winter season and in Lent dinners are constantly given. To those for which formal invitations are issued, an acceptance or regret should be sent immediately. Formal dinner parties begin at 6 and end at 11 P.M., and full evening dress is the usual costume. The customary dinner hour for families is four o'clock, but many do not dine until five and even six o'clock. The custom of dining socially with friends on Sundays prevails, and such dinners, for which invitations are often made as late as the morning of the day itself, are verbal and are generally for four o'clock.

★★★

Theatres. The theatres all commence at 8 o'clock, except the French Opera which begins sometimes earlier when a long opera is to be given. Visiting costume is sufficient for all theatres except the French Opera, where full evening dress (ladies without bonnets) is usual for those in the box tiers. The custom of young ladies attending the theatre alone with a gentleman does not generally prevail, as in other cities.

★★★

Promenades. The hour for promenades in Winter is from 3 to 5 P.M. In Summer from 6 to 8 P.M. Canal street is the usual resort. Up town, Prytania, Jackson, St. Charles and the cross streets are much frequented. Down town, Rampart, and Esplanade streets are the favorite walks.

Driving. The hours for driving vary according to the seasons. In Winter from 3 to 5 P.M. In Spring a little later. In Summer after dinner from 6 to 8 P.M. Driving parties of three or four are often formed.

★★★

Races. The Races commence the Saturday preceding Easter and occupy one week. The last day of the meeting generally closes with a four mile race, and is largely attended. The races take place at the Fair Grounds, and begin at 3 P.M. No ladies are permitted on the Grand Stand, unaccompanied by gentlemen. Members of the Jockey Club are entitled to free admission for ladies accompanying them, and ladies, accompanied by members, are invited to visit the Club House.

Clubs. The clubs are seven in number. All the clubs are on the *open* plan (except for the Pickwick and Louisiana Clubs), and strangers are invited by members for a limited time.

4. From Richard A. Wells, *Manners, Culture and Dress of the Best American Society* (Omaha, NE: Clark, 1891)

Costumes for Country and Sea-Side

We cannot give a full description of the wardrobe which the lady of fashion desires to take with her to the country or sea-side. But there are a few general rules which apply to many things, and which all must more or less observe. Let the wardrobe be ever so large there must be a certain number of costumes suited for ordinary wear. Thus, dresses, while they may be somewhat brighter in tint than good taste would justify in the streets of a city, must yet be durable in quality and of material which can be washed. The brim of the hat should be broad to protect the face from the sun. The fashion of making hats of shirred muslin is a very sensible one, as it enables them to be done up when they are soiled. The boots should be strong and durable. A waterproof is an indispensable article to the sojourner at country resorts.

Bathing Costumes

The bathing-dress should be made of flannel. A soft gray tint is the neatest, as it does not soon fade and grow ugly from contact with salt water. It may be trimmed with bright worsted braid. The best style is a loose sacque or the yoke waist, both of them to be belted in and falling about midway between the knee and ankle. Full trowsers gathered into a band at the ankle, an oilskin cap to protect the hair, which becomes harsh in the salt water, and socks of the color of the dress complete the costume.

5. From Georgene Corry Benham, *Polite Life and Etiquette, or What is Right and the Social Acts* (Chicago: Louis Benham, 1891)

Chapter IV

Society

We have many inquiries from truly anxious people to define what is "good" and "what is bad society." They say that they read in the newspaper of the "good society" in Chicago, Washington, Newport and New York, and that it is a record of drunkenness, flirtation, bad manners and gossip, divorce and slander. They read that our people at popular resorts commit all sorts of vulgarities, such as talking aloud at the opera, and disturbing their neighbors; that young men go to a dinner, get drunk, and break glasses; one young girl remarks, "We do not call that good society in New Orleans."

American Society

***

When you enter society you throw your life into it with all your mental and moral attainments, and those who mingle with you get the benefit of all you have, and you of all they have. Its tendency, therefore, is to make all equal. No young person should deny himself or herself of its benefits. One can never have a complete life without it. But one danger should be avoided, and that is, the danger of giving one's self up too exclusively to society....

Do not forget to have a life of your own—an inner life with which you can commune, and that, too, with pleasure. Some young people assume the outward manners and fashions of society, who are so utterly empty of information or sympathy that they are incapable of being real or interesting....

Chapter XXIII

Visiting

According to the strict rules of etiquette, one call during the year, or a card left at the door in person or in an envelope, continues the acquaintance; although there is no apparent cause for this seeming remissness, society must ask no questions. We can never know what prompts a lady to give up her visiting for a season, it may be sudden calamity, or need of economy, or domestic duties, and she should not be questioned, for no doubt her reasons are purely personal.

There should be uniformity in visiting. No lady is pleased to receive a card from Mrs. Allen and then meet her, making a personal visit (perhaps) to her next door neighbor. If a lady cannot personally visit all her formal acquaintances, she should visit none; for it is not proper to show favors, and the lady receiving the card would certainly feel the slight.

It is rude to ignore the day a lady may designate for receiving calls, and one should try to call on a reception day. Happy the lady, who can give up one afternoon each week to her friends. The person who has established a residence in any town or community should call on the lady or family of subsequent arrivals first, and such calls must be returned promptly.

***

Duty of Visitors

Visitors should conform carefully to the habits of the house, not be out walking at dinner time, nor in bed at breakfast time, and never keep the family up after their hour for retiring. A guest must not show either by word or act that these hours do not suit him, but submit cheerfully. .

A visitor should not appear to notice any unpleasant family affairs that fall under his observation. He should never comment upon them to strangers, nor to the host himself, unless his friend should first broach the subject. Also, if you do not find your friend in as high a state of prosperity as you had anticipated, do not take evident notice of the fact. Your observations may be cruel as well as impolite.

A visitor should, as far as possible, acquiesce in all plans proposed for his amusement or entertainment by the host.

All invitations to either visitor or visited ought to include the other, and either should generally refuse to accept an invitation to him alone.

A visitor should always endeavor to give as little trouble as possible. At the same time he ought not to apologize for the trouble which his presence naturally requires....

***

Duty of Host or Hostess

True hospitality consists in freely and cheerfully giving your visitor the best you have in the way of rooms, provision, and other means of entertainment. Having done this, make no apologies because you have no better. Your general demeanor toward your guests will do more toward making them feel at home and enjoy their visit than any amount of grandeur and luxury. Devote as much time as you can to the amusement and society of your visitors, and let them feel, from your kindness and cheerfulness, that you enjoy their presence.

Kindly, and even urgently, invite your friend to stay as long as you wish; but when a time has been fixed upon for his departure, do not try to break in upon his plans. Assist him in his departure, and ask him to visit you again if you really desire him to do so; otherwise allow him to depart by wishing him a safe journey home.

Appendix D: Louisiana Contexts

[The readings in this Appendix illuminate the Louisiana contexts that inform *The Awakening*, including matters of law, religion, geography, and contemporary views of race, class, and gender. Louisiana has always been set apart from other states in the union: in terms of race and culture, Louisiana is unique because of its history and its tri-racial system codified by law. In order to understand *The Awakening*, readers must be familiar with such terms as Creole, Acadian, and quadroon. The texts in this section not only help clarify these concepts but also describe the geographic locations mentioned in the novel, such as Carrollton and the Louisiana Jockey Club, which is the New Orleans site that fosters Edna's blossoming amorous liaison with Alcée Arobin.]

1. **From *Jewell's Crescent City Illustrated: The Commercial, Social, Political and General History of New Orleans*, ed. Edwin L. Jewell (New Orleans: n.p., 1873)**

The Fair Grounds

The entrances to the Fair Grounds about three miles from the Clay Statue[1] are reached by the street cars which pass down Canal to Rampart, down Rampart to Esplanade, and down Esplanade towards and near Bayou St. John, being the pleasantest railroad ride afforded by the city cars, as well as a delightful drive for carriages. By the Gentilly gate, or the Mystery entrance, the visitor is introduced to a park of 120 acres, (formerly the old Creole Race Course,) studded with magnificent oaks, thickly overgrown with grass, containing a fine tract in complete order, and all the buildings required for fairs, fetes,[2] and exhibitions of all kinds. The race course is an ellipse exactly one mile in measurement, and from the nature and elevation of the ground is usually in good condition. Within the ellipse are the Club House of the Fair Grounds, a platform for music and dancing, and a base ball park. The Public Stand, built by the Jockey Club on the south side of the

---

1 A statue of Henry Clay was originally erected on the corner of Canal Street and St. Charles in 1860. In 1901, it was moved to Lafayette Street where it caused fewer traffic problems. Henry Clay was a nineteenth-century statesman and orator who was considered the "Great Compromiser" because of his stances on issues such as slavery and nullification.
2 French; a festival, celebration, or party.

course, is considered the best stand on the continent, being an enormous three story pile of graceful and substantial carpentry, two stories high, with comfortable seats for more than five thousand people, with ample promenades, broad and easy staircases, roomy saloons, and commanding a view of the whole course and enclosure. The view from the ample and lofty cupola[1] takes in the whole city and its suburbs, a lovely mingling of rivers, bayous, lakes, swamps, forests, gardens, streets, shipping, spires, and railroad trains.

The main building is appropriated to the exhibition of fine and delicate manufactures, paintings, statuary drawings, musical instruments, machinery for household uses, needle work, furniture &c. It is of brick, 200x95 feet, two stories high, amply supplied with light and ventilation from large doors, lofty windows, and numerous skylights through its slate roof. The cost of the building was $70,000.

... Extensive stables on the north side will accommodate more than a hundred horses, and on the same side adjoining the grounds is the live-stock farm ... containing many specimens of thorough-bred and imported animals. The deer park is on the east side ...

... This garden now affords to visitors an exhibition of vigorous tropical shrubs, flowers, plants and trees not to be found elsewhere north of the Gulf of Mexico. The walks are shelled and the grounds symmetrically laid out....

Attached to the garden and furnished from it is the Floral Hall, a walled circular arena, 60 feet in diameter, sheltered by canvass and cooled by numerous fountains. Here during the regular public exhibitions are seen banks and pyramids of the rarest and most beautiful flowers and vines that grow in the garden, field or forest.

Louisiana Jockey Club

This Club was chartered May 15 1871, for the purpose of establishing a race course for the advancement of racing and improving the breed of horses, and the erection or the purchase and equipment of a club house for the social enjoyment of the members....

The Club bought the property adjoining the Fair Grounds, which was once the residence of Mr. Luling, for $60,000. It has a front of 500 feet on Esplanade street, by 2,500 deep, with an area of nearly 30 acres, situated on the Metairie Ridge[2] and exempt from overflow. The grounds are well arranged and thickly set with choice shrubbery. The family mansion has been converted into a club house. It is a substan-

---

1   A dome-like structure on top of a building.
2   A natural levee on the west side of New Orleans that later became a suburb of the city.

tial and handsome three story brick edifice, with a gallery extending entirely around it at each story. The lofty, wide and airy rooms are employed for Reception and Dining rooms, Parlors, Library, Reading and Billiard rooms, Restaurants, &c, all very handsomely and liberally furnished. Most of the oaken furniture being elaborately carved by hand. The other buildings on the premises are carved by hand. The other buildings on the premises are in keeping with the main house, consisting of bowling alley, Pavillion, Kitchen and ten costly stables, with ample room for a hundred horses.

The flower garden contains an extensive collection of indigenuous [sic] and exotic plants and flowers comprising all the rarer varieties to be found in the temperate zone or within the tropics. The adjoining Park has a great number of forest trees of every kind, and orchards of orange, peach and apple trees, and grapevines, all bearing plentifully in their poorer season. In the centre of the Park is a lake of pure fresh water surrounding a small island.

Thus the members of the club have the benefits of a princely private establishment, adorned with all that taste or comfort could suggest or wealth command.

Carrolton

CARROLTON, a distance of six miles by the railroad, is an exceedingly pleasant resort. The line, for nearly a third of the way, passes through the suburbs of the city, and is dotted on either side with beautiful residences—the remainder passes through pleasant pastures, and delightful wood-lands. The road, like the country, is perfectly level shelled and kept in the finest condition. At the end of the route is situated the village; which is principally composed of tastefully built cottages, constructed in every variety of architecture that suited the individual fancy of the owner. Opposite the railroad depot, is one of the handsomest and most extensive public gardens, that is to be found in the vicinity of New Orleans. Here the genial and warm hearted Daniel Hickok presides with that ease and air of hospitality that have made him so popular and so widely known. He delights in showing the rare flours [sic] of his beautiful garden to the many strangers who visit him—and it is always his aim to please those who resort to the Carrolton Gardens for recreation and amusement.

2. From Will H. Coleman, *Historical Sketch Book and Guide to New Orleans and Environs* (New York: W.H. Coleman, 1885)

Creole New Orleans

... There can be no place in America quite like old New Orleans. One who has seen them, can never quite forget the gray stone-arched entrances of the old courtyards, and the houses wrinkled with age and with dusty dormer windows blinking down like faded, aged eyes over which a growth of golden rod leans like a monstrous busy eyebrow. A wild tangle of vines grows in most of these dark courtyards, some of which are given over to complete decay; others, however, being trimly neat and pretty as the homes of prosperous French people invariably are.

Many of the shops contain odd wares. In a house whose round upper windows, covered interiorly with white blinds, look precisely like sleeping eyes, is a music shop. Songs in the windows are French; the master stands within, humming a gay little chansonette,[1] and a curious gray old print, representing a concert in a monastery, gathers a laughing crowd at the show window.

Next door in the jeweler's shop, among the odds and ends, is an exquisite Venetian gondola, done in filigree silver, with gondoliers and all complete.

The down-town people of the poorer localities are great lovers of potted flowers and singing birds. Some streets are fine with color, owing to the brilliant red masses of geraniums that blossom boldly in defiance of the hottest sun; and many a tiny bit of iron gallery jutting in curious fashion out of some tall window is transformed into the coolest of arbors by looped-up cypress vines, which lay their long fingers on everything they can reach.

Here seed dealers do a brisk business in mignonette, morning glory and pansy seeds, while the flower dealers over at the market hard by can, on Sunday mornings, hardly supply the demand for pots of purple Marguerites and pink China asters.

In this French town everything is so widely different from things in new New Orleans. Here the mover's cart is but seldom seen; in a strange, un-American way the people are deeply rooted, and many talk of their ancestry or posterity. Many a young matron lives in the house her great-grandmother occupied, and the passer-by making excursions down some of those long, narrow streets, where there is a hazy perspective of red-tiled roofs tangled together or strung one to the

---

1 French; short song or ditty.

other by freighted clotheslines, has now and again glimpses of quaint interiors.

***

Sauntering down one of the side streets, we glance into *porte cochères*[1] that reveal vistas of beautiful quadrangular gardens, ivy-clad walls, bubbling, sparkling fountains. Stairways lead to galleries, upon which open salons whose proportions dwarf Queen Anne cottage[2] parlors into doll-house apartments. The lower floors, still reserved for business, once the scene of fashion's barter, are now the resort for those in search of oddities in goods and trades.

Placards—"*Chambres garnis*"[3] dangle from long twines tied to hanging balconies, the point of juncture hidden by vines that swing over the railing to catch upon other twines stretched tautly to upper window-sills. Behind their greenery, geraniums blaze and bloom in their improvised beds, as brightly and blithely as if rooted upon spacious lawns.

Windows with contents sacred and secular advertise the stock of interiors near the old French Cathedral. Slate pencils and rosaries, candles and slates, tape and missals, perhaps, one window devoted to those lugubrious tributes to the departed, black and white beads, wreaths and baskets of all sizes and qualities, interspersed with boxes of the tiny nails which fasten them to the tombs....

La Belle Creole

Modest and retired, with but little attempt at architectural ornament, the Creole's home is nevertheless his most sacred possession, about which cluster his most endearing memories and fondest hopes.

***

There comes a time, however, during the warm summer months, when an added charm is bestowed upon the old homestead, a charm that casts over it a spell like that of enchantment.

The pretty Creole maiden born to it some dozen happy years before, returns from the convent where she had gone for her education, to spend the summer vacation at home. Although she may not have crossed the flowery borders of young maidenhood, one can realize the fascination slumbering in her dark eyes, as their fringed lids droop over them, softening, but not diminishing their brilliance. Her

---

1 French; literally a porch gate or carriage porch.
2 An architectural style of home usually rather square with no hallway.
3 Creole French; furnished rooms.

petite figure is formed with the grace and lightness of a fairy, and her voice is as musical as the song of a bird. Of course the little Creole maiden takes kindly to music. She has been as it were cradled in song. It is mother's milk to her. Her earliest lullabies were operatic airs. She comes of a musical family, and, would be untrue to its traditions if she were not a lover of the *art musical*. She is fond of the flowers of every hue that decorate the old garden-walks, which in their delicate loveliness seem akin to her, and of the feathered songsters of the woodlands, who cease their song to listen to hers.

Although the Creole maiden is naturally merry and vivacious, there is none of that wild rompishness about her for which others of the same age, but of different training, are often distinguished. Though at the sound of her voice Sisyphus[1] would rest upon his stone and pause to listen, there is none of that boisterous merriment which in other households defy the rules of etiquette and the frowns of mothers. And yet at all the merry-makings of the neighborhood demoiselle seems at the summit of girlish felicity. In the gay parties given her as she is about to return to her studies in the convent—the feast which ushers in the fast—she is the merriest of all the demoiselles assembled.

A year or two elapses—probably more, as fortune smiles or frowns upon the family. One day there comes into this old Creole homestead, with its oasis of verdure, a young girl, pretty as its flowers, happy as its birds. It is our little demoiselle of the vacation. She has finished her education at the convent, and enjoyed a brief but gay season at home or with some of her schoolmates. Orange blossoms shine like stars in the midnight of her hair, and a single rose-bud nestles in the white wonder of her bosom. She returns to her home with the benedictions[2] of Holy Church, a Creole bride.

Travel where you will, you will not meet with one so fair, so fresh, so smiling, so graceful, merry and easily contented as she. See her once, whether in the happy family circle or in the dancing throng, and it is a picture framed in memory undimmed forever.

Of course here is at once one of the brightest names on the illuminated page of society. In accordance with the law and custom of her peculiar circle, she selects her acquaintances and makes up her list of visiting friends, and is fastidious in her selection. She could not be more so if the destinies of the republic were at stake. None but the select are to be found at her receptions, and to be admitted at her reunions is a much coveted honor. All the surroundings of her home,

---

1   Famous king from Greek mythology whose punishment was to roll a boulder up a hill and then watch it roll back down so that he had to repeat the task forever.
2   A short prayer for help or guidance.

even down to the little bits of porcelain of rare "*Faïence de Diane de Poitiers*"[1]—the heirlooms of honored ancestors—are *comme il faut*,[2] elegant and refined. Her days are passed in fêtes and entertainments of every description.

Is the fair Creole bride given over to the gauds and fripperies of fashionable life? Nay. The brighter parts of her character, which shine with increasing lustre with each passing year, have had their source in another school. Her unbounding generosity, her true nobility of thought and feeling, her courage and her truth, her pure, unsullied thought, her untiring charities, her devotion to parents and friends, her sympathy with sorrow, her kindness to her inferiors, her dignified simplicity—where could these have been learned save at the altars of her faith? And as the family increases does the Creole matron give up her pleasant receptions and *bals dansants*?[3] And has the fashionable world only left to it a memory and a tear for what was so brilliant and recherché?[4] Not so. Not for her the recluse life of the household cipher or the nursery drudge—

> "Retired as noontide dew,
> Or fountain in the noonday grove."[5]

She unites the duties of home with the pleasures of social life. Her graceful influence is felt in both, pleasantly reminding one of the orange tree of her own sunny groves, which bears in its beautiful foliage in the same month the golden fruit of maturity with the fair blossoms of its spring.

With all her wealth of maternal affection the Creole matron is not imprisoned in her nursery to be devoured by her children. In them she has renewed her youth. With her maternity

> "Another morn
> Has risen upon her mid-noon."[6]

Her motherly virtue is her cardinal virtue. Care of her children seems to have contributed indeed to the number and the sensibility of the chords of sympathy and affection.

---

1 Famous French pottery.
2 Proper.
3 Dances.
4 Sought after.
5 From William Wordsworth's "A Poet's Epitaph" (1799).
6 From the sixth book of William Wordsworth's *The Prelude*, first written in 1805 and then revised by the poet in 1850.

The Creole matron, however, does not squander upon the infancy of her children all the health necessary to their youth and adolescence, nor does she destroy their sense of gratitude and her own authority, and impair both their constitution and temper by indiscriminate and indiscreet indulgence. She economises her own health and beauty as she adds both to her offspring.

She is all the fonder of what many deem frivolities, because of her children. For them the gay reception, and the graceful dance are pleasant and harmless pastime. In such indulgences her children learn that ease of manner, grace of movement, and the thousand little prettinesses which are so adorable in after years. She has nursed her babies, prepared them for their studies in the convent school, and she thus finishes an important branch of their education which the school books could not furnish.

And thus another belle Creole grows up to womanhood under her loving eye. She is not permitted to form intimacies outside of home.

The watchful care of the Creole matron may be somewhat relaxed as the mind of demoiselle becomes more perfectly formed, but the invisible rein is still held with a firm, though gentle hand.

The Creole matron is the inevitable duenna of the parlor, and the constant attendant chaperone at all public assemblies; an ever-vigilant guide, and protector against aught that may offend the fine feeling, the noble pride, or the generous heart of demoiselle. And when the time comes for *la belle* to marry she does not trust her own unguided fancies, although she may have read in story books of gallant knights, and had many pleasant dreams of such heroes as live only in the pages of poetry and romance. The Creole matron saves her all the trouble in the perplexing choice of husband, and manages the whole affair with extreme skill, tact and ability. The preliminaries arranged, the selected husband *in futuro* is invited to the house, the drawing-room cleared of all superfluities, and the couple left to an agreeable tete-a-tete, during which they behave like sensible children and exchange vows and rings. The nuptial mass at the church follows, as there is no breaking of engagements or hearts in Creole etiquette.

The Creole matron grows old, as she does everything else, gracefully. She has not been shaken by the blasts of many passions, or enervated by the stimulants of violent sensations. There is no paled reflex of her youthful warmth in the glance she gives to the past, with its buried joys, or the present, with its all-pervading contentment and happiness.

Although an increased *avoirdupois*[1] has added magnificence to her *embonpoint,*[2] and her waltzing days are over, her pretty, well-shaped

1 Body weight.
2 Plumpness.

feet still beat time in unison with the spirit of its music. She is an artiste of conversation, and her *bon mot*[1] is uttered with such natural avoidance of offense, and the arch allusion is so gracefully applied that she gives one the idea of a new use of language, and yet she is a marvelous listener. Her complaisance is ever ready; words come of themselves upon your lips merely from finding themselves so obligingly listened to; and whilst others follow the conversation, it is she who directs it, who seasonably revives it, brings it back from the field from which it has strayed, restores it to others without ostentation, stopping with marvelous tact precisely at the proper point. And the world may not know how much of the stately dignity, the polished ease, the refined elegance that reign supreme in her household is the inspiration of its gay mistress, who remains, in age as in youth, the life and ornament of it....

The Creoles

The original masculine portion of the population was well enough; it was, for the most part, honest but adventurous Canadian *voyageurs* and *courreurs des bois*[2]—sturdy, bold, energetic men, who fought and worked their way overland and down the river, through an endless desert wilderness, peopled with dangerous savages. They came alone and without families, since none but men could endure the fatigues and hardships of this arduous journey. Here, they languished away in single blessedness and melancholy bachelorhood as long as they could stand it, save a few led astray by the dusky charms of some forest maiden. At last good King Louis[3] took mercy on their loneliness and shipped, as an experiment, several cargoes of females; and just here comes in the bar sinister, for these females were prisoners from the royal prison of La Salpétrière.[4] Such were the first women of Louisiana, of whose morals the less said the better, for, as Gov. Cadillac[5] declared to the parish priest when he proposed the purification of the colony by shipping these home: "If I send away all the loose females, there will be no women left here at all, and this would not suit the views of the king or the inclinations of the people."

---

1 Witticism.
2 The literal translation means "runners of the woods," but the term connotes an adventurer.
3 French king (Louis XIV) who shipped women to Louisiana to keep his explorers from chasing Native American women.
4 French hospital and women's detention center opened in the 1650s that served as a facility for beggars and the poor.
5 Antoine Laumet de la Mothe (1658-1730), French explorer who governed Louisiana from 1710-16.

However, for want of better wives, the colonists welcomed these with open arms; but although these satisfied *them*, they did not, by any means, satisfy the directors of the Louisiana Company, as they proved a failure in one of the most important needs of the new country—children.

To supply the deficiency a cargo of girls, known in Louisiana history as the *filles de la cassette*, or casket girls, were sent over by way of experiment—girls, poor but virtuous. The experiment proved a signal success—the girls commanded fancy prices and supplied the needed want. In the infancy of the colony a Louisianian felt proud indeed if he could only trace his origin back to these "casket" instead of to the "correction" girls.

Such was the lowly origin of the first native-born Louisianians—a queer cross between the staid, sober Canadian and the gay, fickle Parisian.

It was some half a century after this that the first Acadian found his way to Louisiana. He came a persecuted wanderer, without country or home; he was so hospitably received, fed, clothed and lodged, that, well pleased with the country and the people, he pitched his tents upon the soil of Louisiana and peopled its western prairies.

The Acadians

The Acadians were a sturdy, stalwart race, showing in their disposition and in every feature their Northern or Norman descent. They were bony, sinewy, with high cheek bones, and their complexion swarthy and bronzed, all their features bearing so close a resemblance to those of our aborigines as to give rise to a somewhat wild theory that the climate of America had an Indianizing effect on Europeans, and that a few centuries of it would convert us in complexion and disposition, into Sioux and Modocs.[1] The true explanation of this undoubted Indian physiognomy is perhaps more easily and naturally explained in the frequency, in the earlier days of Choctaw[2] wives—a custom so prevalent in the colony at one time as to beget a schism between Church and State on this point—the parish priest coolly suggesting that if a man could get no better wife than an Indian squaw he had better remain single altogether.

The Cajan was as prolific as his Canadian cousin. In 1765-66 some 866 Acadians arrived at New Orleans; in 1788 a few more came, making altogether, perhaps 1,000, who, to-day, after the lapse of less than a century, number at least 40,000 covering the whole western portion of the state, and extending even to the Red and Mississippi rivers.

---

1 Two Native American groups.
2 Native American group.

All will remember the story of the Acadians, so beautifully told by Longfellow[1] in his "Evangeline." In Louisiana the expelled people were free from the persecution of the Americans and found a kindred tongue. They settled in the western portions of the State, on the prairies of the Opelousas,[2] where they mainly live to this day, wonderfully increased in numbers, but the same primitive people they were when they left Nova Scotia.

Their homes are substantially-built cypress houses, the walls of which are sometimes reinforced with a thick layer of mixed mud and moss as a mortar. They cultivate cane, cotton, and vegetables, but as the marsh is approached, greater attention is paid to herding, as cattle thrive easily there in winter. Along the many intricate bayous leading out into the marsh around New Orleans, frequent cheniers[3] or live-oak groves are found, like islands in this sea of waving rushes and reeds. In some places these cheniers assume larger proportions, and become known as islands. Lying back some distance from the Gulf, they can be approached from that direction only by the bayous, but by land the marsh inside is of firmer consistency, and affords foothold for horses and cattle. It is here that the Louisiana herdsmen, or what in Texas would be called "the cowboys," thrive. They differ essentially from their Texan brothers, as few of them speak anything but French. They are daring, skillful riders, and drive herds through marshes and swamps which, to the uninitiated, appear impassable. Swimming bayous is to them pleasant sport. Their horses are the small Creole ponies, descendants of the mustang, that never weary, and are as active and quick as panthers. Perhaps no horse has the peculiar, springy gait of these ponies. To the rider it is as if he were sitting on a chair of most delicate springs, and in long journeys this adds much to the comfort of the trip. This motion is the result of continued travel through the sea marshes, where at every step the pony sinks deeper than his knees. To keep from bogging or miring, a quick recovery of the feet is necessary, so that hardly has the entire weight been placed on one leg than it is rapidly withdrawn. This necessitates a quick, elastic step, so rare to highland horses. Where these plucky little fellows travel mile after mile, the larger and stronger horse would fall and hopelessly flounder, rendering it impossible for the rider to retain his seat.

They, like all cattle ponies, are drilled to sudden turnings and wheelings, and can perform intricate movements which would confuse the manege horses of the circus. A slight movement of the hand or the leg, and a sharp turn in his own tracks is made; a slight prick of the spur, and he will take a plunge forward. All this is necessary for the

---

1 Henry Wadsworth Longfellow (1807-82) was an American poet.
2 Town in south-central Louisiana named for a native tribe.
3 Sandy ridges.

safety of himself and rider, for Attakapas[1] cattle have a reputation for belligerency not to be disregarded.

3. From Eliza Ripley, *Social Life in Old New Orleans: Being Recollections of My Girlhood* (New York: Appleton, 1912)

"When Lexington Won the Race"

Every Kentucky woman loves a horse, and when Lexington was entered in the great State stake in 1854 a crowd of the *crème de la crème*[2] of the Blue Grass country clamored to be present at the race....
... Every man, it seemed, in the place, that could spare the time, wanted to see the great race. "Lee Count," as a good many Kentuckians call Le Comte,[3] was the most prominent rival of their boasted and beloved Lexington, and he showed mettle that astonished even those blind partisans, and added zest to the wagers. Ladies had never been in evidence at a horse race in Louisiana. The bare idea was a shock to the Creole mind, that dominated and controlled all the fashionable, indeed, all the respectable, minds in New Orleans at that day. But the Kentucky belles had minds of their own. Every mortal one of them felt a personal interest, and a personal pride, and personal ambition in that Kentucky horse, though probably not ten out of the scores who rushed to see him race had ever seen him before, and when he did appear on the paddock he had to be pointed out to those enthusiastic admirers.

What a host of dashing, high-bred, blue-blooded Kentucky women swarmed the parlors, halls, rotunda of that, the finest hotel in all the land! How they talked, in the soft, Southern accent, so peculiarly their own! How they laughed! How they moved about seemingly knowing everybody they met. How they bet! Gloves, fans, money, too, on their horse, when they found any one in all the crowd that was not a "Lexington horse" man. Those bright women dominated everything in their enthusiasm.

★★★

According to my recollection the Kentucky women were the only females present, so very unfashionable it was for ladies to go to races in the extreme South. There may have been some *demi-mondaines*[4] scattered here and there, in inconspicuous places.

The race, the only one I had ever witnessed, was tremendously excit-

---

1   Native American group in Louisiana, predominantly along the Gulf coast.
2   The upper echelons of society.
3   Like Lexington, a famous racehorse.
4   Worldly women.

ing, and as the gallant horses swept round the last lap, Lexington, ever so little, in the lead, the uproar became quite deafening. One of the Johnson women, beautiful and enthusiastic, sprang upon the bench and said to her equally excited escort, "Hold me while I holler." He threw his strong arms about her and steadied her feet. "Now, holler"—and never did I hear the full compass of the female voice before, nor since. Such excitement, as we all know, is contagious, and it continued for days after the great achievement that put dear old Lexington in the front rank, and filled the pocketbooks of his owners, abettors and admirers.

4. From Alice Dunbar-Nelson, "People of Color in Louisiana: Part 1," *Journal of Negro History* 1.4 (1916): 361-76

The title of a possible discussion of the Negro in Louisiana presents difficulties, for there is no such word as Negro permissible in speaking of this State. The history of the State is filled with attempts to define, sometimes at the point of the sword, oftenest in civil or criminal courts, the meaning of the word Negro. By common consent, it came to mean in Louisiana, prior to 1865, slave, and after the war, those whose complexions were noticeably dark. As Grace King[1] so delightfully puts it, "The pure-blooded African was never called colored, but always Negro." The *gens de couleur*, colored people, were always a class apart, separated from and superior to the Negroes, ennobled were it only by one drop of white blood in their veins. The caste seems to have existed from the first introduction of slaves. To the white, all Africans who were not of pure blood were *gens de couleur*. Among themselves, however, there were jealous and fiercely-guarded distinctions: "griffes, briqués, mulattoes, quadroons, octoroons, each term meaning one degree's further transfiguration toward the Caucasian standard of physical perfection."[2]

***

But already the curse of slavery had begun to show its effects. The new colony was not immoral; it may best be described as unmoral. Indolence on the part of the master was physical, mental and moral. The slave population began to lighten in color, and increase out of all proportion to the importation and natural breeding among themselves. La Harpe[3] comments in 1724 upon the astonishing diminution of the

---

1 Louisiana author (1851-1932) who primarily wrote fiction and nonfiction essays about the white Creoles of New Orleans.

2 [Grace] King, "New Orleans, the Place and the People during the Ancien Regime," 333. [Dunbar-Nelson's note.]

3 Bernard de la Harpe (1683-1765) was a French explorer of Arkansas, Louisiana, and the Gulf Coast.

white population and the astounding increase of the colored population.[1] Something was undoubtedly wrong, according to the Caucasian standard, and it has remained wrong to our own day.[2] The person of color was now, in Louisiana, a part of its social system, a creature to be legislated for and against, a person lending his dark shade to temper the inartistic complexion of his white master. Now he began to make history, and just as the trail of his color persisted in the complexion of Louisiana, so the trail of his personal influence continued in the history of the colony, the territory and the State.

★★★

It is in the definition of the word Creole that another great difficulty arises. The native white Louisianian will tell you that a Creole is a white man, whose ancestors contain some French or Spanish blood in their veins. But he will be disputed by others, who will gravely tell you that Creoles are to be found only in the lower Delta lands of the state, that there are no Creoles north of New Orleans; and will raise their hands in horror at the idea of being confused with the "Cajans," the descendants of those Nova Scotians whom Longfellow immortalized in Evangeline. Sifting down the mass of conflicting definitions, it appears that to a Caucasian, a Creole is a native of the lower parishes of Louisiana, in whose veins some traces of Spanish, West Indian or French blood runs.[3] The Caucasian will shudder with horror at the idea of including a person of color in the definition, and the person of color will retort with his definition that a Creole is a native of Louisiana, in whose blood runs mixed strains of everything un-American, with the African strain slightly apparent. The true Creole is like the famous gumbo of the state, a little of everything, making a whole, delightfully flavored, quite distinctive, and wholly unique.

---

1   Ibid., [Charles Gayarré, "History of Louisiana,"] I, 365-366. [Dunbar-Nelson's note.]
2   In 1900 a writer in Pearson's Magazine in discussing race mixture in early Louisiana made some startling statements as to the results of the miscegenation of these stocks during the colonial period. [Dunbar-Nelson's note.]
3   Most writers of our day adhere to this definition. See Grace King, "New Orleans, etc.," and Gayarré, "History of Louisiana." [Dunbar-Nelson's note.]

Appendix E: The Great Hurricane of 1893

[Much of *The Awakening* is set on Grand Isle, a popular resort and vacation area for wealthy families of New Orleans during Chopin's lifetime. This area of Louisiana and its surrounding islands, including Chênière Caminada—then the largest village on the coast of the Gulf of Mexico—were devastated by the hurricane of 1893, which altered the landscape forever, both geographically and metaphorically. The hurricane received a remarkable amount of national attention and helps to date and define the novel's temporal and imaginative settings. The texts in this section provide contemporary descriptions of the 1893 hurricane as well as Hearn's fictional evocation of the destructive storm of 1856. They also provide insight into the type of people who vacationed in this area and the types of activities in which they participated.]

1. **From Rose C. Falls, *Cheniere Caminada, or The Wind of Death: The Story of the Storm in Louisiana* (New Orleans: Hopkins Printing Office, 1893)**

Chapter I. Cheniere Caminada

... The wind blew stronger and stronger until it swept across devoted Cheniere[1] a hundred and fifteen miles an hour; and the water, churned to a foam by the merciless storm king, rolled across the whole peninsula in towering waves which beat on the frail homes of thin board and fragile latania[2] like hammers of destruction. At last the assaults of the elements began to tell upon these frail habitations, built only for such slight protection as was ordinarily needed in that land of perennial summer.

Following the sweep of some wave mightier than its fellows, or some blast which shrieked across the sedge grown morass like a demon of destruction, would come a crash, which told of the ruin of a happy home. Torn plank from plank by the wind it was scattered in the inky darkness, or, beaten from its supporting piles by the angry sea, it disappeared in the raging waters, and its occupants were face to face with death.... Then came a lull and the inexperienced hoped that the worst was over. But

---

1 A small community on the mainland in southeast Louisiana near Grand Isle.
2 A species of palm tree.

nature was but resting for a mightier effort than she had yet put forth. Again came the wind, this time from off the land; and again the waters swept Cheniere. The debris of the homes previously wrecked, with the huge trunks of trees torn from the earth on the shore north of the Cheniere, battered down the dwellings which had withstood the first assault, while a ghastly procession of white faced corpses drifted by out to sea. When morning broke and the sun again looked down on the storm-swept strip of sand, it shone upon but five houses, all that was left of the five hundred that dotted the peninsula the evening before.

***

This was no overdrawn picture, as was seen by the rescuing parties which went from New Orleans when the tale of destruction reached that city two days later, and whose work will be told later on. On Monday the few survivors, worn out by their long and terrible battle for life, found and buried one hundred and fifty bodies.... Six hundred human beings, men, women and children, on this strip of sand, cut off from the mainland by impassable marshes, with their boats destroyed and the nearest help over fifty miles away as the crow flies, near a hundred by the bayous, the only avenue of communication, and no means of making their plight known! Can the human imagination picture a condition more terrible? For twenty-four awful hours no help arrived. Then a lugger[1] which had gone to New Orleans before the storm for ice, with which these fishermen preserved their catch, returned. This ice was the salvation of the people who had escaped the fury of the tempest.

Chapter II. Grand Isle

... Fortunately most of the summer guests had left Grand Isle before the great storm, and this alone is the reason why the mortality there did not nearly approach that at ill-fated Cheniere Caminada. Had the storm occurred a month earlier, its consequences would have been appalling; for when the large summer hotels were wrecked by the winds and their timbers tossed about by the angry waters, had they been filled, as they were during August and September, with women and children, those who would have escaped could have been counted on the fingers.

***

When the storm struck Grand Isle on that terrible Sunday night there were about three hundred people on the island, most of them permanent residents. Of these only some twenty-eight or thirty were killed, but many were badly injured and all suffered severely for food

---

1 A small sailing boat.

and water before the arrival of the relief boats. They retire early at Grand Isle, and when the tempest came nearly all the inhabitants were in bed and many were asleep....

**

The island was engulfed. Houses were washed away, cattle were drowned, trees were torn from the ground and tossed like straws in its boiling surface. The railroad track leading from one of the hotels down to the beach was utterly destroyed: the ties were torn from the ground and splintered as if by axes in the hands of a thousand woodmen; the rails were wrenched apart and, borne like corks by the angry waters, and tossed hundreds of yards away, some of them wrapped and twined around trees, as if some mighty Vulcan[1] had done it in sportive derision of his human imitators.

**

Just to the east of Grand Isle lies Grande Terre, also an island. Here the storm was equally severe. But no lives were lost, owing, no doubt, to the fact that but few persons were there, and these few took refuge in the fort built there by the United States government on the west end of the island to guard the channel which passes between Grande Terre and Grand Isle into Barataria Bay. But as solid as was this massive work it could not withstand the furious assaults of the ocean. For a while, the sturdy fortification repulsed the attacks of the waves as they thundered up the beach against its grassy sides. But at last a breach was made; the works of man could not stand forever before the irresistible assaults of nature in her might.

2. From Mark Forrest, *Wasted by Wind and Water: A Historical and Pictorial Sketch of the Gulf Disaster* (Milwaukee: Art Gravure and Etching, 1894)

"A History of the Disaster"

On Sunday, October 1, 1893, a rainstorm of exceptional severity raged in the City of New Orleans. As the night drew on the storm increased, the rain fell in blinding sheets, and the wind rose till it raged with all the impetuous wrath of a hurricane. The sidewalks were flooded and blocked with fallen branches and other *debris*; many of the streets resembled small rivers; signs and awnings were blown broadcast, and fences leveled with the ground. By the time it was dark the storm had

---

1 Roman god of fire.

developed into one of the most violent and dangerous tempests the city had ever known.

★★★

By morning the fury of the wind had diminished and the citizens began to breathe more freely as they figured up the damage the tempest had caused. Though it was far less than many had feared, it was yet more than grave enough.

★★★

But now, thick and fast, came such rumors of storm-wreck and disaster from the coast as completely shadowed, in the minds of those in the city, all thought of their own trouble; and with every hour that passed, for days after, the horrible certainty grew and deepened that warring elements had wrought upon the coast-towns and adjacent islands every evil that man could fear from war, famine or pestilence; for all their horrors were now coming in one!

★★★

[T]here were reasons to fear that an awful fate had befallen Grand Isle and Cheniere Caminada—a fear that was all too sorrowfully verified! The rumor ran that the large hotel on Grand Isle had been shattered by the storm and fully 100 had died in the ruins; that the various fishing settlements had been wiped out with a loss of many hundreds of lives.

★★★

At Cheniere Island, out of a population of 1,300 but 400 or 500 had been saved, and those rescued had lost everything but life. 150 luggers had gone to the bottom, together with their seines; and the number of skiffs that had capsized and sunk could not be counted.

★★★

That the destruction had been so unparalleled seemed to be beyond the bounds of reasonable belief. The hearers were first aghast and then incredulous. Yet the rumors were so insistent that it was not possible to wholly discredit them till the matter had been investigated.

The first to take definite action to that end was the *Picayune*, which arranged for a boat to go at once to Grand Isle and Cheniere, with a corps of reliable men, to secure an accurate and detailed account of the damage done by the storm. Even then, however, it was not deemed possible that nearly so much damage had been done as was rumored, or that more than a possible dozen lives were lost.

All along Grand bayou the water stood on a level with the prairie on both sides. Some seine-boats and luggers were passed, bottom up or lying out on the prairie, and a few luggers were seen sailing through Grand Lake and bayou Cavenage searching for bodies. By 5 o'clock Grand Isle and Cheniere were in plain view. The tedious voyage had been rendered still more trying by the feelings of anxiety and suspense which all shared, and the first sight of their destination created an intense excitement on board the boat.

Grand Isle is but little more than an overgrown sand-bar, so that it lies almost even with the lake. From the opening it looked like a long thread of brown, dotted with a few stray trees, with the white shaft of the lighthouse glittering above. Farther to the right the dim outlines of Cheniere were discernible, and even from that great distance signs were apparent of the awful disaster that had befallen it.

When the steamer reached Grand Isle, it was dusk; and having laid out upon the sands the body of a dead fisherman which had been picked up just before they reached the shore, the reporters commenced their investigations. It soon became apparent that the rumors had even underestimated the evil wrought by the storm, for everything bore the impress of an immense horror; and the historic gale of 1856,[1] while terrific indeed, was but a *bagatelle* in comparison.

Everywhere property had been wrecked. The ruins of the Grand Isle Hotel[2] were awful to contemplate, the buildings being heaped together in inextricable confusion. The church was wrecked, and one of the cottages had been thrown from its foundations and carried 300 feet on to the further bank of a canal, 75 feet from the track.

***

But even worse was met at Cheniere! Terrific as had been the work of the storm elsewhere, on Cheniere Caminada it reached a climax of horror that baffles the descriptive power of any pen.

***

On the return of the McSweeny[3] to the city, measures were found to be already in active progress for relieving the sufferers, and the more detailed account than had yet been received which it brought only served to definitely confirm what was already generally known. The report certified to 950 known deaths at Cheniere Caminada, 27 at Grand Isle[.]

***

---

1 See the excerpt from *Chita* in Appendix E3 for a description of this storm.
2 Possibly one of Chopin's models for the Klein Hotel.
3 The boat being used for the transport of stranded people from the island back to New Orleans.

It is not the purpose of this work to give statements in detail of the havoc wrought by the storm, or lists of the killed or injured. The full story of the destruction to life and property on that terrible Sunday night will never be written, for it will never be wholly known, but to relate even a tenth part of what is known would far exceed the limits of the space at our command. Nor could it answer any useful end. Such general statements as we have given tell but part of the story, but more than sufficient to show how horrible and widespread was the devastation and how pitiful the plight of those who survived.

Most of those who have been able to leave Grand Isle and Cheniere have done so with the declared intention of never returning. The Cheniere, they declare, is nothing but wreck and ruin, and no inducements would tempt them to stay there, for the place is so thick-strewn with hastily made graves that not a house could be built unless it stood over, or in sight of, one of them. They call the place a graveyard, and it is looked upon with horror by them all.

The hurricane devastated some 500 miles of the Gulf coast-line, from Barataria Bay, in Louisiana, to Pensacola, in Florida, and wrought havoc and disaster in four of the great States that bound the Mexican sea. But its most terrible fury fell upon Louisiana, and was especially wreaked upon the waters and shores of Bayou Lafourche to the Balize of the Mississippi River. Within these limits the death-roll is possibly far up on the way to 2,000....

It was such a storm which, in the fell darkness of that awful Sunday night, burst upon them. There was no warning of danger, nor was there any harbor of refuge to which they could flee. There was no shelter from the resistless winds, nor any means of staying the impetuous waves....

3. From Lafcadio Hearn, *Chita: A Story of Last Island* (New York: Harper, 1889)

[From VI]

... Almost every evening throughout the season there had been dancing in the great hall;—there was dancing that night also. The population of the hotel had been augmented by the advent of families from other parts of the island, who found their summer cottages insecure places of shelter: there were nearly four hundred guests assembled. Perhaps it was for this reason that the entertainment had been prepared upon a grander plan than usual, that it assumed the form of a fashionable ball. And all those pleasure-seekers,—representing the wealth and beauty of the Creole parishes—mingled joyously ... But the hours passed in mirthfulness; the first general feeling of depression began to weigh less and less upon the guests; they had found reason to confide in the solidity of the massive building; there were no positive terrors, no outspoken fears.

★★★

... Night wore on: still the shining floor palpitated to the feet of the dancers; still the piano-forte pealed, and still the violins sang,—and the sound of their singing shrilled through the darkness, in gasps of the gale ...

★★★

Half an hour might have passed; still the lights flamed calmly, and the violins trilled, and the perfumed whirl went on.... And suddenly the wind veered!

★★★

... Some one shrieked in the midst of the revels;—some girl who found her pretty slippers wet. What could it be? Thin streams of water were spreading over the level planking,—curling about the feet of the dancers.... What could it be? All the land had begun to quake, even as, but a moment before, the polished floor was trembling to the pressure of circling steps;—all the building shook now; every beam uttered its groan. What could it be? ...

There was a clamor, a panic, a rush to the windy night. Infinite darkness above and beyond; but the lantern-beams danced far out over an unbroken circle of heaving and swirling black water. Stealthily, swiftly, the measureless sea-flood was rising.

—"*Messieurs—mesdames, ce n'est rien.* Nothing serious, ladies, I assure you.... *Mais nous en avons vu bien souvent, les inondations comme celle-ci; ça passe vite!* The water will go down in a few hours, ladies;—it never rises higher than this; *il n'y a pas le moindre danger, je vous dis! Allons! Il n'y a—*My God! What is that?"...

For a moment there was a ghastly hush of voices. And through that hush there burst upon the ears of all a fearful and unfamiliar sound, as of a colossal cannonade—rolling up from the south, with volleying lightnings. Vastly and swiftly, nearer and nearer it came,—a ponderous and unbroken thunder-roll, terrible as the long muttering of an earthquake.

★★★

Then rose a frightful cry—the hoarse, hideous, indescribable cry of hopeless fear,—the despairing animal-cry man utters when suddenly brought face to face with Nothingness, without preparation, without consolation, without possibility of respite.... *Sauve qui peut!*[1] Some

---

1 Run for it.

wrenched down the doors; some clung to the heavy banquet-tables, to the sofas, to the billiard-tables:—during one terrible instant,—against fruitless heroisms, against futile generosities,—raged all the frenzy of selfishness, all the brutalities of panic. And then—then came, thundering through the blackness, the giant swells, boom on boom! ... One crash!—the huge frame building rocks like a cradle, seesaws, crackles. What are human shrieks now?—the tornado is shrieking! Another!—chandeliers splinter; lights are dashed out; a sweeping cataract hurls in: the immense hall rises,—oscillates,—twirls as upon a pivot,—crepitates,—crumbles into ruin. Crash again!—the swirling wreck dissolves into the wallowing of another monster billow; and a hundred cottages overturn, spin in sudden eddies, quiver, disjoint, and melt into the seething.

... So the hurricane passed,—tearing off the heads of the prodigious waves, to hurl them a hundred feet in air,—heaping up the ocean against the land,—upturning the woods. Bays and passes were swollen to abysses; rivers regorged; the sea-marshes were changed to raging wastes of water. Before New Orleans the flood of the mile-broad Mississippi rose six feet above highest water-mark.

★★★

[From VII]

Day breaks through the flying wrack, over the infinite heaving of the sea, over the low land made vast with desolation. It is a spectral dawn: a wan light, like the light of a dying sun.

The wind has waned and veered; the flood sinks slowly back to its abysses—abandoning its plunder,—scattering its piteous waifs over bar and dune, over shoal and marsh, among the silences of the mango-swamps,[1] over the long low reaches of sand-grasses and drowned weeds, for more than a hundred miles.

★★★

There is plunder for all—birds and men. There are drowned sheep in multitude, heaped carcasses of kine.[2] There are casks of claret and kegs of brandy and legions of bottles bobbing in the surf. There are billiard-tables overturned upon the sand;—there are sofas, pianos, footstools and music-stools, luxurious chairs, lounges of bamboo. There are chests of cedar, and toilet-tables of rosewood, and trunks of fine stamped leather stored with precious apparel.

★★★

---

1 Mangrove-swamps.
2 Archaic term meaning cow or cattle.

... Suddenly a long, mighty silver trilling fills the ears of all: there is a wild hurrying and scurrying; swiftly, one after another, the overburdened luggers spread wings and flutter away.

Thrice the great cry rings rippling through the gray air, and over the green sea, and over the far-flooded shell-reefs, where the huge white flashes are,— sheet-lightning of breakers,—and over the weird wash of corpses coming in.

It is the steam-call of the relief-boat, hastening to rescue the living, to gather in the dead.

The tremendous tragedy is over!

Select Bibliography

Anderson, Maureen. "Unraveling the Southern Pastoral Tradition: A New Look at Kate Chopin's *At Fault.*" *Southern Literary Journal* 34 (2001): 1-13.

Beer, Janet. *Kate Chopin, Edith Wharton, and Charlotte Perkins Gilman: Studies in Short Fiction.* New York: St. Martin's Press, 1997.

———. *The Cambridge Companion to Kate Chopin.* Cambridge: Cambridge UP, 2008.

Biggs, Mary: "'Si tu savais': The Gay/Transgendered Sensibility of Kate Chopin's *The Awakening.*" *Women's Studies* 33.2 (2004): 145-81.

Bloom, Harold, ed. and intro. *Kate Chopin's The Awakening.* New York: Bloom's Literary Criticism, 2008.

Boren, Lynda S., and Sara deSaussure Davis. *Kate Chopin Reconsidered: Beyond the Bayou.* Baton Rouge: Louisiana State UP, 1992.

Bradley, Patricia L. "The Birth of Tragedy and *The Awakening*: Influences and Intertextualities." *Southern Literary Journal* 37 (2005): 40-60.

Bunch, Dianne. "Dangerous Spending Habits: The Epistemology of Edna Pontellier's Extravagant Expenditures in *The Awakening.*" *Mississippi Quarterly* 55 (2001/2002): 43-61.

Camastra, Nicole. "Venerable Sonority in Kate Chopin's *The Awakening.*" *American Literary Realism* 40.2 (2008): 154-66.

Chopin, Kate. *At Fault.* St. Louis: Nixon-Jones, 1890.

———. *The Awakening.* Chicago: Way and Williams, 1899.

———. *Bayou Folk.* Boston: Houghton Mifflin, 1894.

———. *A Night in Acadie.* Chicago: Way and Williams, 1897.

———. *A Vocation and a Voice.* Ed. Emily Toth. New York: Penguin, 1991.

Church, Joseph. "The 'Lady in Black' in Chopin's *The Awakening.*" *Explicator* 66 (2008): 196-97.

Clark, Zoila. "The Bird That Came Out of the Cage: A Foucauldian Feminist Approach to Kate Chopin's *The Awakening.*" *Journal for Cultural Research* 12.4 (2008): 335-47.

Dalrymple, Theodore. "Just Saying No." *BMJ: British Medical Journal* 336 (2008): 895.

Davis, Doris. "The Enigma at the Keyboard: Chopin's Mademoiselle Reisz." *Mississippi Quarterly* 58 (2004/2005): 89-104.

Disheroon-Green, Suzanne. "Mr. Pontellier's Cigar, Robert's Cigarettes: Opening the Closet of Homosexuality and Phallic Power in *The Awakening." Songs of the Reconstructing South: Building Literary*

Louisiana, 1865-1945. Ed. Suzanne Disheroon-Green and Lisa Abney. Westport, CT: Greenwood Press, 2002. 183-95.

——. "Whither Thou Goest, We Will Go: Lovers and Ladies in *The Awakening*." *Southern Quarterly* 40.4 (2002): 83-96.

——, and David J. Caudle. *At Fault by Kate Chopin*. Knoxville: U of Tennessee P, 2001.

——, David J. Caudle, Lisa Abney, and Susie Scifres Kuilan, eds. "Special Issue: Remembering Kate Chopin on the Centennial Anniversary of *The Awakening*." *Southern Studies* 8.1-2 (1997): 1-121.

Elfenbein, Anna Shannon. *Women on the Color Line: Evolving Stereotypes and the Writings of George Washington Cable, Grace King, and Kate Chopin*. Charlottesville: UP of Virginia, 1989.

Elz, A. Elizabeth. "*The Awakening* and *A Lost Lady*: Flying with Broken Wings and Raked Feathers." *Southern Literary Journal* 35.2 (2003): 13-27.

Emmert, Scott D. "Naturalism and the Short Story Form in Kate Chopin's 'The Story of an Hour.'" *Scribbling Women & the Short Story Form: Approaches by American & British Women Writers*. Ed. Ellen Burton Harrington. New York: Peter Lang, 2008. 74-85.

Evans, Robert C., ed. *Kate Chopin's Short Fiction: A Critical Companion*. West Cornwall, CT: Locust Hill Press, 2001.

Ewell, Barbara C. *Kate Chopin*. New York: Ungar, 1986.

——. "Storm Stories: Chopin and Faulkner in New Orleans—and on the Gulf Coast." *Faulkner and Chopin*. Ed. Robert W. Hamblin and Christopher Rieger. Center for Faulkner Studies. Cape Girardeau, MO: Southwest Missouri State UP, 2010.

——, and Pamela Glenn Menke. "*The Awakening* and the Great October Storm of 1893." *The Southern Literary Journal* 42.2 (2010): 1-11.

——, and Pamela Glenn Menke, eds. *Southern Local Color: Stories of Region, Race, and Gender*. Athens: U of Georgia P, 2002.

Gale, Robert L. *Characters and Plots in the Fiction of Kate Chopin*. Jefferson, NC: McFarland, 2009.

Gaskill, Nicholas M. "'The Light Which, Showing the Way, Forbids It': Reconstructing Aesthetics in *The Awakening*." *Studies in American Fiction* 34.2 (2006): 161-88.

Gray, Jennifer B. "The Escape of the 'Sea': Ideology and *The Awakening*." *Southern Literary Journal* 37 (2004): 53-73.

Hailey-Gregory, Angela. "'Into Realms of the Semi-Celestials': From Mortal to Mythic in *The Awakening*." *Mississippi Quarterly* 59 (2005/2006): 295-312.

Holtman, Janet. "Failing Fictions: The Conflicting and Shifting

Social Emphases in Kate Chopin's 'Local Color' Stories." *Southern Quarterly* 42 (2004): 73-88.

KateChopin.org. Kate Chopin International Society. 7 March 2011. Web 7 March 2011.

Killeen, Jarlath. "Mother and Child: Realism, Maternity, and Catholicism in Kate Chopin's *The Awakening.*" *Religion and the Arts* 7.4 (2003): 413-38.

Koloski, Bernard. *Kate Chopin: A Study of the Short Fiction.* New York: Twayne, 1996.

——, ed. *Awakenings: The Story of the Kate Chopin Revival.* Baton Rouge: Louisiana State UP, 2009.

Louisiana Literature. Special Section on Kate Chopin. 11.1 (1994).

Margraf, Erik. "Kate Chopin's *The Awakening* as a Naturalistic Novel." *American Literary Realism* 37.2 (2005): 93-116.

Mathews, Carolyn L. "Fashioning the Hybrid Woman in Kate Chopin's *The Awakening.*" *Mosaic: A Journal for the Interdisciplinary Study of Literature* 35.3 (2002): 127-49.

McGee, Diane. "The Structure of Dinners in Kate Chopin's *The Awakening.*" *Proteus: A Journal of Ideas* 17.1 (2000): 47-51.

Menke, Pamela Glenn. "The Catalyst of Color and Women's Regional Writing: *At Fault, Pembroke,* and *The Awakening.*" *Southern Quarterly* 37 (1999): 9-20.

Muirhead, Marion. "Articulation and Artistry: A Conversational Analysis of *The Awakening.*" *Southern Literary Journal* 33.1 (2000): 42-54.

Ostman, Heather, ed. *Kate Chopin in the Twenty-First Century: New Critical Essays.* Newcastle upon Tyne, UK: Cambridge Scholars Press, 2008.

Parmiter, Tara K. "Taking the Waters: The Summer Place and Women's Health in Kate Chopin's *The Awakening.*" *American Literary Realism* 39.1 (2006): 1-19.

Parvulescu, Anca. "To Die Laughing and to Laugh at Dying: Revisiting *The Awakening.*" *New Literary History* 36.3 (2005): 477-95.

Petruzzi, Anthony P. "Two Modes of Disclosure in Kate Chopin's *The Awakening.*" *LIT: Literature Interpretation Theory* 13 (2002): 287-316.

Petry, Alice Hall, ed. *Critical Essays on Kate Chopin.* New York: G.K. Hall / Simon and Schuster, 1996.

Pizer, Donald. "A Note on Kate Chopin's *The Awakening* as Naturalistic Fiction." *Southern Literary Journal* 33.2 (2001): 9-13.

Seyersted, Per, ed. *Kate Chopin: A Critical Biography.* Baton Rouge: Louisiana State UP, 1969.

——. *The Complete Works of Kate Chopin*. Baton Rouge: Louisiana State UP, 1969.

——, and Emily Toth. *A Kate Chopin Miscellany*. Natchitoches, LA: Northwestern State UP, 1979.

Shaker, Bonnie James. *Coloring Locals: Racial Formation in Kate Chopin's Youth's Companion Stories*. Iowa City: U of Iowa P, 2003.

Stein, Allen F. "Kate Chopin's 'A Pair of Silk Stockings': The Marital Burden and the Lure of Consumerism." *Mississippi Quarterly* 57 (2004): 357-68.

——. *Women and Autonomy in Kate Chopin's Short Fiction*. New York: Peter Lang, 2005.

Streater, Kathleen M. "Adele Ratignolle: Kate Chopin's Feminist at Home in *The Awakening*." *Midwest Quarterly* 48.3 (2007): 406-16.

Taylor, Helen. *Gender, Race, and Region in the Writings of Grace King, Ruth McEnery Stuart, and Kate Chopin*. Baton Rouge: Louisiana State UP, 1989.

Toth, Emily. *Kate Chopin: A Life of the Author of The Awakening*. New York: William Morrow, 1990.

——, and Per Seyersted. *Kate Chopin's Private Papers*. Bloomington: Indiana UP, 1998.

——. *Unveiling Kate Chopin*. Jackson: UP of Mississippi, 1999. xix-xxii.

Tritt, Michael. "Kate Chopin's 'Cavanelle' and The American Jewess: An Impressive Synergy." *Mississippi Quarterly* 59 (2006): 543-57.

Walker, Nancy A. *Kate Chopin: A Literary Life*. New York: Palgrave, 2001.

Weinstock, Jeffery Andrew. "In Possession of the Letter: Kate Chopin's 'Her Letters.'" *Studies in American Fiction* 30 (2002): 45-62.

Wyatt-Brown, Bertram. *Hearts of Darkness: Wellsprings of a Southern Literary Tradition*. Baton Rouge: Louisiana State UP, 2003.